TC

"Bleek!"

Cordelia paused in mid-step. She'd never heard an animal's cry quite like that one, and she turned, trying to find its source.

"Bleek! Bleek!"

Where in the world—?

Movement flickered in the corner of her vision and her eyes widened in disbelief as she saw the source of the cries.

It's a . . . a treecat*!*

That was all it could be, she thought. She'd seen enough imagery of them to know that! But what had it so upset? It raced toward her for a couple of meters, then turned around and ran in the opposite direction, looking over its shoulder at her.

What in the world—?

Cordelia Schardt-Cordova felt herself smiling hugely as she realized the treecat wanted her to follow it!

My God, they really are *intelligent!* she thought.

She took one more step, and that was when Barnaby's war cry snarled through the clearing. For an instant, she thought it was aimed at the treecat. She whipped around in the Rottweiler's direction, eyes wide, and then froze as the entire shoreline of the near-beaver pond exploded with movement.

IN THIS SERIES by DAVID WEBER

THE STAR KINGDOM:

A Beautiful Friendship
Fire Season, with Jane Lindskold
Treecat Wars, with Jane Lindskold
A New Clan, with Jane Lindskold

HONOR HARRINGTON:

On Basilisk Station • *The Honor of the Queen*
The Short Victorious War • *Field of Dishonor*
Flag in Exile • *Honor Among Enemies*
In Enemy Hands • *Echoes of Honor*
Ashes of Victory • *War of Honor* • *At All Costs*
Mission of Honor • *Shadow of Freedom*
Shadow of Victory • *Uncompromising Honor*

HONORVERSE:

Crown of Slaves, with Eric Flint
Torch of Freedom, with Eric Flint
Cauldron of Ghosts, with Eric Flint
The Shadow of Saganami
Storm from the Shadows • *A Rising Thunder*

MANTICORE ASCENDANT:

A Call to Duty, with Timothy Zahn
A Call to Arms, with Timothy Zahn & Tom Pope
A Call to Vengeance, with Timothy Zahn & Tom Pope
A Call to Insurrection, with Timothy Zahn & Tom Pope

EDITED BY DAVID WEBER:

More than Honor • *Worlds of Honor*
Changer of Worlds • *The Service of the Sword*
In Fire Forged • *Beginnings* • *What Price Victory?*

House of Steel: The Honorverse Companion, with BuNine

To purchase any of these titles in e-book form,
please go to www.baen.com.

A NEW CLAN

A Star Kingdom Novel

DAVID WEBER &
JANE LINDSKOLD

BAEN

A New Clan

This is a work of fiction. All the characters and events portrayed in this book are fictional, and any resemblance to real people or incidents is purely coincidental.

A Baen Books Original

Baen Publishing Enterprises
P.O. Box 1403
Riverdale, NY 10471
www.baen.com

ISBN: 978-1-9821-9275-4

Cover art by Bob Eggleton

First printing, June 2022
First mass market printing, May 2023

Distributed by Simon & Schuster
1230 Avenue of the Americas
New York, NY 10020

Library of Congress Control Number: 2022002999

Printed in the United States of America
10 9 8 7 6 5 4 3 2 1

A NEW CLAN

1

HEART OF STONE

<*You must go, Stone Shaper.*>

<*No.*>

<*You must!*>

<*I am here. I am* staying *here.*>

<*Please, beloved.* Please *leave me.*>

<*No.*> Stone Shaper ran his true-hand gently down Golden Eye's muzzle, his eyes dark. <*You are my life. I will not leave you. I will* never *leave you, so* you *must not leave* me.>

<*But I have no choice.*> His mate's mind-voice was weaker, her mind-glow darker, and he lay down beside her, wrapping her limp body in all six of his limbs, burying his muzzle against the side of her neck. <*I have no choice,*> Golden Eye repeated, <*but you do. Our children, the clan. They need you, and you* must *stay.*>

<*I am in the only place I "must" stay,*> he told her. <*You are my life. I will never leave you.*>

<*I do not want you to die, too.*>

<I know that.> He tasted the pain in her mind-glow, her desperate wish for him to live, but he could not give her what she wanted. Not after so many hands of hands of seasons when she had been the center of his entire world. He could not save her, and he knew that, but this much he could give her, that she did not die alone.

<I know that,> he repeated gently, *<but we are one. We have been since first I tasted your mind-glow, and we have always been there for one another. I will not be less than we have been here, at the very end. So rest, beloved.>* His arms tightened about her. *<Rest, and I will be here, holding you safe.>*

<I love you.> He could scarcely hear her mind-voice now, and he pressed his muzzle closer against her neck. *<I love you.>*

<I know.>

✧ ✧ ✧

"Have either of you seen Mack or Zack this morning?" Lady Danette Schardt-Cordova, Baroness Schardt-Cordova, asked, poking her head into the farmhouse breakfast nook.

"Mom, it's not even nine o'clock and it's a *Saturday*," Dana, the oldest of her three daughters, replied, looking up from her book reader. "You really think we're going to see either of them before noon?" She cocked her head. "You haven't been sampling the hard cider again, have you?"

"I have not," Danette retorted with admirable calm. "I never sample it before *ten* a.m., and you know it, young lady!"

"Just wondering what makes you think either of them are going to show before afternoon on a weekend. I honestly don't think Zack got back much before dawn. Is there something you need that Natalie and I"—she twitched her head in her youngest sister's direction—"could take care of?"

"Oh, Gee, thanks," Natalie said, looking up from her corn flakes. At fourteen T-years, she was ten T-years younger than Dana. She was also ten centimeters taller, which Dana considered a gross miscarriage of genetic justice. "It's not like *I* had anything planned this morning, either."

She rolled her eyes, and her mother chuckled.

"Actually, I need to talk to the boys about the logging pattern for the firebreak. Do either of you know if Mack got the software upgrade on the saws loaded?"

"No," Dana said in a more serious tone. "I know he copied it, but he said something about needing to tweak it." She snorted suddenly. "I think what he *actually* said was 'Those saws are so ancient they wouldn't even recognize this app if they—you should pardon the expression—saw it.'"

It was Danette's turn to roll her eyes. She could just hear Mack Kemper saying *exactly* that in the full expectation that Dana would repeat it to her. Zack was the more flamboyant brother, but Mack had a quietly mischievous streak which had served him well over the years.

The temptation to smile faded. The Schardt-Cordova and the Kemper families had been friends since before the colony ship *Jason* ever departed the Solar System. They'd invested in the colony early and settled adjacent claims, and Danette and Bart Kemper had both been first-generation Sphinxians.

But the Plague Years had been hard on both families. Danette had lost three siblings and her mother in the first wave, and the Kempers had suffered an equally severe death rate. She was one of the people (there were quite a few of them, especially on Sphinx) who'd thought the new Constitution's provision ennobling the survivors of the original shareholders was silly, and it certainly couldn't compensate for all the loss and grief they'd suffered, but it had been ratified only after the worst was over. She'd thought of the title as the bookend for the long, bitter battle against the Plague. After all, they'd finally perfected an effective vaccine in 1496, hadn't they? Which had only made the final outbreak on Sphinx in 1510—the one that had hit fourteen years *after* the vaccine, when everyone thought it was over, the monster had been slain; the one the vaccine *hadn't* stopped dead in its tracks—hurt even worse.

Stringent quarantine and a medical system built and honed in the face of the Plague's original onslaught had kept it tightly confined, restricted to an isolated geographic area on a single one of the Star Kingdom's inhabited worlds, and prevented the sort of pandemic which had made the original plague so horrific. The death rate had been only a hiccup, compared to the staggering death tolls of the Plague Years, but it had hit hard before the medics managed to tweak the vaccine . . . and Danette had found herself a single mother at the same time Zack and Mack had found themselves orphans.

It had seemed so bitterly unfair, so *cruel*, of the universe to deal them such a blow once they'd finally begun to trust life once more. To be confident there would be a tomorrow, and another tomorrow after that, for the people they loved. Yet Danette had survived that blow as she had so many others, and she'd done it by refusing to give in. By refusing to break and fail the people she still had to love.

That had been twelve T-years ago, when Mack had been only six and Zack had been only four. There'd never been any question who was going to take the boys, and not just because they were on adjacent claims, and "Aunt Danette" had never regretted her decision.

Like many of the Plague's survivors, they had their own share of psychic wounds. Mack was very much the quieter of the two, but even Zack—who delighted in his exuberant, artistic (or "artsy-fartsy," to use Mack's occasionally repressive term) personality—had people to mourn, and not just his own parents. Neither of them allowed that to get them down, however, and they had injected a welcome dose of mischief into the Schardt-Cordova household.

Oh, they *could* be a handful, and she would never admit to them how big a place they had in her heart. They *knew*; she'd just never admit it! And they'd more than earned their keep as she struggled to keep both claims up and running. She was going to miss them—a lot—when they moved back onto their own claim again in another T-year or so. The Kemper homestead was located on the East Ridge River in the now-Barony of Kemper's southeastern quadrant, only about ninety kilometers (barely ten or eleven minutes by air) from this very breakfast nook, and she knew they'd still be around, if only because neither of them was a particularly good cook. But it wouldn't be the same, somehow.

"You say Zack didn't get back until dawn?" she asked after a moment, and Dana nodded. "And you know this because—?"

"Because she got back about the same time the boys did," Natalie offered.

"You did?" Danette looked at her older daughter speculatively, and Dana flushed slightly.

"Mom, I'm twenty-three!"

"I didn't say you weren't," Danette said mildly. "I was only . . . expressing a parental interest. Do you plan on introducing him—whoever he is—to us sometime soon? I only ask so that I can plan the number of place settings for dinner tomorrow, you understand. No rush."

"Mom!"

"Okay. Okay! Just teasing." Danette smiled broadly, but the truth was that she had a pretty fair idea where—and with whom—Dana had been, and she approved wholeheartedly. Not that she had any intention of giving up such excellent ammunition!

"And do either of you know where Cordelia might be this fair morning?"

"She's out on that survey you asked for. She grabbed some cold cereal and left about thirty minutes ago. She took a couple of sandwiches with her, too. Said she probably won't be back until after lunch."

"She went alone?" Danette frowned, and Dana shrugged.

"I offered to go with her, but she said she's fine. She took her rifle and Barnaby."

Danette nodded, although not in complete satisfaction. They really needed that survey along the Red Bank Bottoms completed before the loggers moved in, but it was a long way from the house—or help—if something went wrong. On the other hand, all three of her girls were excellent shots—people in the Sphinxian bush tended to take marksmanship seriously—and Barnaby was a Meyerdahl Rottweiler. The huge dog stood almost eighty centimeters at the shoulder and, at seventy-three kilos, outweighed Natalie by a considerable margin. He was also both smart and fiercely protective. Between him and her rifle, Cordelia should be fine, but that didn't mean she wasn't going to experience a rather firm mother-to-daughter counseling session when she got home.

Or maybe not, Danette thought. *She* is *eighteen now, and you know darned well she's an awfully mature eighteen. All the girls are. That's what happens when you grow up on a planet where forty percent or so of the people died in a plague before you were even born.*

And aren't I *a cheerful soul this early in the morning?*

"Okay," she said out loud. "What are you two planning for the day?"

"I told Nat I'd run her into Twin Forks after lunch," Dana replied. "That swim club they've been trying to set up is having an actual organizational meeting at the Y this afternoon."

"Great!" Danette nodded enthusiastically. The planetary data net, coms, uni-links, and computerized classrooms let kids from all over Sphinx "meet" one another, but the Schardt-Cordova claim—only it was now the "Barony of Schardt-Cordova," of course—was a hundred kilometers on a side, and it was still smaller than a dozen other claims she could think of right off hand. Distances like that meant young folks stuck out in the bush got less physical "face time" with their age cohorts than she wished they could. VR was better than nothing, but it just wasn't the same. She'd experienced the same sort of isolation, growing up, and she was in favor of anything that might involve actual group activities for *her* kids, although swimming wasn't the very first one that would have sprung to mind.

Sphinx's enormous orbit imposed lengthy seasons, and its average temperature was significantly lower than that of either Manticore or Gryphon, the Manticore Binary System's other two habitable worlds, to begin with. Gryphon experienced a far more extreme seasonal swing each year, but Sphinx was the dictionary definition of "really, really, *really* cold" over the course of its sixteen-T-month-long winter. Even at the height of summer, Sphinx's natural bodies were scarcely what anyone would call warm, but at the moment, they were halfway through *autumn*. True, this summer had been exceptionally hot (for Sphinx) and dry, with far too many forest fires. The fall weather was continuing the same drought pattern, but at least it was cooling toward something a native-born Sphinxian considered comfortable . . . and anyone else would call "brisk." Which meant that even though Twin Forks was almost four hundred kilometers away from Schardt-Cordova—a good forty-five-minute flight, one way—the Y's indoor heated pool had much to recommend it.

And so does the ice cream at the Red Letter Café, she reflected. *Well, they work hard, my girls. They deserve an afternoon or two off, especially on the weekend.*

"All right, that works for me. But let me know before you leave. I need a few things from town. I'll put a list together."

"Gotcha," Dana agreed.

"And now to go beard the hexapuma. We've got to get those saws up and running by Monday, so wish me luck!"

✧ ✧ ✧

"Dang, I wish you hadn't kept us out so late," Mack Kemper groused as he landed the air car in the clearing. The original Kempers and Schardt-Cordovas had chosen their claim sites in no small part because of how well watered they were, and despite the drought, enough moisture hovered in the air to produce a cool mist, and sunlight slanting through the towering crown oak canopy created gilded bars of gold.

"*I* kept us out so late?" Zack looked at him. "Who was that guy you were sitting with, again?"

"I don't know what you're talking about." Mack pressed the button and his nostrils flared appreciatively as the canopy slid back and the earthy scent of the forest reached them. "And his name, as you know perfectly well, was Brad. Jealous?"

"Not my type, man," Zack replied. "Way too nerdy."

"*Nerdy?*" Mack looked at him in disbelief as he climbed out of the air car and took his rifle from the rack. "This from the guy who came in second in the planetary *Call of Earth* competition? You seriously want to call someone else '*nerdy*'?"

"Asks the guy who came in *first* in the planetary competition," Zack observed to no one in particular as he collected his own weapon—he preferred a shotgun rather than a rifle—and checked the chamber. "I, unlike certain other people, game because my sensitive and artistic nature craves expression. *Some* people, on the other hand, game because they don't have much of a life outside VR. I mention no names, of course. That would be tacky."

"I am *so* gonna smack you upside the head the next time we square off in Death Match, buddy!" Mack warned him with a chuckle.

"Yeah, yeah, yeah. Heard it all before."

Mack tapped the remote and the canopy slid shut. Most dangerous Sphinxian wildlife tended to be on the large side, like hexapumas and peak bears. There were a few smaller critters who could be decidedly unpleasant, however, and finding one of them perched in the air car when they got back to it was not high on his Good Things list. Besides, they weren't far from several of the bigger near-beaver ponds. The sleek, six-limbed beasties had a pronounced fondness for chewing air car upholstery into shreds, and the near-possums were even worse.

"So, let's go kick some saws in the ass," he said, and Zack shrugged.

"I'm just here because someone dragged me out of my hard-earned sleep to make sure nothing ate him," he replied. "But that's okay! Don't mind my sleep-deprived state. Nothing I'd rather do than keep an eye on my brother's back!"

"I sure wish Cordelia hadn't grabbed Barnaby this morning," Mack said thoughtfully, leading the way through the misty sun shafts toward the hulking mass of the nearest robotic logger. "He's a *lot* quieter than you are!"

✧ ✧ ✧

Stone, who had once been called Stone Shaper, lay stretched along the net-wood branch in the sunlight. He would have to change position soon if he wanted to stay in its warmth, and he did. The world had moved into leaf-turning hands of hands of days ago. The cold days would not be upon him tomorrow, but soon enough. Soon enough.

So I have seen yet another green season, he thought,

looking out through the forest. *I suppose that is an achievement.*

He rolled onto his back, presenting his belly fur to the sun, and closed his eyes as he remembered. There were memory songs about others like him. Not many, but a few. He had always wondered why those other People had so stubbornly survived. Now it was his turn, and he could no more answer the question now than he could have then.

I should have ended and gone with her, he thought yet again. It was not a helpful thought. He knew that... and he could no more stop thinking it than he could have flown.

The truth was that he had expected to do exactly that, even if the gray death had not taken him, as well. People seldom survived the loss of their mates, especially when they were as deeply bonded as he and Golden Eye. Indeed, he had not *wanted* to survive when he realized he must lose her.

The gray death struck only rarely, but the People knew its signs well... and that almost all of those touched by it died. None of the memory songs told what caused it. It wasn't like eating death weed or any of the other poisonous plants. It didn't come from bad water, or from death sting venom. It just... happened, and it spread like wildfire in fire season. The only defense against it was to stay away from those afflicted by it. That was why the rest of Bright Water Clan had moved its nests from the golden-leaf in which he and Golden Eye had built their own nest. Neither he nor Golden Eye had blamed them for that decision. The clan's hunters and scouts had brought food and left it for them at a safe distance, and their friends and the mind-healers had stayed close enough to mind-speak them every day. Bright Water had not *abandoned* them. In fact, it had *refused* to, and it had done only what it must to save the rest of the clan.

Stone Shaper understood that. It was what had happened later that had driven him from the clan and its central nesting place forever.

And that was not Bright Water's fault, either. It was his own, because he had not died.

The gray death was not the only sickness that could kill. True, it killed far more of those it struck than most of those other sicknesses. Yet what made it especially terrifying to the People was what happened to so many of the tiny number of People it did *not* kill.

He remembered the day he had finally reemerged from the darkness he had thought was death. He remembered awakening, remembered the aching, awful silence where his beloved mate's mind-glow had been. Remembered the terrible grief, the need to follow her back into the darkness, never to emerge.

Yet he had not. Something had stopped him. Perhaps it was Golden Eye's forever-silent mind-voice whispering to him out of the stillness, telling him to live. Perhaps it was simple obstinacy on his own part. Golden Eye had always told him he was the most stubborn Person she had ever known, so perhaps that was the reason.

Or perhaps I just needed to make my life a curse upon the world. Proof that it cannot kill everything *I love only because it could kill the Person I loved more than all the rest of it combined.*

He had borne Golden Eye's still, stiff body up from their nesting place to the fork at the very top of the golden-leaf and placed her where the cleansing wind, the bright sunshine, could bear her spirit to that other place where he hoped she awaited him. And then he had returned to their empty nest, waited the double-hand of days that proved the gray death had left him, mourning her in silence, before he went out once more to meet the clan.

And discovered that the gray death had taken something far crueler than his life. It had stolen his mind-voice. And not just the ability to mind-*speak*, as was most common among those who survived the gray death. No. It had taken his ability to mind-*hear*, as well. The constant flow of mind-voices, the presence of all those other mind-voices around him, among him, *part* of him...

Gone. Simply... gone. Gone into a great, dark emptiness. Into a silence he had never known. And, perhaps worse even than that, he could still taste mind-glows. He knew exactly what the People around him felt, but for the first time in his life, he did not know what they *thought*. They could not speak to him, tell him, and he could not ask.

They had been horrified by how the gray death had maimed him, and his very presence had only added to their horror. There was no hatred, there was no resentment, no one *wanted* him away from them... yet his mere presence had frightened them, however hard they strove against their fear. Or against sharing it with him. He was the reminder of what might happen to any of *them*, as well. Almost worse, he had tasted their compassion—their pity. Their need to somehow comfort him... and the knowledge that they could not. They could no more avoid sharing their mind-glows than he could avoid tasting them, and the guilt they felt—the guilt about which neither he nor they could mind-speak—had only made it worse.

And so he had left.

Those same mind-glows had implored him not to go. The People well knew how unlikely a single Person was to survive. There were so many perils in the world, so many of them bigger and far stronger than any Person. Without the rest of the clan to watch and ward and aid, death almost always came quickly, and despite his silence, he was a part of their lives and their hearts. They had already lost Golden Eye, and their hearts had cried out against losing him, as well.

Yet he could not stay. Not tasting their mind-glows so deeply from his world of silence. Besides, without his mind-voice, he could no longer serve as the leader of Bright Water's flint shapers, anyway. How could he, when he could no longer hear what was needed or explain the other flint shapers' tasks to them? And so his place as one of Bright Water's elders had passed to Stone Biter. That was good. Stone Biter was his and Golden Eye's eldest surviving kitten, with a good heart, a strong mind-glow. He would do well by the clan.

And so he had changed his own name, in the silence of his own mind. It was not the name by which the rest of the clan might know him, but he no longer knew what they might call him now. So he had become simply Stone. A stone wrapped in stony silence, cast out not by the clan, but by his own heart and will as he set out to find the death awaiting him.

But it had refused to find him, and he had discovered that he could not simply wait passively for it. He had nothing left except the stony determination that the world would not slay him as easily as it had slain his beloved. He would *fight* death, every step of the way, with bared fangs and claws, because it was the only purpose left to him.

He knew that. He accepted it. And yet that empty, bleeding silence within him longed for the day when he lost that fight at last.

And is that not a pleasant way to begin your day? he asked himself. *Perhaps you should be thinking about your next visit to the two-legs, instead.*

Stone doubted the rest of Bright Water would have approved of his raids upon the two-legs, but he was far away from Bright Water's range. Nothing that happened with these two-legs was likely to impact the rest of the People. Besides, the People had been raiding the two-legs' plant places for cluster stalk long before Golden Eye left him. True, Stone had been a flint shaper, without the stealthiness of a scout or hunter, but there was also only one of him, and he had been careful in his forays.

And the two-legs were the only reason he had survived so long, actually. Their plant places provided many plants, some of them pleasant tasting and some not so pleasant, even at the height of the cold days. And there were other... interesting possibilities.

He had been very tempted to sample one of the long-eared creatures who reminded him of grass runners. They were somewhat smaller than a Person, yet large enough that one of them might have fed him for quite some time, and they smelled delicious. Unfortunately, he was sure the two-legs would notice if any of them disappeared, and while they might blame it on bark-chewers or sharp-snouts, it was unlikely. Neither of them would have been able to open the simple but effective closures the two-legs had constructed to keep them out. And so, regretfully, he had left them unsampled.

On the other hand, there were the flutter-wings. It wasn't a very good name for them, but it was the only one he had. They were ridiculous creatures—fat, excitable, and for something with wings, unbelievably clumsy. Certainly they were nothing at all like a death-wing or wind-glider! They smelled even more delicious than the long-ears, though. And unlike the long-ears, they also laid eggs. Whatever the flutter-wings might *smell* like, their eggs truly *were* delicious, and they produced a lot of them. A short visit to the flutter-wing nest place with his carry net could feed him for a full hand of days without taking more than an egg here or an egg there.

He had also availed himself of other treasures courtesy of the two-legs. There was a place behind the main nesting place where they seemed to discard things they no longer wanted. They had some sort of made-thing that crunched up their discards, for some reason. Perhaps it was simply to make them take up less space, but a flying thing collected the eaten pieces every double-hand of days. The important point was that they only used their made-thing the day before the flying thing came, and he had found any number of useful things while prowling through the discard place. He had used them to build a nest that was both larger and warmer than anything a single Person truly needed—enough to shelter him easily even through the coldest of cold days—and he had gathered up other tools he needed to survive inside it, like the marvelous blade he used now instead of the stone tools of the People.

There were actually days when he was almost content.

Almost.

He suspected that he had learned more about two-legs than any other Person. It was a pity he would never be able to share what he had learned with the memory singers. But—

His thoughts broke off and he rolled over onto his hand-feet and true-feet as he felt the approach of a mind-glow. That was one of the things he could never share with a memory singer—the discovery that two-legs had mind-glows. Well, of course they did! Every creature that lived had a mind-glow, of sorts, at least. But two-leg mind-glows were much stronger than those of any other creature Stone had ever encountered. In fact, they were at least as strong as those of the People, although they were very different. Of course, he had no mind-voice, nor any ability to listen for *their* mind-voices, so he had no idea how similar to or different from the People the two-legs might truly be, but it *was* interesting.

Now he watched as one of what he'd come to think of as "his" two-legs made its way along the streambank with a thunder-barker slung over its shoulder. The big, black barker Stone took great pains to avoid in his excursions into the flutter-wing's nesting place scampered in and out of the low growing brush, ranging ahead of the two-leg but always circling back to it.

Now what are you doing out here today, two-leg? he thought.

No doubt the answer was some other incomprehensible two-leg thing, but at least following it would give him something to do.

✧ ✧ ✧

"There!" Mack said.

"Oh? Are you finally *done?*" Zack inquired.

"I didn't notice you breaking a sweat to help," Mack observed.

"Not my job! You're the software guy. I'm the bring-my-shotgun-and-watch-your-back-with-steely-eyed-concentration guy. Remember?"

Since at that very moment Zack was sprawled comfortably in the shade of one of the logging robots with his hands clasped behind his head while he chewed a near-sage stem, his older brother might have been excused for the eye roll he gave him.

"Yeah, sure. But, as it happens, we *are* done here. So why don't we head back? It's almost lunchtime. Besides, I need to talk to Aunt Danette."

"And you broke your uni-link!" Zack said sorrowfully, spitting out his near-sage stem and climbing to his feet. "I didn't even notice!"

"You really are full of yourself today, aren't you?" Mack shook his head. "In this instance, however, I need to show her some diagrams on my pad while we talk. You know how visually oriented she is. There are a couple of trim patterns in this software I didn't realize were included. I think we're going to have more flexibility than we thought we were, but I really need her input to decide which ones we want to prioritize."

"Makes sense," Zack said a bit more seriously. "But you know she's really going to want to hear from Cordelia before she makes any decisions about that."

"Yeah, she is." Mack nodded.

Unlike some Sphinxians, Aunt Danette took her responsibilities as a custodian of the planetary wilderness dead seriously. That was why she wanted an eyes-on report from the ground to back up the drones' aerial scans. She wanted to know exactly what needed to be cut and what didn't, rather than resorting to the "cut it all down and let God sort it out" approach some of her fellow "nobles" would have adopted.

"There's enough daylight left we can still get back out here this afternoon to make any tweaks she wants," he pointed out, and Zack nodded. Sphinx's day was the next best thing to twenty-six hours long and, despite their late start, it was barely midday. "We need to start cutting Monday," Mack continued, "and I have plans for tomorrow."

"Plans that include what's-his-name? Brad?" Zack asked mischievously.

"*Plans*," Mack said repressively, and his younger brother relented.

"All right. Then why don't you and I head on over and give Cordelia a hand? I know she really prefers wandering around the woods alone, but she'd probably forgive us for horning in on her this afternoon. As long as we don't get into the habit!"

"You know, that's not a half-bad idea," Mack agreed. "C'mon."

✧ ✧ ✧

Cordelia Schardt-Cordova made her way cautiously along the game trail. The Sphinxian near-deer, which she understood didn't look a great deal like the terrestrial species it had been named for, preferred flight to fight in the face of any threat. It also ran to around ninety kilos, however, and upon occasion its version of "flight" might be more accurately described as "run-right-over-the-threat-and-trample-it-on-my-way-out."

She figured the odds of any such encounter today were slim, partly because the trail didn't seem to have seen much recent use but even more because Barnaby would spot any near-deer—or anything else large enough to pose a threat—well before Cordelia did. The Meyerdahl Rotties had been genetically modified for a heavy-gravity environment, and although it hadn't been part of the modification's original objectives, the breed's already considerable intelligence had been tweaked in the process. The result was the almost perfect settler's dog for Sphinx, in Cordelia's opinion.

Now Barnaby came bounding back down the trail toward her like a furry, black-and-tan thunderbolt. He slid to a halt, and she braced herself as he rose on his back feet and planted his front paws on her shoulders, tail wagging and ears pricked.

"Don't even *think* it!" she warned him as he cocked his massive head, clearly contemplating whether or not to give her a lick. She scratched him behind his right ear and he decided to close his eyes and luxuriate in the caress, instead.

"Smart move," she told him.

He chuffled happily, then dropped back to all four feet and nosed her rucksack. She glanced down at him—it wasn't that far; he stood well above waist-high on her—and he waggled his head, flapping his ears at her.

"Well," she checked the time on her uni-link and discovered it was later than she'd thought, "I guess it *is* about lunchtime. Let's find a place with a view."

Barnaby sneezed explosively in agreement and went trotting along the trail ahead of her once more, and she shook her head as she followed him.

She kept her eyes open as she went, and not just to make sure nothing untoward pounced upon her. The drone dodging through the canopy overhead was actually as responsible for collecting the survey data she was out here to get as she was, but the impressions of a human observer were bound to play a role in its interpretation. Besides, humans had been on Sphinx for less than a T-century, even now. There were still plenty of things they hadn't figured out about their new planet. The Sphinx Forestry Service was constantly identifying new species of flora and fauna, many of which only reemphasized the need to treat the planetary biosphere with wary respect. And one reason Cordelia loved running surveys for her mom was the possibility of spotting new species herself. There was a bounty for identifying useful plants or animals, although it didn't amount to a whole heap of money. But Cordelia wasn't interested in the money. She wanted the naming rights that accompanied the bounty. A species' discoverer was allowed to propose the official name for her discovery, and Cordelia was appalled by how little imagination some of those discoverers displayed.

Tell the truth, she told herself now. *What you're really hoping is to turn up something like the Harringtons did, aren't you?*

Well, maybe she was. She wasn't sure she accepted the theory that these "treecats" were tool *makers*. Tool *users*, maybe. There were plenty of species on planets humanity had settled who displayed that behavior, using sticks to dig, for instance. But if young Harrington was to be believed, her "treecats" went well beyond that, and that level of sophistication was far rarer. The Forestry Service seemed to agree with her, though. She was actually a Ranger now herself, despite being a couple of years younger than Cordelia, and she and her friends were fierce "treecat" advocates. Cordelia was willing to admit the possibility that they were right about the critters actually making tools; she just wanted firsthand confirmation of it before she signed off on the theory.

The woods began to thin ahead of her as the game trail angled back toward the streambank. More near-beaver work, she thought. For beasties that never exceeded a body length of fifty centimeters or so, they could be incredibly destructive. But the ponds they impounded were often enormous—the one she was approaching was well over two kilometers in its longest dimension—and they nurtured the wetlands that were key to much of the forests' lifecycle. That was one reason she was out here. The last summer had been decidedly too dry, and there'd been a lot of fires, especially over on the far side of Twin Forks. So far, the autumn had been just as dry, with precious little of the rains they normally expected. The parched undergrowth the summer had turned into kindling was in the process of turning into tinder, and the Forestry Service was warning everyone they were far from out of the danger zone. The higher elevations had seen some relief—snow was already falling up there, although there was less of it than usual and it was still mostly melting each morning—but the lower claims were in just as much danger as ever. In fact, in many ways it was worse than it had been at the height of the summer.

Feather-bramble was a critical component of the Sphinxian plant cycle. The resinous, low-growing shrub provided a dense ground cover and the combination of its shade and deep root system played a major role in capturing and conserving rainwater. When there *was* any rain, at least. But it also died back every fall, leaving a skeletal lacework of highly combustible dead leaves and twigs. It was well into that annual die-back cycle now, and it was moving east as the season deepened, which meant it was all too likely to lead a fresh spate of fires in the same direction.

The Red Bank Bottoms lay directly athwart that threat axis. They followed the north-south course of the river for which they had been named, and while the Red Bank was only a modest stream (by Sphinxian standards), tribes of beavers had strung their ponds along it like beads on a necklace to produce the Bottoms. The water in those ponds was always critical for wildlife during dry summers, and the band of wetlands also provided a potential firebreak that guarded over a third of her mom's barony's western perimeter.

The problem was the feather-bramble along the *Bottoms*' western perimeter and number of crown oaks growing alongside the river. Actually, the problem was the crown oak *branches* which extended clear across the river. Coupled with the picketwood thickets which exploded into the clearings the near-beavers' logging efforts produced, they created altogether too many bridges by which flames could leap the water barrier if the feather-bramble caught fire. A crown oak took decades—more probably centuries—to reach full maturity, so the decision to harvest one usually required careful consideration. Picketwood, on the other hand, grew so fast it could become a serious nuisance, and the long, dry summer had turned the blankets of fallen vegetation under the thickets into yet another pile of tinder waiting for a spark. Once Mack and Zack had the logging robots' new software loaded and certified, they'd move into the area to cut back the picketwood and clear out that tinder as a fire precaution. At least some of the crown oaks would be going, as well, though. Cordelia regretted that. As on most recently colonized planets, timber was a primary building material on Sphinx, but a typical crown oak was at least eighty meters in height and eight meters in diameter. Just one of them could provide thousands of board-meters of lumber, and they might be going to drop as many as a half dozen of them. That was an awful lot more timber than anyone was going to need.

In fact, that was really what she was looking for: places where the majestic trees could be topped or pruned to get rid of the fire bridges without taking them down completely. That would be far better for the forest in general, and Cordelia would feel less as if they were desecrating their planet.

Barnaby emerged from the picketwood thicket into a near-beaver-provided clearing, and Cordelia followed him gratefully. She loved the dim-majestic aisles of the crown oaks, but the temperature was decidedly on the cool side, even for her Sphinx-born sensibilities, this early in Sphinx's long day, and a little direct sunlight would be welcome.

She stepped out of the shade and found herself on the brink of the beaver pond she'd been working her way toward for the last forty-five minutes. It was even more impressive down here at ground level than from the aerial shots. In fact, its northern limb ran farther back into the crown oaks than she'd realized. It might well be the biggest single pond she'd ever heard of, she thought, making her way through the knee-high scrub that had taken advantage of the supply of sunlight. Near-beavers tended to take down the trees they intended to use and then let them season. They stripped off branches and leaves for immediate use, but the trunks often lay where they'd fallen for as much as a planetary year before they were hauled off for the current construction project. From the overhead drone's imagery, these beavers had been kind enough to leave several suitable benches from which to choose her luncheon perch.

✧ ✧ ✧

Stone flowed along the net-wood, watching the two-leg and tasting its mind-glow. This was the closest he'd actually come to one of them, although he had seen them moving through the forests on more than one occasion. It was also the closest he'd been to one of their mind-glows, and it was even stronger than he had thought it was. Indeed, it seemed to be stronger than one of the People's mind-glows!

And perhaps it only seems that way because it has been so long since you tasted another Person's mind-glow, he reminded himself. Still, it was astonishing that he could taste it so clearly from this distance.

It tasted . . . nice. That was the only way he could describe it to himself. He suspected that this must be a young two-leg, judging by the bright edges of its mind-glow. This two-leg was still seeing things that were new to it, and he tasted its anticipation of seeing still more of them.

Strange that I can tell that is what it wants so clearly. Even another Person's mind-glow would reveal less about his actual thoughts.

On the other hand, he was close enough now to be confident that the two-legs had no mind-voices. In fact, they must be totally mind-blind, poor things. If not, the two-leg would have to have tasted his own mind-glow by now.

He eased a little closer, confident from their mind-glows that neither the two-leg nor the barker had detected his presence, and his ears pricked as the comforting warmth of the two-leg flowed over him. And that was what it was, he realized—comforting. It was as if he warmed his true-hands over a welcoming fire. Like the fire, the two-leg's mind-glow was not even aware of him, yet its brightness—its warmth—reached into the inner chill where Golden Eye had left him. And if it was not aware of him, neither did it feel pity for him. It simply was, and he followed even more closely through the dappled sunlight and shade, gazing down upon the crown of its head from almost directly above.

He was so lost, so enwrapped in his study of its mind-glow, that he did not realize where it was headed until the trees began to thin ahead of them.

He froze when he did realize, and shock and alarm rolled through him. Was the two-leg *crazed*? How could it—?

And then he realized something else.

It does not know, he thought. *It does not know! And neither does the barker!*

Their mind-glows made that obvious. And even if they had possessed mind-voices, *he* had none. He could not even warn them! Unless—

✧ ✧ ✧

"Bleek!"

Cordelia paused in mid-step. She'd never heard an animal's cry quite like that one, and she turned, trying to find its source.

"Bleek! Bleek!"

Where in the world—?

Movement flickered in the corner of her vision and her eyes widened in disbelief as she saw the source of the cries.

It's a . . . a treecat*!*

That was all it could be, she thought. She'd seen enough imagery of them to know that! But what had it so upset?

"Bleek! Bleek, bleek, bleek!"

She didn't know why she was so certain its agitation had something to do with *her*, yet she was. Maybe it was just that she couldn't think of any other reason for it to be making so much racket—or to have revealed its presence to her in the first place! And now it was flowing back and forth along the branches of the picketwood. It raced toward her for a couple of meters, then turned around and ran in the opposite direction, looking over its shoulder at her.

What in the world—?

She turned and took a step toward it.

✧ ✧ ✧

Yes!

Relief boiled through Stone as the two-leg paused, looked up, and saw him. He bleeked at it again, running back along the net-wood, and tasted the surprise and curiosity that erupted through its mind-glow. There was delight mixed with the surprise, and a sense of wonder that went beyond simple curiosity, and he tasted it turning to follow him.

Good! If he could only get it—

✧ ✧ ✧

Cordelia Schardt-Cordova felt herself smiling hugely as she realized the treecat *wanted* her to follow it!

My God, they really are *intelligent!* she thought.

And this one wants to show me something? Is that what it wants? But why—?

She took one more step, and that was when Barnaby's war cry snarled through the clearing. For an instant, she thought it was aimed at the treecat. She whipped around in the Rottweiler's direction, eyes wide, and then froze as the entire shoreline of the near-beaver pond exploded with movement.

✧ ✧ ✧

No! He had come so close to saving it!

Horror erupted through Stone as the needle-fangs swarmed out of the undergrowth.

Needle-fangs were among the world's most deadly hunters. Not because of their size—they were no more than half a Person's size—but because of their numbers . . . and their hunger. They would attack anything that lived, hands of hands of them swarming over it, pulling it down, literally devouring it alive, especially in mating season.

They were the reason there were no longer any lake builders here.

✧ ✧ ✧

"Barnaby! Come!" Cordelia shouted, un-slinging her rifle and suddenly wishing she'd brought a shotgun instead. *"Come!"*

Near-weasels! She should have realized! That was why she'd seen no sign of near-beavers, why nothing was using the game trail! Normally, near-weasels were seen only in relatively small numbers, but in mid-autumn, the peak of their breeding season, they could run in packs of dozens or even more.

Barnaby's hackles had gone up the instant he scented the near-weasels, but he responded quickly to her call, bounding toward her as she backed toward the open ground where the crown oaks' canopy choked out the undergrowth. Near-weasels were territorial—that was why their packs grew during breeding season as they staked out territory and hunting grounds in which to bear their young—and if she and Barnaby could just get beyond the limit of the territory they'd claimed here—

Barnaby stayed between her and the oncoming near-weasels, flowing back and forth, rumbling his war cry, and it looked as if the creatures were slowing. Or maybe she just wanted to believe that. Maybe—

She was watching the threat. She didn't notice the root growing across the game trail until the heel of her right boot caught on it.

✧ ✧ ✧

No!

The two-leg stumbled, then sprawled backward, dropping its thunder-barker, and Stone tasted the bolt of pain that shot through its mind-glow. Not from the fall; from its ankle.

It fought to climb back to its feet while the needle-fangs surged closer, and he heard it cry out in pain. It managed to scramble back upright, but it swayed, fighting to stay there while anguish ripped through it.

✧ ✧ ✧

Cordelia sobbed in pain as she crawled back to her feet and knew that she and Barnaby were about to die because of a simple stupid, *stupid* fall.

She didn't know if the ankle was broken or just horribly sprained, and it didn't matter. What *mattered* was that she could barely stand, far less run. She'd managed to recover her rifle on her way back up, and her hand found the pistol grip while her thumb snapped off the safety, but that was more a reflex act of defiance than anything else. Near-weasels were fast, and they were small targets. And—

Barnaby's rumbling snarl rolled up like thunder as the outliers of the near-weasel tide reached them. His massive jaws snapped shut with an audible crunch. His victim's squeal died abruptly, and he tossed his head, flipping it back into the pack. His jaws closed again, and then the near-weasels were upon him. They were small foes, but their teeth were needle-sharp. His thick coat and hide offered some protection, but not enough, and Cordelia raised her rifle.

✧ ✧ ✧

"CRAAACK!"

The two-leg's thunder-barker bellowed, and Stone felt a flicker of hope. But the needle-fangs came on, undeterred. They had no idea what a thunder-barker was . . . and if they had understood, they wouldn't have cared. Their mind-glows were minimal at the best of times; now they were filled with nothing but rage and hunger.

✧ ✧ ✧

"What the hell?!"

Zack Kemper bolted upright in his seat as the alarm pinged. He jerked up his wrist and tapped the face of his uni-link.

"What?" Mack asked tautly.

"It's Cordelia."

"What's wrong?"

"She doesn't say. In fact—" Zack tapped again, and his face tightened. "It's her fall alert on auto, Mack."

"*Shit.*"

The brothers looked at each other. Aunt Danette's rules were inflexible. No one ever went into the bush alone without activating the fall alert function on his uni-link. The younger members of her household might occasionally roll their eyes over the precaution, but they didn't really feel like arguing. Falls were one of the most common accidents that could overtake someone in the bush, and in Sphinx's 1.35 gravities, that sort of "accident" often meant broken bones—sometimes a *lot* of them—for humans who hadn't been genetically enhanced for heavy-grav worlds. So if the uni-link detected a fall and its wearer didn't tap the "Are you okay?" prompt within ten seconds, it automatically broadcast a homing signal.

"Where?" Mack demanded. "I don't see—" He broke off as an icon flashed on his navigation display. "Got it! Ping Aunt Danette and tell her we're on it!"

✧ ✧ ✧

Blood stained Barnaby's coat in a dozen places, but he was a Rottweiler. Not just a Rottweiler—a *Meyerdahl* Rottweiler whose person was in danger. He was far stronger, far tougher than any terrestrial Rottweiler, yet he possessed every iota of his ancestors' fearless, go-for-broke nature, and he ignored his own wounds, whipping around Cordelia, snatching away the near-weasels that tried to swarm up her boots and the tough, no-rip fabric of her trousers.

They moved too fast, were too elusive, for her to target them with her rifle, so she used it as a club, instead, sobbing with terror but refusing to panic. She smashed one near-weasel after another, trying to keep them off of Barnaby, but there were always two more in place of each one that she clubbed.

✧ ✧ ✧

Stone snarled in fury as he tasted the mind-glows below him.

The two-leg's terror surged over him like a tide, but for all its fear, it was that mind-glow's focus that caught Stone by the throat. He recognized the despair in it. He had known that same despair as Golden Eye sank into her final sleep in his arms. Had felt it himself when he longed to never awaken and find her gone. But there was no surrender in the two-leg. It would fight against the needle-fangs until it could fight no more, and not just for itself. Stone tasted its desperate determination to protect the barker even as he tasted the barker's bloodred, furious determination to protect the *two-leg*.

They were mind-blind. Neither could taste the other, know that the other would die rather than abandon them. And it didn't matter. Not to them. They would fight, and they would die, together, as surely as any of the People would fight and die together.

And as he realized that, he realized something else, as well.

He could not let them fight and die alone. He knew too much of what that meant.

✧ ✧ ✧

Even through Barnaby's howling fury and her own panic, Cordelia heard another sound. It was like tearing canvas. She'd never heard it before, yet a corner of her brain recognized what it had to be and she wanted to cry out. To reject what she knew was about to happen.

The treecat followed its battle cry down out of the picketwood.

It hit her shoulder, but only a glancing blow, a carom shot that landed it perfectly poised on all six limbs right at her feet.

And then it exploded into action.

✧ ✧ ✧

Stone had no idea if the barker would realize that he wasn't simply one more needle-fang, but he had no choice but to take that chance. He flung himself into the mad swirl of needle-fangs around the two-leg's feet, slashing with razor-sharp claws and fangs as sharp as any needle-fang's.

✧ ✧ ✧

Cordelia clubbed another near-weasel, sobbing for breath. The creatures had gotten through her trousers in several places, and she felt blood flowing down her legs, but her wounds were nothing beside Barnaby's. The Rottweiler was coated in blood, now, and the savagely fighting treecat was already bloodied, as well.

They were going to die. She knew they were. But if they were, then by God, they would go kicking and clawing to the end! Barnaby would never abandon her, she would never abandon him, and neither of them would abandon the treecat who had made their hopeless fight his own.

✧ ✧ ✧

Stone squealed in pain as the needle-sharp fangs sank into his right leg.

It wasn't the first time he'd been bitten, but this time those fangs had reached the big tendon in the back of his leg. The leg went out from under him, and he went down, rolling and lashing out with five sets of claws. The big, black barker's jaws ripped away one of his attackers even as two more of them swarmed over the barker, and Stone managed to lunge upright. Two of the needle-fangs took advantage of the opening, breaking past him and the barker, swarming up the two-leg's legs until they could reach its arms. It cried out, dropping its thunder-barker, beating at them to keep them away from its throat, and Stone flung himself upward, swarming up the two-leg in pursuit of the near-fangs.

He reached the closest and sank his right true-hand's curved claws into its haunch, jerking it back, severing its throat with his left true-hand while he clung to the two-leg's body covering with both hand-feet and the one true-foot that still worked. But he couldn't reach the second needle-fang as it eluded the two-leg's grip and lunged for its throat.

Stone leapt. It was not the strongest leap he had ever made—not with only one leg that worked—but it was enough. He hit the needle-fang, gripping it with both true-hands, ripping the life from it as he arced outward. Then he landed, too far from the two-leg or the barker for either of them to reach him.

The needle-fangs were waiting.

✧ ✧ ✧

"*No!*" Cordelia screamed as the treecat disappeared into the sea of near-weasels. "*No!*"

She knew exactly what the treecat had done . . . and why. It hadn't had to join the fight at all, and now it had died to buy her a few more seconds.

More fangs chewed through her trousers, and three of the little monsters clung to Barnaby's back, biting and tearing. The Rottweiler was slowing as his blood loss mounted. It was only—

BLAM!

Her head jerked up and her incredulous eyes flared wide.

BLAM! BLAM!

It was *Zack*! Where—? How—?

✧ ✧ ✧

Zack Kemper killed his counter-grav unit and hit the ground outside the perimeter of the near-weasel pack surrounding Cordelia, and unlike Cordelia, *he* favored a shotgun. In principle, it was identical to the shotguns which had been used on Terra for thousands of years, but the design was rather more advanced, and he had dialed in what one of his Terran ancestors would have called an "improved cylinder choke." The weapon's cartridges were slimmer than those of an old-fashioned shotgun, as well. There were fifteen of them in his magazine, each loaded with razor-sharp, aerodynamically stabilized flechettes, and because Zack, for all his levity, was dead serious about watching his brother's back in the woods, it was also selective fire.

He went to one knee and a burst of fully automatic flechettes ripped a swath of shredded near-weasels across the pack attacking Cordelia.

Recoil hammered his shoulder, and he emptied the magazine, hit the release button with his right index finger without ever letting go of the pistol grip, and slammed in a fresh magazine with his left hand.

✧ ✧ ✧

Cordelia sobbed in disbelief. She'd been so focused on the near-weasels that she'd never even heard the air car! Now it hovered above her, canopy open, and she saw Mack standing in it. He leaned over the side, shooting downward, and if he didn't have a shotgun like Zack's, his rifle was firing on full auto, and he'd attached the hundred-round drum magazine Cordelia had always teased him about. His fire sawed into the other side of the pack, and that torrent of death and destruction was enough to get through even to near-weasels.

The survivors began to break away, shock and terror

finally penetrating their ferocity and hunger, and Cordelia stumbled. She went to her right knee, ripping at the near-weasels still clinging to her legs, feeling them chewing at her hands as she tore them free and hurled them away. But then she saw Zack changing his aim point toward the biggest remaining cluster of the creatures.

"No!" she screamed. *"No, Zack!"*

He didn't hear her. Or realize what she was saying, anyway.

And he didn't know about the treecat . . . or that it was what the near-weasels were attacking.

✧ ✧ ✧

Fury roared through Zack Kemper as the blood soaking Cordelia's trousers, arms, and hands registered. He dropped his holo sight onto the cluster of near-weasels. His finger tightened, and—

"Barnaby!"

He managed—somehow—not to squeeze the trigger as the bleeding, wounded Rottweiler leapt squarely into the near-weasels he'd been about to shoot. Zack jerked his muzzle up and surged to his feet. He didn't know what had possessed Barnaby to hurl himself right into the middle of his sight picture. Maybe he'd figure that out later. For now, though—

He charged across the swath of carnage his fire had left and brought the shotgun's butt down, clubbing the near-weasels still ripping at Barnaby.

At Barnaby and something *else*, he realized. The Rottweiler's blood-dripping jaws ripped a near-weasel away, tearing it almost in two, and Zack's eyes widened as he saw the mauled, blood-soaked creature—the *treecat*—at the bottom of the pile.

✧ ✧ ✧

"Zack! *Zack!*" Cordelia sobbed, hobbling toward him as quickly as her ankle allowed. "Oh, Zack!"

"It's okay, Cordy," he said, shotgun in his right hand as he threw his left arm around her. "It's okay."

"Oh, Zack," she said again, burying her face against his shoulder.

"Bet *you* don't complain about setting the fall alert again!" he said, but his voice was gentle, and she shook her head hard.

"Never!" she gasped.

"We've got to get you to a doct—" he said, but she surprised him. She pulled back, shaking her head again, and went to her knees.

"No," she said so fiercely he blinked.

She was digging through the dead near-weasels. Barnaby was beside her, pawing at the bodies, and Zack realized what they were after as Cordelia scooped up the treecat in torn, bleeding hands and cradled it against her chest.

"Cordy," he started to say gently, "I'm afraid he's—"

"No he *isn't*!" She glared up at him. "He's *not*! He's still alive! I *know* he is!"

"But—"

"He's alive! And we have to get him to Dr. Harrington, Zack! He saved my life!"

"But—" Zack began, then cut himself off as the bleeding treecat stirred feebly in Cordelia's arms.

"*Now*, Zack!" she said fiercely. "Him and Barnaby both! We can worry about me later!"

✧ ✧ ✧

Stone floated unwillingly up toward the surface of his dreams and stirred in protest.

He should not be alive. The darkness for which a

part of him had longed so hard since Golden Eye left him should have taken him, and he would have been glad. He would have perished doing something worth the doing, and he wished he had. He knew how badly he had been hurt, and that meant death would find him soon enough. There was no other possibility for a single Person alone in the world. And if he must die anyway, why could he not have died in his dreams? Died and been restored to his bond with Golden Eye, if only in a dream?

He could have died so happily in a dream.

But that had been denied him, and something touched his muzzle.

He opened his unwilling eyes and blinked, trying to focus. And as he tried, he tasted a familiar mind-glow.

His eyes popped fully open, and he stared in astonishment at Climbs Quickly!

What was the Bright Water scout doing this far from the clan's range? And—

Stone's thought broke off as he realized they were in one of the two-leg nesting places. It was night outside a transparent part of the wall, but the overhead light was daylight-bright. He lay on his side, strange scents surrounded him, many of them sharp enough to hurt his nose, and the surface under him was soft and warm.

Climbs Quickly stroked his muzzle again, and Stone blinked. He had not seen the scout in almost a hand of turnings, and it was obvious Climbs Quickly had been as badly injured as he since last they'd seen one another. One of his forelimbs was missing, and his pelt was swirled with the telltale traces of scars beneath it.

It is too bad I cannot hear his mind-voice, Stone reflected. His thoughts were oddly unfocused, and he wondered why the pain he felt seemed so distant, almost unimportant. *It would be nice if he could explain what is happening!*

From the taste of Climbs Quickly's mind-glow, he was thinking much the same thing, and Stone tasted a flicker of amusement—of *shared* amusement, he realized—at their predicament.

And then he recognized what he had just felt. Amusement. In the face of this fresh proof of how the gray death had maimed him, he had felt *amused*! What was *wrong* with him?!

The question burned through him, but then he realized something else. He had awakened from his dream of Golden Eye, yet the warmth, the love, the focus of her mind-glow remained with him. It was back . . . and that was not possible.

He twitched as Climbs Quickly touched him again, this time on the shoulder, and he tasted the scout's compassion. And something very like . . . joy?

This was all wrong. Not possible! Golden Eye had been taken from him, so how could he taste her mind-glow again? *He could not!* He—

But, no. It wasn't Golden Eye's mind-glow. And yet—

Climbs Quickly looked down at him, then pointed, and Stone turned his head, eyes following the gesture, and froze.

No, it wasn't Golden Eye's mind-glow.

It was the two-leg's.

This is not possible, he thought. *Surely it is not! It is a* two-leg*!*

Yes, it was a two-leg, not a Person, and the People

could not bond with any other creatures who walked the world.

But the two-legs are not of *our world.* The thought trickled through his mind. *They are not like any other creatures who walk it. We have known that for turning upon turning.*

He stared at the two-leg—*his* two-leg, he realized, tasting the joyous strength of the bond between them. She—he knew now that his two-leg was female—was asleep on some sort of sitting thing beside the flat, soft surface upon which he lay and Climbs Quickly sat. She had wounds of her own, wounds which had been treated as his own had, he realized, and he tasted her exhaustion. Yet even as she slept, her mind-glow sought his. It was not the conscious, knowing seeking of another Person, and yet it was actually stronger in so many ways. Her mind-glow was so bright, so intense, even in her sleep, and it was *his.* It reached out, enfolded him, welcomed him. It was focused upon him, deeply concerned about his wounds and yet totally devoid of the pity which had driven him from Bright Water so long ago. Because the two-leg had no mind-voice of her own, he realized. She did not know what he had lost, and so she did not mourn it for him . . . and she never would. Her mind-glow was not Golden Eye's, and it never would be, and that was a good thing. This, whatever it was and however it had happened, was too bright, too special and precious, to be compared to anything else.

He opened to it, felt it flooding through the dark places deep within him, washing away the fear and the grief and the anguish, and knew he had come home again at last.

✧ ✧ ✧

Cordelia twitched, then snorted, as a feather touched her face.

Her mom and her sisters had teased her about her snoring for years, and from the feel of things, she'd been snoring again, she thought drowsily. Now why had she been doing that? And why was she sleeping sitting up? It was—

The feather touched her again, her eyes popped open, and it all came flooding back. The terror, the pain, the—

The feather brushed her cheek yet again, and she felt . . . *something* else. She didn't know what that "something" was, but it was there. She knew that much. And it was coming from—

She turned her head, and her eyes widened. It wasn't a feather brushing her cheek. It was a long, wiry finger. One armed with a sheathed, razor-sharp claw. A claw she'd seen rending and tearing near-weasels in her defense.

She straightened in the chair and reached out very carefully, wondering how he had gotten into her lap. Dr. Harrington said he'd put twice as many stitches into this treecat as into Lionheart on the day he'd saved Stephanie from the hexapuma, and his right rear leg was immobilized where the tendon had been repaired. He had to be in a lot of pain, despite the anesthetics, but somehow he'd gotten from the table beside her into her lap, and she heard a soft, buzzing sound—a purr, she realized—as her arms went cautiously around him.

She held him close, cradling him like the most precious thing in her world. Because, she realized, that was what he had just become. She and Stephanie and Karl Zivonik had talked while Dr. Harrington worked on both the treecat and Barnaby. Stephanie had tried to explain her bond with Lionheart, but Cordelia had known she hadn't really understood what the younger girl was trying to say.

Now she did, she realized with a sense of awe. She understood *exactly* what Stephanie had been saying... and knew *she* would never be able to explain it to someone else, either.

And that didn't matter at all.

"Hello," she told the treecat—*her* treecat—softly, eyes burning. "My name is Cordelia." She kissed him gently between the ears. "Thank you for the rest of my life."

✧ ✧ ✧

Stone pressed his nose against her, listening to her mouth sounds, wondering if that was how the mind-blind communicated with one another. It was an interesting thought, and perhaps one day he would know.

But that didn't matter at all.

<Hello,> he thought in the silence of his broken mind-voice. *<My name is Heart Stone. Thank you for the rest of my life.>*

2

"DAD," STEPHANIE SAID SOFTLY, STARING THROUGH THE window to where Cordelia drowsed, her dark hair still mussed, the battered and bandaged treecat in her lap, "that 'cat's going to make it, right?"

Although she tried hard not to, her voice choked up. She was honest enough to admit that feeding her grief and fear was the memory of how *she'd* felt when Lionheart had been the one injured while defending her.

"No promises," Richard Harrington said, "but the prognosis is good. And in the meantime, kiddo, I've got a job for you. I cleaned up Cordelia's injuries after the 'cat was stabilized, but I'd be happier if she saw a doctor who specializes in humans before she goes home, and she looks like she's waking up. Do you think you could convince her to leave my patient here while you take her to the hospital? Mack Kemper is off getting her a change of clothes and some supplies they'll need for the convalescents. It would be nice if Cordelia was ready to go when he came back."

"Absolutely," Stephanie replied. "Glad to."

"I'll call ahead to the hospital and warn them she's coming," Richard said. "I know it would be best if Cordelia's away from her 'cat as briefly as possible."

"Yeah," Stephanie agreed, remembering her eleven-year-old self, arms wrapped so tightly around the injured Lionheart that the blood from their wounds had run together. "You've got that right. I'll go talk to her now."

Cordelia looked up when Lionheart bleeked greeting to Stephanie. "Hi, Stephanie."

"How're you feeling?"

"Sore. Amazed. Part of me still believes I'm weasel-chow and dreaming all of this from heaven or somewhere. I mean..." The young woman gestured toward the treecat in her lap. "When I woke up, everything you and Karl told me came back, and I can't believe it. I mean, he's a wild...not animal, but alien? And he's sort of in love with me, and I'm in love with him and that's just impossibly great, and super-incredibly weird all at once."

Stephanie grinned. "I was only eleven when it happened to me, so I don't think I ever thought about how weird it was, but you're right. It's weird. Lionheart and I are a unit. Anybody else, even Mom and Dad or my best friends, they're one remove. Speaking of removes...Dad wants you to go to the hospital so they can look you over, especially your leg. Thing is, you'll need to leave the 'cat here. He's really fragile still."

"Sure, that's no problem," Cordelia began gently setting "her" treecat back on the nest of pillows that had been set up for him when she froze, panic visible in every line of her body. "Or is it a problem? My heart's racing all of a sudden."

Cordelia sagged back against the back of the sofa,

still holding the 'cat, panting slightly. Moving stiffly within his bandages, the 'cat rose on his hindmost pair of legs, pressed his frontmost paws against Cordelia's chest, and began emitting a loud, thrumming soothing purr. He rubbed his face against Cordelia's, then hunkered down, still purring.

Stephanie grinned ruefully. "Yeah, it *is* a problem, sorta kinda. Earlier, when Karl and I told you about the bond, we didn't get into the details. Short version. This bond isn't just for real, and for life, it's . . ." She scratched the nape of her neck, trying to find the words to explain something that she'd taken for granted for five years. Given that she was not quite sixteen, that meant about a third of her life, which was a strangely sobering thought.

Stephanie started again. "You and your 'cat really *are* a unit, and not in the symbolic way humans talk about for marriage. A married couple can live on different worlds, in different solar systems, heck, possibly in other galaxies or universes. You and your 'cat are going to always need to be on the same planet, within a limited number of kilometers from each other. If you're not, the strain gets uncomfortable. While you're getting to know each other, you're going to need to stay closer, especially at times, like now, when you're worried. Later, well, you'll be able to be apart, just not too *far* apart."

Cordelia's expression flickered through disbelief, lingered on a touch of dismay, then settled on bemused resignation. "I believe you. I mean, I feel in my gut or heart or something that you're right, but wow . . . This could have a lot of complications. I wonder how Irina Kisaevna feels about Fisher being sort of the third partner in her marriage with Scott MacDallan. That's kind of kinky."

Stephanie laughed. "Not really. I mean, I'm not

married or anything, but when I was dating Anders, Lionheart didn't seem to feel jealous about that. The bond's not competitive or anything—maybe because nothing can threaten it."

"How would you feel if Lionheart got 'married'?" Cordelia asked, genuinely curious.

Stephanie thought before answering. "I think I'd feel like I would if any good friend found someone special, but better, because I know how Lionheart feels about me. I know that nothing is going to change or weaken our bond. I think for me, his 'getting married' would mean I'd be getting extra friends and family. Love is one of those things that multiplies when shared, especially when you know you're not going to lose the person you love."

Stephanie didn't add how she'd felt when Anders started dating Jessica. Then she *had* wondered if she would lose not only her boyfriend, but one of her best friends as well. So far things were working out. In fact, if she was losing Jessica to anything, it was to the other girl's newfound passion for becoming a doctor. That reminded her; they needed to get Cordelia to the hospital.

"So, Cordelia, what you started feeling when I asked you to leave your 'cat behind? That's part of the bond, but intensified because the bond is new, and because you know that your 'cat is injured so you don't want to leave him. Can you take a few deep breaths? Tell yourself that he's perfectly safe here, safer than he would be if you carried him along to the hospital? I get the feeling that Lionheart's going to stay with your 'cat, so he won't be alone. My dad will be here, too."

Cordelia closed her eyes and began to breathe

deeply and rhythmically. Stephanie smiled when she realized that the breathing was falling into a cadence with the 'cat's purr. This time, when Cordelia gently lifted the 'cat and set him on the pillows, the panic reaction was there but under control.

Cordelia turned, locked eyes with the 'cat, then said slowly, "I'm going away to see a doctor about this"—she touched the bandages on her leg—"and these." She tapped various scrapes and scratches. "I'll be back. You get some rest."

She pressed a fingertip very gently against one of the few unwounded places on the 'cat's head, encouraging him to lie down. Lionheart bleeked, curling up in the pillows near the other 'cat, thrumming the soothing purr. Stephanie remembered that Jessica had told her how Valiant and Fisher had done the same thing when the 'cat Karl had dubbed "Survivor" was recovering from surgery. She saw how Cordelia relaxed, even if the lines of panic didn't completely fade, and guessed that meant Cordelia's 'cat was calming both himself and her.

Having been on the receiving end of a treecat's ministrations, she knew how effective they could be. "Ready? Dad's calling the hospital to let them know we're coming, so we won't be gone long."

"Ready," Cordelia replied firmly. "After all, I have responsibilities to my new partner, and I won't do either of us any good if I get sick."

"Any idea what you're going to call him?" Stephanie asked as she helped Cordelia to the Harrington's air car. Like Karl, Cordelia had the musculature of the "born-on-Sphinx," but today she was relying on a counter-grav unit to take the weight off her injured leg and sculling along with a crutch.

"I'm not sure," Cordelia said. "I wish I knew what he called himself. I'm sure that treecats have their own names for themselves."

"Me, too," Stephanie agreed, "and I bet they have their own names for us, too. I just hope mine isn't 'Source of Celery.'"

Cordelia giggled. "My sister Natalie claims that our dog, Barnaby, calls our family 'The Foodbringers,' but after today . . . Wow. Barnaby's paid in advance for a lifetime of premium chow." She shook her head in wonder. "I bet Nat never makes that joke again. Barnaby and my new treecat pal were the real heroes today." She paused, bit thoughtfully into her lower lip, as she eased into the passenger side of the car. "What about 'Hero' for a name? No. That's not quite right. I'll keep thinking about it though. He deserves a name, if for no other reason than to remind humans that he's not just 'Cordelia's Cat.'"

✧ ✧ ✧

Like every member of Bright Water clan, Climbs Quickly knew the tragedy of Stone Shaper and Golden Eye. Stone Shaper had been among the finest flint shapers Bright Water had had in generations of memory songs, which was why his early names had vanished. He had been called by the same name as the craft he had perfected, and as a youngster, Climbs Quickly had loved to watch the older Person at work. Indeed, there had been a time when he had thought he, too, might become a shaper of stone.

That had not been destined to happen, however, yet on the day he had officially been named a scout of Bright Water, Climbs Quickly had been awarded a knife of Stone Shaper's making. He had treasured it for many turnings. But then, on the day he met

Death Fang's Bane, that knife had been lost in his wild charge through the net-wood to reach her. He could not regret its loss, not when that day had brought so much joy into his life. Even so, he had grieved for it, because the gray death had meant it could never be replaced—not by the true-hands which had made it with such loving skill. Yet now Climbs Quickly felt only joy at reconnecting with this hero of his youth.

Stone Shaper had no mind-voice to tell Climbs Quickly what had happened, but the scent of needle-fangs had been heavy upon both him and the barker, and it was not hard to deduce what must have happened. The impressive wounds Stone Shaper had incurred in saving the young female two-leg and her barker made it impossible to tell just how harshly the turnings of isolation had treated the older Person, yet the fact that he had fought so well testified that he had managed not only to survive, but to thrive.

Back when Stone Shaper had chosen to leave Bright Water, Climbs Quickly had been among the many who had been puzzled and even a little hurt. The idea of choosing to live apart from the clan would—then—have never occurred to him. How could any person *choose* to be separated from the mind-glows, the heart warmth, of the People of his clan? And how could he take his own mind-glow away from them, like the last scrap of sunlight disappearing into the darkness?

Sings Truly, at that time only a junior memory singer, but already wiser than her years, had sought out Climbs Quickly and tried to explain why Stone Shaper would have separated himself from his clan and his young.

<*It is easy to forget,*> she had explained, <*because*

we can no longer hear what Stone Shaper says or share his memories, that he is still able to feel our reactions to his plight. However, there is every evidence that he can still taste our mind-glows.>

<But I cannot help how I feel,> Climbs Quickly had protested. *<I do feel sorry for how the gray death crippled him. I pity him for the loss of his mate.>*

Sings Truly tugged Climb Quickly's tail—hard. *<Idiot brother-mine! How would you feel if you were subjected to pity, grief, and even indignation, and could not explain the landscape of your mind, when before all about you knew what you truly thought, not just what songs sang in your heart? He can no longer do that, no longer share that part of him which* knows *things, as well as that which feels . . . and we can no longer mind-speak him to share that part of ourselves with* him. *Moreover, I am proud that Bright Water clan is so loving, but I fear not all clans would think Stone Shaper made the right choice when he lived on after Golden Eye, especially as what many People would see as a cripple who would burden the clan. Perhaps it is best he not face the taste of disdain or aversion in their mind-glows.>*

His sister's wisdom had not satisfied him, then, yet Climbs Quickly had learned much from these seasons' turning of his bond with Death Fang's Bane. He was accustomed, now, to having a friend—his best and dearest bondmate at that—be unable to use mind-speech or even to taste mind-glows. The same was true of Fisher, who had lived with Darkness Foe for many seasons' turnings, as well as Dirt Grubber, who had now been over a season with Windswept or Keen Eyes who had recently bonded with Shining Sunlight.

All of them had tasted much of the frustration Stone Shaper must have endured when those he loved could no longer mind-hear him, and they knew how bitter it could be. Yet they had also learned that even the mind-blind loved, and loved deeply. And they had also been forced to find ways to communicate with their two-legs despite their mind-blindness.

They were, he realized now, the first People who had ever done that. The first who had ever *had* to find a way, other than the union of the People's mind-voices and mind-glows, to "speak" to another.

We are a clan of sorts, Climbs Quickly thought with amazement. *A new clan of People who are a bridge with the two-legs. And perhaps what we have learned trying to communicate with* our *two-legs will help us do the same with Stone Shaper!* Hope for the other Person burned like a tiny flame inside him as he watched the other sleep, and he curled a bit closer to him. *Welcome into our clan, Stone Shaper,* he thought. *You have come home to rejoin us at last.*

✧ ✧ ✧

Cordelia was glad that Stephanie interpreted her reaction solely as being due to separation anxiety from "her" new 'cat. Cordelia wished it was that simple, but the truth was that she had very bad memories about the hospital.

The Plague that had wiped out part of her family, killed so many of her friends and neighbors, had stretched Sphinx's medical system. Hospitals had been reserved for those in most grave danger of dying. Cordelia had been so young that, for her, hospitals were imprinted on her soul not as places for healing, but as where people went to die.

"What the heck?" Stephanie exclaimed as she led them in via the emergency room entrance. "When Dad called, he was told to bring you around here, because things were pretty quiet."

Whatever Richard Harrington had been told a scant quarter hour before, now the emergency room displayed organized chaos of the sort Cordelia imagined was reserved for battlefields: professionals reacting to a crisis with efficiency that didn't hide their concern.

Background to it all was a woman wailing while trying to trail after a gurney that was bearing off a younger woman, somewhere in Stephanie and Cordelia's general age-range, in the direction of a pair of doors marked "Operating Room."

"Know that girl?" Cordelia said softly.

Stephanie shook her head. "You?"

"Nope. Maybe vaguely familiar from one of my online classes, but . . ."

A new voice, speaking with quiet authority cut in. "Paschel Trendane. Her family are relatively new settlers. I think they're steading near the Franchittis' land while they wait for their own petition for a grant to come through."

Cordelia and Stephanie wheeled as one. Cordelia was astonished to see that the speaker was a young woman, probably a little younger than herself, wearing scrubs. A treecat peered placidly over her shoulder. Her appearance—thick, light-auburn hair, barely subdued by a braid, hazel-green eyes—was vaguely familiar, and Cordelia placed her as Stephanie spoke.

"Jessica!" Stephanie exclaimed, her tone alive with affection. "I'm so glad you're here! Jess, this is Cordelia Schardt-Cordova, who . . . No, later; long story.

Cordelia, this is Jessica Pheriss, another treecat adoptee. The 'cat is Valiant."

Cordelia held out her free hand. "You're the one who went into a forest fire to help rescue some stranded 'cats, and got adopted."

Jessica was speaking at the same time, "'Another'?" Her ready grin faded as she took in the skin-coat bandaging where the near-weasels had mangled various parts of Cordelia's epidermis, as well as the bulky wrappings around her ankle. "Looks as if you signed on for Extreme Violence: the official Stephanie Harrington Treecat Recruitment Method. I recommend near-suffocation, myself. Much less painful, with the bonus that it leaves fewer scars."

"Karl handled adoption easiest," Stephanie added, laughing at Jessica's teasing. "He and Survivor . . . I still don't know what brought them together like that, but whatever linked them, the bond has been terrific for them both."

Treecat/human bondings were far from usual, so Cordelia had seen news stories about all three of these. For the first time, it occurred to her that she and her Nameless Hero would likely come in for their share of attention as well. She winced. She'd always been the most introverted of her family—Zack Kemper would have *loved* the attention.

Jessica saw the wince, and looked at Cordelia with concern. "I was sent down here as escort when the word came that Stephanie was bringing someone in. I'm supposed to take you to one of the examination rooms, so you can get more comfortable while we wait."

She motioned for them to follow her.

"Do you work here?" Cordelia asked, swinging her

sound leg and then the cane Dr. Harrington had given her as a stopgap.

"Volunteer. I'm shadowing various doctors. I want to go to med school. It's never too early to build my vita, especially since I'm going to need a scholarship or two or three. No way my family can afford to put me through med school, especially since I'm going to need to go off-planet."

Cordelia nodded. Owning a barony was nice, but her own family was richer in land than in credits. There were lots of post-Plague families on Sphinx in the same situation. Recently, the Kemper boys had been thrilled when an off-planet biologist had offered to rent use-rights on some of their vacant land. It meant income that was all the more necessary as they prepared to move from the Schardt-Cordova home back into their deserted holding.

The examining room was decorated with a lovely print of a lace willow transformed in spring. Stephanie pointed to it with evident pride. "My mom's art. She's a botanist, but a really great painter, too. She started doing scientific drawings, but her art took on a life of its own."

As Jessica took Cordelia's vital signs, Stephanie prattled on about the "Old Man," which was what her family called the specific lace willow that had served as the model. Cordelia guessed that underlying the cheerful commentary was Stephanie's awareness that Cordelia was feeling very nervous.

Being famous hasn't made her self-centered. I like her. From how the newsies portray her, I never really thought I would, but I do like her.

Jessica clearly felt the same way.

You can judge a person by their friends. Even on this small sample, these are two people I'd like to know better. Cordelia felt surprised. Unlike Natalie and Dana, she'd never really missed having friends, maybe because she and Mack were close enough in age to be twins, and Zack only slightly younger.

The doctor who came in a short time later was a tall, lean, long-jawed man with dark brown skin and eyes that contrasted with hair so startlingly silver that Cordelia wondered if he bleached it. The bulge of a counter-grav unit under his outer tunic and relative lack of overt musculature identified him as a newer settler.

"I'm Thomas Flambeau," the doctor said, holding out his hand. "I'm sorry I've kept you waiting, but I was called to help with an emergency. I know Jessica, of course, but you young ladies?"

Stephanie offered her hand. "Stephanie Harrington."

"Cordelia Schardt-Cordova," Cordelia said in turn. Gesturing to her various bandages she added, "I'm the patient. Stephanie drove me over from her father's clinic."

"Looks as if Richard did well by you, but let's take a look at the leg in particular. Jessica, would you like to work the scanner?"

Jessica beamed, then grew immediately serious. "Yes, sir!"

The examination that followed was facilitated because, after cutting away Cordelia's damaged clothing, Richard Harrington had supplied her with a loose caftan in an astonishingly brilliant purple and gold pattern. Tests were run, readings taken, resulting in Dr. Flambeau deciding that he'd like to do some further treatment on the worst of Cordelia's lacerated leg muscles.

"I'll also give you a crutch, which will free-up your cane hand. You've had a bad break in that ankle, then walked on it. It's going to take at least three weeks to heal, even with quick-heal—longer if you don't go easy on it."

When Jessica and Valiant darted off to get the necessary equipment, Stephanie, possibly, Cordelia thought, by way of a distraction, asked Dr. Flambeau:

"Is the girl in emergency badly hurt?"

"I can't speak to specifics," the doctor replied, "but sadly yes. She apparently forgot about how serious a fall can be in Sphinx's higher gravity." His expression became rueful. "I've had a few near-misses myself when I thought I could manage without my counter-grav unit for just a little. Apparently, she made the same mistake...but without the 'miss' part."

Jessica and Valiant returned then. Before long, Cordelia had undergone a session of nerve stimulation, had had her wounds freshly patched, and was feeling just a little light-headed from the pain meds. When her com unit chimed as they were heading back to Stephanie's car, she had to think about what the sound was. She read the text and smiled.

"Mack will be picking me and Barnaby up at your dad's clinic. He's bought me a change of clothes, so I can give your dad back this amazing caftan." She frowned. "Uh, do I need to have Mack pick up treecat kibble or something?"

Stephanie laughed. "Not really. We'll give you a list of recommended foods, as well as ones that treecats like but aren't exactly recommended."

"Like celery?" Cordelia laughed, remembering Stephanie's earlier comment.

"Like that. Just like we can eat Sphinxian foods, treecats can eat ours, but there can be—uh—digestive consequences."

✧ ✧ ✧

Mack was waiting at the veterinary clinic when they arrived. His dark-brown hair, which as a boy he'd worn so it tumbled over his forehead, had been recently cut much shorter, a practical concession to his self-appointed role as the family tinkerer. Cordelia had always thought Mack's best feature was his smile, which was wide and open. Today, his relief at seeing her scudding briskly along on her crutch, had put that smile on full display.

"I'm here to pick up the Three Musketeers," Mack announced. "If my sister, Pathos, there will relinquish that so fetching robe and deign to don this more humble attire I have acquired for her..."

"That's it!" Cordelia interrupted, pausing in the middle of reaching for the bag Mack extended. "Athos! I'll call the 'cat 'Athos.' He and me and Barnaby really were like the Three Musketeers, facing down the Cardinal's guard."

She didn't add that she somehow felt that the treecat had more in common with brooding, romantically betrayed Athos, than with either boastful Porthos or self-consciously intellectual Aramis.

"Then I shall be D'artagnan," Mack announced. "He really was the smartest one of the lot, or at least the most practical. Zack can be, oh, what was his name? The clever servant."

Mack extended the shopping bag again, and this time Cordelia took it. "Stephanie, is there somewhere I can change?"

"Sure," Stephanie replied. "Why not Athos's room?

I'll come along if you'd like, help you with fasteners or whatever. Your leg is probably feeling like dead wood about now."

Cordelia nodded, remembering what Jessica had said about "the Stephanie Harrington" method of treecat adoption. Stephanie was doubtless speaking from firsthand experience.

Mack made a shooing gesture to urge them along. "If I'm not here when you come out, I'm fetching Barnaby. Ping me."

The treecat—Athos—was looking right at her as Cordelia came through the door, but that didn't surprise her. Even with all the pain meds in her system, she'd felt him, too, long before she'd entered the room. She grinned at Stephanie, shaking her head in something between bemusement and amazement.

"It's real. That connection. It's like a glow, a light that I don't see with my eyes."

"You don't mind, do you?" Stephanie asked, a trifle anxiously.

"No way! It's only been a little while, but I already know I'd miss it."

After she'd finished helping Cordelia into her change of clothes, Stephanie shuffled her feet, showing a shyness that surprised Cordelia. "Um, if you want, I could come out to your place, sort of tell you things about living with a treecat. Jessica could come, if she's not shadowing someone, or maybe Karl. He's a new adoptee, like you, too."

Cordelia hesitated, not wanting to impose more than she had already. Stephanie, who'd hunkered down to let Lionheart climb where he could look over her shoulder, continued in a rush.

"I don't want to be bossy. It's just that there are things that are useful, like how you can wear a padded brace, so your 'cat can ride resting his legs on that rather than your needing to carry him or him trying to run alongside." Stephanie paused, bit into her lower lip, then went on. "But you're injured, probably super tired and stressed. I don't want to butt in. Karl always says I act like because I made first contact with the treecats I think I own them. Seriously, if you want, I'll just message you stuff."

Cordelia waved Stephanie down. "Chill. If you want to come all the way out to our homestead, you'd be welcome. But I know you're busy. School. And you have a job with the Forestry Service, too, right? We live like four hundred kilometers south of town, but I'll need to come into Twin Forks so your dad can check Athos over again, so we could meet here."

Stephanie laughed, obviously relieved. "I'd love to come. Seriously. I could even help with the firebreak you were surveying for when you got attacked. That's a job my bosses at the Forestry Service would completely approve of."

✧ ✧ ✧

I'm glad Cordelia's okay with me visiting, Stephanie thought as she walked out the door of the clinic, carrying Athos so Cordelia could make her way to the air car without putting too much weight on her broken ankle and near-weasel mangled limbs. *I should arrange a meeting with all of us adoptees. We're going to need to clue Cordelia in on the Great Treecat Conspiracy.*

Her thoughts were broken into by a soft hiss from Lionheart that she felt with her soul before her ears caught the sound. At the same moment, she became aware that Cordelia and Mack, who had been a few steps in front of her, were slowing. Her heart sank as she realized why. José "Nosey" Jones, the self-proclaimed "Ace Reporter of Sphinx," was standing outside the clinic.

Nosey's tall, lanky build proclaimed that he had not spent his early growth years on Sphinx. His most notable feature was the large, slightly hooked nose that was so prominent that it was easy to overlook his expressive blue-gray eyes and sensitive mouth. His skin was dark, with tints taken from the "red-brown" palette rather than the peach of Stephanie's own.

Nosey was in his mid-to-late twenties, and a private courier by trade. During the recent wildfires, he'd taken it upon himself to deliver supplies and personnel where the need was greatest. In the process, he'd discovered the joy of seeing people flock to him, wanting his eyewitness account of how the wildfires were being handled. Later, after the worst of the fires had been beaten back, he'd actually done a lot of good, bringing attention to circumstances where fire damage had left freeholders needing additional assistance, whether in clearing away ruined trees or rebuilding homes and outbuildings.

Now that fire risks wouldn't be as bad, and the most tragic situations had been dealt with, Nosey had been sniffing around to find ways to keep his eyewitness reports central to Twin Forks and surrounding areas. Today, he clearly thought he'd found an item of interest to his audience.

He wasn't rude enough to actually block the small group as they headed toward their waiting air car, but instead dropped alongside.

"Cordelia Schardt-Cordova? I was at the hospital covering another emergency and heard about your being attacked. Is it true that near-weasels did all that damage?"

Cordelia nodded curtly.

"Wow!" Nosey continued, not in the least put off by her lack of encouragement. "Hey! That's one seriously messed up treecat. How did it get so badly hurt? Ms. Harrington, does this mean you'll have two pet treecats? I guess your Lionheart will enjoy the company. From what we know, treecats are social creatures. It must be hard for Lionheart living all alone with just humans for company. Of course, you do seem to be collecting a nice little group of human friends with pet treecats. Maybe you can start a club for treecat fanciers. It seems that even wild-born treecats can make excellent pets..."

Stephanie, rarely at a loss for words, found herself momentarily floundering under this flood of mingled assumptions and misinformation. Once again, she felt the sinking sensation that always hit her when she realized that the majority of people couldn't help but think treecats made excellent pets. Explaining that they weren't pets, that they were closer to symbiotes... No. That was right out.

Worse, she wasn't eleven anymore, dealing with super-annoying kids like Trudy Franchetti. She couldn't fly into a rage or sulk. Or punch anyone in the nose. She was a member of the Sphinxian Forestry Service, a badge-carrying probationary ranger, and the treecats—all the treecats—were hers to protect, up to and including—no, *especially*—the ones that wanted nothing to do with humans.

Cordelia could use her injury as a reason not to answer, and Mack was occupying himself with Barnaby. But Nosey wasn't going away, and Stephanie knew ignoring him would just give him an excuse to write whatever he felt like. She decided to hazard a reply to the simpler question.

"No, I'm not going to have another 'pet,' treecat. Athos, here, will be returning to the area where Cordelia and Mack's family holdings are. That's where he came from."

No need to mention that Athos would be staying with Cordelia. Cordelia had slipped into the passenger seat, and Stephanie handed her Athos. Mack had gently loaded Barnaby into the air car's back seat and hopped agilely into the driver's side.

"We're off," he said to Stephanie, pointedly ignoring Nosey. "See you!"

Stephanie waved back, then turned, expecting to find Nosey at her shoulder but, when she turned, braced for more questions, he was gone. Somehow, that worried her a whole lot more.

✧ ✧ ✧

Later that day, Stephanie discovered that her instincts had been right on target when Nosey's latest *Sphinxian Oracle* column appeared in the feeds. The headline story was "New Settler In Critical Condition" but, right after it, were two stories that hit much closer to home. "Severely Injured Treecat Finds Human Home" was headed with a holovid of Cordelia cradling Athos as she and Mack drove off from in front of the Harrington Veterinary Clinic. The opening paragraph was deceptively warm-spirited:

Treecats in the Twin Forks area are lucky to have

Dr. Richard Harrington to tend to their injuries. His latest patient came from some 400 km south of our bustling town. The treecat, dubbed "Athos" by Dr. Harrington's daughter, Stephanie, was injured in an attack (see following story) by near-weasels at the height of their breeding frenzy. Also injured in the assault were Cordelia Schardt-Cordova and her family dog, Barnaby. Details on precisely how the incident occurred will be forthcoming.

Given the severity of "Athos's" injuries, it seems unlikely that he will be returned to the wild any time soon, if at all. If he remains in human care, this will make the fifth such treecat taken into human custody. Although xeno-anthropologists are still severely divided as to where on the intelligence scale these furry Sphinxian natives should be classified, there is no doubt that they are both appealing and clever enough to make fascinating pets. But should keeping treecats be permitted?

In the case of Lionheart, the first captive treecat, his injuries were severe enough that releasing him into the wild, especially in the dead of winter, would have been a sentence of death. That his caretakers include a veterinarian and his daughter, a young woman who has shown herself so dedicated to Sphinxian wildlife that the post of probationary ranger was, many say, specifically created for her, makes Lionheart's situation admirably well-suited to the crippled treecat's needs.

"Fisher," the treecat who resides with Dr. Scott MacDallan of the Thunder River region, does not appear to have any injuries that justify his continued association with humans. However, as far as this reporter has been able to learn, no effort to repatriate Fisher has been made. Nor has any release effort been made for

"Valiant," who resides with Jessica Pheriss of Twin Forks, although he also shows no apparent injuries.

More justification for continued human-associated dwelling can be made in the case of "Survivor," who very recently came into the custody of newly promoted SFS Ranger, Karl Zivonik. Although not an amputee like Lionheart, Survivor shows evidence of recent injuries.

How these widely varied prior cases have been handled raises the question as to what the fate of Athos should be. Should he be left in the custody of the Schardt-Cordova family, simply because Cordelia Schardt-Cordova found him injured and took him to the vet? Or should there be some process to be followed before these wild animals can be kept by humans? Perhaps an educational or orientation program could be instituted? If so, who would be in charge of said program? The SFS is an obvious candidate, but their resources are already spread thin.

Those of us concerned about development on Sphinx, including how spreading settlement will mean increased interaction between humans and the native wildlife of our adopted home planet, feel these are matters that need to be addressed. We must protect the treecats and other creatures who may find their lifeways interfered with by well-meaning humans.

Less personally intrusive was the article "SFS: Falling Down on Educational Duties?" which immediately followed. The gist of this piece was that accidents like that which had recently hospitalized Paschel Trendane wouldn't happen if new settlers to Sphinx were better educated as to the hazards that came with settling in their new home.

Since Stephanie had already decided that her future lay with the Sphinxian Forestry Service, she felt personally offended by this criticism of the SFS, even as she reluctantly agreed that Nosey did have a point. Even Cordelia had nearly gotten herself killed, and she had taken reasonable precautions because she understood the normal risks. But the near-weasels had surprised even her, so what about newer settlers who hadn't grown up here the way she had? Stephanie herself, for example. She'd been nine T-years old, going on ten, when her family arrived, and she'd taken *way* too much for granted. An older and wiser Stephanie knew how right her father had been to order her not to go into the bush by herself, uni-link or no uni-link! But right after she'd arrived? Heck, even two *T-years* after she'd arrived!

Looked at in that light, Nosey had a point about newer settlers who, equipped with counter-grav units, so often forgot just how many additional hazards came from living on a planet with 1.35 Old Terran gravities.

"It's just all so complicated," she complained to Karl when he looked up from his own uni-link. "The SFS doesn't have the budget to teach 'Welcome to the Dangers of the Sphinxian Bush' classes to new arrivals."

"And the budget isn't there because two major waves of the Plague, in addition to the minor ones, really hit our population hard," Karl agreed. "Believe me. I've heard it. Lack of funding comes up at every SFS weekly briefing, every time someone has a great idea for an SFS program. No money. No program."

"Worse," Stephanie griped, "the immigration and outreach office doesn't dare emphasize too heavily how many hazards there are here, because if Sphinx is perceived as dangerous, then bye-bye to tourist credits, research grants, business investment, and immigration. Back when you and I were taking the accelerated ranger training program on Manticore, I heard more than a few people muttering that Manticore itself was still largely unexplored. Why did Kingdom funds need to be diverted to Sphinx and Gryphon? Let those planets prove their value to the Star Kingdom before money gets wasted on them."

Karl blew out his breath so hard that calling it a "sigh" was like calling a hurricane "strong winds." "It's complicated; that's for sure. Well, you and I can't do much about the SFS budget, but we need to do something about the treecat adoption problem. Annoying as he may be, Nosey has a point. When treecat adoptees were just you and Scott MacDallan, that was one thing. With me and Cordelia getting 'cats within a few weeks of each other? It's not going to be long before people are going to at least insist there be a 'fostering' list rather than what it seems like now, which is 'finders keepers.'"

"Worse," Stephanie said, hugging Lionheart tightly enough that he bleeked in protest. "How long before someone decides to injure a treecat, just to make an excuse to 'rescue' it?"

3

"DO YOU MIND IF I STAY THE NIGHT WITH SCOTT AND Irina?" Cordelia asked her mother. "He thought it might be nice if Athos had a 'play date' with Fisher. It's possible some of the other treecat people are going to come, too, sort of an orientation for me."

In the few days since Athos had come to live with Cordelia and her family, the treecat had definitely become a part of the family. That he would be Cordelia's shadow surprised no one, but he also seemed to have decided that Barnaby was his responsibility as well, standing by and purring loudly whenever the Rottie's bandages were changed, as well as apparently encouraging the big dog not to spit out his medications. The threat that Athos might be taken from them—as a variety of responses to Nosey Jones's post had suggested—made it all the more important that the Schardt-Cordovas show that they were doing their best by the injured 'cat.

"That seems more than reasonable," Danette agreed. "I certainly can't complain about your going to the doctor's, can I? Sure you can fly yourself? The ankle not bothering you too much?"

"I'm good for flying," Cordelia assured her. "I'll message when I get there, though."

Cordelia hurried away before Natalie, who had been making "I want a treecat, too" noises, could suggest she come along. Although neither Scott MacDallan nor Stephanie Harrington had said anything specific, Cordelia had a feeling that more was going to be discussed than what laxatives were best for a treecat who had scored an entire bunch of celery.

✧ ✧ ✧

Athos clinging to her shoulder, Cordelia walked around the rambling stone structure which served as home, clinic, and studio for Dr. Scott MacDallan and his wife, the potter, Irina Kisaevna. Scott wasn't currently Cordelia's family's doctor, since they lived south of Twin Forks, while he was north, closer to Thunder River, but they'd come to know him well during the final, tragic stages of the Plague, where his dedication to his professional duties had been nothing short of heroic. Later as the second human to be adopted by a treecat, he had become something of a celebrity.

Today, as Cordelia walked around the building to the residential entry, she felt a little awkward, like when she'd been invited to a party of a school friend she knew mostly from the planetary data net. She became aware that Athos was softly buzzing where he rested with the foremost of his three sets of paws on her shoulder and found herself relaxing. Unlike those parties, she wasn't going alone to face a group of people who already knew each other well. She had a friend.

Cordelia was raising her hand to knock when the door swung open. Irina smiled warmly at her. She was a little shorter than Cordelia and, like her, shared the well-muscled build of someone who had grown up on Sphinx. As often, she wore her straight, dark-brown hair swept up and back, a style that not only kept it out of her clay, but displayed her enormous, expressive brown eyes to good advantage. She greeted Cordelia as if they were old friends who met often, rather than mere acquaintances.

"Stephanie, Karl, and Jessica are already in the living room," Irina said, holding up her hands to take Cordelia's jacket, "as you can doubtless hear . . ."

Stephanie's voice carried. She wasn't quite whining, but she did sound distinctly exasperated, "Nosey's article about treecats as pets was fair enough. I admit that. He even raised some good points. But these 'letters to the editors' that he posts without any attempt to provide balance or commentary are a real problem. Listen to this one." Her voice shifted as she read in a tone of voice so carefully neutral that it provided a subtext of its own. "We get that Stephanie Harrington 'discovered' treecats, but that was five years ago. She's no longer the sole expert. Isn't it just a little suspicious that all the adopted treecats end up going to friends of hers? Does that mean everyone has to suck up to a fifteen-year-old to get a treecat for a pet?"

"Annoying, I admit," said Jessica, laughter rippling under her words. "Especially since I don't suck up. Don't let them get you so riled, Steph. This problem is never going to go away, because the 'cats have too good taste to adopt a loser, right, Karl?"

"I agree," came a deep male voice. "I don't know Cordelia well, but we've had data net classes together. She seems very solid, actually more well-balanced than Stephanie. I'll never forget how the first time I saw Stephanie, she was getting into a rumble with a bunch of kids."

Stephanie made a rude noise, but she was laughing, too.

Irina cleared her throat loudly. "Speaking of Cordelia, she and Athos have just arrived. I'll call Scott in from his office." She gave Cordelia a gentle shove. "Go on. Refreshments are there. You've already met just about everyone."

Paradoxically, the praise she'd heard made Cordelia even more shy, but she was used to pretending to be more social than she actually was. Raising her chin just a little, she marched out to meet what she would soon come to think of as the Great Treecat Conspirators.

Stephanie and Jessica sat side by side on one of the comfortable sofas, each sipping steaming mugs of cocoa. Lionheart and Valiant sat behind them, each messily tearing into a stalk of celery.

Unlike their first meeting on the day Cordelia and Athos were hurt, Karl Zivonik wore his SFS uniform, which initially made him seem very grown-up and formal, an impression somewhat undercut by the fact that "his" treecat, Survivor—showing evidence of his fur growing back from recent injuries—was perched on Karl's knee, daintily eating a piece of sashimi. Karl rose politely to greet Cordelia, and his height, combined with the powerful build of a born-Sphinxian, made him an imposing figure. A life spent mostly outdoors had tanned his skin, which provided a nice contrast to his gray eyes and dark hair.

As he rose, Karl automatically picked up Survivor

and held him loosely in one arm. The sudden image of Karl as a boy with a very battered stuffed toy flashed into her mind, and Cordelia stifled a smile.

Karl seemed to feel the smile and grinned back. "Good to see you looking less battered and bitten," he said. "And Athos is looking a lot better, too."

"Thanks," she said. "We are—better I mean, both of us."

Stephanie waved Cordelia to take her choice of one of several comfortable overstuffed chairs. "Coffee? Tea? Cocoa?"

"Coffee, please."

Jessica shoved a tray of cookies over toward Cordelia. "Try these. Be honest. My mom and I have been experimenting on ways to use some of Sphinx's human-friendly plants. These are pseudo-doodles, sort of a variation on a snickerdoodle, but made with range barley flour."

And as easy as that, Cordelia found herself welcomed and drawn in. Athos left her long enough to get a slice of smoked river trout and touch noses with Fisher, Lionheart, and Survivor, but he returned and snuggled into her lap, tufted ears moving as he tracked the conversation.

Scott MacDallan joined them as they were analyzing the cookies. (The general verdict was that they were pretty good, but needed more work to cut the astringent taste of the range barley.) Scott had red hair that burned with a fiery hue rarely seen in adults. That, along with his freckles, made him seem boyish. As he helped himself to some strong black tea and his share of the pseudo-doodles, Scott asked about Cordelia's and Athos's injuries, then sank back into his chair. His next statement transformed what had been a purely social occasion into a meeting.

"Cordelia, you must know that the question of just how intelligent treecats are is of serious interest right now. And you've had several days now to observe Athos up close."

Cordelia couldn't hide her enthusiasm about her new friend. "He's smart. Incredibly smart." She told them about how quickly he had adapted to her household's routine, how he helped with Barnaby, how she'd seen him actually making what looked like some sort of stone tool.

"He wasn't happy with it, tossed it away, but I thought it was incredible, so I saved it. When he saw what I was doing, he sort of snorted, came over, took it from me, picked up a piece of stone and rubbed it along the edges and gave it back. I think he was deliberately blunting it, so I wouldn't hurt myself like some dumb kid."

She pulled the partially-finished stone tool from her pocket and showed it to them. "I'd never believed treecats were toolmakers. But this is something more. From the way Athos acted, how he figured out what I was doing and what he needed to do to, well, protect me from myself. That was really, really smart!"

"Did you tell anyone about what Athos did?" Stephanie asked, sounding a trace apprehensive.

"Just my older sister, Dana, but she basically rolled her eyes and said I should tell her when he learned to talk." Cordelia looked sheepish. "I've been, well, sort of enthusiastic about Athos."

"How would you feel if we told you that we"—Scott's gesture encompassed all present—"thought that the best thing we could do for the treecats would be to conceal just how smart they are?"

"What?" Cordelia exclaimed. "That's crazy. Having them acknowledged as fully sentient would be the best thing for them. Have you been reading the comments to Nosey Jones's articles? It's not going to be long before there's going to be a craze for pet treecats. My little sister is already hinting about what she wants for her birthday."

"Um," Stephanie said, and Cordelia looked at her. "That's the problem," the younger girl said. "They *aren't* pets. They'll never *be* pets."

"I've already figured that out," Cordelia replied, just a bit more sharply than she'd meant to, and Stephanie waved a hand between them.

"I know you have," she said quickly. "I only have to watch you with Athos. But you're right—way too many people are already like your sister. They really, really want a neat 'pet' of their own, and a lot of them aren't likely to be too particular about how they . . . acquire one. The SFS is doing its best to protect the treecats, and they're *way* too smart to walk into any obvious traps." *Especially*, she didn't add aloud, *after Lionheart's clan spread the word about Bolgeo's traps*. "But that doesn't mean they won't keep trying. It doesn't mean those of us who end up adopted by one of them aren't going to be under a microscope, either, and trying to explain to someone who hasn't been adopted that we *can't* be separated, is . . . well—"

She shrugged, and Cordelia nodded in understanding, irritation fled.

"That's a big enough problem to be starting with," Karl chimed in, drawing her eyes back to him, "but there's more. Maybe even worse." He twitched his head in Stephanie's direction, his expression very serious. "Steph's dad was right when he reminded her about what happened to the Amphors."

"Amphors?" Cordelia repeated. Her brow furrowed. The name was vaguely familiar, but...

"Barstool," Stephanie said grimly, and Cordelia inhaled sharply.

She hadn't thought about Barstool in a long time—not since her last history class, four T-years ago. History, unfortunately, had never been her favorite subject. She was too focused on "now" and rebuilding her world in the Plague's wake. But she remembered now. The Amphors had been an amphibian species native to the planet named Barstool by its human settlers. They'd built their homes underwater as protection against predators, and—like the treecats—they'd been missed in the early planetary surveys. Their eventual discovery, and the realization that they were toolmakers and users, had created a furor, and that furor had included demands from some quarters that the human settlers leave the planet entirely. Others had demanded that huge portions of the planet be set aside as habitat for its native sentients. Even more moderate voices had called for a moratorium on further human settlement or development on the planet until examination could determine just how intelligent—as humans ranked such things—the Amphors truly were.

No one had ever completed that examination. That was because the human government had solved the "Amphor problem" by officially declaring them animals, and the species had been hunted into extermination in less than thirty T-years.

Barstool had paid for that with near universal condemnation, trade boycotts, even the official condemnation of the Solarian League Assembly. Indeed, it was *still* paying for it. But that hadn't brought the Amphors back.

"Do . . . do you really think that could happen here?" Her arms tightened protectively around Athos, and he looked up quickly. He touched her cheek with his nose, his purr buzzing loudly, and she kissed him between the ears.

"We don't know," Stephanie said somberly. Cordelia looked back at her, and she shrugged. "One thing that's different from Barstool is that there are three habitable planets in this star system. It's not like humans wouldn't have other places to live if some or all of Sphinx got set aside for the 'cats. At the same time, there are people who have plans for the planet, and then there are those of us who already live here."

"This is what you really invited me here to discuss, isn't it?" Cordelia said slowly, and Stephanie nodded.

"We're still in the really early stages of figuring things out about the 'cats, Cordelia, but we already know they're supersmart, just like you've said about Athos, and the Forestry Service knows they're tool-users. So does the government on Manticore. So far, they're going really slow, and Dr. Hobbard—she's the xeno-anthropologist heading the official government study teams—is on our side. But sooner or later, the question of just how smart they really are, where they fall on the sentience scale, is going to have to be determined. Dr. Hobbard says the fact that the treecats can't talk and don't seem to have any kind of writing or record keeping argues they probably rank pretty low, but her own observations—and ours—of their actions and interactions argue exactly the opposite.

"The problem is that if we can't demonstrate where they rank, and if it isn't high enough, then they'll just be 'animals' to way too many people . . . just like the Amphors. Maybe there won't be some kind of organized extermination campaign, the way there was on Barstool, but they'll be protected *only* as animals. This is their world, it belongs to *them*, and if we can't prove they're 'smart enough,' humans will just keep pushing in and take all of it away from them!" Stephanie's eyes flashed, and she shook her head hard. "We can live here with them, but they were here *first*!"

"Of course they were," Cordelia said sharply.

"But until and unless we can figure out a way to prove they're intelligent enough to be considered Sphinx's rightful owners, they're at risk," Scott said. "Some of the inclination to classify them as animals, not sentients, is inevitable and natural, but there are also people who will push that idea just as hard and as fast as they can because of the way an official recognition of the 'cats' sentience would interfere with *their* plans for Sphinx."

"So what do we do about it?" Cordelia asked tautly.

"What we're doing so far is to go as slow as possible," Stephanie said. "We're trying to dodge any questions about how smart they really are because we hope that as long as people in general think of them as cute, adorable little animals, the folks who might want to kick them out of the way won't feel threatened. Won't come out into the open and start campaigning to have them *officially* classified that way. And the whole time we're doing that, Dr. Hobbard and some of her friends—and us, of course—are recording everything we can about the 'cats. We're keeping records of their interactions with us and studying them 'in the wild' as closely as we can. We're trying to build up enough data to demonstrate that even without a spoken language or writing, they *are* truly sentient, and the longer we have to do that, the stronger our case will be. Most of the SFS is in on it, and so are at least a couple of off-world xeno-anthropologists, but keeping a lid on what we're doing while simultaneously protecting them *and* integrating them into human society as our friends—*not* pets—is . . . hard."

"That's our Steph," Jessica said dryly. "As always, the mistress of understatement."

Karl and Scott both laughed, and Lionheart and Survivor bleeked with what was clearly laughter of their own. It was a welcome break in the tension, Cordelia thought, and settled back into her chair.

"Well, it *is* hard," Stephanie said with a grin. Then the grin disappeared. "And it's going to get even harder if Nosey and his friends try to set up some sort of Treecat Protection Society. If they really were just animals, just pets, I'd be a hundred percent on his side, actually." It seemed to irk her to admit that, but she did it without flinching. "I can think of dozens of people who'd just *love* to have a treecat 'pet' . . . and shouldn't be allowed within a hundred kilometers of one of them! Fortunately, the 'cats seem pretty picky about who they choose, and they're really good at disappearing when they need to, so most of *those* people probably won't *get* within a hundred kilometers of them. But—"

"But if somebody sets up something like a protection

society to start looking over our shoulders, that 'going as slow as possible of yours' goes out the window," Cordelia said.

"Maybe. Maybe not. But probably, yes," Stephanie said. Then she exhaled and sat back on the sofa beside Jessica.

"So there it is, Cordelia," she said. "Welcome to the club."

"Gee, thanks." Cordelia shook her head with a grin of her own. "Boy, I figured you guys wanted to talk about more than just the care and feeding of tree-cats. Didn't see *this* coming, though. On the other hand"—her grin vanished as completely as Stephanie's had—"sign me up. Is there a membership card and everything? Or just a secret handshake?"

✧ ✧ ✧

That José "Nosey" Jones had embraced the seriously unkind nickname he'd been given in middle school said a lot about him. That he'd transformed it into a career said the rest: Nosey Jones—Your Nose for News. Nosey Knows You Want To Know.

He'd raced over to the Harrington Clinic because Stephanie Harrington was rumored to be prone to losing her temper, and she might say something eminently quotable. Despite keeping a treecat as a pet, she was well-known to have "opinions" regarding the attractive little beasties, opinions quite at odds with her own behavior, or so many people saw it. Differing opinions led to hits on newsfeeds, especially when there was a lack of "real" news; hits led to micropayments from his advertisers, which Nosey turned around into funding his research.

But Stephanie had kept her cool, and the Schardt-Cordovas and Kempers had proved unreceptive to being interviewed. Nosey was considering pushing harder for a few quotes, even going out to the Schardt-Cordova's homestead to take some long-range shots of the site of Cordelia's encounter with the near-weasels. Thing was, that was private land, and trespassing was . . . discouraged on Sphinx. Those Schardt-Cordovas and Kempers had a reputation for being quick on the trigger, and he had no desire to be the subject of one of his own news stories.

For the time being, he decided to focus in on a safer topic. A nice tearjerker follow-up piece on Paschel Trendane would fit the bill. He had an opening there, which helped. The Trendane family was one of the many he'd assisted both during and after the recent spate of fires. They were relatively new settlers on Sphinx, but they were from Manticore itself, not immigrants from out-system, with every prospect of becoming landowners. While they were waiting for the paperwork to go through, they were residing on land owned by the Franchittis.

Jordan Franchitti had turned a deaf ear to their requests for help, saying that he had his own family to look after, and that the terms of the Trendanes' lease did not obligate him to assist with repair to their damaged home. Nosey knew better than to directly attack a powerful landowner like Earl Franchitti, so he went about shaming the earl into helping by arranging a sort of "barn-raising" event to help the Trendanes with repairs. Once Jordan Franchitti realized everyone assumed that he and his family would be partaking, he'd shown up, all forced affability and fake smiles. No one ever directly referred to what Nosey had done, but the Trendanes viewed him as a sort of hero for the underdog.

When Nosey dropped by, Paschel's mother, Maisha, greeted him warmly, motioned for him to come inside, then handed him a stoneware mug full of the rich clove-scented, honey-sweet tea she knew he liked, almost before he had taken off his outdoor gear. She was a lovely woman, with dark skin and eyes. Rumor had it that her family was related to the Manticoran Royal family but, if so, they weren't trading on the relationship to get their request for a land grant expedited. To Nosey's way of seeing things, this made the connection more, rather than less, likely, since the Wintons were renowned for believing in doing things themselves.

"How's Paschel?" Nosey asked, reaching into his messenger bag to remove a small box of nut clusters he'd purchased at the Red Letter Café, after consulting with the owner, Eric Flint, about what sort of treats Paschel liked. "Up and about?"

Maisha's brave smile couldn't conceal her worry. "She had some bad bone breaks, but tests show she's healing. Still, she doesn't seem to be bouncing back. Why don't you go see her? I'm sure she'd love a visitor."

Nosey wasn't certain that was the case. Of the three younger Trendanes, Paschel was definitely the shy one, but he hefted his mug and said in a hearty tone of voice, "Point me in the right direction."

Paschel was ensconced on a daybed on the sunporch. Her skin was several shades lighter than her mother's, but her enormous eyes were the same melting dark. As she looked up from her holovid-screen, Nosey was reminded of a wild animal peeking out from the underbrush.

"A visitor for you, dear!" Maisha chirped. "You remember Nosey Jones, don't you?"

Unspoken in her inflection was, "And everything he did for us."

Paschel managed a shy smile. "Hi, Nosey."

"Candy for you," he said, sliding the box over the table and feeling fully rewarded by the smile that lit her features. "How're you feeling?"

"For somebody who left her c-gee off?" Paschel spoke so softly that if Nosey hadn't trained himself to listen, he wouldn't have heard her. "Dumb."

"Ouch!" he said. "Sympathies. I'm not sure there's a pill for that. If there was, I'd have a whole bottle in my pocket."

Once again, he was rewarded by Paschel's shy smile, but doubt shaped her expression, too, saying as clearly as if with words, "You? Seriously?"

"On my honor," he replied, hand over heart. "You don't die from it. You just wish you could."

Paschel murmured. "I almost did."

✧ ✧ ✧

Several days after the meeting at Scott's, Stephanie and Karl flew out to the Schardt-Cordova holding to visit Cordelia and Athos. Stephanie had hoped Jessica would come along, but she was babysitting her little brother, Nathan, then going by the hospital for a volunteer shift.

When Stephanie and Karl arrived at the Schardt-Cordova holding, they were invited in for snacks. As soon as the tiny fruit pies and cold drinks were set out, Natalie, Cordelia's younger sister, materialized as if my magic. Zack Kemper wasn't far behind.

Superficially, Zack resembled his older brother: brown hair and eyes, the classic Sphinxian muscular build. He was shorter than Mack but, at sixteen, he still might shoot up. As if determined to set himself apart from Mack, Zack wore his hair longer, with a side part. He'd bleached the upper portion a pale golden brown, which contrasted to make his brown eyes seem even darker. For all this flamboyant flare, his smile was shyer than his older brother's, although no less friendly.

Then Mack came in, grabbed a couple of pies, and positioned himself where he could finish off something on his computer, although this didn't keep him from firing in random quips.

Noticing how easily Karl—who most people tended to think of as the "strong, silent" type—joined in the familial banter, Stephanie saw the influence of his own mob of siblings. Back on Meyerdahl, where she'd been born, Stephanie's only-child status was more normal than not. Here on Sphinx, she was definitely an oddity. In their circle of friends, only Anders was also an "only," and he was from Urako. If recent rumor was correct, he might be going back there soon.

Anders was Stephanie's former boyfriend. He'd broken up with her a short time before, and was now courting Jessica, for whom he had fallen hard while Stephanie had been away, studying on Manticore. Stephanie had been really hurt at first, but she'd more or less gotten over it. After all, Jessica wouldn't be her best human friend if she wasn't a pretty fantastic person. Making her adjustment easier was that Stephanie wasn't certain if Anders was outcompeting Jessica's new obsession with getting into med school.

As soon as they had arrived, Lionheart had accepted a stick of celery, then climbed up a nearby crown oak with Survivor and Athos. Without him to pat, Stephanie felt oddly lonely, acutely aware of how awkward she was in a crowd where there was nothing to do but make idle chatter. Now if there had been an activity where she could *do* something...

She remembered an offer she'd already made.

"Cordelia, you and the Kempers were marking timber to be cleared when you were injured, right? Do you need any help? I mean, not just with the marking, but with the cutting?"

Zack answered as if the question had been addressed to him, one of those weird sibling dynamic things Stephanie still didn't understand. "If you wanted to, that would be fantastic. Cordy's not supposed to put a lot of weight on that ankle yet, and Aunt Danette doesn't want just me and Mack out in the bush, especially with Barnaby on the sick list, too. Dana's got a job in Twin Forks, and..."

"A beau," Mack added, rolling his eyes.

Cordelia intercut Mack's comment, neat as steps in a dance, swinging back to Stephanie's question. "Normally, we'd trade favors with some of the neighbors, but with Athos..."

She trailed off. Stephanie suspected that Mack, Zack, and Natalie would "read" the unfinished sentence as Cordelia not wanting people goggling at a wounded wild animal, but that Cordelia was letting her and Karl know she was taking what she'd learned at the recent meeting seriously.

"Terrific!" Stephanie said enthusiastically. "Where do we start?"

"Normally," Mack said, "I'd say we should get to work on feather bramble clearing down where Cordy had her encounter with the near-weasels. The survivors made themselves scarce. But, if you don't mind, Zack and I have a job to do on our own holding that needs to be done ASAP."

"We have a tenant," Zack explained importantly. "Have had for a couple of months now. She's a mycologist, researching mushrooms and fungi, and not just for the bounty for new discoveries, like you might think. She's crazy interested in the squishy things. Someone at the SFS sent her to us, because she was looking for land not that far from a town, but that hadn't been in use for a fair while."

Karl paused in mid-reach for a mini-pie and said, "I remember that coming up at a briefing. The mycologist had an interesting name . . . Glynis . . . Glynis . . ." He snapped his fingers. "Glynis *Bonaventure*! That's it. Nice lady. Rich as can be. She wanted to set up her operation on SFS lands, but after the bit with the Whittaker Expedition, Chief Ranger Shelton is leery about having off-worlders roaming around the bush, unsupervised. But we knew with her money she wasn't going to be stopped, so a few suggestions were made, places that would suit her needs but weren't just dumping her in unexplored bush. I hadn't kept track of what happened, though. I'm glad you guys got her as a tenant."

"So are we," Mack said. "We're hoping to shift back to living on our own homestead full-time by next T-year. Aunt Danette has done right by us financially, keeping most of, well . . ." He gulped a little, then forged on. "Our parents had life insurance. She's invested most of it for us, so we have a grubstake, but we can use more."

Stephanie bounced in her seat. "I've met Glynis. She's

come to consult with my mom a bunch of times. Mom's more into leafy plants than fungi, but the two fields are interlinked. I liked Glynis, even if she's inclined to be fanatical. To listen to her, you'd believe that mushrooms can solve every problem from affordable meat substitutes to cleaning up industrial pollutants."

"And she may be more than half-right," Mack said seriously. "I've learned more than I ever knew there was to know because I've been helping out, part neighborly goodwill, part to keep an eye on what they're doing over there."

"And don't forget," Zack poked him, "because she pays extra for labor, and you can always use pocket money."

"True, true," Mack admitted. "Anyhow, today's job is putting up a new prefab building. Parts have been delivered, but the job will go faster with a bunch to help. Otherwise it would just be us two and Herman. That's Herman Maye, Glynis's assistant. He's the one who actually lives at the lab while Glynis goes mushroom hunting."

"I have time today," Karl said. "Full shift tomorrow. Can we get on it now?"

"Sure thing!" Mack said, reaching for his uni-link. "I'll let Herman know to expect us, then we'll grab some tools and be off."

✧ ✧ ✧

Up in the reaches of a towering golden leaf, Climbs Quickly concentrated on flooding his mind-glow with his pleasure in his piece of cluster stalk. Keen Eyes amplified his pleasure. The way Stone Shaper ripped into his own stalk demonstrated that he was pleased that his guests were enjoying his hospitality.

When the cluster stalk was only a soggy memory and fur had been groomed back into place, Climbs Quickly presented a small carry net containing a chunk of stone to Stone Shaper. As a scout, he had been taught to recognize resources of all sorts, and he knew this to be one of the types of flint that skilled artisans among the People turned into tools.

When Stone Shaper realized what the net contained, he bleeked aloud, pleasure evident in the taste of his mind-glow.

Keen Eyes pointed to the stone, then play-acted the art of making stone tools.

Stone Shaper nodded, a gesture that the treecats had rapidly adopted to facilitate communicating with the two-legs.

Keen Eyes mind-spoke, as if Stone Shaper could understand him, but augmented speech by mimicking using an imaginary pressure flaker. *<Do you have the tools you would need?>*

Stone Shaper tilted his head to one side as he watched, then his mind-glow brightened. He scampered up the tree trunk and came back with a carry net that had been tucked into a small hollow in the tree's trunk. Within were a tidy selection of pressure flakers, hammer stones, as well as a few pieces of partially worked flint. Doubtless this was the kit he had used to make tools for himself during the days of his self-imposed exile.

Climbs Quickly filled his mind-glow with excitement. Taking Keen Eye's example, he mind-spoke as he would have if Stone Shaper could understand him but, as he did so, he took out his own well-worn stone knife, and indicated the unworked stone.

<I hoped you still practiced your craft! Perhaps now I may earn a new knife.>

"Bleek!" Stone Shaper said, his mind-glow cheerful, but then he puffed out his fur as might an adult reprimanding a kitten.

Climbs Quickly was momentarily confused, then he understood and bleeked laughter. *<I see. If I'm a good boy you'll let me have one of your creations! I see you have not forgotten my . . . mischievous youth. I assure you, I am a reformed Person.>*

He let his laughter spill out, and Keen Eyes joined in. Soon Stone Shaper was laughing as well, his mind-glow warm and bubbling. Who needed speech when the desire to understand was there?

The bough of the golden leaf was comfortably broad, and without further delay, Stone Shaper began examining the piece of flint Climbs Quickly had brought. Although not a toolmaker himself, Climbs Quickly's basic education had not been neglected, and he knew that some types of flint needed to be immersed in hot fires before they could be worked. He hadn't been certain if this was one such type, and wondered what Stone Shaper's two-leg would think if her bondmate came and put a chunk of stone on the fire. That reminded him . . .

<Keen Eyes, while I am certain that Stone Shaper has a name for his bondmate, he cannot tell it to us, nor do I think we should even try to ask. Can you think of a name for her?>

Keen Eyes paused to scratch vigorously where new fur was growing in, an itchy process as Climbs Quickly himself knew all too well.

<We have only met her a few times, but we know

she is brave or she would not have taken on a nest of needle fangs.>

<We already have my Death Fang's Bane,> Climbs Quickly said, *<and Swift Striker's Darkness Foe. I suppose we could keep with tradition and call this one Needle Fang Biter.>*

Keen Eyes bleeked laughter. *<From what I have heard, that name better suits her big, black barker. Shall we call him that? He is hero enough to deserve a name.>*

<Needle Biter he will be, then,> Climbs Quickly agreed. *<But what of the two-leg female? She not only fought bravely, but she seems to have given Stone Shaper a new will to . . . not just live. He has faithfully done his best to stay alive since he left our clan. This is more. I felt his mind-glow when he awoke to first discover his bond. There was joy, then confusion, even a touch of sorrow. But then he reached for the bond and accepted it with determination.>*

<In Shining Sunlight,> Keen Eyes said, looking down from the tree to where his tall two-legs was just now emerging from the human nest, *<I found someone who understood the despair into which I had been driven but, more than that, I found desire to move out of darkness into light. Neither of us could do it alone, but we could make the journey together.>*

<We will never know precisely why Stone Shaper decided to risk his life to fight alongside his two-legs and her barker. I believe that Death Fang's Bane and I had bonded before our own faithful battle, so the battle was not the reason for our bond, only the confirmation. But from what I tasted when Stone Shaper awoke, his bonding happened in the course

of that battle. Perhaps just when he was ready to throw his life away in a noble cause, he discovered how much he valued that life.>

<*Reason For Living is quite a cumbersome name,*> Keen Eyes mused, <*although no less so than Death Fang's Bane, I suppose.*>

<*Awakening Joy,*> Climbs Quickly said suddenly. <*That is what I felt from Stone Shaper. A fresh awareness that there could be not just life but joy.*>

<*I like it!*> Keen Eyes agreed. <*Awakening Joy she will be . . .*>

And, almost as if he could understand them, although doubtless what he felt was the happiness in their mind-glows, Stone Shaper looked up from his handiwork and bleeked satisfaction.

✧ ✧ ✧

Fruit pies and drinks finished, the two Kempers, Cordelia, Natalie, Stephanie, and Karl—laden with a variety of tools—headed out to the vehicles. The Kemper holding might border the Schardt-Cordova, but that didn't mean it was in walking distance.

"Who wants to ride with us over to Mr. Ack's?" Mack said.

"Mr. Ack's?" Stephanie asked.

Zack grinned. "The official name is the Glynis Bonaventure Mycological Research and Analysis Center but, since that's a mouthful, GBMRAC or MRAC. After I had a taste of one of the samples—which tasted horrible raw, though a lot better cooked, I will admit—I decided that Mr. Ack's fit, 'cause 'ack' was definitely what I wanted to say. Besides, that makes it rhyme with Mack and Zack, which is cool. Now, who wants to ride with us?"

"In the Garbage Truck?" Natalie asked, rolling her eyes.

Mack stiffened. The refurbished vehicle was one of his many pet projects, although that didn't mean he didn't tend to toss empty food bags and cups into the little used back seat.

"It's been thoroughly cleaned!" he protested.

After hauling me, Barnaby, and Athos off to Twin Forks after that attack, Cordelia thought, *and us bleeding all over everything.*

"I'll go with you," she said. "C'mon, Athos."

The treecat, who had scampered down from the crown oak with an ease that was a tribute to Richard Harrington's skills as a vet, came over to join her. He still limped from where his tendon had been damaged, and his fluffy gray fur looked as if he'd lost a battle to a swarm of moths, but his green eyes were bright and his whiskers curled with interest.

"Can I ride with you, Stephanie?" Natalie wheedled. "And Karl and"—the longing that flooded her voice left no doubt at the real attraction—"the treecats?"

"Sure," Karl said, "if you don't mind sitting in the middle. They like to hang their heads out the window if we're not going too fast."

"Can I hold one?" Natalie begged. "Please!"

"That," Stephanie said firmly, "is up to the treecats. They're not tame and, while they're too small to be peak predators, having to compete with creatures like hexapumas and condor owls for that honor, they're plenty dangerous."

Natalie looked unconvinced, but Cordelia saw her take a second look at the scars both Lionheart and Survivor sported. She nodded solemnly.

"I'll remember, but it still would be cool to cuddle one."

Cordelia waved as she headed over to the Garbage Truck. "Don't disgrace us, munchkin."

✧ ✧ ✧

Cordelia had been over to the area the Kemper boys had leased to Glynis Bonaventure a couple of times, helping set up the cluster of buildings that would become the mycology lab. The area selected was on the northern edge, to be more convenient to Twin Forks, as well as a couple of kilometers from the original Kemper residence. That meant that even when the Kemper boys started spending more time in the childhood home they barely remembered living in, no one would feel crowded.

There had been enough for her to do on the Schardt-Cordova homestead that Cordelia hadn't been over recently and she was impressed by the changes. Initially there had been just two geodesic dome structures—one to serve as a caretaker's cottage, the other as a work and propagation area—now several others had appeared, as well as a sign proclaiming the facility's official name.

"Is it my imagination," Cordelia said, leaning forward for a better look through the front windscreen, "or have those domes been painted to make them look like mushroom caps?"

"Got it in one," Mack said languidly, pulling to a halt in the designated parking area. "Glynis said that we set up the first geodesic domes so quickly that it seemed as if they had sprouted overnight. After that there was no stopping her. When Herman said that he needed dedicated space for the propagation lab—something about needing to recreate proper microclimates—she had some customization done *and* ordered cosmetic kits to enhance the original two. Zack's been doing most of the arty stuff."

"Unlike some," Zack said, chuckling as he moved around to unload tools from the Garbage Truck's trunk, "I am not afraid to express myself. Anyhow, it gave us extra work, and it was sort of fun. I like the effect. Geodesic domes are great—easy to build and adapt; they shed snow easily, too—but they *are* a bit drab."

"Artists!" Mack sighed theatrically. "I still haven't gotten over the suspicion that you put the idea into her head."

Zack's unusually broad grin was answer enough. "But we got paid for the work, just like we will today."

"Did you invite anyone else to the building party?" Cordelia asked. "I don't recognize that van."

"How could we," Mack asked sensibly, "when we didn't know we were going to do this today until Stephanie got the fidgets? Must be someone visiting Herman."

Karl pulled in while they were talking. Stephanie hopped out, moving with an energetic grace that made Cordelia wonder if she had a counter-grav unit on under her jacket, even though she hadn't been wearing one before. Now Stephanie paused in mid-step and stared at the air van, brow furrowed in thought.

"That looks sorta familiar but . . . No, can't be."

"Can't be what?" asked a deep voice that somehow managed to make those three conversational words sound like an insult. "Can't be your old pal, Frank?"

The speaker had curly black hair and tanned skin. Black eyes studied them mockingly from beneath heavy brows. Cordelia thought this "Frank" could have even been considered handsome, except for something loutish and leering in his manner. She guessed he was in the same general age group as the rest of them, maybe closer to her and Mack than Stephanie, but when she searched her memory she couldn't remember meeting him in any of her virtual classes. Of one thing she was sure: from how Stephanie was bristling, she didn't consider Frank any sort of pal.

Frank had been towing a counter-grav sled laden with a stack of low, hard-sided boxes. Now he dropped the pull and came toward them, hand extended.

"Frank Câmara," he said, "of Câmara's Comestibles and Produce. We've probably crossed paths around town. Steph and I used to be in the same hang-gliding club, but I quit. I'm working in the family business now. You two fellows must be the Kempers. Are you going to introduce me to your sister?"

Before either Mack or Zack could reply, Athos hissed from where he was peering over Cordelia's shoulder.

"Whoa!" Frank said, reeling back theatrically. "I remember hearing about your sis on the news: she's the chick who stumbled on a bunch of *near*-weasels and *nearly* got herself and the family dog eaten. That must be the heroic furball. I know scientists keep saying these treecats are smart, but if they keep getting themselves nearly killed rescuing females that aren't even their own species, I just don't see it."

Frank clearly thought he was being hilariously funny, hiccoughing laughter as he reached for the sled-pull. "Look, it's been real, but I've gotta get these 'shrooms to the shop. Later." Without waiting for a response, he trotted around them, and started loading the flats into the back of the van.

Cordelia had the strange feeling that, for all his bravado, Frank was afraid of something. Athos? It must be. Mack and Zack had long-ago learned what battles were worth fighting, and Karl clearly agreed. Natalie had retreated to within Karl's air car and was staring out wide-eyed and frightened. Stephanie stood, a pint-sized fury, flexing and unflexing her fist. When Lionheart bleeked softly and patted her on the side of her face, Stephanie shook herself.

"Lead on, Mack," she said with false heartiness. "From the stink in the air, I think this is the perfect time to cultivate another giant mushroom."

As she spoke, Herman Maye popped out of the office dome. Clearly, he'd been hoping to catch Frank, but when he saw the Kempers he stopped short.

"Have you fellows come to put up the building already?" he said. He was a small, pale man, wiry, with reddish curls that poked every which way from under the cap he'd hurriedly jammed on his head. "I wish all the landlords I've had were as responsive."

Mack grinned easily. "I know where the prefabs were dropped off. We can get started if you need to . . ." He jerked a thumb at where Frank was snapping the sled onto the roof of the air van.

"Oh, no worry. We've been selling off some of the surplus of the approved varieties," Herman said. "We're producing some of the promising new types. I can text Frank just as easily later. I don't want to keep you and your crew waiting."

This time, Mack was quick with introductions. Herman greeted Cordelia and Natalie warmly as the neighbors they were, and expressed delight in meeting Karl and Stephanie. Unlike most people, he seemed only mildly interested in the treecats. Cordelia guessed that, like his employer, for Herman anything other than a fungus just wasn't interesting.

Certainly Herman was proud of GBMRAC. On the way to where the new geodesic dome was going to be assembled, he took them into each of the various labs. In one, he demonstrated how newly collected specimens were recorded, even letting Natalie set up a spore print. There were different growing environments as well, with the smart tiles from which the domes were built programmed to maintain appropriate light and moisture levels.

"The new building is going to be dedicated to experimental growing environments," Herman told them. "Once we've identified a fungus as having a useful property, then we want to discover if it could be grown other than in its native habitat."

"Useful?" Natalie asked. "You mean like good to eat?"

"Or for medicine," Herman replied, "or, even better, as a means of converting or reducing a material. Fungi are amazing that way. Back when Terra was being overwhelmed by industrial waste and artificial materials, mycologists discovered fungi that would break down plastics or chemicals, rendering them to a more benign form. But we can't just go around introducing off-world flora into our new environments. We *do* introduce familiar plants, but only after we've thoroughly evaluated their possible ecological impact. But that doesn't mean we can't find similar fungi—fungi with equivalent value—right here in our own star system. Wouldn't it be wonderful to have a fungus that could eat your trash, then be sliced up and eaten as part of a tasty omelet or veggy burger?"

"I guess," Natalie replied, wrinkling her button nose just a little. "I'm not super crazy about mushrooms."

"I'll change your mind," Herman declared. "I'm growing one that reduces wood pulp and, in the process, creates a fruiting body that, when dried, tastes amazingly like vanilla wafers."

"No way!" The disbelief was general.

"Way," he said complacently. "What makes for the flavor is the *type* of wood pulp used as the growing medium."

Herman nattered on until they reached where the tiles and support struts for the new dome had been dropped off. Mack tapped his uni-link to download the instructions. Zack popped open a footlocker-sized case that, so Cordelia saw when she looked over his shoulder, contained a variety of bright decals, stencils, and spray color coat applicators.

"Leave the art supplies for later, bro," Mack called. "Work first, play after. The materials for the foundation are on this flat. Let's unpack those."

Stephanie and Karl immediately started cutting the restraints on the barrels. Zack, with a last wistful look at the decoration case, went to help wrestle containers of ceramcrete medium off the pallet.

Cordelia was about to join them when Mack waved and pointed to a tidy little backhoe fitted with a roller attachment. "You get to operate that, Cordy," he said. "Save your gimpy ankle. We chose an area that was already pretty even and clear cut, but it's going to need packing down so it won't settle under the dome's weight."

Cordelia gave him a brisk nod, not wanting to admit her relief but feeling it nonetheless. She glanced around for Athos and found that he was up in another crown oak with Survivor and Lionheart, apparently involved in some task of their own that involved twisting lengths of bark.

It's fun getting to know new people, she thought, feeling curiously happy. Then, thinking of Frank Câmara, unaccountably, she shivered.

4

THE COMMENTS TO HIS FOLLOW-UP ARTICLE ABOUT Paschel's accident were filled with anecdotes about an uptick in peculiar accidents. While Nosey had been happy enough to have such a strong reaction to what he'd thought about as a lightweight human interest piece, he was too conscious of his reputation to simply ride the wave without checking facts. Rumor had an amazing ability to blow events out of proportion.

One of the great things about his job as a courier was that he had a lot of air time during which he could set his air car on autopilot and do research. He started by downloading accident reports for the last three T-months, restricting his area of interest to Yawata Crossing, Twin Forks, and the surrounding holdings. Since not all accidents would be reported as such, he added police and SFS reports where officers and rangers had been called to assist. Inevitably, there was overlap, but this gave him an ample body of material to work with.

That done, he started culling. Out went obvious work-related accidents and traffic accidents, unless there was something a little different about them. He flagged those that—like Cordelia Schardt-Cordova's encounter with the near-weasels—involved encounters with local wildlife. He wasn't trying to get the SFS in trouble, but there was a perennial fascination with clashes between humans and wild animals. He also noted those incidents that had an odd element that made them that little bit more newsworthy.

As he went on his rounds, he also did some old-fashioned sniffing about for unreported incidents. Since one of his most reliable jobs was picking up medical samples to be taken to labs for testing, the subject of how everyone was doing came up almost without his needing to ask. Sometimes he heard more than he needed about some oldster's high-gravity stressed heart or smoke-damaged lungs, but since he genuinely liked people, that wasn't much of a trial. More than once, he eased his conscience about snooping by relaying what he'd been told or observed when he dropped off a sample, figuring the doctors would like having more information, rather than less. Most of those who had settled on Sphinx viewed themselves as hardy pioneers, and didn't want to be seen as whining.

Eventually, he narrowed his list down. He found his next candidate in the Simpson family of Yawata Crossing. They had been among the few families to take advantage of the early round of assisted immigration, settling on Sphinx in 1495, a full year before the second-generation of the plague vaccine had been perfected.

The accident in question had happened to seventeen-year-old Jake. It had been an unlikely accident for someone born on Sphinx, as Jake had been, and even less likely for someone who, like Jake, was considered a good all-round athlete. The improbability of the incident was what had prompted Nosey to try for an interview.

Happily, he knew the Simpsons fairly well. Sports news always did well, and on a planet that didn't yet have the population to support professional teams, school sports were followed avidly. Since Jake played on several teams, as well as being a member of the hang-gliding club and showoff skimmer club, Nosey had featured him not long before in a series on exceptional athletes.

On his way over to the Simpsons', Nosey reviewed the accident report. Jake had taken a spill while practicing at the Twin Forks skimmer park. He'd gone late, when he'd have the space mostly to himself. That made sense only if you didn't know Jake. Jake was highly social. The likelihood he'd been completely alone didn't fit, so Nosey guessed that Jake had probably been horsing around with someone—or more than some-*one*—else.

Next Nosey reviewed what he knew about skimmers. Like most kids, he'd played with a basic model as a kid, but that experience was as different from what athletes like Jake did as "Old Maid" or "Go Fish" were from a high-stakes poker game.

Skimmers were usually considered to have evolved from something called a "skateboard," a narrow elongated oval platform fitted with wheels. In reality, skimmers bore about as much resemblance to these distant ancestors as an atlatl did to a rifle. About the only thing they had in common was their purpose: to carry the rider over the ground, with the only manipulation and steering coming from shifts in the rider's weight and posture.

Skimmers were delta-form platforms that spread from a sharp point, just wide enough to accommodate the rider's feet, one on each of the outward flaring panels or "wings." Skimmers were equipped with compact maglev units that, in Nosey's childhood model, had lifted the skimmer a maximum of twelve centimeters off surface level. Greater heights were possible, but not without substantially increasing the size of the unit and—especially—its power supply. And, of course, it could be used only on specialized tracks fitted with the necessary magnets. The basic tech had been around since literally before humanity left Old Earth and was about as mature as a technology got, and skimmer parks were common, but there was a vast difference between the standard skimmer park and the parks in which skimmer riders like Jake played.

Nosey was making certain his jargon was up-to-date when his air car pinged him that they were approaching the Simpsons' homestead. He tucked his notes away, checked his messenger bag to make certain that his little present for Jake (a particularly revolting confection made with dry ginger, sugar *and* salt, courtesy of the invaluable Eric Flint's Red Letter Café) was inside, and parked.

He had hardly departed his air car when the house's front door flew open and Jake emerged, riding his lift-chair with a cocky ease that made the medical aid seem like the latest sports accessory. Someone—Nosey suspected Jake himself—had used holographic flashing tape to give the chair racing stripes, and Jake spun the chair in place so that he was haloed in rainbows.

Really, Nosey thought, *you'd never guess the kid is undergoing some really intensive therapy.*

When Nosey had written his feature article on Jake, he'd struggled with how to describe him. Jake was capable of being both goofy and intensely focused, often with little time between. He was a warm person, except when he was being competitive.

Although Nosey hadn't used the comparison, he'd privately decided that Jake reminded him of one of the more overbred species of bird dogs. Silly, bouncy, and enthusiastic—until called to the job, then intent and almost frighteningly focused. The comparison had been helped along by Jake's physical appearance: large brown eyes and a lean, muscular build. That Jake's thick wavy hair was cream on top with a lower tier of sky blue—colors of the Twin Forks School district teams—did nothing to dispel the general impression.

If Jake had had a tail, it would have been wagging wildly as he soared his chair over to Nosey's side.

"So terrific you're here, man! I am six times six dying of boredom. I mean, I've been hurt before but usually they spray on the skin-coat, dose me with quick-heal, and *bam*!" Jake made a sort of "whooshing" gesture with both arms, then spun his chair again. "This time I'm not allowed out of this chair, not even to sleep! It reclines. I don't even get a break to pee. I'm hooked up like a spacer getting ready to go into battle. It sucks. Absolutely sucks!"

He giggled at his own pun.

"But," Nosey said, "the prognosis is good? I mean, you're going to heal?"

"Am!" Jake assured him. "If I'm a good boy and stay in the chair, do my PT and take my meds. And, you know, I am. I've decided PT is my new favorite sport. I'm going to kill it, be the all-time champ. Seriously, my PT person says she's using me as an example to others. I like that."

"You're a good idiot," Nosey said fondly, reaching over to tousle the youth's hair. During Jake's effusion, they'd progressed from the parking pad to the house. Nosey thought they were going to go in the front door, but Jake swerved his chair around the side of the house, toward a secondary entrance.

"Game room! Pool table," Jake explained. "I'm getting superior at making shots without violating my promise not to leave my chair. I'll even spot you a couple of balls. Wanna play?"

Jake looked so much like a dog holding his favorite Frisbee in his teeth that Nosey didn't have the heart to admit that he hadn't played pool since he was in college and that, even if Jake spotted him more than a few balls, he'd still lose.

"Sure, but I should say 'hi' to the rest of your family," Nosey said, "let them know I'm here."

"No problem! Vernon just made a bunch of some terrifying-looking cookies for his chem class. We're all going to be subjected."

And, indeed, when Vernon—age eight, white-blond, with bright blue eyes the color of his brother's hair—came bouncing in with a plate of cookies, the rest of the Simpsons followed. The cookies did, indeed, look like a science experiment, being red on one side, blue on the other, bleeding into purple at the middle, but they tasted of butter and vanilla and weren't too scorched. When the cookies had been eaten, the rest of the family swirled away as suddenly as they had appeared, leaving Nosey and Jake to their interview.

"So, Champ," Nosey said, lining up a shot, "tell me how you nearly broke your back."

"Wow! You make it sound so dramatic!"

"That's my job." Nosey grinned. "Anyhow, wasn't it dramatic?"

"Not really. I was trying a newish sort of move. Uh, you know that skimmers can be tweaked, right?"

Nosey did, but if he got Jake talking about the finer parts of his hobby, he'd be more likely to forget if he had anything to hide.

"A little, I mean, it has something to do with modifying the limiters, right?"

Jake elevated his chair, tilted it at an angle, and made a shot that set off a ricochet that looked random right up until balls started falling into various pockets.

"Oh, I forgot to call that," Jake said, chagrined. "Call this warm-up?"

"Sure. You were telling me about how you adapted your skimmer."

"Right." Jake focused along the length of his pool cue, as intense as if he was on the playing field. "Well, the stock limiters are pretty tame, probably because of the makers' liability concerns, but competition skimmers routinely modify them, because we need more power and speed for the really high scores."

"And the skimmer parks are okay with that?"

"Sure, as long as we tell 'em about it ahead of time and we sign the waivers. It's not like it's usually *that* risky, anyway, with all the safety regs." He paused and glanced up at Nosey. "You know about the basic safety regs, right?"

"Not a lot," Nosey confessed as he set up what should have been an easy shot, managed to scuff his cue on the green cloth cover of the table, and nearly hit himself in the face instead. To his credit, Jake didn't laugh.

"Oh, bad luck, man. Try this." The next few minutes were given over to a tutorial, but Jake was deeply interested in skimmers, and came back to the topic without Nosey needing to prompt. "So, yeah, safeguards. Okay, first there's safety equipment you gotta wear—helmets, pads, gloves, and here on Sphinx, counter-grav."

Nosey nodded understanding of that part, and Jake went on.

"Second, there's power settings. Unless your tweaks are approved and you sign that waiver, the parks automatically shut you down if you try to run at anything above a pretty tame level."

He paused again until Nosey nodded once more.

"Okay," Jake resumed, "those're the basic safety parameters. Actual operation's pretty simple, at least at the basic level, too. You control attitude by shifting your balance, but you control *altitude* by adjusting the power. That's one reason we wear the gloves. The power controls are built into them, and you've gotta learn to play 'em like a guitar if you want to compete at the highest level. There's a lock on how high you can push the board that's a factor of its power and the surface's magnetic density, and the parks have to maintain a strong enough field to support the boards over the entire area of the court or the track. Can't be any 'blind spots' where you'd lose lift, except for some really limited things like—oh, like a water jump."

He raised an eyebrow at Nosey to be sure he was following, and Nosey nodded.

"Well, all that's fine for kiddies, but it's pretty tame, once you know what you're doing. Takes the sport out of it. High-level skimming gets a lot more challenging, especially where the track shifts are involved."

"Track shifts?" Nosey prompted.

"Changes in the base track," Jake replied. "The layout and density of the mag field. You don't really have to make it a big, boring circle, like they do for the kiddies, or even a contoured track with fixed features. You can lay it out more like an obstacle course. Make it a point-to-point race even on one of the flat baby rinks by shutting down parts of the track to make lanes that have to be followed. Or you can lay out an entirely new lane across any open ground—one with switches and shunts built in—for cross-country races. And you can program a competitive track to shift the lanes on the fly."

"They do that? Shift them 'on the fly'?" Nosey asked.

"For the high-end competitions, sure."

"Do the riders know when and how they'll shift?"

"Nope." Jake beamed. "That's part of the fun. Your helmet display shows you the shifts ahead of time, but the warning interval gets shorter and shorter as the level of the competition goes up. Same thing for the cross-country races. The track comes in both big rolls and individually conformable tiles, you know?" Nosey nodded, and Jake shrugged. "Well, you can roll out a really complicated pattern—one that winds around all kinds of obstacles and crisscrosses all over the place—and the riders won't know which part of it is currently live till they get there. Higher the ranking, shorter the warning."

"And the faster you're traveling, the less time you have to react, right?"

"Sure! But that's all pretty flat and boring, almost as bad as the baby rinks, once you get used to it. The real competitions usually include that, but only as a launch point. Where they get *really* tricky is when they send you down different chutes."

"Chutes?"

"The competitive courses. Not just obstacle courses, but ones with real challenge features. Could be pools, or ramps, or bowls, spirals, jump hazards—you know. Most parks have at least three or four chutes live at any one time, but here in Twin Forks, it's usually only two. Well, they only have *three* total, so I guess that makes sense." Jake's expression drooped for a moment, then brightened with his usual enthusiasm. "In the unlimiteds, though, they don't tell you which chutes are live, or how they're configured till you actually run the course. You've gotta ride 'em cold, no prep or practice runs, and you don't even know the order they're coming up in—you've gotta ride the lanes to find out. And they usually reconfigure between heats." Jake shrugged. "Not hard to do. The track units are built on smart tiles. Their shape at any given moment's what their programming tells them to be, and they're flexible enough for just about any conformation you want. It only takes a few minutes for a good control room tech to swap 'em around completely, and that way you can't watch your competition running the course ahead of you, 'cause it's a *different* course for each heat. Takes a lot longer, and a lot more people, to unroll one of the obstacle course tracks, but reconfigging the chutes in place is easy."

"So you have to run the course and the chutes without knowing what they're going to be till you get there, and the winner's the guy who gets through fastest?"

"Usually." Jake nodded. "But you get points for the variations you can pull off *while* you're running the course, too. Once you're in a chute, it's not gonna change till you're done, but since you don't know what's coming next, you can't really plan your jumps and recovers ahead of time. You can either run 'em straight, as fast as you can, as you come through, or you can be more creative and improvise moves, find ways to cross back and hit the same feature two or three times, a different way on each pass. You can collect a *lot* of points if you manage really cool variations on the basic 'just run the course' approach because of the difficulty mods built into the scoring. Enough to put somebody with a slower overall time but really good on the aerobatics and conversions in the lead. That's usually where we do the most tweaking to the power settings, because the more power you're ready to burn, the faster and higher you can go. 'Course there are limits in everything, and even today, a board's charge is only good for a couple of hours. But if you press the board, ride the 'high' effect, you get points for elevation, as well. Kills your power supply faster, which can be a downer for the longer courses, but the higher you push it, the more creative you can get on those variations. So if you're really serious, you practice running the course just like you would in a competition, as fast and as hard—and as high—as you can, with as little warning about the track layout as possible." He shrugged. "Works best if you can get to the park late enough there aren't a lot of riders around. That's when management will let you and a buddy play with the track and switch it around on each other."

"So that's what you were doing when you got hurt?"

"In one," Jake agreed.

He went into some of the details involved in the course he'd been running—something about "vert ramps," "six-meter bowls," "aqueducts," and "free jumps"—and Nosey's thoughts wandered. He hadn't been born on Sphinx. His family had moved to Sphinx from Nova Terra when he was fifteen T-years old, so Nosey definitely remembered what it was like to live on a planet where park management that allowed the sort of extreme course-modding Jake and his pals were doing, apparently without adult supervision, would have been severely reprimanded, probably even fined.

The frontier mentality of Sphinx was different. As long as Jake didn't whine about his injuries or try to blame someone else for not protecting him from his own choices, then even extreme skimmer-riding fell into the category of acceptable risks.

Except something's not right here, Nosey thought. *They're* supposed *to wear counter-grav units with the fall alert set to switch on automatically if they wipe out on one of those ramps or bowls. Some of the kids moan and complain about "training wheels," but I've watched Jake perform before, and he* always *wears his. He might seem like an idiot, but he's not. Far from it. In fact, according to the accident report, he* was. *So why didn't it kick in? Did he just not set it on automatic? But that's not like him, either. And if he did, what could've made him forget his basic safety procedures? And why is he dodging around saying who was there?*

Because Jake did evade each of Nosey's probes, as skillfully as he would have the ball in a game of dodge 'em. Even Nosey's promise he wouldn't put anything in his article, that he was just trying to give Jake a chance to get the full story off his chest, only merited a look of wide-eyed innocence from those big puppy eyes.

A *girl? Was he showing off for a girl, maybe? Or did someone dare him? Well, I've got enough for a good story, and I won't rat the kid out for not having his counter-grav unit set right. Even the accident report only says a "probable malfunction."*

But after Nosey left the Simpsons, promising to come back and visit soon, the problem still niggled at him. He decided that for his next article in the series on accidents, he was going to see if anyone else might have experienced a counter-grav unit malfunction. Now *that* would be a major story, wouldn't it?

Humming to himself, Nosey programmed the air car to take him back to Twin Forks and started writing.

✧ ✧ ✧

"I have a job for you two," Chief Ranger Shelton announced, motioning for Stephanie and Karl to follow him into his office, then shutting the door.

Stephanie's imagination raced. The last time he'd called them into his office for a private meeting like this, he'd wanted to send them to Manticore to attend that special accelerated training program for Forestry Service personnel. What might he have in mind *this* time? Perhaps a new group of xeno-anthropologists were due to arrive to study the treecats. Or maybe someone was up to something unethical out in the bush.

Stephanie sat in one of the two chairs facing the

desk and felt Lionheart move to recline across the back. These chairs were new, and she found herself wondering if they'd been acquired because Shelton now had two rangers with treecats.

Or maybe Shelton had something more routine in mind, like going to do on-site confirmation checks on some new type of plant or animal that some enterprising settler wanted to claim a bounty on. That last wouldn't be nearly as exciting, but it was valuable work. Shelton's next words startled her back to the moment.

"Stephanie, do you remember how we first met?"

"You bet! My parents and I came to see you so you could tell me to my face that you wouldn't be able to let me be a junior intern with the SFS." Stephanie looked theatrically hurt. "Not a great day for me."

"Well, great day or not," Shelton said, "how do you feel about creating a program for other kids that will do for them what I couldn't do for you?"

"You mean create a junior internship program?"

"Or at least lay the groundwork for it." Shelton leaned back in his chair and emitted a gusty sigh. "Not much has changed for the SFS since you came in here, thirteen and a half T-years old, all big eyes and boatloads of determination. We still don't have a large enough budget, sufficient numbers of rangers, or excess equipment. But one thing *has* changed. The population of Sphinx is rising, both resident and nonresident. Tourism, both of the holiday sort and of those who want to see if Sphinx will suit the needs of their particular business, is climbing. All of this puts considerable pressure on the SFS to keep everyone safe, even if only from their own stupidity."

Stephanie, thinking about how Anders's father, Dr.

Bradford Whittaker, had nearly gotten his entire xeno-anthropological team killed, nodded understanding. She heard Karl give a nearly inaudible chuckle, and guessed he could list his own examples.

Shelton went on, "So what I'm proposing isn't make-work. Never think that for a moment. In a way, it's a covert operation. What I need you to do is design an educational program that will be presented not in the classroom but as club activities. Ostensibly, our audience is going to be kids, but we're targeting the adults as well." Shelton grinned slyly, obviously pleased with himself. "In my experience, there's nothing like a kid when it comes to showing off new knowledge. We'll start with something exotic to capture their attention, perhaps highlights on the more dangerous of Sphinx's wildlife."

"Hexapumas," Stephanie said with growing interest, "peak bears, swamp sirens."

"That would definitely capture attention," Karl said. "Even out in the bush, most people don't see those live. We could get images of them on the prowl."

"We could," Stephanie agreed happily. "I'm good at getting live images of wildlife. After the big predators, we could move onto flyers like albatrosses, mountain eagles, and condor owls."

"And compare them with the Terran creatures they're named after," Karl said. "Then we encourage discussion—perhaps linked to a project like building computer models—of how and why a Terran mountain eagle wouldn't be able to fly on Sphinx."

"Which would let us educate about some of the hazards of living on a high-gravity planet," Stephanie cut in, "without being—uh—dare I say 'heavy-handed'?"

Her pun scored the groans it deserved.

Shelton nodded. "We're definitely on the same wavelength. If we promoted these talks as educational or cautionary, they'd pretty much be ignored except by the sort of kid who would be fascinated anyhow. If we make them a club event, give out badges for related activities, even prizes, then eventually have uniforms and contests, we'll get the information out just the same, and everyone will have a lot more fun. Eventually, we can evolve a junior internship program like the one Stephanie asked for a few years ago, presenting it, quite honestly, as a gateway into the SFS."

"Why choose us, sir?" Stephanie asked. "Karl and I did take those classes on Manticore, but neither of us are trained educators."

"That's precisely why I want you," Shelton replied. "Teachers and parents will inevitably serve as club moderators, but you two are actual SFS rangers—probationary, in Stephanie's case—but actual rangers with field experience, formal certification, badges, and some darn dramatic experiences behind you. It also helps that you're both wildlife celebrities, courtesy of Lionheart and Survivor there."

Karl said stiffly, "We're not showing off the treecats, though, sir. You do understand that. Until their status is settled, drawing even more attention to them is not a good idea."

Shelton raised both hands in a gesture of surrender. "I absolutely agree. But nothing changes that Stephanie is the treecat discoverer, that you're both adoptees. That gives you a certain aura. I'm sure the 'cats could be convinced to stay out of the way. Lionheart was remarkably cooperative about that when Stephanie took him with her to Manticore."

"Will the club activities be live or on the planetary data net?" Karl asked.

"Both," Chief Ranger Shelton said. "Live performances will be in different locations, but all the sessions will be archived. I'd like to shift the live meeting among various locations, including—maybe especially—the urban areas, since that's where new arrivals tend to gather. Actual locations can be worked out, but most SFS sub-headquarters have a meeting room."

Stephanie found her enthusiasm mounting. She hadn't forgotten her thirteen-year-old self, how much the idea of being a junior intern had meant to her, how crushed she'd been when her family moved from Meyerdahl, robbing her of the chance to join that much-anticipated program. This wasn't as exciting as fighting fires or as intellectually stimulating as taking college-level courses on another planet, but it was important, too. After all, she didn't want to be known for the rest of her life mostly for something she'd done when she was eleven. Discovering the treecats had been special, but this could be, too.

"Thank you for believing I can handle this," she said, and meant every word. She wondered if Shelton realized how much of an effort it had been for Stephanie to learn how to get along with people her own age. As an only child, and a smart one, she'd gravitated to adults. People her own age had to work twice or even three times as hard to prove themselves her equals.

I really was, she thought with amusement, *a serious snob.*

"Karl will be senior on this project," Shelton said, "since he's a full ranger. However, we can't spare him from all his other duties, so a lot of the planning and research is going to fall to you, Stephanie. Perhaps you could ride along sometime when Karl's on patrol or doing rounds, then you could use the air time to consult. You both will host the club meetings."

Since Stephanie already rode along with Karl—as she was certain Shelton knew—this would be no hardship. In fact, since Karl's family lived in Thunder River, over a thousand kilometers from Twin Forks, Karl stayed with the Harringtons often enough that one of the spare rooms had been pretty much turned over to him. Stephanie sighed happily at the idea of days and evenings spent cozily together, assembling the materials for their first several club meetings.

"Can we have the first meeting in Twin Forks?" she asked. "I'm sure we can recruit a bunch of younger kids to attend. Jessica Pheriss has a ton of sibs. The hang-gliding club has some younger members, too. It would be better if we didn't recruit only through the schools or it will look too much like a school activity."

"We'll definitely use word of mouth," Shelton said. "We won't ignore the schools, but we won't push too hard there. I'll drop a hint into the ears of some of the more ecologically-minded instructors to make sure their students learn about the club—I was thinking we could call it the SFS Explorers—without realizing they're being tipped off."

The next quarter of an hour or so was spent working out logistics, including what their starting budget would be. The money wasn't much, Stephanie realized, but she knew how strapped the SFS was for funds. Even being trusted with this relatively small amount made her feel very determined to make the project pay.

As they were rising to go, Karl halted in mid-step.

"Sir, would it be all right with you if I contacted Nosey Jones and offered him an interview about the new club?"

Stephanie felt her mouth dropping open in surprise and clamped it shut. Nosey Jones? He was the enemy! She wouldn't be surprised if his recent series of articles on accidents—which, although they never criticized the SFS directly, certainly led others to do so—weren't part of the reason Chief Ranger Shelton was starting the program at this time.

"Good idea," Shelton said. "Don't let Nosey get away with thinking we're being reactive. You could even hint that we've been planning this since a certain brown-eyed immigrant from Meyerdahl asked if we had a junior internship program like the one on her homeworld. Handled right, you might even make an ally of him, part of your informal recruiting drive."

Karl nodded, but Stephanie doubted she'd ever think of Nosey Jones as anything other than a pest.

✧ ✧ ✧

As Stephanie and Karl were leaving SFS headquarters, already deep in discussion, a tall young man, drop-dead gorgeous, with golden hair and eyes of such a dark blue that in some lights they seemed black, stepped from the shadows and moved to intercept him.

Despite herself, Stephanie felt her heart lurch, then beat faster, but with Lionheart's purr thrumming against her back, she managed to summon what she hoped was a relaxed and easy smile.

"Hey, Steph," said Anders Whittaker, "Karl. Lionheart. Survivor. I . . ." He paused, looking at a loss. Then he blurted out, "I was wondering if I could talk with Stephanie. Alone. I could give her a ride back to Twin Forks, I mean, if you two don't have plans."

Anders's obvious discomfort surprised Stephanie. His mother was a politician on their homeworld of Urako. Normally he had the poise of someone far older than his sixteen, almost seventeen, T-years. Now, however, he looked nearly as uncertain as he had on the day, a few weeks back, when he'd told Stephanie that he'd fallen in love with Jessica.

For a fleeting moment, Stephanie wondered if Anders wanted to get back together. Maybe he was learning that it wasn't much fun dating a girl who, between her family duties, school, and volunteering at the hospital was hardly ever available. Stephanie wondered if she *wanted* to get back together with Anders. He still made her heart race uncomfortably fast, but getting dumped had *hurt*.

Stephanie glanced up at Karl, who looked bemused.

"Whatever Steph wants," he said. "She and I can meet up tomorrow. I have some work to do, then I was going to drop by the Schardt-Cordovas, see how Athos is doing, give him and Survivor a little face time. They're both new to being adopted. I thought it might be good for them both."

Almost unconsciously, Stephanie reached to feel what Lionheart thought. The treecat was not in the least upset, which meant Anders didn't mean her any harm. As sometimes happened, she thought that through Lionheart she could feel something that might be what Anders was feeling: an uncertainty, confusion, pain?

"Sure, Anders," she said, "I was just going to hang out with Karl until he was done with work, then ride home with him. As long as we stop for something to eat, I'm fine with hanging out with you instead."

"I'll buy you lunch or whatever," Anders replied

promptly. He then made a visible effort to relax. "I remember how regular feedings are key to a Happy Harrington."

"Then, later," Karl said with a wave. "Steph, I'll call. We've got a lot of work to do."

"I'll message," she agreed. "I have a bunch of ideas I don't want to forget."

"As if," Karl said, and got into his air car.

Stephanie swallowed hard, then turned to Anders. "How about seafood? Maybe Yawata Bay Baskets?"

The place she'd named was right on the bay and renowned for enormous baskets of crisply fried, newly-caught Terran seafood, harvested from aquaculture net-tanks that prevented the contents from escaping into the wild. If you ordered the catch of the day, even the Jumbo wasn't too expensive.

"Sounds great," Anders replied. "I love their hush-puppies."

They managed to make small talk on the way to Bay Baskets, an easy enough task, since Anders could ask why Shelton wanted to see her and Karl. Their orders—Jumbo Puffy Tempura Shrimp baskets for them both, with sesame-drenched seaweed crisps for Stephanie and coleslaw for Anders, along with a side of raw shrimp for Lionheart—came quickly. Stephanie wasn't surprised when Anders suggested they eat in his car. He'd been very polite thus far, but he had asked if he could talk with her alone. He parked his air car at a spot overlooking the waves crashing against the rocks, watched a near-loon flap up with something wriggling in its beak, absently crunched into a shrimp, then the words started spilling out.

"I told you, didn't I, that my mom has been making

noises about wanting me to come back to Urako? Well, as of a week ago, she and Dad settled it. We're both going back. Not immediately, but she wants us back in time for her reelection campaign. Dad couldn't really complain. He's been back briefly, but well . . ."

Stephanie nodded. Dr. Whittaker's return had been to answer to a board about the disastrous results of his decision to go examine an abandoned treecat site—without telling the SFS, which would have forbidden him to do so. Although Stephanie herself had been known to advocate the creed "sometimes it's better to ask forgiveness rather than permission," she prided herself that she hardly ever did so for selfish reasons, and she really did try to put no one but herself at risk.

"Not exactly great for your mom's image, right? I mean, your dad did end up officially censured."

Anders snorted a laugh. "Honestly, Dad never has been what you'd call a 'political asset,' but she really loves him. It was hard for her to let him go, not just off-planet but out-system, but she did. And she let me go with him because . . ."

"I remember why," Stephanie said, so Anders wouldn't need to fill in the gap. Anders had come to Sphinx hoping to see treecats—and to meet Stephanie. Dr. Whittaker's interest had been pure and fanatical xeno-anthropology, but Anders had been more idealistic. He'd loved the idea of a new species that just might be intelligent, and he'd romanticized Stephanie herself.

And then I pretty much threw myself at him, but he didn't mind. Okay. We can take that all as read. Now to push for why he wanted to talk with me.

"So?" She dragged the single syllable into three, then bit into the largest of her remaining shrimp so she wouldn't be tempted to steer the conversation. She still didn't have the least idea what Anders was working his way toward, but she didn't think it was going to be a suggestion they start dating again.

"So... Jessica," Anders began. "So she wants to go to med school. So, I think, why does she need to go to med school here in the Star Kingdom? Urako has been settled much longer. It didn't have two waves of plague to set it back. Her grades are excellent. My mom sent me a test that I had to take to make sure I'd go back into my lessons at at least the level I was when I left. Jessica wanted to take the test, too, see how she measured up."

"I bet Jess did well," Stephanie said, realizing that all she felt at the confirmation that Anders wasn't about to suggest they get back together was relief.

"She aced it," Anders enthused. "I mean, I was even a little surprised because her family has moved around so much, but she told me—and a little tartly, too—that because her dad kept moving the family around she'd learned not to depend on anyone except herself."

He visibly deflated at this, and moodily bit into another shrimp. Stephanie, remembering how Anders had thrown himself protectively between Jessica and an insane treecat, how he had admitted he wanted to protect her, knew that his ego must have been singed at her calm declaration of independence.

"Go on," Stephanie prompted, taking a long pull on her iced spikethorn tea. "So Jessica did great on the test and then..."

"And I sent my mom the results, and I explained about Jessica, and about med school," Anders said, letting the words stream out with hardly a breath between, "and how I thought she'd benefit from Urako's educational system and how I thought her family could manage without her, because they were going to need to do so pretty soon because she'd need to go off-planet to get the advanced studies she needed and . . ."

He paused, focusing on his cooling hushpuppies, leaving Stephanie to fill in the next part in her head. *And how you are in love with her and if you had to leave Sphinx and the Star Kingdom, maybe you could at least take Jessica, and . . .*

"And?" Stephanie said mildly, although she had a pretty good idea now what was coming. What she wasn't sure was what Anders wanted from her.

"And my mom was actually interested. Mom said if Jessica wanted her to, she could arrange something in the way of an exchange student program. She even sent me the documentation, so Jessica would have something to share with her parents."

"And?"

"And Jessica shot me down. She said she wasn't interested in leaving Sphinx, that she certainly couldn't leave Valiant, and really maybe we should not even try dating because since I was definitely leaving, it would just make my leaving harder on both of us."

"That sounds like Jessica," Stephanie said diplomatically. "She's pragmatic. Remember, it's not like this is a new situation for her. She's had to give up close friends before. Don't take it personally."

"But"—and suddenly Stephanie felt sure that Anders was now reaching the key point, the reason he'd wanted to speak to Stephanie—"I couldn't help but feel that if all things were equal, Jessica would have gone. But the one thing that wasn't equal was Valiant. I mean, I think I'm being thrown over for a treecat!"

With a start, Stephanie realized that Anders's instinct was right. Maybe Jessica would have been interested in trying out Urako, but there was no way she could take Valiant with her. Treecats had been discovered by humans in 1518. This was 1522. Four years was hardly any time as far as politics were concerned. Moreover, treecats weren't relatively benign creatures like wood rats. They were dangerous carnivores, quite capable of killing an adult human. No way Urako would want one brought planetside, even a relatively mellow treecat like Valiant.

And then there was the bond. Anders understood more about treecats than most of those without the bond, but he didn't understand on a gut level what it meant. It wasn't that Jessica *wouldn't* leave Valiant. She *couldn't*, not without serious consequences to herself.

Well, this is awkward. When we were dating, Anders got a hint of the way Lionheart can feel my emotions, but I never let on more. I won't now, not when Anders is leaving, especially not with his dad's interest in the 'cats and what they can do. Whoo-boy... I need to make sure Jessica isn't suddenly feeling as if she's acquired not a new buddy, but an alien ball and chain.

With complete sincerity, Stephanie said, "If you want me to talk to Jessica, make sure she's really certain..."

"Would you, Steph? Really? That's big of you. I was thinking, maybe you can get Jessica to leave Valiant with you or with Karl? Or maybe that Cordelia's family could take him? I saw that she had a couple of sisters. It might be nice for the new 'cat, Athos, to have a resident friend."

With an effort, Stephanie restrained herself from sighing. That wasn't going to happen, but she couldn't tell Anders that, not now, probably not ever.

"I'll talk to Jessica," she said. "I promise."

But what I can't promise is that I'll make her change her mind. All I can hope is that I won't find her angry and full of regret for a bond that happened in a moment and will last for life.

5

WHEN SHE'D VOLUNTEERED TO HELP WITH GETTING THE Kemper house in order for the boys to eventually take up residence, the last thing Cordelia had expected was a steady stream of visitors. In fact, she'd taken on the job in part because, until her ankle was completely healed, she'd been forbidden to go on even a short hike, and her mom, meaning well, would keep coming to check on her. The "checking" was usually disguised as something else: asking an opinion on dinner or bringing a cup of tea "because I was brewing some for myself," or some other completely innocuous excuse, but Cordelia knew the attention for what it was: Lady Danette's need to reassure herself that Cordelia was fine.

When Cordelia had made the mistake of complaining to her older sister, Dana had been tart and unmerciful. "Brat! You're too young to remember the Plague. It's a story to you. But I'm just that little bit older, and what I remember best is the sense of uncertainty. You didn't plan for anything, big or small, beyond the next day, especially fun things like birthday parties, because it was all too possible that the person wouldn't be there or would be too sick or whatever. When you planned it was for scary things, like running out of supplies or having to move. I had an evacuation bag in my room. Mom gave it some silly name, like 'sleepover bag,' but she knew and I knew what it was: it held all I could take if I had to go somewhere else because Mom was sick, like Dad had been sick, or Uncle Bart had been or . . ."

Dana's voice had trailed off, soft and tight, and she had dashed tears from her eyes without realizing they were there.

Cordelia had drawn in a deep breath. "Sorry. I get it. PTSD. And I triggered all that again by nearly getting myself and Barnaby killed and because I'm a *brat*"—she'd stressed the word—"who had a thing about not wanting to set my Fall alarm." She'd shaken her head. "That was a *joke*, Dana! Of course I always set it when I was out alone. You know that!"

"Yeah?" Dana had cocked an eyebrow, then shrugged. "Okay. You're right; I did know, or I'd've raised Cain over it when I got you alone. But are you sure *Mom* knew that?"

"Well, I *thought* she did," Cordelia had said. "But even if she did, I know it's not funny anymore. And I know, Mom's not only haunted by what actually happened, but what might have happened, how you here would have wondered why I didn't turn up for dinner and gone looking and . . ." She'd thrust out her injured ankle and imagined the healing flesh as it had been, red and oozing, imagined all of her like that, maybe her eyes ripped out, bald patches on her scalp, or bones showing. "Doesn't Mom know that every time she comes to check on me I feel guilty all over again for scaring her that way? I get it. I'm sorry. I won't do it again, but what can I do?"

And Dana, because she was Dana, because she was sensible and understood both sides, had come up with the suggestion that Cordelia could make herself useful over at the Kemper house. Lady Danette had agreed because she, too, was sensible, and because she knew her middle daughter needed some time to herself.

So Cordelia had taken to spending a few hours a day at the Kemper farmhouse. It was a large, rambling structure. Even today, stone and timber were much easier to get on Sphinx than prefab, especially given freight costs and how strapped for hard money most Sphinxians were. It was another sign of Glynis Bonaventure's wealth that she could import so many of her geodesic domes. Fortunately, counter-grav made it possible to haul raw materials to be built into sturdy, solid, surprisingly lovely homes, insulated by massive walls against both the cold and the monsters that prowled in the bush, and that was exactly what the Kemper farmhouse was.

After the boys had come to live with the Schardt-Cordovas, the house had been cleaned and sealed. The original furniture was still in storage: knickknacks and practical goods alike boxed up because an empty structure didn't offer as much temptation to thieves and vandals. Although the house had been alarmed, Lady Danette had insisted on a visual check at least once a T-week, a ritual that Cordelia now suspected had been intended as much to keep the Kemper boys connected to their heritage as it had been to care for mere real estate.

Now that Mack was eighteen, he wanted to take

up part-time residence in a home he barely remembered. Like many of the older houses on Sphinx, the Kempers' had been built in stages. The plan was to open the oldest part: kitchen, bathroom, living area, a couple of bedrooms, and leave the rest for later, so the boys wouldn't need to maintain as much.

Or be as aware of all the space their parents had expected to fill with the siblings they'd never had.

Cordelia had taken on the task of room by room triage, starting in the kitchen, checking which appliances would need to be replaced or refurbished, washing down surfaces, and estimating how much paint and oil would be needed to freshen walls and wood floors. It was good, tiring work, and she'd thought that, even with Athos for company, she might get lonely.

But, of course, she'd discovered her expectation of solitude had been sadly misplaced. Both Mack and Zack had dropped by, although they'd vanished when she'd suggested they grab a scrub brush instead of gloating over how much space there was in the pantry. Herman Maye from Mr. Ack's had stopped by, twice in one day. The first time had been to make sure no one had broken into the house. The second had been to give Cordelia some excess Portobello mushrooms to take home with her. He'd popped in and out, hardly a distraction at all. Then Karl Zivonik had dropped by to talk treecats. Unlike the Kemper boys, he knew how to chat with a scrub brush in hand, which nudged him up in Cordelia's estimation. Karl was due to come back today, so when Cordelia heard an air car coming in for a landing, she figured it was either him or the Kempers and didn't even look up.

Then she heard the front door open and close. Footsteps came down the hall toward the kitchen, and she began backing out of the cabinet where she'd been putting contact paper down on the newly freshened shelves to greet her visitor.

"Hi!" she began. "I didn't—"

She froze, still on her hands and knees, as she found herself looking up into the amused and somehow predatory gaze of Frank Câmara. A bag dangled from his fingers, and from it came the earthy scent of fresh mushrooms.

"I knocked," he said. "And let myself in when no one came to the door."

Cordelia knew he'd lied. She'd been listening for a knock because a knock would have been Karl, while the Kemper boys would simply have thundered in. She felt vulnerable down on the floor, and adjusted her counter-grav to bring her to her feet without the need to put weight on her ankle. She'd progressed from crutch to cane, but her gut feeling was that she didn't want to look the least gimpy. Once she was on her feet, though, she casually wrapped her fingers around the length of polished red spruce that her mother had supplied for her.

"Your dad's," she'd said, far too casually, "from when we were building the house and he broke his foot."

Now Cordelia felt a strange courage, as if her dead father was standing right behind her, whispering in her ear, telling her to face bullies, not shrink back.

"If you run, they will chase. It is the nature of the beast, but look them squarely in the eye and they will wonder if you are more dangerous than they had believed."

So Cordelia met Frank's insolent gaze. As she did so, she tried to remember where Athos was. Outside, she thought, messing about with stones, as he seemed to enjoy doing. She hadn't wanted to pry into what it was he did in his private time. That seemed too... anthropological or something, like Athos was a something to be studied, not a new friend, who would show off what he was doing when he felt like it.

Frank's arrogant leer was fading into a quizzical expression that just barely masked something cat and mouse in his posture. Momentarily, Cordelia wished her rifle wasn't near the front door with her outdoor things, then she realized that if she pulled a gun, she'd just show how scared she was. So she forced what she hoped sounded like a casual laugh.

"I didn't hear you. Uncle Bart built solid cabinets, I guess."

"Looks like it," Frank agreed. "Really solid house."

His tongue moved quickly over his upper lip. Cordelia fought a shiver. What was wrong with her? She didn't know much about Frank Câmara, but surely even he wouldn't try anything. He had to know she'd report him if he did... Or did he? There was something odd about him, slightly unfocused. She struggled to find a topic of conversation and pointed to the bag still dangling from his fingers.

"Mushrooms? Did Herman send those over? Were you making a pickup for your father?" She stopped herself short of adding "Like the last time we saw you?" She didn't want to remind him of that last meeting, of the cutting things he'd said to Stephanie and about injured treecats.

"Mushrooms, yeah," Frank echoed, looking at his

own hand as if it was new to him. "Mushrooms. From Herman. He had them set by, was going to bring them, but I said I'd do him a favor. I wanted to see what this place looked like, check on you, a young woman, all alone . . ."

This time the innuendo was plain, but there was nothing Cordelia could call him on, even if she'd felt like doing so. One thing for sure, this was the last time she'd leave the door unlocked.

"Are you going to live here, too?" Frank asked, still holding onto the bag of mushrooms, "with Mack and Zack? That could be . . . fun."

Again, he'd said nothing Cordelia could call him on, but his inflection turned the words into something lewd. She felt dirtied by his obviously lecherous imaginings, and wondered if her cheeks were turning red.

"No," she said, and found the one syllable almost impossible to articulate. How could she change the subject, get him out of the house, without giving Frank the pleasure of knowing he'd scared her? That would give him power over her, and more than anything else, she didn't want that.

The bag of mushrooms that was swinging forgotten again from Frank's left hand gave Cordelia an idea.

"I'd better put those mushrooms in the cooler," she said, plucking the bag from his slack fingers before he could think to tighten his grip. "Let me call Herman to make sure that's the right thing to do. I'd hate to spoil them."

She was proud of herself for managing to make her tone matter-of-fact, slipped the bag on her wrist, and got out her uni-link in one smooth movement. Frank jolted slightly, as if he'd been asleep on his feet.

C'mon, Herman. Answer my call, Cordelia thought desperately. *Don't let this go to message. Answer, answer. . . .*

When Herman answered, Cordelia had to fight to sound casual. "Hi, Herman. Cordelia. I wanted to thank you for sending over the . . ."

Frank moved, blinked. Cordelia hardly knew what she was saying because Frank, realizing that they were no longer alone, was moving toward the door. She trailed after, managing to chatter back at Herman, who was giving her some sort of recipe. Then Frank was out, walking across the porch, down the steps, over to the same air van he'd been driving the last time. Cordelia snapped the deadbolt shut, then scurried to make sure the kitchen door was locked as well.

Herman must have heard something in her voice, because he stopped in the middle of explaining why browned butter was so important to bringing out the flavor.

"Are you all right, Cordelia?"

"I'm fine," she lied. "I heard something on the roof. I need to run upstairs and open a window for Athos. That recipe sounds great, but I'm not much of a cook. Can you text it to me? I'd like to try it."

Herman looked very pleased on the uni-link's tiny display. "I would have brought it myself, along with the mushrooms, but Frank left before I could . . ."

Something changed—ever so briefly—in Herman's voice, something that made Cordelia wonder whether Frank restricted his bullying to young women with broken ankles caught all alone. But surely Frank couldn't bully Herman. Herman was an adult. He had a responsible job. Frank needed Herman as a source of exotic produce for the family business, right?

She disconnected the call and adjusted her counter-grav unit so she could float upstairs and open a window—a small window—for Athos. The moment it was open, the treecat flowed through the narrow gap and butted his head against her arm, purring loudly.

Cordelia collapsed down onto the windowseat built into the thick wall of the house and let Athos onto her lap. Only then, to her astonishment, did she begin to shake, then burst into tears.

✧ ✧ ✧

If Heart Stone had nurtured any doubt that his two-leg bondmate was young, her eagerness to be up and doing even before the ache of her wounds had faded from her mind-glow was proof enough. He had been interested when she had taken them in one of the flying things to a seemingly vacant nesting place of the sort the two-legs built for themselves. The nesting place in which she resided with a group of two-legs that felt like a clan group to him was indeed busy, especially when various outliers came to visit, but he did not think it was so crowded that Life Shaper needed to go elsewhere.

Could it be that she was of breeding age? Her lack of interest in any of the young males who visited her clan's nesting place had made him think she was young for such things, but despite his distant observation of Life Shaper's clan during the seasons in which he had scavenged their leavings, Heart Stone did not consider himself an expert on the two-legs. He wished he could ask Climbs Quickly, whose two-leg also seemed young, but that was not to be. He would need to figure out Life Shaper's needs for himself. His curiosity, which had dimmed after Golden Eye's death, had been stimulated by the puzzle of two-legs and why they did what they did, even before he had bonded with Life Shaper.

He wondered what his new friends called his bond-mate, for he was certain they would have given her a name by now. His name for her represented not only the new shape she had given his life, but also a tie to his own former name, for he envisioned her as shaping him into something useful and even beautiful, just as he shaped flint.

On the first day they had come to Second Nest, after assuring himself that nothing dangerous resided within the vacant nesting place or its immediate surroundings, Heart Stone had scampered up one of the spreading golden leaf trees that surrounded the nest, taking himself far enough to escape the stench of the various fluids Life Shaper was spreading on every surface, only to wipe them away with much water and even more effort. Here, he could continue work on the stone knife he was making for Climbs Quickly without leaving sharp chips of stone where they might cut the delicate skin of his bondmate.

Heart Stone had been leaning back against the tree trunk, admiring his newly finished project, when yet another of the flying things came to rest on the flat area near the nesting place that was their designated roost. Even before the flying thing had disgorged its two-leg, Heart Stone had recognized the stink of the young male human's mind-glow from their first brief meeting at Rich Dirt Grove. He had bristled and set the newly finished knife aside, thinking he would drop down and enter the nesting place when Life Shaper came to open the swinging flap that covered the entry.

What Heart Stone had not counted on was that the young male—Stench, as he thought of him—would push the flap and enter the nest himself. Up to this point, the only ones who had entered without banging on the flap had been the members of Life Shaper's own clan. Disturbed, Heart Stone had swarmed down the tree trunk so quickly that some of his treasured tools plummeted down. He had left them to be retrieved at some future time.

The next breaths of time, short as they were, had been greatly disturbing. He had tasted how Life Shaper had begun as startled, then become afraid. Stone had raced from point to point on the nest, seeking an entry that would not involve him having to break anything. He had known he would do his best to rip loose whatever part of the nest he could if the threat to her went beyond fear. Even feeling her tolerating fear had been almost more than he could endure. Had he not been a senior Person and an injured one as well, he might have tried to rip through the walls. But Heart Stone *was* older, and he had known all too well that fear was danger's herald, not danger itself. If Stench was the source of Life Shaper's fear, then frightening Stench might have set loose the very menace Life Shaper feared.

When Stench took his leave, Heart Stone stood guard until he confirmed that the flying thing had definitely left the area, not merely prowled around for another approach. As he did so, he heard the covering over one of the smaller upper openings in the nest snap open, and Life Shaper softly calling. She often made the same noise, and he was more and more certain that it was her name for him.

"Ah-thos" meant no more to him than did the mating song of a peak-wing or the chitters of a bark chewer, but it warmed him just the same. He bounded to that summons, slipped in through the opening, and pressed against Life Shaper, purring as once he had purred to soothe his kittens when they were frightened by the wind screams of an early snow-time storm. Life Shaper was a very brave two-leg, for all she was young, and soon responded to his purrs with mouth noises. He was puzzled when he realized that once her fear ebbed, she began to feel a different sort of fear, a protective one. Given how hard she gripped him (although ever careful for his mending injuries) he realized that the fear was for him. Heart Stone sensed that somehow she was relieved that he had not been close enough to confront Stench. While he was glad that she did not feel he had failed to protect her, he also believed this confirmed his conjecture that Stench might have offered some threat to Life Shaper.

Eventually, they went back to the lower portion of the nesting place, and Life Shaper finished the task she had been doing before Stench's arrival. At her insistence, Heart Stone went outside, but she made a point of showing him where she had left one of the smaller flaps arranged so he could come and go as he wished, without letting the weather inside.

He was burrowing through the duff beneath the golden leaf, looking for the pressure flaker he had dropped, when he heard the sound of another flying thing approaching. This one though, held the cheerful mind-glows of Climbs Quickly and the Person Heart

Stone had decided to call Sharp Sight because of his obviously keen vision and tendency to note details others might have missed, as well as of their two-legs. He was glad. Life Shaper would be glad of friends at this time, and he could tell from the excitement in the mind-glows of his two new People friends that they had something they were eager to share with him. He wondered if it might be cluster stalk, but maybe it was some other treat.

Tucking his tools in his carry net, Heart Stone slid inside the nest so he would be with Life Shaper when she realized she had guests. When the signal drumming sounded against the entry flap, he felt the flash of panic in Life Shaper's mind-glow. He purred reassuringly at her, then jumped down to lead her, tail high, to the entry flap. He heard her make the soft, low pleasure sound that he was coming to think was the equivalent to a Person's bleek of laughter, then some mouth noises. She then rose to follow him, taking with her the heavy stick she sometimes used to relieve the pressure on her injured ankle.

At the entry flap, she took the time to survey outside before snapping open various things that must be intended to keep someone from entering without permission. She made a happy noise when she saw that those without included the young male who had been adopted by Sharp Sight and Climbs Quickly's young female. Their mind-glows held confusion at Life Shaper's reaction, then grew concerned as she made mouth noises at them.

Climbs Quickly's and Sharp Sight's mind-glows also held confusion and concern, followed with a faint touch of frustration. Heart Stone felt certain they had tried to ask him what had happened, only to remember that he was deaf to their mind-voices. However, none of the pity Heart Stone loathed followed, only a warm practicality. He wondered if it was the fact that Climbs Quickly and Sharp Sight were both scouts, a calling that demanded a degree of adaptability, that made them so quick to accept his limitation.

Instead, Climbs Quickly leapt down from where he had perched on his two-leg and made a quick, short bound in the direction of the golden leaf he knew was Heart Stone's favorite perch. Heart Stone paused, uncertain if he should leave Life Shaper. But although she was making rapid mouth noises at her friends, she hadn't missed what was going on with the three People. Again she made the happy sound, then followed it with a shooing gesture that was easy to understand. Heart Stone decided he would take her suggestion. He didn't yet know these two two-legs well, but both of their mind-glows radiated strength and determination. The little female had barked very fiercely at Stench when they had encountered him before. If she had possessed hackles, surely she would have raised them. Life Shaper would be safe with these two, and perhaps even relax more easily if she didn't guess how concerned Heart Stone was about her peace of mind.

Perhaps I shall call the little female Fierce Fighter, for whatever else there is to her—and there is a brilliance to her mind-glow that is astonishing in one who is mind-blind—she is both those things. What to call the male? Determined Defender feels right. He is less quick-tempered, I think, but I would not want to be the death fang that went after his clan.

Pleased with the decision that finally gave him suitable names for Life Shaper's friends, Heart Stone bleeked agreement to Climbs Quickly's suggestion, then leapt ahead to lead them to his little nest, as was polite when hosting guests.

Once they were comfortably settled, he reached into the cranny in the golden leaf's trunk where he had stashed his most recent handiwork. The flint Climbs Quickly had given him had proven sufficient to make blades for two knives. These he had mounted on handles made from the shed horn blade antlers that he had scavenged in those seeming long-ago days before he had met Life Shaper. He had been finishing polishing them shortly before Stench had arrived.

Even before he had come to live with Life Shaper and her clan, Heart Stone had noted the many tools the two-legs created to enable them to compensate for their lack of fangs and claws, including knives, one of which he had found hardly at all damaged and now used for himself.

The two-legs had other knives he looked forward to getting a closer look at. These looked like a handle without a blade until the two-leg did something to make it come alive. Then there was a humming, and those bladeless knives cut better than did flint or obsidian, or even the marvelous stuff of which his salvaged knife was made. Although Heart Stone had not witnessed such for himself in the short time he had lived with the two-legs, he guessed that the two-legs would use their knives as weapons as well, especially at times when their formidable thunder barkers might be inappropriate or excessive.

By contrast, People used knives as cutting tools, not

as weapons. No mere knife could compete with the drawing edge of a Person's claws for sharpness, but claws were short. Something longer was often needed, and while teeth could be used to cut, if necessary, that was messy, and plant matter often tasted quite terrible. So knives were useful, if not absolutely necessary.

When Climbs Quickly had presented Heart Stone with the piece of flint some days before, Heart Stone had been puzzled why the scout, who surely had access to not-stone knives, would want something made of stone. But then he had felt the eagerness in Climbs Quickly's mind-glow and been flattered to realize that Climbs Quickly valued Heart Stone's work for its beauty, not merely for utility. Therefore, when making these knives, he had taken great care that the flaking was symmetrical, and the pattern of the knife blade also displayed the beauty of the flint.

For once, Heart Stone was happy he couldn't mind-speak, because he surely would have been tempted to say something apologetic, for he was definitely out of practice. At the same time, he believed he had done a good job. Fleetingly, he wondered if Life Shaper might like a stone knife, or perhaps something to hang from her earlobes or around her neck for adornment, as he had seen her littermates do when going forth.

Climbs Quickly and Sharp Sight bleeked with pleasure when he slid the knives over to them, handle first, as was customary. They patted their true hands together in a gesture that looked both odd and strangely familiar, until Heart Stone realized that they were borrowing a gesture the two-legs made when pleased or excited.

Interesting, Heart Stone thought. *We People do not need gestures, because we can read each other's mind-glows, but even if the mouth sounds are indeed a peculiar form of communication, gestures would augment them, perhaps provide emotional content.*

As he had in the healing place, when he was still hardly aware of his new bond to Life Shaper, Heart Stone found himself wondering how he could learn more about how the two-legs managed to understand each other. Sound alone would be so very limiting, and would only work when within hearing.

No wonder Life Shaper was so frightened when Stench was stalking her. Unlike a Person, she could not call to any within range, as Musty would have been if he were a Person. They are so fragile, so isolated, poor kittens.

He came out of his reflections when he realized that Climbs Quickly was gently tapping one of his true feet with the tip of his tail. Again, Heart Stone was struck by how two-leg the gesture was. A Person would have no need to get another's attention by touch.

"Bleek?" Heart Stone offered to show he understood that Climbs Quickly wanted his attention.

Climbs Quickly's earlier excitement was once again flooding his mind-glow. Rising to his true-feet, he turned, carefully orienting his body and then raised both true-hands and hand-feet to point in the same direction in which he had angled his nose. Sharp Sight imitated Climbs Quickly, then Climbs Quickly bounded down from the golden leaf and leapt to the top of the flying thing where it slept. There he resumed the point, carefully indicating the same direction. Sharp Sight then rose to his true-feet and did a remarkable imitation of Life Shaper shooing the three People off to enjoy themselves.

Climbs Quickly and Keen Eyes want me to go somewhere with them. Somewhere we must use the flying thing to reach, so it is not merely to see some local curiosity or to go hunting for some tasty tree hopper.

Heart Stone felt a roiling storm of emotions within him. He was no fool. He knew what lay in that direction: Bright Water, the clan he had left behind him. Climbs Quickly and Sharp Sight were asking him if he wanted to go to Bright Water, indicating that the two-legs could close the great distance between this place and the clan's lands with their thing.

Would I go with them to Bright Water? I will not. I have left that life behind me. For the second time today, I am happy that I do not need to speak. For now, let them believe that I am reluctant to go chasing about in the forest when Life Shaper is unsettled.

But he thought that even though he pointed to where Life Shaper was and wrapped his tail around his toes, they were not fooled. Nor did he think this was the end of their asking. But he would keep refusing. He was glad for his new friends, but there was no going back, neither for him, nor for the family he had left because he could not bear their pity.

6

NOSEY'S INTERVIEWS WITH PEOPLE WHO HAD SUFFERED accidents were starting to show him a pattern, one he wasn't at all comfortable with. He'd talked with numerous accident victims since Paschel Trendane and Jake Simpson, and published many of their accounts, especially when he felt there was a human interest angle.

Some information about just how those accidents had come to happen, though, he'd deliberately suppressed. He didn't think it was his place to add insult to injury—in the most precise and literal sense of the phrase—when someone was recovering from damage that could be seen as being caused by being just plain dumb. And a lot of it had been just that. Even if he didn't call it that, those Commenting on an article would surely do so. He could moderate those Comments posted to his article, but he could do little about what people chose to say on their own feeds, and so he had avoided mentioning the victims' more . . . questionable decisions.

Besides, there was something about those decisions. Something they all seemed to have in common.

Nosey had decided that the thing to do was look

for a pattern, then see if he could confirm what he was coming to suspect. After that, he could take his suspicions to the appropriate authorities... Whoever that might be.

It was in pursuit of that larger pattern, as well as of a potentially touching news story, that Nosey headed off to his next interview. This one had tied in neatly with one of his courier jobs. The accident victim was recovering at home, and Nosey was bringing medical supplies, including some nano-tailored painkillers.

He knew the Yazzie family slightly. As with Jake Simpson, the eldest daughter was a noted athlete, specializing in dance and gymnastics, rather than team sports. Like Jake, Eldora Yazzie's accident seemed highly unlikely for anyone who had followed her career. Nosey's excuse for talking with her was that he wanted to do a piece about when her next recital would be held, but his goal was getting some information about just how she had come to be so badly hurt.

Eldora's family were relatively new colonists, but both parents possessed specialties that Sphinx needed, and they'd been actively recruited for their skill sets. Her father was a biomechanical engineer, specializing in prosthetic devices but with a broad background that lent itself to a wide spectrum of needs, and her mom's background in IT applications—especially biomechanical control systems—made them a formidably effective team, so they were doing very well.

When he rang the bell, there was a pause, then Oliffe Yazzie answered the door. She was a tall, slim woman with straight, dark hair blunt-cut right at her jawline. On many women, the style would have looked terrible, but on Oliffe it looked fantastic.

"Sorry," Nosey said. "I think I'm a little early. The pharmacy was ahead of schedule for once."

Oliffe smiled warmly. Wiping her hands on her apron, she motioned for him to come in. "Thanks for bringing the painkillers and lung therapy gear. Pirney is off-planet at meetings, and I don't like to leave Eldora with only the little ones. They're good kids, but they're kids . . . They forget that their big sister needs looking after. Usually, it's the other way around."

Oliffe made as if to take the container from him, but Nosey held onto it.

"It's awkward to carry. Let me take it into the kitchen, maybe? The contents should be kept in a cool area with a regulated temperature."

"Kitchen would be fine," Oliffe said, turning and leading the way. "Forgive the mess. I've been baking. I find there's nothing like handwork to free up my mind when I get stuck on some project. Happily, the kids never get tired of cookies."

"Those smell terrific," Nosey said, honestly. He hoped Oliffe didn't think he was hinting, but it seemed ruder not to comment. "How's Eldora doing?"

"Honestly, not as well as I hoped she'd be by now."

Nosey had put the cooler on the counter and Oliffe started unpacking it without really looking at what she was doing.

"She's still having breathing issues. Her lungs were damaged in the fall, because several of her ribs splintered. The surgeons say they got all the fragments, but lung damage can be serious in high-gee. Eldora's morale is low. She's never liked living on a high-gee planet, because she needs to use a counter-grav unit. Now that using one is not merely a matter of moving more easily, but is a medical necessity, she's become decidedly grim."

"Are you sure Eldora wants to see me?" Nosey asked, but he was good enough at reading people to tell that Oliffe—if not Eldora—had been looking forward to his visit.

"Absolutely! You want to interview her about dance and that's her favorite topic—one that, if I may be honest, the rest of us are talked out about. You'll be doing more than just her a favor. She's on the sun-porch. Let me show you the way."

✧ ✧ ✧

Eldora didn't look exactly thrilled when Oliffe announced Nosey's arrival. She was a dramatically lovely young woman, with hair like wet ink and long, dark, almond-shaped eyes. Semi-reclined as she was on a daybed heaped with cushions, she looked more like a painter's idea of an invalid, rather than an actual invalid: lips slightly pouting, eyes half-shut to display the curve of her lashes.

As they went through the usual greetings, Nosey searched through his mental thesaurus looking for the right word to describe Eldora's affect: Bored? Apathetic? Indifferent? He decided that "impassive" fit best.

He had a faint sense that Eldora had been hoping for a visitor and, while she wasn't unhappy to see Nosey, her impassivity was at least partially meant to hide that he wasn't the person she'd hoped to see. Nosey tried to remember who her friends were, and realized with a start that he couldn't place any. The type of dance she did certainly had team elements, but from the start Eldora had wanted to be a soloist. Did she have a romantic interest? There was something about how she'd displayed herself so carefully that made him wonder if Eldora had anticipated the arrival of a sweetheart. If so, Oliffe hadn't been told. She had clearly expected Nosey's arrival to be a treat.

Nosey settled onto the chair next to the daybed, and turned on his charm. "How're you doing, Eldora?"

"Is this 'on the record'?" she sniped, trying to sound as if she was making a joke, but failing.

Oliffe had been on her way back to the kitchen, but now she paused and stiffened. "Eldora!"

Nosey dismissed Oliffe's protest with a wave of one hand. "No worries. I get that all the time." He smiled at Eldora, dropping her the slightest wink. "Anything you say will be off the record unless you say so. Otherwise, I'm just here to talk about dance."

Possibly embarrassed into good behavior by Oliffe's reaction, Eldora produced an almost convincing smile. "Thanks. That's nice of you. Sitting around by myself gets old fast."

Oliffe resumed her retreat. "I have some cookies in the oven. Excuse me."

As her footsteps retreated, tapping lightly on the hardwood floor, Eldora rolled her eyes theatrically.

"Cookies in the oven!" she mimicked. "I swear! Sometimes the culture on this planet is so retro I could just scream. It's like we're all supposed to forget we live in the age of space voyages, and instead play Happy Pioneers. My dad's taken up wood carving, if you can believe it, with a steel knife and everything. And he's a biomechanical engineer! He could probably *grow* wood carvings if he put his mind to it."

"So, you don't like living on Sphinx?"

"Off the record?"

"Sure."

"I hate it." The way she bit off the three words left no doubt she meant them. "Back on Thule, I'd been involved in dance and theater since I could walk, practically. I did ballet until I was twelve. Then I decided that a wider emphasis on theater and dance suited me better. Then, just as I was getting to the age where the really good ingénue roles would be opening up for me, my parents move me to a planet where I feel like a rock all the time."

"There're counter-grav units," Nosey said mildly, indicating the one he wore, rather than the one that encircled Eldora's trim waist.

"It's not the same. Even if I set it for Thule normal, I know it's a cheat. Anyhow, even if I did manage to keep up with my practice, what would it matter? Everything on Sphinx is, frankly, bush league. Even Manticore is bush league. You know what I'm hoping?"

"What?"

"I'm hoping this accident will provide me my excuse to go home. High-grav planets and damaged lungs aren't a great mix. Anyhow, I'm nineteen. Legally, I could have skipped out a year ago, but my parents won't come up with a ticket and the jobs I could get here aren't going to earn me a ticket home."

She trailed off, despair etching every line of her face. For the first time, she looked genuinely unwell.

Nosey asked a question to which he already knew the answer. "Your family has been here, what? Two T-years?"

"Two T's, seven months."

"Did you want to immigrate?"

"Not really, but I didn't exactly have a choice. Parents."

The final word comprised what Nosey felt certain was a wealth of arguments, compromises, and more. He didn't ask if Eldora's siblings felt the same way she did. He knew they didn't. There were two, a brother and sister, both younger. Both were involved in various community activities, including sports. Doubtless their adjustment to Sphinx and its myriad challenges only made Eldora feel worse about her own situation.

Nosey deftly steered the conversation to dance. After a few questions that demonstrated both that Nosey had seen her performances and that he'd bothered to learn something about her art, Eldora loosened up amazingly and even became fun to interview. Several times, Nosey tried to work her around to exactly how she'd managed to take such a serious fall, but each time Eldora danced away from the issue.

The closest she came to saying anything substantial was an airy, "Oh, I was so caught up in the euphoria, the music, the memories, that I forgot that I was here in Lead Foot Land. I certainly can't forget now—no matter how much I wish I could."

By the time Oliffe arrived with a plate of fresh-from-the-oven oatmeal raisin cookies and a pot of oolong tea, Nosey had Eldora laughing. But he didn't miss how her gaze kept straying to where an approaching air car would first be seen descending on the Yazzie property, and he wondered who she was waiting for—and why Oliffe seemed to have no idea Eldora was expecting a guest.

✧ ✧ ✧

"I would rather," Stephanie said to Lionheart, slicing through the thick, crusty loaf of sourdough bread with enough force to nick the cutting board, "fight a hexapuma armed only with this bread knife than have a 'relationship chat' with Jessica."

"Bleek," Lionheart replied agreeably from where he lolled on one of the designated cat platforms set around the Harringtons' kitchen. Early on in the treecat's residence, Marjorie had insisted that no matter how much she loved Lionheart and was grateful to him for saving Stephanie's life, she was not going to have everything she ate liberally seasoned with gray and white fur. *Long* gray and white fur, at that.

Stephanie knew Lionheart didn't understand what she was saying, but who else could she talk to? Her mom and dad were great, but what if they just gave her one of those "You really need to learn how to deal with interpersonal relationships, dear" lectures? Or worse, hinted that Stephanie's problem was that she wasn't really over Anders yet? After all, he'd only dumped her a few weeks before . . .

Astronomically awkward.

When Jessica's air car began its descent, Stephanie had a moment of panic during which she considered locking all the doors and pretending she wasn't home. Of course, that wouldn't work, because Valiant and Lionheart would know perfectly well the other was there. They might even think Stephanie was inviting them to play some sort of hide-and-seek. That would seriously suck. And be seriously unfair to Jessica, who had seemed so happy to have time to hang out with Stephanie.

So Stephanie squared her shoulders and was ready when Jessica gave the kitchen door a *pro forma* tap and let herself in. Valiant slipped in before his human, bleeked at Stephanie, then sprang up to a platform adjacent to Lionheart's. Then the two treecats sat up, straight and tall, nearly identical except for Lionheart's scars and the greater number of rings on Valiant's tail, two sets of leaf green eyes focused on the celery stalks that Stephanie had prepared earlier and put in a glass vase, like a peculiar bouquet.

Jessica gave Stephanie a quick enthusiastic hug, then rummaged in her shoulder bag and pulled out a large bottle full of some bright pink liquid. "Mom sent along a batch of her latest tea blend. You wouldn't think spikethorn and spearmint would go well together, but with just a little honey to cut the sharpness, it's great."

"You want to set up a pitcher?" Stephanie asked, giving her an appreciative grin. "I'll finish prepping the food. There's all sorts of stuff for sandwiches. I just need to get out condiments and side dishes. Mom said she wouldn't mind if we ate everything. She's picking up the latest grocery order on her way back from the Eisenbergs'."

Jessica bustled over to where one of Irina Kisaevna's pottery pitchers was displayed on a shelf. "Actually, this time I may actually give you honest competition. I grabbed a nutribar before my morning physiology class. I had questions for the teacher after, so I was almost late for my hospital shift—it's been crazy there—and then I dove into the air car and came straight here. Archie must have found my secret stash of emergency snacks, so I'm seriously starved."

"Help yourself," Stephanie said, setting a basket of ice potato chips, along with a creamy dill dip, where both she and Jessica could reach them.

Then she got out individual bowls of mixed fruit salad and a covered plate of double dense chocolate cupcakes. Jessica poured them both tea, and for a brief while there was silence as they constructed their sandwiches. Stephanie concentrated on piling alternate slices of roast capricow, sharp "moon" cheese (so called because it was distinctly green and had holes that looked like craters), and arugula between thick slices of sourdough bread until the sandwich was a fair rival to the Dagwoods at the Red Letter Café. She took her first bite, and sighed with pleasure, largely because as long as her mouth was full, she couldn't be expected to talk.

Through all of this, the two treecats watched patiently, but when Stephanie went for her next bite, Lionheart bleeked, then stood up on his rear set of paws, curling his one remaining upper true-hand and both hand-feet in mimicry of a cute gesture he'd seen a miniature poodle do when she and Karl had been putting up flyers at a popular eatery in Yawata Crossing. Stephanie suspected that Lionheart knew she found the pose completely nauseating and was doing it on purpose because she'd overlooked him and Valiant.

"The question is," she said to Jessica, who was giggling uncontrollably at the sight, "do I reward annoying behavior? What do I do if Lionheart tries this in public? We have enough trouble convincing people that treecats may be fluffy but they're not meant to be pets, without this sort of behavior. Imagine if Nosey Jones got a holo of it? We'd be doomed!"

"I will bet you my share of all future cupcakes," Jessica said, handing each of the treecats one of the stalks of celery from the vase, "that Lionheart will never do that in public—especially since he's got to know it annoys you. He's jerking your chain because you were ignoring him and his guest. And, hey, you seem seriously distracted. Is anything wrong? Having trouble getting recruits for the SFS Explorers? Should I ask Melanie-Anne who else you might invite?"

Here it was: her opening—and her out. Stephanie waivered, then decided that if she could face a poacher, a hexapuma, forest fires, and muggers, surely she could talk honestly to her best friend.

"Uh-mmm." *Eloquent, Steph. Really, really eloquent.* "So, how do you feel about Anders going back to Urako?"

Jessica ate a few bites of her sandwich, then several chips in a very thoughtful manner. She was quiet for so long that Stephanie finished her first sandwich and started to build a second. She was wondering if she should apologize for bringing up the subject when Jessica started talking.

"Honestly? I've been trying to figure that out. I mean, I knew he wouldn't stay here on Sphinx forever. Don't tell him this, but one of the reasons I was okay with dating him—because, I mean, we *had* gotten to be close, when you were off on Manticore, and I wanted to figure out if that was *just* because you were off on Manticore—was because I knew there was a natural break-up point. I've lived a lot of places, and knowing you're going to move on makes it easier to try a relationship."

"Not harder?" Stephanie blurted, honestly curious.

Even back on Meyerdahl, she hadn't had a lot of friends her own age. She was still trying to figure what was normal or not. She tested how she'd feel if Buddy Pheriss announced his family was going to move again, and felt a sharp pang of loss.

But Jessica can't *leave,* Stephanie thought, *because*

of Valiant. And part of this conversation is to find out if she realizes that.

After crunching another chip, Jessica went on. "Not harder, not really, not unless someone becomes a really close friend. Like you are, I mean. I'd feel worse about leaving Sphinx than just about anywhere since I was five and had to leave my bestie from kindergarten."

"So you agreed to date Anders because you knew that there would be a natural breakup?" Stephanie had to make sure she understood. When she'd fallen for Anders she'd thought this was It, the one, the true, just like in those serials that fade out with the dramatic declaration of love and never get into the details of mortgages or diapers or whatever.

"Kinda," Jessica said. "You probably don't know this, but Anders started declaring how he felt right after we'd been through a really horrible experience together. Suddenly, he's babbling about wanting to protect me and all . . . It was sweet. It was also intense. And I was having my own revelations, and honestly, they had nothing to do with Anders."

"That's when you decided to become a doctor," Stephanie said. It was hard to believe how little time had actually passed. Jessica's decision was such a natural fit that it seemed as if she'd announced it at their first meeting.

But then, we haven't been friends very long, really, have we? It wasn't until my fifteenth birthday party that I realized Jessica wasn't a complete zork. And I won't be sixteen for a few more T-weeks.

Stephanie spoke her next thought aloud, without really thinking. "Funny. It's really more like you've been dating future med-school than Anders, isn't it?"

"Yeah." Jessica finished her sandwich, looked at the makings, then shook her head. "You win the eating contest again. I want to save room for a cupcake—or two."

The manner in which Jessica had taken the subject of Anders had relaxed Stephanie. She'd expected resentment or—horrors!—tears, but this calm, even calculated, response put her at her ease.

"Anders doesn't feel that way," Stephanie went on. "He actually snagged me, asked me to sound you out on an idea he'd had. I promised I would, do you mind?"

"Go ahead, but I'll tell you right now, I'm not taking any promise ring and waiting for him to finish college and come back."

"Oh, it's not that." Quickly, Stephanie sketched out Anders's plan to take Jessica with him to Urako.

Jessica frowned. "Oh, so that's why he keeps mentioning all the neat things on Urako. He's trying to get me interested in advance."

Stephanie nodded. "He's even talked with his mother. He thinks she could get you a scholarship to finish school, even to med school. Do you want me to be the one to tell him that it won't work or do you?"

Jessica was staring at Stephanie. Her hazel-green eyes had gotten wider and wider as Stephanie had detailed Anders's plan. Now she froze.

"Won't work? Because it would be leading him on to take the scholarship, but not be sure I wanted to be a couple?"

Stephanie felt her heart start racing. *Uh-oh.*

"Won't work, because of Valiant. You can't leave him, and you can't take him. For now, I think the farthest any of us who've been adopted can go is someplace in-system. Maybe later we can go out-system but, even if Urako would let you take Valiant there—and Anders's mom didn't think that would be possible—it's not likely the Star Kingdom would clear a 'cat for export, not now, not while their status is so uncertain."

She kept talking, even though she saw that tears were flooding Jessica's eyes, then spilling down her cheeks. Valiant leapt down from his perch and raced to her, making small worried sounds, similar to those Stephanie had heard mother treecats use to soothe their very tiny kittens. For a terrible moment, Stephanie thought Jessica might fling him away, but the bond was true. Jessica opened her arms and hugged Valiant to her, crying into his thick, soft fur while he patted her with whichever of his true-hands he could get free.

Eventually, Jessica choked out, "He saved me. I'd be dead without him. But I never asked for this. I never asked for my life to be lived in prison. But . . ."

She started sobbing again. To give her a moment, Stephanie rose and put on the kettle for what her father would jokingly call "a nice cup of tea." She was rattling the cups onto a tray when she heard Jessica say, her voice muffled by the thickness of Valiant's coat:

"I guess what I feel for Valiant must be real love because, while I could leave Anders in a heartbeat, I could never, never, never leave Valiant. And I wouldn't want to." Jessica laughed, a funny, strangled sound. "Add this to the list of things the Great Treecat Conspiracy is going to need to figure out—how to explain why we can't travel without each other, without giving away the 'cats' secret before its time."

Stephanie understood. She'd already dealt with

that issue once, but then it had been an internal SFS thing. "Explaining's going to be rough on Anders because we can't tell him all the details of the bond. We just can't risk Dr. Whittaker learning about it and publishing what he'd surely view as important scientific information."

"Poor Anders," Jessica managed between sobs and giggles. "I'll try and find a way to break it to him gently. I think I'd better just tell him I don't care for him like he does me and leave Valiant out of it."

"Yeah," Stephanie said, "probably best, but Anders is smart. He's going to suspect. You know he's going to suspect."

✧ ✧ ✧

The skimmer park was as noisy as usual, so that Karl had to raise his voice slightly to be heard over the music that accompanied the skriders as they rode over the curves and convolutions of the complicated course.

It should be raw cacophony, Cordelia thought. *I wonder what the base programming is, because no matter how many skriders, no matter where they are on the course, it never is.*

"So where is Dia?" Karl asked. His tone was completely reasonable, but there was steel under it.

Cordelia, standing a few steps behind Karl, noticed that Survivor, perched on the pads set into Karl's SFS uniform, was twitching his tail—not all of it, just the lower part, with its single ring. She thought that if Karl's younger sister, Anastasia, could have seen the treecat's reaction, she might have read her brother's mood better than she did. Then again, maybe not. Staysa was something like thirteen and a half, an age when a lot of kids thought they were smarter they were.

"Dia? Nadia?" Anastasia said, looking side to side as if she'd just noticed that her older sister was not in the skimmer park. "She must be around here. Maybe she's in the bathroom? I wasn't really paying attention. Nadia's so good on her skimmer, you know. I have to concentrate to keep up with her when we're skimming."

"Hmm . . ." Karl said, tapping his uni-link. "I'll message her. If Dia's not here before Cordelia and I come back from getting a frozen custard, she's going to have to figure out if she's good enough on her skimmer to get home on it—that or tell the folks why she wandered off, leaving you younger kids on your own."

Cordelia's sister, Natalie, piped up. "I'm almost Nadia's age, only eight months younger."

"Hmm . . ." was Karl's only reply as he began to walk toward the concession stand at the far side of the park, motioning for Cordelia to join him. She noticed how he kept from breaking into his usual long stride out of consideration for her still-healing ankle. The passage of time had made a difference, but after being careful for so long, Cordelia sometimes felt as if she was learning to walk again—or not so much to walk as to trust that stepping wrong wasn't going to send shooting pains up her leg.

"Do we get custard, too?" Anastasia called after them hopefully.

"Nope. You knew the rules for your and Dia's coming to the skimmer park. I'm not going to reward breaking the rules." Karl grinned back at his little sister, an easy, almost impish expression. "Besides, I'm betting you've already had at least one. There's a spot on your shirt."

Cordelia glanced over her shoulder and saw Anastasia scrubbing at her shirt. What caught her attention, though, was how Natalie was looking after them, her expression guarded and thoughtful.

Nat knows something, but she doesn't want to rat out her new friend. Later, if it's important I'll push but, for now...

Once the younger girls couldn't see his face, Karl let his annoyance seep into his expression. "Dia is becoming a problem. She's fifteen now and boy crazy. I guess hormones turn on then or something. That's when Stephanie went nuts for Anders, too. And Sumi..."

He stopped speaking abruptly, so Cordelia filled in before it could get awkward.

"Who's the boy Dia's crazy about?"

Karl's frown deepened. "I don't know. That bothers me a little. She's had crushes before. Usually we could tell who the lucky person was because his name would come up every other sentence. Of course, most of those were 'safe' crushes—actors or music stars, not real people. But even the couple of times some 'real' person caught Dia's eye, we weren't kept in the dark."

"Does she have a type?" Cordelia asked. "I mean, Mack always gets crushes on the same type: tall, dark, and handsome. He'd probably go for you in a moment."

"Sorry," Karl grinned, "he's not my type. Nice guy and all, but... What's Dia's type? At least a few years older than her. A challenge in some way—maybe he has a girlfriend already or like that. Preference for the sophisticated sort, rather than your typical fifteen-year-old zork."

"Which probably explains why she likes the older guys," Cordelia said. "She can at least imagine they're sophisticated. Can you talk to Dia? Do the big brother act?"

"Not if she's interested in someone she doesn't think I'd approve of," Karl said, "or if she's head over heels. I tried probing once, and she just snapped at me, 'What do you know? When you were my age, you were practically engaged!'"

He stopped, as if he'd said too much, then visibly pushed himself to continue. "It was a situation not all that different from yours with the Kemper boys. Sumiko's family and ours were close. She came to live with us after they died in the Plague. Same age. She made up her mind we were destined for each other. I was, well, me. It didn't mean the same thing to me. I mean, I was fond of her, loved her, even, but when she started pushing for us to get engaged young, even hinted about our getting married before we were done with college, I balked."

"And . . ." Cordelia had noticed the past tense. She couldn't remember anyone mentioning a Sumiko, and she'd been spending a lot of time with the Zivoniks lately.

"She died. An accident. For a long time I blamed myself. Lately, I've been trying to forgive myself, but . . ." He shrugged.

They'd reached the frozen custard stand. Choosing flavors and sizes gave breathing space. Cordelia noticed Survivor nuzzling against the side of Karl's face, making that loud, thrumming purr that was so curiously soothing. Karl visibly relaxed, the shadow that had gathered over him as he talked about Sumiko vanishing.

Cordelia remembered what Stephanie had said about Karl and Survivor's bond: "I still don't know what brought them together like that, but whatever linked them, the bond has been terrific for them both."

I bet Stephanie knew perfectly well what brought them together. The name Karl gave Survivor says it all: They've both survived tremendous grief and loss. And I'll bet anything that they both had a fair share of survivor's guilt to top it off. Karl's admitted it, and who's to say that a treecat isn't capable of feeling something like that? Maybe they even feel it even more. If they can feel other people's emotions, they'd have to be able to feel when those they're close to are sick or starving.

But Stephanie couldn't explain without talking about Karl's past, and even if they're buddies, she isn't going to abuse that trust. There's a lot to like about that kid. And about Karl, too . . .

Cordelia thought how relieved she'd been when, the day after Frank Câmara's unwelcome visit, Karl had "just happened" to show up again. And he kept showing up. He always had a perfectly good excuse: patrol route in the area; getting her and Natalie's opinion on some aspect of the SFS Explorers; offering to drop Natalie off after some event she'd been at with one or both of his sisters; bringing a treat Athos might like or a spare cat bed or sweater, or, like today, suggesting they pick up the girls together.

If they had lived in the same area, this might have seemed completely normal, but Karl's family lived way out near Thunder River, while the Schardt-Cordova holding was pretty much in the opposite direction, on the other side of Twin Forks. Maybe as a ranger Karl was used to putting in the kilometers and the distance didn't matter to him, but Cordelia couldn't help but wonder.

Is there something going on, more than just protectiveness or because we're both the newest members of the very exclusive Treecat Conspiracy?

She didn't know what she thought about Karl maybe "liking" her. Unlike Dia, she'd never been boy crazy. Or girl crazy. She'd dated a little, but romance just wasn't her thing.

Maybe I had too much of it from all of Mack's crushes? He was always either over the moon or down in the dumps. It didn't make falling in love seem like a lot of fun.

Karl handed her a chocolate and mint frozen custard piled high in a waffle cone. "Shall we amble back? My uni-link pinged, and Dia has returned. She *says* she was in the ladies' room with an upset stomach and thanks me for my concern. Tartly. With appropriate emojis."

"You're not going to ask her where she was, are you?"

"Nope. Stupid as the day, that's me." He lifted his custard so Survivor could sniff it, then brought it down, unlicked. "But I won't forget. I promise you. I won't forget."

7

WHEN NOSEY JONES SAW THE TWO VISITORS IN SFS uniforms waiting on the covered porch of his A-frame house, he set his air car down on the landing pad next to their nondescript vehicle. The weather wasn't bad, and he was curious as to what would bring the rangers to his home, rather than just asking him to drop by headquarters. He'd garage his air car later.

It was only after he'd started walking briskly toward his visitors that Nosey realized he'd made a horrible mistake. The trousers and shirts they wore, along with the serviceable boots and neatly holstered sidearms, had looked very much like SFS uniforms from a distance. However, the impression didn't hold up from even a few paces closer, especially when they turned to face him and he saw that their features were curiously blurred.

No fool, Nosey didn't pause, but immediately started backing toward his air car. A warning shot froze him in his tracks.

"Hold it right there, Jones," said a distorted voice, deep and mechanical. "We've got a few words for you. Then we're going to have you deliver a message."

"What?" Nosey struggled for his usual poise and managed a poor facsimile. "I consider it my duty to help everyone be heard. You could have texted me. No need for this . . ."

He started to say "melodrama," but saw the gloved trigger finger of the hand holding the firearm begin to curl. The spokesman laughed, a guttural, ugly sound.

"Glad you see the wisdom in cooperating. Here're the words for you—just for you. Leak them to anyone, especially to the law, and we'll know."

Nosey nodded, his mouth suddenly powder dry.

"You've poked that honker of yours into someone else's business, someone who doesn't want you nosing around anymore. Got that? Accidents are accidents. None of those who've had one of these unlucky incidents didn't know exactly what they were doing. Got that?"

Nosey stood frozen. All the way home, he'd been thinking about the pattern emerging from his interviews with accident victims, how some of the senseless accidents made sense if looked at in a certain way. He'd even begun to think he knew why some of the victims were victims. What he didn't know was the "how," and the "what," and the "where." Even so, he'd been thinking he had enough to take to the SFS or one of the local municipal law enforcement agencies. News stories were great but, if what he suspected was true, then getting someone official to look into how these weren't really accidents was much more important than any ad revenue.

Nosey didn't realize that he'd been standing motionless, soundless, until the spokesman repeated in an aggressive bark, "Got that?"

"Sure. Got that. Drop the accident stories." Nosey

drew a deep breath. Maybe if he asked a question or two, he'd get a clue as to who these men were, who they represented, because he was sure they weren't the top of the food chain. "You said you had a message you wanted me to deliver?"

The man holding the gun, silent to this point, gave a coarse chuckle. As if that was a cue, the spokesman strode forward, moving with a leisurely, muscular gait that reminded Nosey of one of the hexapumas at the local wildlife center. The man talked as he moved closer.

"Yeah. I've got a message for you—one I gotta deliver up close and personal. Don't do anything stupid like try running. My buddy there said that we should shoot your kneecaps out. He bet me a six he could do it with only two shots. I told him we wouldn't bust your joints unless you were stupid. Soft tissue heals a lot faster, but, y'know, I think I'll give you an excuse to have that big nose of yours fixed."

As he drew closer, the spokesman clenched his right fist. Nosey swallowed hard and heard himself whimper. He'd been beaten up before, back when he'd been a lot younger. The bullies had backed off after he'd taken some self-defense classes. Even after the bullies moved on to easier prey, Nosey had kept up with his training. He'd learned to shoot as well, because couriers carried expensive or sensitive packages—the sort of things that couldn't be trusted to the bulk shipping firms.

Neither his ability to fight hand-to-hand nor his skill on the shooting range mattered one bit right now. His handgun was locked in the glove box of his air car. Even if he'd had it right there, in his hand, he didn't think it would help, and it would probably make matters worse.

The spokesman was closing in at an angle that gave the shooter a clear line on Nosey. If he'd had his gun, Nosey might have gotten a shot off, but he felt absolutely certain that if he did, then the shooter wouldn't have settled for a knee. He'd shoot to kill. They'd probably steal Nosey's air car and make the whole thing look like a carjacking. The only thing that was keeping him alive was that they were going to use him as an example.

The bullies were back, and he was a little boy with a big, funny nose who, even then, had liked to ask too many questions. But unlike that little boy, Nosey Jones didn't plead or cry or scream for help. Waiting stoically for what was going to happen was a small thing, but after that one terrified whimper, he didn't make a sound and held his ground. Nosey studied his attacker as he drew closer, grabbing every detail he could. Maybe, later, there would be a chance to get even.

Then the first punch came, a right to his solar plexus. Nosey doubled up, took a fist to his nose. Blood spurted out, and his hands flew up as if he could somehow catch it. There was a kick to one of his knees, delivered from the side. As he fell back, the next kick squarely hit his groin. He was down now, and not getting up but, nonetheless, his attacker kicked him in the head. There was something methodical, almost scientific, about the sequence of blows.

That's information, Nosey thought. Then there was nothing but pain shooting fireworks behind his eyes, and, finally, an almost welcome darkness.

✧ ✧ ✧

<*I am sure,*> Climbs Quickly began, <*and Keen Eyes is as well, that Stone Shaper understood that we were suggesting that he come visit Bright Water. Whatever the gray death did to him, it did not make him less intelligent.*>

He and Death Fang's Bane had ridden her folding flying thing to spend a lazy day at Bright Water. From their earliest days together, Death Fang's Bane had taken great care that Climbs Quickly would not be completely cut off from his birth clan, even though he had chosen to nest with her. Now he sat in the ornate nest of his littermate, Sings Truly, and regaled her with the tale of his and Keen Eye's failed attempt to coax Stone Shaper to come visit Bright Water.

Sings Truly twitched her ears. <*I do not disagree with you. From what you describe, Stone Shaper should have been able to understand, but let us not jump to conclusions. You say his new two-leg bond-mate was very upset that day. He might not have been rejecting your suggestion that he visit Bright Water as much as indicating that he would not go anywhere at that time.*>

<*How* could *we have gone anywhere at that time?*> Climbs Quickly protested. <*When Stone Shaper left Bright Water he made an amazingly long journey before settling near where his new two-legs has her family nest. Even though the netwood is well-connected in that part of the forest, we would have needed to run for many days to reach Bright Water. Surely he did not believe I was suggesting that I could make the flying thing do my bidding?*>

<*Could Stone Shaper know that for certain?*> Sings Truly countered. <*Remember, he has lived in isolation*

for almost a hand of turnings of the seasons. You said his mind-glow was full of surprise when he met you at Healer's place of healing.>

<*And he studied my injuries carefully as well,*> Climbs Quickly admitted, <*so he had no awareness of the shape of my personal song.*> His usual ebullient nature rose and he bleeked laughter. <*Perhaps he* does *believe that I could make the flying thing do as I wish. After all, he did seem puzzled when I asked for one of his stone knives. I saw his gaze rest on my not-stone knife and on the little not-stone axe Death Fang's Bane gave me at the time of many presents her family celebrates. You may have a point. I forget that while he and Keen Eyes bonded with their two-legs within a hand of days of each other, Keen Eyes can ask questions and receive answers, while Stone Shaper must watch and arrive at his own conclusions.*>

<*I have been thinking,*> Sings Truly said, <*I would like to meet with Stone Shaper myself. He lives too far from Bright Water for me to make the visit myself. The clan accepts that I will not be limited to the clan's central nesting place as Memory Singers traditionally have been. However, asking them to accept that I go that far would make the traditionalists unhappy. Since Stone Shaper's son, Stone Biter, is one of those traditionalists, and our goal is a reunion for Stone Shaper and his children—as well as with the clan—I think it would be unwise to create controversy. Stone Shaper would feel the tension, but we could not explain that it had nothing to do with him.*>

<*Yes, we must take care. Being able to read mind-glows without mind-speech might be worse than*

being completely mind-blind as the two-legs are. Partial information would be interpreted not based on knowledge but on what one imagines to be knowledge.> Climbs Quickly twitched his tail thoughtfully. <*There is one way to bring Stone Shaper closer to Bright Water, whether he wishes to come or not. If Awakening Joy came to the nesting place of Death Fang's Bane and her clan, then he would have no choice but to come with her. One of our scouts is almost always close enough for me to mind-speak from Death Fang's Bane's nesting place. If he is, then I could get a message to you when Stone Shaper is here, and you could come.*>

<*It would still take time for me to make the journey,*> she reminded him. <*My escort would not be happy if you and he had flitted in and out again before we could arrive.*>

<*I am learning to read the signs that Death Fang's Bane is expecting guests who live with People,*> Climbs Quickly said. <*For one, she always prepares a choice selection of cluster stalk, more than she ever lets me have for myself. If I saw those signs, then I could send word to you and you could come part way. Then I would let you know if Awakening Joy and Stone Shaper were among those visiting.*>

<*A good plan,*> Sings Truly agreed. <*Returning to the subject of those of the People who have bonded with the two-legs, I was surprised that Keen Eyes was not with you today, nor has he been with you on any of your more recent visits. I know we are not his birth clan, but Shining Sunlight often comes with Death Fang's Bane on these journeys, and Keen Eyes with him.*>

<*Shining Sunlight has been spending far less time with Death Fang's Bane and her clan,*> Climbs Quickly replied. Knowing that Sings Truly would read that he was deeply troubled from his mind-glow, he went on to explain. <*Death Fang's Bane's mind-glow is clouded, yet I feel she does not realize how much she misses Shining Sunlight's companionship. He was the first person close to her age for whom she did not feel a touch of—Scorn? Detachment? Aloofness?—sometimes it is difficult to understand how the mind-blind perceive each other. Season turnings passed before she really befriended anyone else close to her age. Now she has Windswept and Bleached Fur . . .*>

<*Except she does not,*> Sings Truly completed for him, <*Windswept is spending much time in the place where two-legs go for healing of grave illness or injury. Bleached Fur has chosen to pursue Windswept, although from what Dirt Grubber has told you about Windswept's feelings—or perhaps her lack of deep feeling is a better way to put it—I think Bleached Fur's pursuit will be one without a tasty morsel at the end.*>

<*As do I.*> Climbs Quickly flicked his tail toward where Death Fang's Bane rested at the base of a netwood, absorbed in one of her things. <*Death Fang's Bane aches because where her friends once set a warmth she is now cold. But, because for so long she did without friends of her own age, she may not even be aware of that cold. I do what I can, but I fear my comfort only makes it easier for her to deny how much she misses them—especially Shining Sunlight. When they meet, as they do meet, still almost daily, she flares up. Even when he makes mouth noises at*

her through the little thing she carries with her, she feels some of that warmth.>

<She is young yet,> Sings Truly said, *<but I wonder if someday Death Fang's Bane may be drawn to bond with Shining Sunlight.>*

<They would fit each other well,> Climbs Quickly said, *<but unlike People, they do not feel these things clearly. They have no mind song through which they can realize that they resonate in special harmony with another. I am not sure, but sometimes I think two-legs are like near-weasels in mating season, except they confuse being in heat for love. Shining Sunlight is spending much time with Awakening Joy. She is, in her own way, as brave and determined as Death Fang's Bane. There is much to like about her.>*

<And does Shining Sunlight more than "like" her?>

<Shining Sunlight is similar to a forest after snow time. You know how the People first named him Shadowed Sunlight because, for all the warmth of his mind-glow, there was a darkness to him? His bond with Keen Eyes burned away the shadow, as the sun burns away clouds after a storm. I think he "likes" everything, from his food to his family to his friends more than ever.>

Sings Truly reached forward and patted Climbs Quickly gently on one side of his face. *<Then maybe he will also like Death Fang's Bane more than ever. We can only hope she gives him a chance to see her brilliance and does not lock it away out of fear of being abandoned.>*

✧ ✧ ✧

The outing to Twin Forks had not started really well. Stephanie had ridden into town with her dad in the Vet Van to do some work on the SFS Explorers. She'd hurried over to the SFS station eager to meet with Karl.

He'd greeted her with his usual casual wave and smile. But when he'd moved from the shelter of the building's overhang toward her, someone had come with him: Cordelia Schardt-Cordova, Athos peering over her shoulder. Cordelia's ankle was still wrapped, but she'd given up using a cane, and Athos was beginning to fuzz his wounds. They'd all reached Karl's air car at the same time and, when Karl had popped the canopy, Athos had jumped into the front seat with the ease of long routine. As he did, Stephanie felt her heart give a funny squeeze. That was *her* place.

Cordelia hadn't followed her 'cat, but had gotten into the back seat, sliding into the middle to leave the windows for the treecats. She patted her lap to bring Athos to her, then indicated her right, so there would be room for Survivor behind Karl. Stephanie wondered if she'd been overreacting but no . . . Did Karl look just a little disappointed?

If so, he didn't say anything, but slid into the driver's seat, while Survivor hopped into the back behind him. Lionheart, ever sensitive to Stephanie's moods, stayed with her, softly thrumming his soothing purr. She wrapped her arms tightly around him and hoped she didn't look as much like an insecure kid as she suddenly felt.

Karl spoke as the air car lifted. "Hey, Steph. I met up with Cordy when we were both dropping sisters off at the skimmer park. She had some errands to run, so I said I'd take her into town. That way she didn't need to find parking."

Too much explanation, Stephanie thought, *especially from Mr. Strong and Silent.*

"Hi, Cordelia," Stephanie said, forcing herself to turn around and sound friendly. "You're really walking well now. No one would ever guess you'd had such a bad break. Dad said, after that last time you brought Athos in, that Athos is healing fantastically."

"We both do our PT," Cordelia said. "Every day and every way. But doing all those stretches gets *old* really, really fast. You know, though, better than most."

Stephanie felt the weird, lonely ache easing. She liked Cordelia, she really did. And 'cats knew how to find good people. If Karl wanted to date Cordelia, Stephanie was going to encourage him all the way. She'd make sure to invite them both over. Maybe if Cordelia wasn't too busy, she would like to join the SFS Explorers as a counselor. That would avoid having all the adults involved be teachers or parents.

She brought up the idea and Karl beamed. "I'd been thinking that, too. I was going to bring it up to you when we had our next planning meeting. What do you think, Cordelia?"

"Sure! I'm a firsthand example of why we all need to know what to look out for in the bush. A really excellent object lesson, because I was born here and I've played in the bush all my life, but if it hadn't been for Athos"—her hand drifted over to stroke the treecat from the top of his head to the base of his bushy tail—"I'd be dead and so would Barnaby."

Talk about the SFS Explorers kept them all busy on the drive to the skimmer park. Since this was on the edge of town, on the opposite side from the flying field the hang-glider club used, Stephanie had never been there before. She'd seen it from the air, but never from the ground, where she could really appreciate the tracks' layout. Now she gaped in awe—and just a little bit of envy.

"Wow! I never realized how steep they get!" she gasped in admiration as she watched the skriders guide their deltoid craft up, over, and along the sides of a series of fluid, curving tracks. "I never thought I wanted to take up skimmers, but this could make me change my mind. Sure, I've seen holovids, but it's different in person."

"Harder than it looks, too," Cordelia said. "It's all about balance and velocity. You've got to be moving pretty darned fast to do something like *that*." She pointed at a rider who'd just shot up the surface of a steeply curving bowl. The lip of the bowl curled back over, like a breaking wave, and the young man followed it up. He sailed up the inside of the concave shape, then broke contact with the maglev field and sailed free in a complete, elegant loop that landed him back on the track. His legs flexed as he took the shock of the sudden braking effect in Sphinx's heavy gravity, but he landed with hummingbird grace and rode his momentum into a sharp switchback that sent him shooting back out on an exactly 180-degree reversed course.

"The park requires riders to wear counter-grav units," Cordelia continued, "and the track's surface underneath is padded, but scratches and scrapes are still common."

"Look," Karl said, pointing. "There goes my sister, Staysa. She's going to try a triple."

The three humans leaned forward, watching intently

as Anastasia shot down a steep ramp, gaining velocity, and then rode her skimmer into a circular, twisting tube. Momentum kept her stable, shooting around the inside of the tube like a bullet, while she made three complete loops inside the tube, then went scooting out the other side in a semi-crouch, arms outstretched for balance, while her long dark hair streamed out below her helmet.

"That was impressive," Stephanie said sincerely.

"Yeah, I know," Karl said. "And she keeps telling me it's perfectly safe. I believe her—really, I do—and I've ridden the same course. But I have to say, skimmers are *not* my choice of hobby, and my stomach still turns flip-flops when I watch her. Want some frozen custard? I mean, Steph, you haven't eaten in at least twenty minutes."

"Almost an hour," she corrected solemnly. "Just remember, I'm a growing girl."

"Very slowly growing," he teased.

The familiar banter felt good. Stephanie grinned at Cordelia. "How about you?"

"I think I'm done growing," Cordelia said solemnly, "but I have mending bones. I need the extra calcium. Custard isn't a snack, it's medicinal."

They laughed together. When Karl didn't come up with his own creative excuse, Stephanie glanced over and saw he was staring at the skimmer course, worry furrowing his brow.

"Karl?"

"I was looking for Dia and Natalie. I thought I'd get them something from the snack stand, too. I've spotted Natalie, but I can't find Dia. I thought she was with that huddle of girls over on the left, but they've just broken ranks to start skimming again, and she's not there. If she's gone AWOL..."

Cordelia bounded from the back seat. "I'll check the facilities. You call the other two over and ask if they know where Dia is."

"What's up?" Stephanie said, hurrying to stand by Karl as he waved to Natalie, then waited until he could catch Anastasia's eye without putting her at risk during a tricky part of the course. "You and Cordelia are both acting like Nadia not being right here is a reason to worry."

"It is," Karl said. "This isn't the first time. Last time she claimed to be in the rest facilities, which is why Cordy went there. This time Dia won't be able to use that as an excuse. Worse, I've commed her. She's not answering, but the locater on her uni-link says she's here in the park."

"So you really think she's where she shouldn't be?"

"Since the only place she should be is this park, and I don't see her—no matter what the uni-link says—yes. Cordy's had enough time to ping if Dia was in the rest area. So... Dia's probably gone off. Probably with a guy. Probably a guy we wouldn't like her going off with."

Stephanie had known Nadia Zivonik for almost three years, but she'd never really paid too much attention to her, even though they were close to the same age. It wasn't that Nadia wasn't a perfectly decent person, but Stephanie gravitated to people older than herself.

"We'll find her," she said.

"Oh, we'll find her," Karl agreed. "And then I'm going to stay very, very calm, and I'm going to take her home, and let my parents do the parent thing because right now I'd shake that girl so hard I'd rattle her teeth right out of her skull."

Stephanie was reaching up to squeeze his arm in comfort when Karl's uni-link pinged.

Cordelia spoke with the crispness of a bridge officer reporting to the captain, "Nadia's not here. I've checked the restrooms, locker area, and the little eatery. No way I would have missed her. There aren't that many people back here."

"Got you," Karl said. "Natalie is almost here, and Staysa is finishing her loop and will be a bit after. I'll find out what they know. Come join us."

"Right. I'm stopping for a tray of custard cones. Those two are going to need sweetening." Cordelia laughed, but it sounded forced. "And Steph and I really do need a snack."

They converged by the exit gate from the skimmer park, from which Karl all but frog-marched the two sweaty younger girls over to his air car.

"Where's Dia?" he demanded when they were in relative privacy.

"I don't know," Anastasia said, but there was something in her tone that Stephanie recognized as speaking the sort of absolute truth that nonetheless withholds information. She and Natalie looked nervous.

"Me, neither," Natalie added. She looked at Cordelia, something pleading in her expression.

Cordelia frowned. "Is something bothering you, Nat? You look as if you have an upset stomach. Want me to take you to the restroom?"

Natalie hesitated, then nodded. When the sisters started moving away, Stephanie glanced at Karl, decided he might get more out of his sister if there weren't witnesses, and trailed after Cordelia. Although the two treecats attracted a certain amount of attention, no one slowed the group down and soon the three humans and two 'cats had claimed a small changing room and shut the door.

"You have something to say, Nat?" Cordelia said, leaning back against the wall, Athos in her arms. "Something you didn't want to say in front of Staysa?"

"Yeah . . ." Natalie hesitated, then the words tumbled out. "Staysa wasn't lying. Not really. We *don't* know where Dia is. But we do know she isn't here and that she left with Loon. We've been worrying for the last hour because she promised us that this time she'd be back early, so even if Karl showed up early there wouldn't be a problem. But she wasn't back."

"Did you com her?"

"Couldn't. She left her uni-link with us. She knew Karl's been checking up on her, remote, and this way it wouldn't show her where she shouldn't be."

Cordelia's sigh was gusty enough to blow ripples through Athos's fur. To give her a moment to compose herself, Stephanie asked a question of her own.

"Loon? Is that a person's name?"

"Nickname," Natalie said, obviously relieved to have a perfectly normal question to answer. "When he was a baby—or at least this was what Dia told us—he was really chubby, so his family called him 'Balloon,' and it stuck. When he got older, he couldn't shake it, but he did manage to get most people to call him 'Loon.'"

"I guess a little better," Stephanie said. "A waterbird, right? I've seen near-loons in Yawata Bay."

"Balloon Villaroy?" Cordelia exclaimed. "Nadia went off with Balloon Villaroy? He's older than I am!"

"Dia thought that was cool," Natalie said. "I mean, that a college guy thought she was interesting. They met when he was coaching swimming at the Y. I think he's one of the ones who organized the swim team. She's crazy about him."

Loon for a nickname makes more sense now, Stephanie thought, thinking of the long-necked, sleek-bodied aquatic avians she'd watched what seemed like ages ago with Anders.

"Four or five years' difference doesn't matter much when you're, oh, Dana's age," Cordelia said, "but what would Loon see in Dia? She's only fifteen."

"Hero worship?" Stephanie offered, trying not to be offended by that "only fifteen," after all *she* was nearly sixteen. "Maybe she also looks really good in a swimsuit."

Cordelia looked at Natalie. "I am not going to say that it's your job to rat out a friend except, y'know, maybe I am. Not for having a crush on an older guy, but for sneaking off. The one is connected to the other. Don't think Mom's not going to hear about this. Whether Karl tells his mom is his business, but if you don't tell Mom, I will. I'm not going to be an accomplice."

"But . . ." Natalie began, obviously seeing her new freedoms possibly being limited.

"But nothing. Two words: Fall Alarm," Cordelia said. "I griped about setting mine for years. Having you and the others in a group, that was, well, a sort of social fall alarm. But you didn't set it."

"That almost makes sense," Natalie said, "but it's not like we're alone here at the park. There are lifeguards and all that."

"But there are no lifeguards wherever Dia is," Cordelia snapped. "She's out there, somewhere, with a fellow who, no matter how nice she thinks he is, didn't care enough about her to get her back here in time to keep her from getting in trouble. If he's that much of a zork, what else might he do?"

While Cordelia dressed Natalie down, Stephanie had been messaging Karl about Loon. His reply came back promptly.

"Karl says 'thanks.' He suggests we see if we can find Dia ourselves before calling in a search party. He's taking off with Staysa to start a search pattern."

"Have him send coordinates," Cordelia said, hustling Natalie out in front of her. "We'll set up a complementary pattern."

Stephanie did so, then loped a few steps to catch up with the Schardt-Cordova sisters. As they were getting into the air car, Toby Mednick, one of Stephanie's friends from the hang-glider club, came hurrying up. He was wearing the uniform of a local concession stand.

"Karl told me to tell you, that I'm keeping a lookout in case Dia comes back here. I'll ping you if she does."

"You're an angel on earth," Stephanie said, letting Lionheart jump in first, then flinging herself into the back seat of Cordelia's car, "as well as in the air."

Toby's large brown eyes flashed and he gave her a thumbs-up.

"He's cute," Natalie said, looking after the lithe, dark-haired young man as he hurried back to his post at a falafel and cheese curds stand. "I've seen him before. Do you know him well?"

"It seems like forever," Stephanie replied, a little surprised, "but really only a few years. He was one of the younger members of the hang-glider club when my dad and Mayor Sapristos started it up. Now he's one of the ace flyers, captain of the Blue Flight."

"I wonder how old he is?" Natalie said with a sidelong glance at her older sister.

"Younger than you, I think," Stephanie said, laughing. She saw that Karl had copied Cordelia on his post to Stephanie, and that Cordelia had linked the search pattern to the larger screen of the air car's HUD. "Natalie, we're going to be twisting through a lot of trees, so there's only so much Cordelia can see while driving. I'll look down from Cordelia's side, you do yours."

"Right," Natalie said, suddenly serious.

Lionheart joined Stephanie at her window. Athos had climbed up to the back of the driver's seat and was thrumming at Cordelia. The sound was so soft that if Stephanie hadn't been attuned to it, she doubted she would have heard it.

So for all Cordelia is being cool, she's worried.

Stephanie herself wasn't exactly worried. Although she'd missed the Plague years, she'd had her share—more than her share, according to her parents—of life-and-death adventures since she'd come to Sphinx. She was perfectly aware that something could be wrong. What she didn't doubt was her and Karl's—and maybe even Cordelia's—ability to handle whatever they would find.

Karl's voice came over the audio on her and Cordelia's uni-links: "We've found an air car, parked mostly under cover. Matches general description in the SFS database for one belonging to Loon's family. I'm going down. Join us soon as you can."

"Roger!" Cordelia snapped and wheeled the air car through an admirably tight turn and roll. "We'll be there in less than five. Nat, why didn't Staysa tell right off who Dia was with?"

"Dia has something on her," Natalie replied. She was pale now, as if she suddenly realized how serious this could be. "They did the whole, 'you know I know what the folks would like to know' thing. Staysa didn't exactly tell me what Dia's threatening her with, but later Dia needled her again. I think it had to do with some sort of heirloom that no one admitted breaking and that finally got blamed on the dog. Like that."

When they landed, Anastasia was in Karl's air car, visibly weeping. Karl stood to one side, surveying the area through the SFS drone he always carried in his air car while he waited. Stephanie knew him well enough she could almost physically feel his need to already be tearing through the bush, looking for his sister. But he wasn't. Instead, he was methodically mapping the terrain while he waited for reinforcements. Although today he wasn't in uniform, his whole stance shouted out his training as an SFS ranger, and Stephanie felt her heart swell with pride. Their various instructors back on Manticore would have been pleased.

"Loon's air car is empty," Karl reported tersely. "I waited until you all were here to make a search. Staysa, get in Cordelia's car. You and Natalie stay there until you're told you can get out. And try to stop wailing. We need to focus on finding what happened to them. Cordelia, your ankle's a lot better, but we don't want to stress it. You stay here by the cars with Athos. Steph and I will do an area search."

Neither of the Schardt-Cordova sisters argued.

Athos, however, when he saw Survivor and Lionheart swarm into the upper reaches of the near-pines that dominated the area, joined them. Stephanie got out of Cordelia's air car then stood alert, awaiting her own orders. One of the things she and Karl had learned in their law enforcement courses on Manticore was how following orders saved a lot of energy. She knew how much Karl must have wanted to go find his sister, but he had followed protocol and waited for backup. The least she could do was support him.

"Steph," Karl indicated the area to the east of the clearing with a sweep of one arm, "you take that way." He didn't bother to say he'd take the other side or that she should call in if she found anything. They'd trained with the same teachers and, even better, they trusted each other's common sense.

Stephanie gave him a brisk nod and stepped out. She was aware of Lionheart moving overhead, just a little ahead, alert to whatever dangers might linger in the bush.

Although, Stephanie thought, *any creature that would stay in the area with three air cars and several humans thumping around is going to either be hexapuma dangerous, crazy, or . . . too busy having dinner to pay attention.*

The last thought, which her imagination illustrated with grisly images of Dia's mutilated corpse, made Stephanie want to hurry, but she knew hurrying was the worst thing to do in such a situation. "When there is a potential emergency," Dr. Mordecai Flouret had said, "a balance between speed and thoroughness must be carefully assessed by those executing the search."

Today's search was going to need to be slower

because of the nature of the terrain. Like any forest, those on Sphinx varied according to the dominant trees. Picketwood and near-pine provided a heavy canopy that often meant that their understories were open and it was possible to see for a great distance. This area, however, had a higher concentration of groundwater and so was dominated by feather bramble and other scrub growth. While the forest wasn't tangled with vines or briars like some of the second-growth forests Stephanie had played in back on Meyerdahl, by Sphinxian standards it was relatively dense.

Her 11-millimeter magnum ready, Stephanie began working through a methodical search pattern. This forced her to take some of her attention from potential local hazards, so she was glad to know that Lionheart wasn't far away. The patch of forest Loon had chosen for his tryst with Dia wasn't really remote from settled areas, but that didn't mean there weren't predators.

Once again, Stephanie felt a sense of urgency. She considered setting her counter-grav for a lighter weight, so she could skim along at a faster pace, but then she might miss some crucial detail. When she did find her first trace of the missing pair, she was glad that she hadn't chosen speed because, if she'd been going even a little faster, she would have missed the body sprawled beneath a natural bower made by a mature lace willow.

She spoke into her uni-link. "Found a male. He's down on his back, unconscious. Looks as if he hit his head on a tree root. Breathing ragged. Signs of exterior injuries. I've got my first aid kit, but—"

"Administer first aid." Karl's voice was sharp. "Any sign of Dia?"

Stephanie closed with the young man who she assumed must be Loon. "She's not here. I could keep looking. There are some odd marks in the duff, one set goes off—"

"Make sure Loon isn't in danger," Karl said. "I'm on my way."

The rest of Karl's reply was cut off by a series of sharp urgent bleeks from Lionheart, amplified by Athos. Having assured herself that Loon was not in immediate danger, Stephanie left him where he lay and raced to where the treecats were calling. She noticed that one set of the marks in the duff went in this direction.

Dia's trail, Stephanie thought. *She must have gone this way.*

A blur of gray and white dropped from above as Lionheart sprang down from his arboreal perch to land directly in front of Stephanie, forcing her to pull up sharply—and thus avoid plunging into a cut in the forest floor partially concealed by a host of fluffy near-pine saplings. The opening was neither big enough nor deep enough to be dignified with the terms "crevasse" or "ravine," but it was deep enough that tumbling in unawares would be dangerous.

Dia Zivonik lay in a crumpled heap at the bottom and, from where she stood above, looking down, Stephanie couldn't tell if the younger girl was breathing.

8

ONCE BOTH LOON AND DIA HAD BEEN LOCATED, CORDELIA flew over to join the others. Natalie and Anastasia remained in informal arrest in the air car, while Cordelia hurried to see what assistance she could offer. Stephanie had lowered herself into the hole into which Dia had fallen and was checking her over.

"Dia's breathing, but knocked out," Stephanie said into her uni-link. "Good news is she had her counter-grav on when she fell, so she was at Terran normal gravity. Even better, this gully's thickly carpeted in near-pine needles so, as falls go, she had a relatively soft one. She also seems to have managed to fall with her arms in front of her. They're buried up to the elbows in the pine needles. I don't think she went out right away. Looks as if she rolled partway onto one side before passing out. I've scanned her with the med-ap on my uni-link, and I don't see any obvious breaks. She probably has at least a concussion, though."

"Do you think it's safe for us to move her?" Karl asked, his voice tight. "Or should I call for EMTs?"

"You and I have basic EMT training," Stephanie

replied. "If you feel clearheaded enough to use it when the patient is your own sister, then I think we could move her. Sooner we get her to where she can have a full scan the better."

"I have a stretcher in my car," Karl said, "I'll bring it over."

He left his uni-link open, though, so they could continue planning.

Cordelia offered, "I could take Nat and Staysa in my car, Loon, too, if you want. That way we can slide Dia flat onto the back seat of Karl's air car, and Stephanie can ride along as ambulance attendant."

"Good plan," Karl said, his voice slightly distorted by the bounce of his gait, "but I'm worried that Loon might decide to take himself off. Even if this is the accident it looks like, he's got to know the situation's going to look bad for him. Why don't you take Loon and Steph in your car? Steph can sit in the back seat with Loon; she's on the SFS roll already, and I can deputize her to look after him in case anyone wants to complain later. You can take Natalia and I'll take Staysa. We'll meet up at the SRW Hospital in Twin Forks."

"That leaves you short of medical assistance, if Dia needs it," Stephanie reminded him.

"Anastasia passed basic first aid over a year ago," Karl replied, his voice cold. "I think it will do her good to face the consequences of being a passive participant in irresponsible activities. I'm at the car. I'll be to you in just a minute."

Counter-grav made moving Dia without undue jostling possible. Anastasia assisted, pale but resolute, following her older brother's orders without comment.

Although she obviously wanted to help, Stephanie had gone over to Loon. The young man was beginning to stir. Stephanie checked him over with an efficiency that Cordelia couldn't help but think was more than a little ruthless.

"Dia?" Loon's eyes were unfocused. "Where's Princess Nadia? Where's the music? My head . . ."

His next several words were incomprehensible. Stephanie began asking him the standard self-identification questions. The first couple of replies were so distinctly weird that Cordelia, who was assisting Karl and Anastasia, felt her eyebrows rising into her hairline.

To "What is your name?" Loon replied, "Prince Effervescent Seabird, of the Palace of Forgotten Time."

Only when Stephanie repeated the question did he give his full name. When Cordelia heard that his given name was "Fabrice," she understood why he'd preferred "Loon." He seemed to have equal trouble with his address, repeating the bit about the Palace of Forgotten Time until Stephanie, her voice astonishingly sharp and no-nonsense for a not even sixteen-year-old girl, snapped out the question a second time. After that, Loon's answers were more or less sensible, although he seemed reluctant to give up his fantasy self.

"Could he have hit his head hard enough to cause hallucinations?" Cordelia asked Stephanie when, with the patients aboard, the two air cars lifted and sped to the hospital.

Stephanie shrugged. "Maybe. I'm guessing he was a little drunk. He smelled sour. When we locked his air car we found the foil from what looked like a mini-bottle of champagne in the front seat, along with a couple of fluted glasses."

"Seriously?" Cordelia wanted to ask more, but since Loon was in the back seat, head flung back, a cold compress over his forehead and eyes, she restrained herself.

Later, at the hospital, when Loon and Dia had been taken back to be examined, and Karl had gone to wait with his sister, Cordelia resumed the subject. She kept her voice low so that Anastasia and Natalie, sitting side by side a few seats away, completely silent, guilt and worry wrapped like a shared blanket around their shoulders, wouldn't overhear.

"Are you serious about the champagne?"

"Serious as life," Stephanie replied, idly stroking Lionheart. "There were indications that the two of them shared a lovely little picnic before doing whatever it was that got them hurt."

"Which was . . . what, do you think?" Cordelia asked a bit coldly, and Stephanie snorted.

"I thought the same nasty thought you just did," she said. "Given where we found Dia, it sure looked like she might've been trying to get away from him. Older guy, younger girl, sneaking away, alcohol, he gets all handsy—or worse—and she runs. He falls chasing her, hits his own head . . ." She shrugged. "Yeah, I thought it. And I was pissed off enough at him for worrying Karl that way I didn't want to give it up, either. He should darned well know better, and Dia really could've been killed out there. That would've been terrible enough for anyone, but Karl does *not* need that kind of worry, especially after—"

She broke off and shook her head angrily, and Cordelia nodded in silent agreement.

"Anyway," Stephanie resumed, "I was mad enough

I wasn't about to cut Loon any slack. But then I calmed down and took a look at these." She called up holo-imagery on her uni-link. "I took them at the site. I'm no expert tracker. Karl's far better than I am. But the more I've looked at them, the more I have to say, it *looks* like they may've been dancing."

"Dancing?" Cordelia repeated incredulously. "What sort of dancing gets you knocked out?"

Athos bleeked. Both young women turned to see that Karl, Survivor peering over his shoulder, had come back into the room.

"Dia's conscious?" Stephanie asked. "How is she?"

"Sore. Bruised. A couple of broken fingers. A mild concussion. She came off light. Loon is actually worse off. It looks as he tripped over a root and did a header into a tree trunk."

Anastasia burst into tears and Natalie wrapped her arms around her, her own eyes flooding over.

Karl evidently decided that Anastasia was in good hands, because he sank down on one of the seats near Cordelia and Stephanie. Survivor flowed around to sit in his lap.

"Karl, look at this," Stephanie said, showing him the images on her uni-link. "Does that tell you what they might have been doing?"

"Maybe that would, but I have inside information," Karl replied. "Apparently they were trying to duplicate an old ballet about a misunderstood prince transformed into a bird and the young woman who sees beneath his ugly feathered exterior to the noble nature beneath."

"So they really were dancing?" Cordelia shook her head in disbelief.

"Dancing," Karl agreed. "When I pressed her, Dia

did admit that they'd had a bit too much to drink with their picnic. While they'd been dining, they'd been trying out the idea of performing some sort of water-ballet as a swim club event and, well, one thing led to another."

He grimaced. "Dia's holding something back, so I suspect they were doing a little more than dining and dancing, but there's no evidence that Loon pressed his attentions too far. Apparently, he's to blame for egregious carelessness, but nothing else."

For all the calm in his tone, Karl's right fist kept tightening, as if he was getting ready to punch someone. He'd loosen it, then ball it up again. Cordelia watched the rhythmic motion with fascination, thinking that Karl really was the protective big brother. And Stephanie had been right; what had happened to Dia must have jabbed every single painful memory of how his fiancée had died. Karl was both relieved that Dia was going to be all right, furious at her for putting herself at risk, and probably almost equally furious with her for the scare she'd given him. He'd have liked to be able to blame Loon entirely, but it seemed that he couldn't. Which probably made it even worse.

"So there we have it," Karl said. "My father is close enough to Twin Forks that he's going to come and get Dia and Staysa both. I've been told to make myself scarce. I think some heavy parenting is coming down, and me being present would cramp Dad's style."

Stephanie gave what Cordelia was certain was meant to be a reassuring smile, but her concern was acutely evident.

"So, when Karl's dad gets here, do you two want to go get something at the Red Letter Café? My treat?"

Cordelia shook her head. "Normally, I'd say 'absolutely,' but I need to take Nat home for her own dose of parental justice. We've only stayed this long because I didn't want to leave until we heard how Dia was—Loon, too, but mostly Dia."

"Rain check, then," Stephanie said. "How about you, Karl?"

"Chief Shelton said I'd be useless in the field, suggested that you and I put in a few hours on the SFS Explorers." He grinned. "He's a good boss. Manages to be compassionate, provide me with a distraction, and justify the payroll all in one."

"I'm good for it," Stephanie said. "We can plan at the Red Letter Café as easily as at the SFS branch office, though. Milkshakes and burgers, then, on me."

"Hungry again?" Karl asked, tousling her curls with a brotherly hand. He grinned at Cordelia and lowered his voice. "Steph's been known to order two desserts, and thinks she's fooled the waitstaff into believing one's for me."

Stephanie mock-kicked him in the ankle. Cordelia wondered if either of them were aware just how much affection underlay the teasing. She wondered, too, why the realization made her just a little sad.

✧ ✧ ✧

When Life Shaper brought her flying thing down from the treetops to rest on the flat roosts, Heart Stone immediately felt Climbs Quickly's mind-glow, powerful and welcoming. Sharp Sight's mind-glow also shone with pleasure, but without the same "host" note. From this, Heart Stone deduced that he and Life Shaper had come to where Climbs Quickly lived with Fierce Fighter and her clan, and that Determined Defender was also visiting. Life Shaper was still taking some things out of the carrier part of the flying thing when another flying thing came to roost, and another Person and his human emerged.

Heart Stone had met them before, and had found their mind-glows oddly similar. Both tasted of a certain singlemindedness, not in the negative sense of being narrow, but in the positive sense of having discovered a great passion through which everything else was perceived. It was easy to guess what that was for the Person, for if he wasn't tending a plant, he was examining a new specimen or thoughtfully tasting some bark or berry or leaf. For this reason, Heart Stone thought of him as "Plant Fancier." Since he wasn't certain what central interest drove Plant Fancier's two-leg, he'd named her "Feels Strongly."

So there is to be a gathering of the little clan of two-legs who have bonded with People, he thought and was pleased. These gatherings always made Life Shaper happy. Her initial nervousness about these two-legs had vanished, and her feelings about them were warming, as if they were an extension of her birth clan. He could feel the tension melting from her as she chattered away to Feels Strongly, her pleasure when Determined Defender and Fierce Fighter came out to help her carry all the things she had brought with her. There was so much—and Feels Strongly had more of her own—that Heart Stone wondered if they would be staying here overnight. That would be very pleasant indeed.

He bleeked greeting to Plant Fancier, then the two of them scampered up the trunk of the tall golden leaf where the other People waited for them. Climbs

Quickly had a very comfortable nest near to the two-legs' sprawling nesting place, part of which had been adapted with flaps so that he could go in and out as he wished. Similar adaptations were being made to Life Shaper's clan's dwelling, and Heart Stone appreciated this. He was well-fed, well-loved, but he had lived many seasons' turning with only his own mind-glow and sometimes it was nice to be alone with himself.

This was not one of those times, however. Climbs Quickly bounded from limb to limb, giving a tour of his territory and, by his actions, making clear that he was happy to share it with his friends. Plant Fancier was particularly happy when they came to a place made nearly entirely of the shining clear-stone that the two-legs used to let light into their massive nests. Even before they slipped in through an open panel, Heart Stone had guessed that this was a large and elaborate version of the smaller plant growing place that Life Shaper's clan used. There was a strong scent here of an adult female two-leg, a female whose scent sometimes lingered on Fierce Fighter. Her mother, perhaps?

Further tours brought them to areas in which Heart Stone caught the scent of Healer, who had saved his life after his nearly fatal encounter with the needle-fangs. Heart Stone had already suspected that Healer was Fierce Fighter's father. Now he felt certain.

Eventually, they all went in to join the two-legs. Flame Crest, the healer of two-legs, and his Person had not joined the group, but otherwise all the two-legs who he knew had bonded with People were present. They were heatedly chattering over some point—one of Sharp Sight's false furs, much the worse for wear, was on the flat, polished wood platform on which they had also rested a variety of things to eat and drink. Heart Stone plucked at his own false fur, thinking he took much better care of made things than did the young scout. Still, soon enough, both of them would have enough fur to protect them against the worst of the cold.

Climbs Quickly led his guests to a place which smelled of food preparation. There, as always when they met, were a variety of foods that People enjoyed, including some cluster stalk. None of them were precisely hungry, but everyone had a snack, then Climbs Quickly took out a very nice carry net and proceeded to bundle up some of the provisions.

For later, Heart Stone thought, and did his best to help.

He might not have been so eager if he had known the nature of the gathering that Climbs Quickly had planned.

Later, after all the young two-legs had gone to their sleeping places, leaving only the quiet ebb and flow of their dreaming minds to trickle to their bondmates, Climbs Quickly pointed toward outside. His mind-glow frothing with merry excitement, he settled the net of provisions and indicated that he had something he wished to show them. Doubtless the other two knew what Climbs Quickly was suggesting, for their mind-glows held no overt curiosity, only interest.

Perhaps Climbs Quickly knows of a good place for fishing or for catching toothsome night creatures, Heart Stone thought, *but if so, why bring the food? Still, the night is pleasant and it is good to run under the stars with friends.*

By the time he tasted the carefully muffled mind-glow of the one who waited for them, it was too late for Heart Stone to avoid the meeting, especially since the one who waited had offered him no offense. Indeed, even when they were within sight of each other, he did not know her. Only when she had unmuffled her mind-glow did he recognize her.

His first reaction was complete astonishment. The mind-glow was familiar but, even as the one who bore it was no longer the almost youngling he remembered but a magnificent adult female, so the mind-glow had matured and deepened, containing resonances so powerful that Heart Stone almost believed his damaged mind-voice might hear what she had to say. Certainly her mind-glow was almost blindingly brilliant.

Was this young Sings Truly? Even as he remembered Climbs Quickly as a mischievous young scout, so he remembered Sings Truly as a promising memory singer, one who had been—and surely should still be—under the authority of Song Spinner. What was she doing here? Memory singers never left the clan's central nesting place, yet she was here and there was no doubt that she was also a memory singer.

Climbs Quickly is not the only one of his line to bend and break rules, I think. Sings Truly has risen to the highest rank, and taken it in her claws to rip into old provisions and shred them into fill for a newly born litter's nest.

Heart Stone wished he could ask if his old friend, sometimes old rival, Song Spinner had died and, if so, how she had met her death. Song Spinner had not been young, but she had not been a creaking elder either. Sings Truly astonished him by providing him with an answer to his unasked question. From her carry net she took a section of a peeled branch. The wood was so old and dry that it hardly held any scent of its own, but instead was imbued with the strong scent of Song Spinner, several days old, perhaps, but no more.

"Bleek!" he said, curling his paws around the wood and taking another sniff. Who would have thought how glad he would be to know the crotchety old female was still alive? When last they had met he had been defying her and taking himself into exile. He felt his companions sharing his joy, then apprehension replaced joy. He knew why Sings Truly had made this dangerous journey to meet with him. She wanted him to visit Bright Water Clan.

Almost instinctively, Heart Stone balked and began to turn away. His self-exile from his clan had become as much a part of his image of himself as the pain that twisted deep inside him when he remembered Golden Eye's mind-glow fading into a darkness where he could not follow. He had wanted so much to go into that darkness with her, yet her own rejection of that course had made it impossible. Caught between the two, savaged by the gray death—had there been a part of him that felt he deserved to lose his mind-voice? Had that made the pity he felt in the mind-glows of his fellow clan members particularly loathsome—because he blamed himself?

He braced himself for more unwanted pity, pity that would be particularly terrible coming from such a powerful mind—and he felt none. He felt admiration. (What had he done that was admirable?) He felt joy. (Surely not at meeting him again. As a Bright Water elder, he had known her as he knew all the clan's young, but they had scarcely been close.) He felt welcome. And he felt . . . was that laughter? Not at him, no, but laughter nonetheless, a sense of the ridiculous, perhaps.

Heart Stone's resistance melted before the cascade of emotions. In some ways, he felt as he had when he had awakened after the battle with the needle-fangs, believing himself reunited with Golden Eye. The new bond with Life Shaper had swept through his pain and suffering, proven to him that he was capable of not merely surviving but of *living* fully and joyfully, not with his memories wiped clean, but with them put into a new perspective.

How could he argue with this singer? Arguing with Song Spinner had been easy enough. They'd known each other lifelong, had argued over other matters. But this . . . Memory singers were the true leaders of the People. They governed not through domination, as in a herd of horn blades, nor through mere seniority, as in a group of lake builders, but because they held the memory not only of the clan but of all the People. The clan's elders as a whole decided the clan's actions, but all of them looked to the memory singers, the keepers of its history and precedent.

Apparently, Sings Truly felt that there was a place for him—not living with the clan, she would understand better than any other that his place was with Life Shaper now—but as a welcome guest.

In mid-motion, Heart Stone stopped turning away, rejected his own self-pity. He realized that he'd been unable to live among the People who pitied him because his own bowl of pity was already full to overflowing and theirs had drowned him. Now, in his mind, he took that bowl and tipped it over. Instead of fleeing, he reached into his carry net and found a choice treat which he presented to Sings Truly. She bleeked thanks and sat comfortably back on her haunches to better enjoy the delicacy.

Mind-speech must have been used, for the festivities became general. Heart Stone admitted a feather-touch of relief that apparently they were not going to immediately go racing through the netwood back to Bright Water. Perhaps the distance was too great but, whatever the reason, he was glad to have time to adjust his thoughts, to prepare for seeing his kits again, to meeting old friends—to accepting their pity as a gift, not a burden.

✧ ✧ ✧

A few days after the meeting of the Great Treecat Conspiracy at her house, Stephanie's uni-link lit with a message from Nosey Jones.

Stephanie . . . I'm recovered enough now that I'm getting back to my columns. Karl messaged me about the new SFS Explorers program, and I'd really like to interview you both about it. Can we meet up and chat in person? You can see the column before it goes to press.

Like just about everyone in the Twin Forks area, Stephanie had heard about how Nosey Jones had nearly been killed in the course of a brutal carjacking. It had been especially shocking because carjackings were so rare on Sphinx. There was little market for a stolen vehicle, and the electronics were too easily traced in such a small community to make stripping it for parts profitable, the way it might have been on Manticore itself. On the other hand, the thieves had done an excellent job of covering their tracks, and she supposed it was possible they'd wanted the air car for some one-time use, after which they'd simply disposed of it. No one had a clue who they might have been, though, and Nosey had been in no shape to give details about the incident in the critical fifty-one-hour period following the crime. When he had been sufficiently recovered to be interviewed, he'd offered what he could, but he admitted that his memories of the events were hazy.

Getting as much coverage as possible for the SFS Explorers overcame Stephanie's distinct dislike for anything to do with Nosey Jones. But, as she explained to Karl when asking if he'd be available to go with her:

"Ever since the attack, Nosey has more readers than ever, even if all he's posting are recycled older columns. He said we could review the column before it went live, and I believe him. He's annoying, pushy, irritating, but, when I went back and reviewed a bunch of his coverage of the fire season incidents, he never distorted the facts."

Karl nodded. "The trouble comes in the Comments section. Nosey rarely limits what people are permitted to say. Sometimes the discussions get pretty heated, and some of the more . . . energetic comments end up having a higher word count than the original column!"

"Yeah, idiots will be idiots," Stephanie said, "and since Nosey probably gets advertising money for every return hit, letting the Comments go wild is a great way to garner action."

"Here's what I want to do," Karl said. "I'm the lead on this project. If any Comments need to be responded to, I'll do it. Let's face it, Steph, you've gotten a lot better over the years, but you *do* sometimes lose your temper."

Stephanie nodded. "I do and you're right. If you're willing, then I'll read all the Comments—if we get any—and flag you so you don't need to waste your time."

"Deal."

They made an appointment for the next day. Nosey had suggested that they come out to his house, stating that he was still in bad enough shape that going places "wasn't a lot of fun."

"Let's take him something," Stephanie said. "Flowers? Food?"

"Food," Karl said. "He lives alone. His family is in Yawata Crossing, and his sister, who had been staying with him, went back a couple of days ago. He'd probably love a treat of some sort, especially since he's used to being out and about every day."

When they stopped by the Red Letter Café, Eric Flint suggested that they bring a flash-frozen moussaka. "I know he likes moussaka, and a little bird told me that he's been getting sent all sorts of sweets."

✧ ✧ ✧

Nosey's house proved to be a small but pleasant A-frame, set on a large parcel on the east edge of Twin Forks. An adjoining A-frame housed a garage and probably provided extra storage space. The landscaping took advantage of the area's natural beauty, including a small stand of tanapple trees.

Although Stephanie had spent a fair amount of time around injured people—and even been severely injured a time or two herself—when Nosey opened the door and she stood face-to-face with what a methodical beating could do to a person, it was like waking up to find that a nightmare was real. Nosey had never been what anyone would call "handsome," but bruises turning from rich purple to green and yellow were not a good look on anyone. His famous nose was still set in sprayplast and so looked larger than ever. Part of his wiry dark-brown hair had been shaved so that a long, curving cut on his scalp could be cleaned and treated. His mouth was swollen and both eyes had been blackened. And those were just the injuries above his neck. From how Nosey moved, every little motion caused him pain, even with his counter-grav unit set to minimize the pressure of gravity on his battered brain.

"Come in," Nosey said, moving away from the door toward the interior of the house, then using a remote to lock it after they were inside. His voice was distorted, as if he had a bad head cold, and Stephanie guessed he couldn't breathe through his nose at all. Despite herself, she felt pity for him, then had to remind herself that even so he could be—if not actually an enemy—a serious antagonist.

"Thank you for coming by," Nosey said. "I have a few snacks ready—including celery for the 'cats, if you think it's all right for them to have some."

Stephanie was becoming accustomed to how people often supplied treats for Lionheart, so hadn't let him have any celery so far that day.

"Karl, can Survivor have celery today?"

"Sure," Karl grinned. "If Nosey doesn't mind that the 'cats aren't exactly tidy eaters."

Nosey indicated a tiled section of flooring at one edge of his living room/dining room area, directly in front of a floor-to-ceiling picture window.

"Would they sit there while they ate? It has a nice view."

Stephanie nodded. "We've trained them to follow simple commands." She tried not to sound as if the question threatened her, but knew she didn't quite manage. Making even the most minor admission to Nosey about what the treecats could do seemed dangerous.

Karl covered for her smoothly, as he so often did. "Nosey, are those the promised snacks on the counter? Why don't you let me get them? No offense, man, but you look pretty rough."

"I feel pretty rough," Nosey admitted. "If you wouldn't mind . . . The celery's in the fridge, along with a hummus spread for the pita squares. There's a pitcher of fruit punch, and I've set up a pot of coffee. If you prefer tea, my sister left enough to stock a shop."

"Oh! I nearly forgot!" Stephanie jumped to her feet and presented Nosey with the box from the Red Letter Café. "We brought you a 'get-well' present: moussaka from the Red Letter Café. Eric said you liked it."

"I do." Nosey's battered features tried to shape a blissful smile. "And even better, it's soft but not soup or stew. You don't know how tired I am of soup and stew."

"Should I put it in the freezer compartment?" Stephanie asked. "The instructions say to reheat without thawing first."

"Terrific, thank you!" Nosey looked pathetically grateful, and again Stephanie felt that dangerous pity rising. He settled stiffly into a high-backed, cushioned recliner, adjusted his legs and raised the footrest, then motioned for them to take seats on the comfortable, slightly battered sofa on the other side of the coffee table. "First off, I need you to know I got you here under slightly false pretenses..."

Stephanie, who had been giving Lionheart and Survivor their celery, stiffened again. "If this is about the treecats—"

Karl's warning, "Steph..." overlaid Nosey's anxious, "Not one bit."

Nosey went on. "I'm not as against treecats as you seem to think. I'm actually *for* them. I just feel that if they're going to be kept as pets, the situation should be handled properly. That's an issue for another time, if ever. Why I brought you here has nothing to do with treecats, and everything to do with the sort of person you've always shown yourself to be, Stephanie—Karl, too, but especially you."

"What?" Stephanie barely managed not to goggle in astonishment.

Karl laughed and scooped some hummus onto a whole-grain pita square. "I don't think he means annoying or abrasive or anything like that, Steph."

"I don't," Nosey agreed. "Not a bit. I mean older than your years, reliable, capable of taking on high-pressure jobs. Before I go further, I want you to know my house is secure from surveillance. Even the picture window is tinted so that it can't be seen or scanned through. Privacy is very important to my businesses, both as a courier and as a reporter. Even so, I'm taking a tremendous risk talking to you two, but when I went through my options, I realized you were the best I had."

Stephanie rose and went to join Karl on the sofa. She noticed that Lionheart seemed completely relaxed around Nosey. She'd come to trust the treecat as a judge of—if not precisely character, then intent. Whatever else, Nosey wasn't trying to deceive them or offer any threat.

"Go on," she said, layering several squares of pita with hummus, then offering the little plate to Nosey.

"Just hummus, please," he said. "The dentist said soft foods only for a while. Even soft bread is too much. If you'd be so kind, I'll take a cup of coffee and some of that caramel custard." He paused then, and his tone shifted, sounding very much as it did in the audio portions of his column. "I definitely plan to report on the SFS Explorers program, so anything you can leave me on that will be useful. Why I've asked you here also has to do with your role as SFS rangers. I need to tell someone about why I was attacked."

"It wasn't just a carjacking, then?" Karl asked. "There was some speculation at headquarters. You *have* been known to irritate people."

"It wasn't," Nosey said. "I believe I was attacked because of a story I've been researching, one I stumbled on almost by accident, in the course of covering what, until I looked more closely, just seemed to be, well, accidents."

9

NOSEY FELT RELIEVED THAT STEPHANIE HARRINGTON AND Karl Zivonik were taking him seriously. He knew his occasional criticism of the SFS—although he preferred to see what he'd written less as criticism of the organization than as criticism of its sinfully minimal budget—rankled its members.

"Accidents," Karl said. "According to your column, there have been a lot lately. Honestly, though, are there really more or are you just finding what you look for?"

"You know that better than I do," Nosey said. "I've stopped writing about the accidents, but I'm continuing to track. Your own sister was involved in a rather peculiar accident not long ago, along with Loon Villaroy. That incident was another reason why I selected you and Stephanie. You'll know firsthand whether what happened to Nadia was something that surprised you or one of those things where your whole family sighed and said, 'Again?'"

Karl frowned. "Maybe we'd better start at the beginning, so I can better answer that."

Nosey thought Karl's refusal to answer was as good

as an answer in itself. If Nadia Zivonik was the family klutz, or even the one known for getting into scrapes, Karl would have said so.

"All right," Nosey said, reaching for his notepad, "let me give you some details."

The two young people listened intently as Nosey related the sequence of accidents he'd researched, including those that had received no more than a passing reference in his column.

"Eventually, I started feeling as if I was hearing the same sort of story over and over, yet, really, no two incidents were alike. Once I started reviewing my notes, I realized that what was creating the sense of similarity was how many of the accidents seemed to have been caused less by carelessness or ignorance—say of the consequences of living on a high-gee planet—or bad luck than by a singular, unbelievable stupidity.

"Maybe I hit on it before anyone else did because while any accident is newsworthy, some types of victims are more likely to attract interest and sympathy. Basically, it's the man-bites-dog principle."

"What?" Karl and Stephanie said as one.

Nosey laughed. It hurt, but he couldn't help it.

"It's an old adage in the news business. Dog bites man, that's not news. Man bites dog, *that's* news. A lot has changed about reporting since somebody first coined the phrase, but one thing hasn't: the readership has only so much time, so much attention. If you want them to follow your feed, you need to catch them with something a little unusual or at least something that's going to tug on the heartstrings."

He sipped his coffee, then continued. "So, if I had a choice between interviewing a promising young athlete whose chance of playing in the upcoming season was threatened or a construction worker who dropped a bucket on his foot, I picked the athlete. I was also biased, I'll admit, because I also cover the local sports scene. If I interviewed someone involved in sports or the arts or whatever, then I'd be connecting to my established audience's interests. Since Sphinx doesn't have professional sports, that meant I was talking to a lot of young people. Over time, I began to consider how unlikely it was that any of these people could experience these sorts of injuries. If they'd all been on the same team or the same sport, well, I'd suspect someone was doing something unsafe in an attempt to get an edge on the competition, but they weren't."

"Edge?" Karl asked, his voice tight. Nosey wondered if the young ranger hadn't already had suspicions of his own.

"To be blunt," Nosey said, holding up one hand to forestall the protest he anticipated. "I began to suspect that some of these people had been doing drugs."

"Drugs?" Stephanie blurted out. "What? That's crazy. Anyhow, hospitals run tests for drugs. Surely they'd find something like that."

"They'd find it if they knew to test for it," Nosey countered. "You can't test for something that you don't know might be there."

"So a new drug," Karl said stiffly. "One that I haven't even heard rumors about at work. But that you just manage to stumble on. Where do you think it's coming from?"

Nosey shook his head. "I haven't gotten that far. At first I assumed from off-planet, but the more I noticed that young people were involved and how the 'accidents' seemed to cluster right around Twin Forks, the more I wondered if it might be something local—maybe something cobbled together by a kitchen chemist, being shared by friends."

"That makes a sort of sense," Karl admitted grudgingly, "but I'm reluctant to believe we have a spreading drug culture, targeting the young. Maybe it's something else entirely. A new fad for taking dares or pushing limits."

Stephanie cut in. "Karl, wait. If Dia wasn't *possibly*"—she carefully stressed the word—"involved, what questions would you be asking?"

Then, clearly to give Karl a chance to consider, Stephanie asked a question of her own. "Nosey, why didn't you tell this to the town constables? Surely they interviewed you."

"I didn't want to turn up dead," Nosey said bluntly. "The men who attacked me made it very clear that I was being beaten up as a warning. I'd guessed that the warning was meant either for someone I'd talked to or someone I *might* talk to or both. Also, well, this is going to sound cowardly, but I wasn't sure anyone would take me seriously. Oh, if I got killed, then, sure, but I really didn't want to die just to prove my point."

"What else didn't you tell the constables?"

Nosey forced his swollen lips to smile, although he suspected the expression was grotesque rather than winning. "I didn't tell them one of them held me at gunpoint specifically so I could be beaten, and I didn't tell them that they threatened me with worse if I told anyone what had really happened. I didn't tell them that the two men who beat me up were dressed so that, from a distance, they resembled Forestry Service rangers, either. That's why I set down my air car where I did, rather than parking it in the garage. Since the weather wasn't bad, I didn't want to be rude and keep them waiting. Otherwise, the only outright lie I told was that I'd parked my air car outside and surprised the carjackers in the act. That when I tried to stop them, they beat me up and took the car."

"Hold on," Karl said, his momentary annoyance vanishing. "Did you say that the men who beat you up were dressed as SFS rangers?"

"Enough to pass from a short distance. Right colors, styles, but no obvious insignia. When I came home, they were standing on the porch, near the front door. In the shade of the overhang, any details would have been lost anyhow."

Stephanie had called up the official police report and was skimming it. "This says you didn't see their faces."

"That's right. They were wearing some sort of distortion mask. And, no, before you ask, I wasn't lying when I said I didn't recognize them. I didn't. Maybe if we'd talked longer before they started hitting me, I might have but, even though I've studied some martial arts, I'm no action hero. It's one thing to take a punch in the dojo, a whole lot different when someone's hurting you on purpose."

Nosey shifted uneasily and glanced at the clock. "I'm worried I'm being watched. How long can we justify this meetup?"

Stephanie grinned. "Oh, I'm super-eager, super-annoying when I have a hobbyhorse to ride. Don't worry about that. It would be more suspicious if we left soon."

"And," Karl added, "if you agree, from this point on, you're going to be under surveillance. I have some motion-sensitive recorders in my air car. We use them all the time for the job. Let me run outside now and grab them. Steph, come to the door and yell at me not to forget the spare concept uniforms or something."

"Two birds with one stone," Stephanie said. "We'll get you set up for surveillance and reassure the watchers that you're really researching a perfectly innocuous article."

The two young rangers grinned at each other, then Stephanie added, "Karl, what do you think about letting Lionheart and Survivor out to get some exercise? We can't tell them what we want, but if there are any humans watching, the 'cats will find them."

Forgetting his injuries, Nosey tried to spring from his chair, then sank back, a moan of pain slipping out before he could stop it.

"Don't do that! These people are horrible. The treecats might get hurt."

"I don't think so," Karl said. "The forest is the 'cats' natural hunting ground, and whatever else they are, they're smart enough to avoid attacking just anyone. They'd be more likely to go up a tree and drop nuts or cones to flush someone out of hiding."

Nosey still didn't like it, but he also knew he couldn't forbid them. And he *would* feel better about the young people being here if he knew they weren't being spied on by anyone close enough to do them harm.

"All right," he said. "Do your act, then come back. I've made copies of my research files. Now that I've told you my suspicions, I'll let you review the material and see what conclusions you reach."

They spent another hour with Nosey, with the

young people going outside periodically to "check on the treecats" during which time some very discreet surveillance equipment was hidden.

"I'll set you up with a link to the feed," Karl said, "because it's got to be creepy wondering if someone is watching you from just outside the range of your home security system. Don't let this make you careless, though."

"I won't," Nosey promised, placing one splinted hand over his heart, "I definitely won't."

Stephanie had been reviewing the data summaries, and now she looked up, her expression so serious that Nosey suddenly knew what she would look like as a mature woman.

"I can see what you're getting at," she said, "but I'm not sure I would ever have come to the conclusion that drugs were involved. I mean, aren't drugs a problem for crowded urban societies, places where people are bored, or feel as if they lack opportunity, or maybe are chasing after the next big thrill? Sphinx is full of challenges. Even if you're not into hunting or sports, just making a place for yourself on a frontier world should be enough, shouldn't it?"

If Nosey had been a different sort of adult, he would have laughed at her naiveté, but the fact was, he felt about Sphinx the way she did. He knew he'd have loved to be a reporter anywhere, but knowing that his newsfeed was one of the first attempts of the sort on his home world made him feel as much of a pioneer as someone who found a new species of plant or animal. His sense of kinship with the people who were making Sphinx what it was had been one reason he'd started sharing news. He wanted everyone to see all the varied and wonderful projects going on. But he'd also seen how what was an exciting frontier for him was a prison for others.

"I wish boredom and decadence were the only reasons people take drugs," Nosey said, "but that's far from the case. Some people take drugs because drugs make them feel more confident or to help them relax or even as a reward for working hard."

Karl nodded. "Don't forget, alcohol and tobacco are drugs, even if most people don't think of them that way. And one name for drink is 'liquid courage.' My Aunt Irina has a sneaking fondness for frontier tales set on olden times Earth. She gave me a couple and I noticed that a bar or tavern seemed to be the one standard structure in any newly settled town. Even if the town was too small to have a doctor or a judge or a jail, it had a bar."

Nosey reached for his coffee, thinking as he sipped it that caffeine was also a drug, but he didn't want to get off the point. "So, people take drugs to feel more confident, or to relax, or even to have a little chemical stimulation after a hard day—and there are lots of hard days on the frontier. But, Stephanie, you're making a mistake if you think that everyone on Sphinx is as happy to be here as you are and I am and, I presume, Karl is. Especially among the younger population there are many who feel trapped. They may have been brought here by their parents. Or they may have been born here, and imagine all the wonderful things they're missing 'out there.' Many of the younger 'stupid' accident types I interviewed fit this category. The last one—Eldora Yazzie—was flat-out hostile about being stuck on Sphinx. Moreover, the whole time we were talking I had a feeling that she was waiting for someone, and that it was someone her family didn't know was going to be dropping by. That was just an impression. I could be wrong."

Stephanie started to reply quickly, then stopped and nodded slowly, instead. Yes, Sphinx was full of exciting challenges, and, yes, she was deeply happy meeting those challenges. Especially with Lionheart at her back. But before Lionheart, when all she'd been able to see was the way her parents' decision to emigrate had "stolen" her chance with the *Meyerdahl* Forestry Service . . . Oh, yes, indeed. She'd been miserable enough to embrace any escape then, hadn't she?

"But you think a supplier?" Karl said, following up on Nosey's last sentence. "That's interesting. I don't know how this would fit in with Dia's accident, but it's possible Loon slipped her something. If so, he didn't know how hard it would hit them. I think detailed blood panels were run on them both. Since she's my sister, I can probably get a peek at her results. Or at least ask my dad and mom discreetly—*very* discreetly—about them."

He grimaced at the thought, and Stephanie hid a smile of mingled sympathy and amusement. As a mere sibling, Karl couldn't get around the patient confidentiality rules to view his sister's records, and it was clear he could imagine only too well how Aleksandr Zivonik would react to the notion that his errant daughter might also have been using drugs. Dia would be lucky to get off the Zivonik claim again before she was thirty!

"I'm sure you can think of a way to be discreet," she told him in an encouraging sort of tone. "I don't see any way to get a peek at Loon's, though."

"I could just ask him. And not in any 'official capacity,' either. Just a big brother who's still less than delighted with him." Karl clenched one large fist and looked down at his knuckles, and his smile turned nasty. "I wouldn't worry about being discreet with *him*, Steph! Not after sneaking off with Dia that way!"

Stephanie laughed, and Nosey eased back in his recliner, feeling as if he was relaxing for the first time since the attack. He knew he'd passed on his information to the right people. He could rest now. He just hoped that he hadn't just put these two winning, intelligent young people into danger.

✧ ✧ ✧

When Karl asked if she could meet him to discuss something very important and very, very sensitive, Cordelia didn't really know how she felt. She liked Karl, maybe even more than just *liked* him, but was she ready for dating? She thought about talking it over with Dana, but Dana was at that stage in her own love affair where, having found love for herself, the only thing that could be more wonderful would be for everyone else to be in love. Mack was out for similar reasons, although Cordelia wasn't sure that his nerdy new boyfriend was going to be his One True Love. Based on how Zack was reacting to Mack's new attachment, Zack was definitely too young.

Cordelia might have tried talking to Natalie, since Natalie had spent so much time with Dia and Anastasia—and because of that, with Karl, who often did drop off and pick up, when his job permitted. But Nat was moody lately. Dia's injuries had been relatively minor, thanks to the many seasons of pine needles that had padded the gully, but Mom had come down hard on Nat, showing her maybe a little too clearly that were it not for luck,

Nat might be dealing with a friend crippled or raped or even dead because Nat hadn't spoken out.

This was definitely *not* the time to put Cordelia's maybe sorta kinda romantic feelings for the dashing Karl Zivonik on Nat's young shoulders.

"I'll do this," Cordelia said to Athos as they took Barnaby out for what everyone in the family called PT, but to the big, affable dog was just a delightful walk. "If Karl asks me on a date, I'll accept. But if he suggests anything too, well, romantic, like dinner at Elegant Edibles, I'll suggest something less heavy like a drive up to Yawata Crossing for seafood at Bay Baskets. That way I won't seem like I'm pushing him off, and, even better, we won't be in Twin Forks where there just might be gossip."

"Bleek," replied Athos, patting the side of her face with one of his true-hands. "Bleek, bleek, bleek."

He made the sounds in a conversational rhythm but with no change of sound, so Cordelia didn't think he was actually talking, just mimicking her talking, maybe to let her know he was listening? The members of the Great Treecat Conspiracy had spent a lot of time discussing just how treecats communicated, but even more on how to maintain the general impression that treecats were dog smart or even Terran chimpanzee smart, capable of learning a wide variety of "tricks," and even using primitive tools, but not a lot more than that. However, everyone agreed that the more time they spent with treecats, the more confident they became that they had a genuinely intelligent nonhuman species living right here on Sphinx.

When, later that day, Karl came by to pick Cordelia up, she was surprised to see that Stephanie was with him. Had the younger girl tagged along at the last minute or had Cordelia completely misunderstood what Karl's "very important, very, very sensitive" matter might be? That Stephanie spilled into the back seat, giving Cordelia the front seat, further confused the issue, but as soon as they were underway, Karl's first words made the matter clear.

"Stephanie and I have been given some really sensitive information that we need to investigate. We've talked about it, and if what we've been told is correct, then your family has already been impacted, even if indirectly."

Stephanie cut in, "It seems we're always asking you to keep secrets, but if everything works out, this one won't be forever, like it might be with the treecats, just until we find out how much truth there is in Nosey's suppositions."

Karl set the air car to self-navigate and called up data from his uni-link on the car's heads-up display. Now Cordelia understood that Stephanie had given her the place up front so she could see the screen more easily. A list of names, each followed by a short description, came up in blue.

"This is what Nosey started us with," Karl explained. "The names with the yellow star next to them are the ones he did articles on. This overlay, coded in green, are cases I pulled using SFS databases where formal incident or accident reports were filed. This, in purple, is a little less official. We convinced Jessica to raid the hospital files for incidents that fit the parameters but hadn't been officially reported. She'd only pass the information along if we didn't push her for names or very specific incident descriptions, but she didn't mind giving the numbers, age, and gender of the people involved, and descriptions like 'fall with broken bones' or 'sports injury.'"

Cordelia scanned the material. "There're quite a lot of accidents and just over the last six T-months, too. I had no idea there'd been that many, and *I've* been sort of supersensitive on the subject since I had my own 'accident.' If he dug this kind of uptick out of the background noise, then maybe he's more of a genuine reporter than I thought he was!"

"I agree," Stephanie said, and there was nothing in her tone to indicate that she begrudged her sometime rival his victory. "He *does* have 'a nose for news,' and he notices a lot of stuff other people miss. I even agree with him about treecats, just not how he's handling the issue. And I might not mind even *that* as much as I do if it weren't for the Treecat Conspiracy . . . which he doesn't know anything about. One of the things we wanted to ask you was what you thought about all of this. Take your time."

Cordelia started reading, then stopped. "Uh, I just realized. I have no idea where you're taking me. Not that I mind the outing, but Karl was very cryptic."

Karl laughed. "Sorry about that. I was so focused on what we'd learned, I guess I did sound like someone out of a spy thriller."

Or an awkward hero from a romance novel, Cordelia forbore from adding. Why did she feel sort of sad that Karl hadn't had romance in mind? Hadn't she been determined to put him off? Athos thrummed at her so softly that she felt, rather than heard, his comforting purr, and she ran her hand down his back, feeling the silk and velvet of his patchy coat.

"We're going up to Yawata Crossing," Stephanie said.

"Ostensible excuse is to pick up some stuff from SFS headquarters for the SFS Explorers. Actual reason is to have a meeting with Chief Ranger Shelton. We wanted you along for two reasons: the first is that we needed someone smart who we could run our data by and see what conclusions she reached. The second is, we want to know if you're interested in being recruited into our task force. We already know you're trustworthy, and although Nat wasn't actually involved in the incident with Dia and Loon, you've seen firsthand how this can impact families."

"Shut up, Steph," Karl said with obvious affection but equally obvious exasperation. "Much more and you could be accused of leading a witness."

Stephanie shut up, but Cordelia was aware of her leaning forward, those intense brown eyes focused on the data display, reviewing as intently as if she'd never seen it before. As Cordelia worked her way through the layers of data, occasionally tapping an entry for more detail, she found herself feeling increasingly confused. From time to time, she asked a question, but otherwise Karl and Stephanie kept silent, determined to let her draw her own conclusions.

They were approaching the outskirts of Yawata Crossing when Cordelia said, "Honestly? Especially after reading some of the specific incidents, these people would have had to be on drugs to be so dumb. I mean, I *know* some of these people. They're behaving like the worst sort of new visitor, but in a lot of cases they've lived on Sphinx for years—maybe their whole lives."

Karl's tone was very, very careful as he asked, "I want you to think hard about what you said. Do you mean it?"

Cordelia ran her own statement through her mind, trying to figure out what she'd said that Karl was taking so seriously.

"Do you mean 'be on drugs'? I didn't really mean it. I mean, it's just one of those things people say, but it *would* explain this plague of stupid, wouldn't it? Steph, did Jessica find anything out when she checked the hospital records?"

Stephanie shook her head, but was nonetheless beaming in pleasure. It took Cordelia a moment to realize that Stephanie wasn't happy because Jessica hadn't found anything in the records, rather because Cordelia had confirmed a conclusion Stephanie and Karl had both already reached.

"She didn't," Stephanie went on. "Nosey didn't find anything either, and because he does a lot of work as a confidential courier for medical supplies, he has some pretty good connections of his own. But, as Nosey himself pointed out to us, not finding anything doesn't mean there's nothing to find. A skimmer rider who falls and breaks his back while doing something too daring isn't going to be tested for drugs. The same with a dancer who's known for pushing the limits of what should be tried in high-gee."

"And," Karl said, "drugs metabolize at different rates. It's completely possible that someone like Dia—who was drug-tested because I asked for it, because Loon was saying loopy things—might already have the drug out of her system by the time a test was done."

"I get it," Cordelia said. "And in Dia's case, we don't know for sure how long she was there, knocked out. Karl . . . I've got to ask this, but is Dia, y'know, the kid who raids the family liquor cabinet?"

"I don't think so," Karl said, "and that's not just big brother wanting to put everything in the best light where little sister is concerned. Staysa would almost certainly have at least an idea if Dia was experimenting like that, or sneaking Dad's pipe tobacco or whatever. Our folks came down hard on both of them, and they both insisted they didn't do things like that."

"So if Loon slipped her something," Cordelia said, hesitating, because she couldn't really imagine slightly goofy Loon slipping a fifteen-year-old drugs. "Well, she wouldn't have any experience to guide her, would she?"

"There's no evidence to indicate that he did," Karl said. "I didn't talk to him. That would have been more than useless, but Stephanie did. She can be very sympathetic, can our Steph, when needs drive. Loon was a wreck, worse than a wreck. He really likes Dia and knew that she liked him, but that he was in a position of authority and all that. People with crushes can be incredibly clueless, but I don't think he's the sort to roofie a girl—and even if he was, that doesn't explain what happened to him."

"We're setting up a database," Stephanie said, "to sort the reports by various parameters: by age of victim; type and severity of accident; gender; how long the victim has lived on Sphinx; prior illegal drug use; excessive/irresponsible alcohol use. We're still working on how to classify 'stupid behavior'—that takes a value judgment. But one thing we're seeing is an uptick in accidents involving younger people: mid-teens to early twenties."

"To do this right," Karl said, "we really need a better comparative database, one that goes back a couple of years. One thing we want to ask Chief Ranger Shelton for is access to that information."

"Couldn't you just get it?" Cordelia asked. "I mean, you are a full-ranger and Steph's sort of on staff, too."

"Probably could," Karl agreed, bringing his air car down to rest in the staff parking field at SFS headquarters, "but the Old Man notices an amazing amount about what goes on. I'd rather brief him in advance than have him call me in and ask what I'm doing. Besides, if there *is* anything to all this, he has to be brought onboard. Officially, I mean. Drugs or not, what happened to Nosey constitutes criminal assault for purposes of intimidation. That's extortion under the Crown law code, and that's a felony."

From the way he glanced over his shoulder at Stephanie while he was speaking, Cordelia guessed that they'd disagreed on this point.

Stephanie caught her looking and shrugged. "I just thought we'd have a better case if we compiled more data first, that's all."

"Getting more data without telling the authority figures in your life—even when you had enough to go on—" Karl said, sounding grim, "is what led you to crashing in a thunderstorm and nearly getting eaten by a hexapuma. Yeah, you were eleven then, but you're nearly sixteen now. There's a time to stop being the smartest kid in all the classes, and try to be part of the team."

"I agreed we need to bring in Chief Shelton," Stephanie said. "You win."

Brother and sister or nearly married? Cordelia thought ruefully as she followed the pair into SFS headquarters. *I wonder if even they know how they feel.*

10

"...AND THAT'S ABOUT IT, SIR," KARL SAID, TWENTY minutes later, and Stephanie nodded in silent approval. They'd made a couple of tweaks after presenting their data to Cordelia, and she felt the two of them had given a polished, even professional presentation. But—

"That's very interesting," Chief Ranger Shelton said, tipping back in his chair. "I'm not sure how much we can do about it, though."

"Excuse me, sir?" Stephanie said after a moment. That was the last reaction she'd expected out of him.

"I said I'm not sure how much we can do about it," Shelton repeated.

"Sir, a crime *has* been committed," Karl pointed out.

"Yes, it has," Shelton agreed. "Of course, there is the minor question of whether it was the carjacking Nosey initially reported, or the exercise in extortion that he's *now* reporting. Is he prepared to come in and change his story on the record?"

The three young people looked at each other, then Stephanie shrugged.

"I think he *probably* would, sir," she said. "I can't

be positive about that, though. He came to us—to Karl, specifically—because we were a part of the 'official' system that he trusted, so I'm pretty sure he's prepared to talk to *you*, too. But whether or not he's ready to do it on the record . . . ?"

She shrugged again, and Shelton nodded.

"That's about what I expected," he said. "And the fact is that I'm not the one he'd have to go on record with, anyway. We don't actually have jurisdiction over crimes which are committed on private land. Oh, there are a few offenses where we *would* have jurisdiction, but they all relate to wildlife violations or arson. This one wouldn't come to us. It would go to the Twin Forks Constabulary, and that's where he'd have to go to change his statement."

"Oh." Stephanie frowned in chagrin. She hadn't even thought about who might have jurisdiction! Karl, on the other hand—

"I thought about that, sir," he said diffidently. "I wasn't sure how the jurisdiction on the physical beating would shake out, but I knew which way it would probably go. But if Nosey is right, whatever's going on isn't limited to just Twin Forks. And some of these 'accidents'—like my sister's—*are* happening on Crown lands. If they're the result of criminal actions, or even just criminal *negligence*, the SFS does have jurisdiction, doesn't it?"

"That's a valid point." Shelton nodded. "But you say the drug panels haven't detected any prohibited substances in any of these 'accident victims'' systems?"

"No, sir."

"Well, if it's not a prohibited substance, then providing it to people who want to use it—whatever it is—isn't a criminal offense. Maybe it should be, and maybe someday it *will* be, but until it's at least been identified we can't arrest anyone for distributing it."

"That still leaves the criminal negligence side, though, sir," Karl said with respectful tenacity. "If your actions endanger another person, or lead to their actual physical harm, and you *knew* that they might at the time, then you're still legally liable for endangering or harming them whether or not those actions were illegal. Same thing with 'reckless endangerment,' actually."

"And that's another valid point." Shelton sounded pleased that Karl was sticking to his guns. "At the moment, though, all we have is speculation. I think it's intelligent speculation, and, frankly, I think you three and Nosey are almost certainly right about what's going on. But it's only speculation at this point. Until we turn up something more concrete, there's only so much I can do. You two"—he looked at Karl and Stephanie—"know how tightly stretched our funding is. The planetary financial board has way too many places that need money right now, and not nearly enough cash to cover them all. I've already had to argue for Karl being given part-hours to help with the SFS Explorers, and I managed *that* by pointing out that he'd be productively using what was otherwise travel time. I can think of two or three board members right off the top of my head who'd have a hissy fit if I started funding an all-up investigation into a drug that might or might not exist and accidents that might or might not be its result."

"Excuse me, sir," Stephanie cut in, knowing she was about to be impulsive. Karl could chew her out later, but there was no way she was going to just walk out of Shelton's office without trying harder for his support.

"I understand what you're saying about jurisdiction," she continued. "I should've thought about that, and I didn't. And I understand about the budget, too. What I want to know is whether you'd have any problems if I—not Karl, because he's working—and say, Cordelia, did some research using the SFS databases. Could you just look the other way?"

"No, young lady, I couldn't," Shelton said, then quirked his mouth in a slight smile at Stephanie's reaction. "And the reason I couldn't is that I think you do have a valid basis for an investigation here. The problem is that what we don't have yet is any *evidence*. If we did, and if this fell into our jurisdiction, I could organize a task force, maybe put Frank Lethbridge or Ainsley Jedrusinski on it. The planetary board would cough up the money for an investigation if I told them I had evidence of a potentially serious crime—which extortion certainly is—and that it, or other crimes related to it, had occurred on Crown lands.

"Unfortunately, I can't do that, because I don't have that evidence. However, I'm well aware of the Harrington propensity for charging straight ahead when you think you're right, and I am *not* going to turn you loose unsupervised in the SFS database when I have a certain . . . lively apprehension about where you might go with whatever you found. On the other hand—"

He paused, rocking slightly in his chair, and Stephanie made herself keep her mouth shut.

"On the other hand," he continued after several seconds, "the one person I know can ride herd on you with at least a modicum of success is Ranger Zivonik here. And I don't have to justify how I have him using his hours as long as I'm not adding still more *paid* time to his account. Not as long as it's internal SFS business, at least, which the Explorers aren't. So if it should happen that I were to tell him that I want him to very carefully, very discreetly—and very *cheaply*—look into this, that would be a purely internal affair. And if he wanted to enlist some equally discreet *unpaid* volunteers to assist him, that would be a purely internal affair, too."

Stephanie beamed, and Shelton raised a cautioning index finger.

"I'm confident that what I'm about to say will do only limited good, Probationary Ranger Harrington, but I'm going to say it anyway, and you're going to listen." He smiled, but his tone was very serious. "You are only investigating whether or not there actually is some new drug out there. You are not confronting anyone you think may be making or distributing it. In fact, you're not taking *any* action, except to research our database, without specifically clearing it with Karl ahead of time. And in *your* case, Ms. Schardt-Cordova, as of now, I have no reason to believe that you partake of our Stephanie's impulsiveness. Keep it that way."

"Yes, sir," Stephanie murmured dutifully, and Cordelia nodded. Shelton glowered at his probationary ranger for another moment, then sighed.

"Sir, am *I* authorized to go beyond research?" Karl asked. "I mean, if I develop a lead, or another avenue of evidence opens up, can I follow it up? Interview people I think may know something that could help us? Look for physical evidence in the field?"

"Of course you can."

"And may I enlist some of those 'unpaid volunteers' in the process?"

Stephanie held her breath as Shelton frowned in thought.

"All right," he said finally. "I know perfectly well that Stephanie is constitutionally incapable of not poking her nose where it doesn't belong if she thinks it's the right thing to do. I'll probably regret saying this, but that's actually a fairly good trait to have. But because I know that, I know that if I order you to shut her out, she'll just go off and begin nose-poking on her own. So, yes, you are authorized to enlist your volunteers in fieldwork under the following conditions. First, you'll be in charge and have supervisory authority. Stephanie"—he looked at her sternly—"if you try to do one of your end runs around Karl, I will revoke your probationary ranger status. Permanently. Do you understand me?"

Stephanie nodded silently, her eyes huge.

"Second," the chief ranger continued, looking back to Karl, "you may use them *only* as investigators. They will have no authority to confront or apprehend *anyone*, under any circumstances. They will be fact-gatherers, not law-enforcers."

"Understood, sir," Karl said, meeting Shelton's gaze levelly.

"And, third," the chief ranger said, "you will keep me completely informed of your findings and even of your suspicions, should any new ones present themselves. Understand me, all three of you. If Nosey's telling the truth—now—about what happened to him, these are dangerous people. I know you and Karl have dealt with dangerous people before, Stephanie, but so far, you've been lucky. I don't want your luck running out on this investigation. So, as soon as you've established what's happening—assuming that we're all right and something *is* happening—you back off, you tell me, and I tell whoever else needs to know, whether it's the Twin Forks Constabulary, the Yawata Crossing PD, or the county sheriff. We take it from there; *you* don't. I know your promise means something to you, Stephanie, and that's what I want right now. I want you to tell me that you understand everything I just said and that you *promise* to abide by the conditions I've set."

"I promise, sir," she said solemnly. He looked at her for a second or two, then nodded.

"Then that's good enough for me," he said simply, and Stephanie felt a stir of pride as she realized he meant it. Her promise truly was good enough for him.

Which, of course, meant she had no option but to keep it.

"Now get out of my office," he told them, waving both hands in a shooing motion. "Scat, the lot of you!"

✧ ✧ ✧

"Wow," Cordelia said as the three of them headed back out toward Karl's car. "I hadn't realized how well Chief Shelton knows you, Stephanie!"

"Oh, *everybody* in the SFS knows Steph." Karl chuckled, and Stephanie shook a fist at him. But then she chuckled herself.

"I'm really a lot better than I used to be," she said. "I was a little surprised he was willing to allow us to be officially involved at all, though."

"I think you can probably thank Cordelia for at least some of that," Karl said, reaching down to ruffle her hair. "I think he expects her to be a moderating influence on you."

"I think you're right," Stephanie said wryly, and smiled at Cordelia. "Thanks, Cordy."

"All I did was sit there and nod in all the right places," Cordelia said, and all three of them laughed.

Despite that, Stephanie strongly suspected Karl had a point, and she was grateful for Cordelia's support. Especially because she hadn't needed that odd sensitivity to emotion she sometimes got through Lionheart to know that Cordelia had been surprised—and maybe momentarily upset, when she saw Stephanie was with Karl. That had been part of the reason she'd gotten in the back seat, so Cordelia wouldn't feel like a tagalong.

And they're the same age and both new adoptees and . . . She'd really be perfect for Karl, so why don't I feel happier about the idea?

"Next move?" she asked a bit more brightly than she felt.

"First, we feed the Harrington," Karl said. "I suspect we need to fortify your blood sugar if we're going to get your very best scheming out of you."

✧ ✧ ✧

They stopped at Bay Baskets to pick up what was either a late lunch or an early dinner. Trying to get the memory of her last visit here with Anders out of her mind, Stephanie concentrated on planning the next stage in their investigation. It didn't quite work, though. According to Jessica, Anders hadn't taken her rejection of his admittedly generous offer well and there was some question as to whether he'd leave Sphinx at odds with both Jessica—and with Stephanie, who he blamed for not doing more to facilitate his claim.

Anders is definitely a problem, Stephanie thought, biting a hushpuppy in half, *but he can be a problem for later.*

She leaned into the front seat and studied the list

projected on the HUD. A familiar name reminded her of an idea she'd been holding onto until they found out if Chief Shelton was going to put someone in charge over them—or even tell them to stay away from investigating the possible drug problem.

"I think Jake Simpson's who we should start our queries with," she said. "Karl, you and I know him from the hang-gliding club, which gives us a natural opening. I dropped in on him soon after the skimmer accident to bring him a gift basket from the team. We could see if he's interested in doing something with the SFS Explorers as an opener, then work around to his accident. When I saw him before, he was just home from the hospital and really dopey, not up to chatting."

Karl nodded. "Reasonable. If I'm on duty, you can take Cordelia. I don't think any of us should go alone when we do anything related to the accidents."

Cordelia grinned. "As long as I don't fall too far behind on my studies, my mom won't mind. I think she's glad to see me 'coming out of my shell.' Hanging out with you two is treecat socialization, too. All good. When do we see Jake?"

"Let's try now, if that's okay with you, Karl?"

"Sure, I'm off duty for the rest of the day, and if we tie it into the Explorers the visit's even SFS work. I love showing myself eager and willing and able."

Stephanie made a face at him, then tapped her uni-link. The call connected almost immediately. "Hey, Jake, Stephanie Harrington here. How do you feel about visitors, maybe shortly after dinner?"

She'd put the call on speaker, and Jake's cheerful voice filled the air car's cab. "Oh, wow, Steph, that would be super hexy. You can't believe how bored I get. You said 'visitors'—some of the team?"

"Karl," Stephanie said, "and Cordelia Schardt-Cordova."

"The chick who just rescued a treecat and nearly got eaten by near-weasels while she was doing it? Hey, that would be cool. Three humans, three treecats, I rate! I don't have any celery though. That okay?"

Stephanie laughed. "Honestly, it's more than fine. How about we bring you something?"

"No need. Seriously. I'm losing my manly muscles with all this sitting around. And I've had so many extra calories. Just seeing you guys would be the best. When do I look for you?"

Karl held up several fingers, and Stephanie made the arrangements. Despite Jake's request for no presents, they did pause long enough to pick up a mixed snack pack, so they wouldn't inconvenience the Simpsons.

When they arrived, Jake's dad sent them around to the side door into the pool room. Jake was sitting in his float chair, practicing trick shots.

"Hi, Steph, Karl." He turned a dazzling smile on Cordelia. "And by process of elimination, you're Cordelia. I'm Jake. Glad to meet you."

"Me, too, you," she said. "This is Athos."

"And I know Lionheart and Survivor." Jake motioned to the rack of pool cues. "Want to play? I'm getting wicked good since I've been stuck home, but I'll spot you."

He levered himself up out of the float chair. "I don't really need it all the time now, and the doc says it's not going to be long before I can shuck the brace."

Stephanie, looking for a cue short enough for her to be comfortable with, laughed. "Maybe you should loan the chair to me. You tall people have all the advantages in this game."

"Hey!" Jake said with the natural enthusiasm of the coach Stephanie felt certain he would be one day. "Why don't we all shoot from the chair? Level the playing field and like that?"

Everyone fell in with the idea, and before long they were laughing as they invented rules. Jake really *was* good, but he was also a natural sportsman, eager to show them how to get the best of each shot.

"This is fun," Stephanie said. "Jake, have you heard about the SFS Explorers?"

"That program you and Karl are fronting for the Rangers? Sure. I listened to Nosey's 'cast on it. It sounds pretty cool."

"Maybe you could come talk to one of the meetings," Stephanie said, "about sports, especially the challenges on a high-gee world like Sphinx."

"I thought you guys were going to be all like, 'our friend the range bunny,'" Jake said dubiously, "not a sports club."

"We're a club about Sphinx," Karl said, smiling with satisfaction as he brought the cue ball in with just the right tap to send the solid-colored balls trouping one by one into the side pockets. "And if there's one thing that newcomers need to think about when adjusting to life here, it's the gravity. That's what turns a routine fall into a broken bone."

"Oh, yeah. Hey, I remember hearing that your little sis took a tumble. She okay?"

"Better than we could have hoped," Karl said. "And

she's native born, should have known better. With the influx of tourists and new settlers . . ."

He gave one of those eloquent "guy shrugs" that said, "You can fill in the details, right?"

The treecats had been outside, but now they came scratching at the door. When Cordelia moved to let them in, Lionheart hopped up on an unoccupied chair and gave the yet-unopened snack tray a significant look.

"Hey, the flying tigers are starving." Jake laughed, popping the tray open and offering each 'cat a chicken drumstick.

"Flying tigers?" Cordelia asked, puzzled.

"Oh, sorry. I started calling Lionheart that when he would ride Stephanie's glider with her. Her glider had tiger stripes then. Karl's been showing Survivor the ropes, too. Are you going to take Athos hang-gliding?"

Cordelia laughed. "I've never been, so I guess I'd better learn how to do it first."

"Oh, you've gotta try it. It's terrific when you turn off the counter-grav and it's just you and the wind. And with the counter-grav it's safe as anything. Let me show you some pictures of this year's trainee class. They're not all kids."

There! Stephanie thought. *The perfect opening.*

"Do you use counter-grav in skimmer riding?" she asked innocently. "I mean, I know that the kids at the park do, but what about with the fancy stuff you do?"

Jake reached up and scratched his curly head. "Oh, yeah. I'm always careful, even when doing the fancy stuff. No idea why my c-gee went out on me. You can bet I'm going to double- and triple-check next time. I have seriously not enjoyed all this chair time, even if I'm getting super good at shooting pool. Hey, Cordelia, isn't it your turn?"

Stephanie didn't need Karl's warning glower to make her back off. By the time they left, relations were back to normal—more or less.

Once they were in Karl's air car, heading to drop Cordelia off, Stephanie sighed.

"Well, I muffed that one."

Cordelia chuckled. "Steph, you forget who you are. 'Probationary' or not, you've been an SFS ranger since you were fourteen. Karl is now an official ranger: on the payroll, badge, uniform, and all that cool stuff. Jake is about as likely to tell you he deliberately turned his c-gee unit off while he tried a fancy new move as he would his parents. Heck, he might tell them first, depending on how well they get along."

"But—" Stephanie began.

"Cordelia has a point, Steph," Karl interrupted. "The problem is, some skriders like to show how brave they are—stupid's a better word for it—by riding *without* c-gee whenever they can get away with it. Chance to prove they're so good *they* don't have to worry about little things like broken bones! But that's an automatic safety-violation grounding, no appeal, at the parks if they get caught at it. And it'll get you banned from your team if you get caught. Jake's always been a pretty straight arrow where that rule's concerned. That's what makes his 'accident' so strange, when you come down to it. But you and I have been branded as too squeaky clean for our own good—at least in a case like this. He's not going to tell us anything that might even *sound* like he'd been stunting without c-gee to show how good he is. Cordelia, though, if she doesn't mind twisting the truth a little, she might be able to get something out of those we suspect did something dumb under the influence."

"Jake might be a hard call," Cordelia said. "He's going to be on guard for a while."

Stephanie looked at the list. "What about this one—Eldora Yazzie? She's one of the ones Nosey wrote up. Do you know her? Looks like you're about the same age."

"I do, sorta, kinda," Cordelia said. "From classes. We've never really been buddies, but I could probably work something out. Thing is, if I'm going to be your undercover scout, then I'm going to need to distance myself a little. The treecats are a good excuse for us to keep meeting up, but I might—sorry, Steph—play on your reputation as a bossy know-it-all."

"That's me." Stephanie did her best to sound as if she was joking, but realizing that she had such a reputation stung.

Was there anything wrong with really knowing more than other people about something? Did she need to play dumb just because she wasn't even sixteen? The weird thing was that most of the adults didn't seem to mind, but her "peers" really did.

Ouch. Maybe that's because I don't sneer, even inside, at most of the adults I know, but I'm not really good at hiding when I think some kid is a zork.

She filed that for future consideration. "I think that's a good idea. We just need a lead, some idea of how the drug is being dispensed. If we managed that, maybe we could analyze it, figure out what it was. That might give us a lead as to who's making it."

Karl sighed. "I've tried again and again with Dia,

but nothing doing. Champagne and canapes, then dancing, then passing out. It's getting so I believe her. Loon, too. Same thing. My folks are wise to the ways of the young, and they realize that forbidding Dia to see Loon will just encourage her to sneak around. Instead, she's seeing him, but only supervised: swim team, at our house. The restrictions are being explained as a penalty for her breaking the rules and leaving Anastasia and Nat unsupervised, not as her being interested in an 'older man.'"

Stephanie nodded. Secure in her place in the back seat, she studied Karl.

Older man. Do people think that about me and Karl? She felt her cheeks burning and was glad for the relative shelter of the back seat. *Or maybe, I'm just seen as a sort of kid sister tagging around after a sort of big brother. I wonder what Karl thinks, but he's the last one I'd ever ask.*

✧ ✧ ✧

If Stephanie and Karl hadn't taken Cordelia into their confidence, Cordelia knew she wouldn't have thought twice about the weird relationship between Frank Câmara and Herman Maye. If she was completely honest with herself, Cordelia knew that ever since Frank had invaded the Kemper house, she'd shied away from thinking about him at all. So what if she double-checked the locks on the house if she heard a vehicle passing overhead and she was alone? That was just prudence, right?

But Cordelia knew deep down inside that Frank had scared her. Even more than she hated having been scared, she hated knowing that she *could* be scared. She'd always been comfortable wandering the bush alone. Now she never went hiking without Barnaby, and she took a lot of comfort knowing that Athos would be somewhere near.

Cordelia was working over at the Kempers', thinking about how best to approach Eldora Yazzie, when she heard the hum of an air van passing by. Glancing out a window, she confirmed that it was the one Frank Câmara typically used when he came to pick up mushrooms.

I wonder why Frank—who's the son of the owners of one of the fanciest, most popular restaurants on Sphinx—goes to pick up the mushrooms himself? He's a null, but surely his folks could find something better for him to do, something that would be better training for helping with the family restaurant and grocery warehouses. It's not as if he does any selecting. Herman has the order ready and boxed.

She was pretty sure she was right about this. Recently, she and Mack had been over fixing a waterline to one of the mushroom-growing buildings when Frank had come by to make a pickup. Another time, she'd been over there herself, picking up a truckload of mushroom compost for the Schardt-Cordova gardens when Frank had been loading his air van. Another time, when she'd gone to drop off some interesting mushrooms she'd found when hiking, in case they might be a new type, she'd seen an order boxed and ready to go.

That's another thing. Why does Herman seem so scared of Frank? Come to that, why are Herman's moods so changeable? I've always thought that his mood swings were due to the fact that he's not thrilled with how his job keeps him from getting out and collecting bounties. Or maybe it's not the bounties, as much as the credit for discovering? But what if it's not just job-related? What if Herman is messing with whatever drug that's out there? Certainly, Frank Câmara has a reputation for doing drugs, even for dealing a little.

Having no answer to these questions, not even a sense as to whether there really *were* questions, or just her imagination going wild, Cordelia decided that the next sensible course of action was to snoop.

The obvious place to start was with Herman. The Kemper boys took their role as landlords very seriously, so it was easy to tag along the next time they went over to make some improvement at Mr. Ack's. Today's project was an automatic bagger for the mushroom compost, an addition that Cordelia completely approved of after spending half an hour sweeping remnants out of the bed of the Schardt-Cordova family air truck.

Herman didn't immediately appear to greet them, and Cordelia noticed that the flats on which the boxes of mushrooms were usually stacked were empty today. She felt nervous tension drain away, because that meant it was unlikely that Frank would be coming by. Then anger at her cowardice stiffened her spine.

When they'd unloaded their gear and Herman still hadn't appeared, Mack turned to Cordelia. "Would you mind finding out where Herman is? We don't need him or anything, but it only seems polite to let him know we're here. Tell him we'll be back by the compost heap."

Zack grinned and added, "And if he offers any mushrooms for us to take home, be sure to ask if he has any of those purple portabellas. I'm still dreaming about the stuffed caps Dana made last time."

"Will do," Cordelia promised. She swung out of the back seat where she'd been riding, pleased that her ankle didn't even twinge. Athos swarmed up to ride on the harness Cordelia now wore with all her clothing. At first the thick pad along her back and the matching one on her shoulder had felt distinctly odd, but the other day she'd forgotten to put the harness on and *not* wearing it had been what felt strange. Funny how things changed.

"Bleek!" Athos commented as he settled down, and Cordelia almost would have sworn she could feel that he shared her amusement.

Since Cordelia had the excuse of looking for Herman to poke around, she did so. Most of the mushroom-capped buildings were closed and locked. Tidy signs featuring a talking cartoon mushroom noted: "Please don't disturb. We're growing!" In these, Cordelia definitely saw the peculiar obsessive humor of Dr. Glynis Bonaventure.

Cordelia found Herman working in the lab. Unlike the cultivation buildings, this one was unlocked. She tapped on the door, paused, then, following the easy countryside custom of rural Sphinx, let herself in. She felt a little guilty, given her determination to snoop, as she remembered the way Frank had used the same excuse for coming into the Kemper house uninvited.

Maybe there is *some similarity,* she thought. *But that doesn't explain why he acted so weird. Or the fact that I'm sure he* didn't *knock first.*

Like most buildings on Sphinx, no matter how small, there was an enclosed entryway, meant to provide a barrier between the outside and the interior during not only the nearly sixteen months of winter, but the colder portions of autumn and spring as well. Cordelia came in, reflexively stomped her feet to, as her mother liked to put it, "Leave the outdoors where they belong," then opened the connecting door. This led into a small office, which in turn opened into a door labeled "Lab."

"You stay here, Athos," she said, patting the air in the "get down" sign. "I don't think they'd want 'cat hair in the Lab."

Cordelia knocked again, then peeked around the edge of the lab door. Nearly colorless gray eyes wide over his mask, Herman looked up from where he had been doing something arcane with a solution of something containing flecks of organic matter. He hurried toward her, motioning for her to go back into the main office.

"Oops!" Cordelia apologized, backing up. "Sorry. I didn't mean to startle you. The reverse, really. My brothers wanted me to tell you that they're around by the compost heap, putting together something that Mack swears will sift, sort, and then bag the compost."

Herman pulled his mask down and smiled at her. "I thought I heard a knock, but I was working with this precipitate and, since I didn't expect anyone, I kept on with what I'd been doing."

Normally, Cordelia would have taken her leave, but now, remembering her resolution to snoop, she decided to stay.

He seems okay, she thought, noting that his eyes looked normal, and that he seemed appropriately energetic, *but baselines are useful, too. If I come here another time and his pupils are dilated or something, then I'll have a comparison.*

"What are you working on?" she asked, perching on the edge of the desk and drawing Athos into her lap.

"Analysis of a new shelf fungus," Herman said happily. He launched into a detailed explanation of how each of the Sphinxian fungi were studied on all sorts of levels. He lost her pretty quickly, but Cordelia gathered that fungi were very changeable. Some were even poisonous at only one part of their lifecycle, a mechanism doubtless meant to make them unattractive at a key point in their reproductive or fruiting cycle.

"So, we not only do detailed analysis of every sample," Herman said, "but, once we've succeeded in growing our own cultivars, we repeat the process at each growth stage. Then we do it all over again after propagating in different mediums. What a plant is grown in—and this includes far more than fungi, although most people are unaware of this—can change flavor, texture, even how nutritious the end result will be."

"I think my mom was talking about this," Cordelia said, "something to do with sugars?"

"Sugars are definitely one category, especially in regard to flavor." Herman managed, just, to not sound condescending.

"That's a lot of work," Cordelia said.

"And more all the time," Herman agreed, "since Dr. Bonaventure is more interested in going on safari to find new samples than she is in the dull routine." He must have realized that it was imprudent to speak so of his employer, because he quickly added, "But I don't mind. I don't mind at all. Job security."

"Maybe she'll hire you assistants," Cordelia offered, "and give you some field time."

She expected Herman either to look pleased or

dismissive. What she didn't expect was the look of panic that flashed across his usually mild features.

"Oh, I really don't mind," he repeated. "It's a lot of work but, like I said, job security."

Did he have an argument with his boss? Cordelia wondered. *Maybe he's already been told the budget doesn't extend to more help. Dr. Bonaventure is funding this project out of her own pocket, and if the work is as fussy as Herman makes out, she can't just hire a couple of biology interns to do the work. Maybe he's afraid I'll make a "helpful" suggestion to the boss and give away that he was griping.*

Outside, a faint rumble announced that Mack and Zack were testing some aspect of their machine.

"I'd better go help the boys," Cordelia said, jumping down from the desk. "Mack will probably want me to shovel compost into the hopper or something. I'll tell them you're busy, and we'll knock before we go."

Herman politely escorted her to the door. As Cordelia was fastening her jacket and letting Athos get settled, the outer door slid open, then the inner. Glynis Bonaventure quite literally breezed in, moving with so much energy that an arrangement of dried flowers in a vase on the desk fluttered.

Short and plump, with warm golden-brown skin, Glynis wore her hair dyed a bright red with a scattering of silvery white spots. This remarkable coiffure was styled to curl under near her chin, so that she gave the impression of wearing a mushroom cap on her head. Her clothing was field-practical, right down to her neatly booted feet, the over-powered personal counter-grav unit she used when collecting to avoid compressing the soil and ruining the subterranean portions of her beloved fungi, and the rifle slung over her shoulder.

That rifle's sling was worn and its stock was scratched. Clearly it had seen a lot of use, and Cordelia was glad, although not really surprised, to see it. Mack and Zack had told her Dr. Bonaventure had a "breezy" personality. Indeed, Zack had rolled his eyes at Mack's choice of adjectives. But they'd also told her Bonaventure was an experienced explorer who approached Sphinx's wildlife with a dead serious focus. Karl had told her much the same thing when she'd asked him about it.

"Chief Shelton would rather she wasn't running around the bush on her own," he said, "but this isn't the first time she's been in the field. Not even the first time on Sphinx, really. She can seem like—I hate to say this, but the only term that really fits is an 'airhead'—but I'd trust her to look after herself out there more than I would eighty percent of the folks *born* here."

At the moment, however, that "breeziness" Mack had described was totally front and center.

She was already in mid-speech when she stepped through the door. "Herman, I've found a wonderful new spotted pointed-cap; purple and orange, if you can believe it, but so tiny it's easy to overlook. I printed it in the field, but I want—" She seemed to notice Cordelia for the first time, and stopped, the collecting box she'd been thrusting at Herman held in partly outthrust arms. "Cordelia! My dear! You look so much better than the last time I saw you. No scars from those horrible near-weasels. I'm so glad."

"I came by to tell Herman that the compost bagger is being set up," Cordelia said awkwardly, feeling a little as if she'd walked into a tornado. "I was just leaving."

"A bagger! Wonderful!" Glynis almost sang. "Herman, why don't you go find out how to use the new machine? I can set my little pretty up for spore collection."

She headed toward the lab, but Herman glided to intercept her, taking the box from her hands.

"I'm certain the Kemper boys aren't done yet," he said, "Cordelia only just arrived. I'll take care of this. Maybe you should go see what they're up to. After all, you're the real tenant. In any case, I'm in the middle of an analysis."

"And we don't want me to contaminate anything," Glynis chirped gaily. "Very well. You take this and get to it as soon as is reasonable. I'll go with Cordelia to see what the darling boys have built. We'll chat later."

They said their good-byes and Cordelia found herself being bustled through the fanciful grove of mushroom buildings toward some very odd thumping noises.

Well that's very interesting, she thought. *Herman didn't make a fuss when I opened the lab door, so I don't think he was actually too worried about contamination. Somehow, I feel certain that he didn't want Glynis to see what he'd been working on.*

11

"NO ESCORT TODAY?" NOSEY ASKED PLAYFULLY WHEN he answered his front door to find Stephanie Harrington on his front porch.

"Karl's at work," Stephanie said, then added for any possible eavesdroppers, "and Cordelia and I had an argument about how much junk she's letting Athos eat. Just because treecats . . ."

She stepped inside and closed the door behind her. Nosey nodded to let her know that he'd done his usual sweep for listening devices, and the house and immediate grounds were clear, nor had the hidden cameras shown any sign of anyone around the house. Sometimes, he felt as if he was becoming paranoid but, even though the injuries from the beating he'd been subjected to were healing, he still only had to look in the mirror to be reminded of what had happened.

"And just because treecats?" Nosey asked, curious as ever.

"Just because treecats can eat human food," Stephanie replied perkily, "just like we can eat a lot of what is natural to Sphinx, their diet should be biased in favor of native Sphinxian animals and plants, and not be overprocessed."

Stephanie grinned, a genuine, friendly smile that made Nosey very happy. He'd never wanted Sphinx's girl wonder to dislike him as intensely as she had done. By now, they'd had enough opportunities to talk about the issue of treecats as pets that they understood each other's position a whole lot better, including that Stephanie was—contradictory as it might seem, given the whiskered face that peered over her shoulder—if anything, more passionate than Nosey about making certain that keeping treecats as pets was properly regulated.

"I brought the latest data chip," Stephanie said. "Do you have anything for me?"

"A bunch," Nosey said. "Come on into the living room. I have snacks, including some hardboiled eggs for the celery bandit."

After he brought out the snacks, Nosey placed his coffee mug on the table to his right, then handed Stephanie a neat little file folder. He placed a minute data chip on top.

"The folder contains the first round of entries in the 'Design a Uniform For the SFS Explorers' contest," he said. "Despite instructions, some entries were very low resolution, so I printed them. Some are incredibly hideous, a lot are repetitious, but some are actually pretty interesting. At this early stage, I'm leaning toward the ones that don't involve an investment in a full outfit. That not only makes it easier for families on a budget but also encourages individuality, both of which I'm in favor of."

"Me, too," Stephanie agreed, leafing through the folder and pausing over one crayon drawing of a person of indeterminate age wearing a gray and white hat, complete with carefully drawn treecat ears. "While rangers need to be able to work as a team, initiative is also an important part of the job. Uniforms that remind us that while we're all different, we're all on the same team would be great."

She closed the folder, then looked up at Nosey, her expression a little puzzled. "You sound as if you're really into this contest. I thought the contest was just cover so that we'd have an excuse to drop over to see you."

"I *am* into it," Nosey admitted cheerfully. "When I haven't been crunching data files, I've been busily searching the data net for information about scout groups, both in other systems and back into history. I like the idea of badges for various achievements, too, and was thinking about sponsoring one on constructing clear reports. From what I've seen, SFS rangers spend a lot of time dictating, writing, and otherwise providing documentation."

They discussed the badges idea for a while, then moved on to the real reason for Stephanie's in-person visit. After one exhaustive afternoon of trying to sort through the data they'd gleaned from the SFS archives and making far less headway than they had hoped, Cordelia had suggested that they enlist Nosey.

"He already has the skills and probably thinks crunching data is fun," Cordelia had said, looking at the neat but still rudimentary database they'd taken hours to design. "And he doesn't have homework, either."

Nosey had been thrilled to help, but he had expressed concern that whoever had assaulted him might have some way to intercept data going in or out of his house or, at least, to spy on his net research.

"I've good security programs," he said, "but I still suspect that whoever beat me up was a professional, and professionals might be watching me still."

"Or maybe have flags set if you start researching certain topics," Karl had agreed.

So they'd arranged that anything crucial on either side would be handed off in person. The SFS Explorers had proven good cover, and given that Stephanie had been heard to say more than once that she was determined to educate Nosey Jones on the realities associated with treecats, no one would find the duration of her visits in the least peculiar.

✧ ✧ ✧

As she drove over to the vet clinic to meet her dad, Stephanie mused over what Nosey had summarized for her. Even allowing for Nosey's bias, it seemed pretty conclusive that younger people—ranging from mid-teens to mid-twenties—were being hit by an unusual run of stupid accidents. These were so widely varied that it took looking to find a pattern. Nosey had created a chart from the archived data as a comparison. Even allowing for other changes, such as increased immigration and tourism, there definitely had been an increase in accidents.

Less certain was the cause. Jessica and Nosey had pieced together all the details they could about the accident victims who had actually gone through the medical system, but their ability to dig deep was limited Not all cases had involved comprehensive blood work, and even if they had, patient confidentiality would have prevented them from getting a look at the results without patient permission—which they couldn't get without explaining why they wanted it—or a warrant . . . which they couldn't get without an official investigation of an actual potential crime.

If we had the data to support an investigation, we could demand more blood screens, but to get that data—or even evidence that there's more and different drug use going on—we need blood screen results first. *It's frustrating that none of the people we've interviewed will admit to taking anything. Cordelia hasn't had any more luck than we have. Sometimes I think we're the wrong sort of people.*

The vet clinic's parking area was fairly empty today. The striking exception was a medium-sized air van ornamented with the logo of the Twin Forks branch of Wild and Free, a relatively new organization that rehabilitated injured animals, both native and feral. The latter category was pretty small, but the former was growing as human habitation expanded. Just the fact that such an organization existed showed one of the small ways that Sphinx was changing.

"A few years ago," Richard Harrington had said, "between the final wave of the Plague and the general attitude of many of the earlier settlers, an injured animal either would have been left to fend for itself or found itself in the cookpot. Hexapumas and other, admittedly less dramatic, predators still prowled close enough to holdings or settlements to finish off any domestic animal unlucky enough to go feral."

Had it not been for her activities as a probationary ranger, Stephanie might have signed with Wild and Free. Fostering wild animals, especially with the goal of releasing them into the wild again, definitely appealed to her. As it was, her dad occasionally brought a particularly critical case home, but most of his non-domesticated patients were fostered through Wild and Free.

I wonder what's in today, Stephanie thought, letting herself in through the door marked "Staff Only" that led into the maze of examining rooms, kennels, labs, and offices that was the nonpublic face of the vet clinic. Lionheart chose to stay outside, swarming up a tall crown oak and heading toward a particular limb that was one of his favorites for sunbathing. Although the treecat was welcome in the clinic, Richard Harrington had suggested that he not come in all the time.

"There's always the chance that Lionheart might catch something. We're a long way from knowing all the possible treecat-dangerous viruses on Sphinx and even longer from having vaccinations for them."

"Bleek," Lionheart called down to her, twitching his whiskers and curling his tail around his toes.

"Bleek yourself," Stephanie called back. "Be good."

"Bleek!!" Lionheart replied with more emphasis.

That almost seemed like a warning, Stephanie thought.

When an exam room door popped open and she found herself nearly nose-to-nose with Trudy Franchitti, she had no doubt that it had been. Trudy was nearly a year older than Stephanie, but already had curves like those of a grown woman. She was very pretty, with dark hair and violet-blue eyes that could look knowing and innocent at the same time. Trudy and Stephanie had met when they were both in the hang-gliding club, where they had been, frankly, rivals.

Trudy wore a shirt printed with the Wild and Free logo. Behind her, drowsing on an examination table, was a magnificent near-beaver with a nasty set of stitches running down one flank, and another set girdling its upper left rear hind-leg. Stephanie had researched Terran beavers, and the Sphinxian version looked more like an otter than a beaver. However, since another creature had copped the name "near-otter," and near-beavers did behave a lot like Terran beavers, especially creating landscape-altering dams, the name definitely fit.

The two girls stared at each other. Then, to Stephanie's surprise, because she and Trudy had never been particular friends, Trudy motioned for Stephanie to come into the exam room.

"He," Trudy said, pointing to the near-beaver, "had a nasty encounter with an automatic dredger. He was in such bad shape, your dad said to bring him directly into the clinic. We hope he'll keep the leg. Your dad said it was gloved: that's when the muscles detach from the bone and slide down."

When Trudy mentioned the near-beaver being in danger of losing a leg, Stephanie stiffened, wondering if she was being taunted about how Lionheart had lost his left front true-hand. But, there was no mockery in Trudy's wide violet-blue eyes.

"I'm waiting for the beav to come around, so Richard can give the go-ahead to take him back to Wild and Free. It's creepy sitting with an unconscious creature; they look way too like dead. Wanna talk? I could seriously use some company."

Stephanie sank onto the bench built into the wall, accepting the invitation more from curiosity than out of a desire to be nice. "Sure. I'll ping my dad that I'm here. I'm supposed to get some stuff from him, and take it home, but there isn't a huge rush."

Trudy, Stephanie decided, after they had chatted for a little, had definitely changed. They hadn't had a lot of contact since Trudy had dropped out of the hang-gliding club after her boyfriend, Stan Chang, had announced that it had become too full of itty-bitty-kiddies to be any fun for advanced flyers. When they'd both been in the club, they'd been rivals from the start. It was bad enough that Trudy was a curvaceous boy-magnet, while Stephanie had been boyish. Worse was that Trudy was a complete snob who reminded anyone she could, any time she could, about how her father, Jordan, had been one of the first children born on Sphinx. The final straw had been that Trudy was the sort of kid who collected wild animals as pets, but didn't bother to learn what it took to keep them healthy. Suspicion that the rubbish heap rather than the vet was the destiny of any of Trudy's pets unfortunate enough to get sick, because "there's always another one out in the bush" had sealed Stephanie's aversion.

"I didn't know you were working with Wild and Free," Stephanie said. "That's cool."

"I started after the last fire season," Trudy said. "I needed help because some of my pets got hurt—smoke inhalation, mostly."

Because you had them caged and they couldn't run away or get low, Stephanie thought, but remembering a woebegone Trudy sitting in the vet clinic's waiting room with her animals around her—and the way Trudy had defied her father to *save* those animals from the fire, and been burned herself in the process—she didn't feel the usual anger.

"Wild and Free helped me decide which animals

could be safely released, which needed more care," Trudy went on. "Later, I started volunteering. My dad doesn't get it, but I don't care."

Stephanie found herself thinking how lucky she was to have parents who did understand how important animals and plants—the whole biome, if it came down to it—were. Trudy's decision to volunteer at Wild and Free was, for a Franchitti, an act of rebellion.

They talked for a few minutes about some of Trudy's various fosters, then Trudy said with a trace of her former slyness, "So, rumor is that you and Anders Whittaker split, that he went after Jessica, and that she's not having much to do with him."

Marveling at the efficiency of the local gossip network, Stephanie searched for a reply that would be both honest and not slam either Jessica or Anders.

"I guess Anders was lonely. I mean, I went off to Manticore for a school term."

"With Karl," Trudy said.

"Who isn't my boyfriend," Stephanie said firmly. "But, you know, I think that Anders isn't the type for long-distance relationships. He'll be going home to Urako soon. Jessica hasn't said anything to me about this, but she's probably decided that she doesn't want a short-term thing."

She held her breath, hoping that Trudy hadn't heard anything about how Anders had been making arrangements for Jessica to go home with him. Trudy's next comment was both a relief and a surprise.

"Guys! Sometimes I think they really are another species. Maybe like those types of animals that are sexually dimorphic, they're really different from females."

Stephanie was still trying to not show her astonishment at hearing the term "sexually dimorphic" from Trudy Franchitti, when Trudy went on confidingly.

"I'm really worried about Stan. He's the first guy I seriously dated, and I really thought we were, oh, happily ever after and all that."

Stephanie nodded, thinking about how she'd been so sure Anders was "The One."

"Now, though, he's really changed. I thought it might be that we're almost seventeen, that we're both getting a lot of pressure to 'grow up,' think about what we want to do with our lives. Stan's really resented that. He's got cousins on Manticore, you know, and he says that while they're being encouraged to think about college and all, they aren't getting the same pressure to be adult."

Stephanie nodded, wondering if Trudy expected her to say something, but Trudy was in full spate.

"Lately though..." Trudy's voice dropped, and she pinched her full lips together until they became a white line. "I think Stan's fallen in with a really bad crowd." Her expression became defiant. "I mean, he and Frank were always a little wild, but that bad boy vibe, it can be really tasty. This is different. A few times, we've had a date and he hasn't shown up. Or he's had way too much money. Or..."

Trudy defiantly eyed Stephanie, like she was daring her to criticize. "I think Stan's doing drugs, the sort that mess with your head. I know you're almost sort-of-kind-of law enforcement, but we've all been pals since we were kids in the hang-gliding club, right? You wouldn't rat him out, just because I say I'm worried about him. I mean, maybe he's not my forever-and-ever guy, but we've been friends since Stan's family moved to Sphinx when we were both three and I'm worried, right? That's okay, right?"

Tears, real, genuine tears, not a drama queen pretending, pooled up in Trudy's eyes, and she dashed them away.

Stephanie heard her own voice saying, "Right, right. It's absolutely fine to be worried. It's okay," as her mind was racing about the implications of this for her own investigation.

Trudy told me because *I'm sort-of-kind-of law enforcement, not despite it. She's desperate to tell someone, in case Stan really is in over his head, but she can't go to her folks. Jordan Franchitti is the type to laugh and pat her on the head while saying "Boys will be boys" or something equally stupid. And she's not going to go to the cops. Either they'd just dismiss her as a bimbo trying to get back at her boyfriend, or they'd do something that would get Stan in trouble legally or with his parents, and that would be the end of their romance, and probably of their friendship.*

Awkwardly, Stephanie reached over and patted Trudy on one shoulder. "I get you," she said, hoping the words conveyed her full meaning. "I do. It's rough."

"I knew you'd understand," Trudy said. "I mean, you've been in love, too. You know what it's like to care, to worry, even when he's done you wrong."

Stephanie nodded. "I do. I do indeed."

✧ ✧ ✧

At Stephanie's suggestion, the next meeting of the Great Treecat Conspiracy was held at Scott MacDallan's.

"Scott doesn't have a lot of free time, but I think

he really hates always having to cancel," she'd said. "So if he can't make it to the meetings, maybe we should take the meeting to him, right?"

Agreement had been both enthusiastic and general. And the actual meeting only further demonstrated why it was sometimes so hard for him to get there. Even though the meeting was set for after the doctor's appointments were over for the day, Scott and Fisher were the last to arrive.

"Sorry," Scott said, collapsing into his favorite of the two over-stuffed chairs near the fireplace and gratefully accepting the whiskey and soda Irina handed him. "Lately, if it isn't one thing it's another. It's as if the world has gone down Alice's rabbit hole or something, and people believe the normal rules of physics and good judgment have been suspended."

That was all the opener Stephanie needed. Cordelia and Jessica helped Irina with putting the final touches on dinner, as Karl and Stephanie presented their case, much as they had to Chief Ranger Shelton.

They've gotten really good at this, Cordelia thought, trading grins with Jessica, who clearly was thinking the same thing. The initial presentation finished as Irina was ladling out a thick stew into stoneware bowls of her own making.

"Stephanie, I'm sure you have more supporting data you want to show Scott," Irina said cheerfully, "but tables and charts can wait until after we've eaten."

"Yes, ma'am!" Stephanie replied, shutting off her tablet and coming to wash her hands. "I stand appropriately reproved."

The next quarter of an hour or so was devoted to properly appreciating the stew, crusty dark-brown bread, sweet butter, and mixed salad, the last augmented, as always when Stephanie was one of the group, by interesting cullings from Marjorie Harrington's greenhouse. Only when seconds had been served to those who wanted them—which was just about everyone—did Scott open the discussion to the possibility that drug use might explain the recent rash of accidents.

"I know you don't like Nosey, Stephanie, but he has a good grasp of the realities of emergency medicine. Usually, in the case of an accident, dealing with the damage comes first, what caused it comes second, if ever, especially if it's obvious to the meanest of intelligences why the person got hurt."

"I don't dislike Nosey," Stephanie protested. "I think I've even made headway—without giving anything away—in letting him understand that none of us think that treecats make great pets, but sometimes we get stuck with them. An added advantage to finding out if he's right about why he was beaten up is then we'll have made an even better ally of him."

"Very calculating of you," Karl said with a smile of approval, and she stuck out her tongue at him.

"I can't get around the confidentiality rules and snoop through their records any better than you could, Jessica," Scott said with a frown. "To be honest, I wouldn't if I could. That's not what ethical physicians do. But I *can* sort of float the possibility with the other doctors I know. See if they've seen anything they're willing to share." He shrugged. "That happens to be something ethical docs *do* do—a lot—when it comes to spotting new health threats. The ER docs are actually less likely to notice something like this, unless they're already looking for it, because they usually don't know their patients, recognize that they're acting out of character, the way the family practice docs do."

"That would probably be a good idea." Karl nodded.

"But we don't want too much public attention, yet," Stephanie cautioned. Scott looked at her, and she shrugged. "We need to go public with it as soon as we can, before someone gets killed in one of these 'accidents,' but we also need to establish that's what's actually happening—and how to prove who's behind it—before the ones distributing it figure out we're looking for them."

"Another good point," Karl agreed. "Speaking of which, you texted that you'd thought of someone we might interview?"

"Well, not interview," Stephanie replied, pausing in the middle of slathering soft cheese on her bread, "because he'd never talk to any of us, but check out somehow."

Then she told them about her meeting with Trudy Franchitti, and what Trudy had said about Stan. "Basically, I think she *knows* he's messing with drugs, and that his personality change lately is due to that."

"Huh, remembering how Stan's acted, you'd think any personality change would be for the better." Karl snorted. "Trudy said something about him falling in with a bad crowd? That's worrisome."

"Hold on," Cordelia interrupted, "I don't really know these people, but did you say that Stan Chang and Frank Câmara are friends?" When everyone nodded, she went on. "Frank Câmara has been coming over to Mr. Ack's. Is it possible that Frank could be getting drugs there? I mean, mushrooms can be drugs, can't they?"

Scott MacDallan's eyebrows rose until they merged with his fiery hairline. "Now that's interesting. Mushrooms certainly can cause a wide variety of psychoactive and other reactions. The puzzling thing is that Glynis Bonaventure has an excellent reputation. She's been posting regular updates on what they find, and on subsequent analysis. It's hard to imagine her as a drug pusher."

"Is what she posts available to the public?" Karl asked, leaning forward, eyes shining.

"No, it isn't. Glynis herself asked that the information be restricted. She said that amateur 'mushroom hunters' make themselves sick so routinely that she didn't want to be responsible for encouraging irresponsible behavior. Her long-term plan is to write a comprehensive guide to the fungi of Sphinx, and even teach courses on safe mushrooming."

Cordelia felt deeply unhappy. Despite his essential weirdness, she liked Herman Maye and didn't want to get him into trouble. But if he was involved, voluntarily or not, well, that couldn't be ignored. She remembered seeing Dia crumpled at the bottom of the gully, how terrified they'd been that she might be badly injured—or even dead.

"If the GBMRAC is involved, Dr. Bonaventure might not know anything about it," she said. "Herman Maye might be doing something behind her back. If what he's told me isn't just griping, he's the one who does most of the primary analysis, while she gallivants around finding new samples."

"It's just a two-person operation, then?" Scott asked.

"Pretty much," Cordelia said. "I think Glynis planned on hiring some more help, but she found that Mack and Zack are very serious about their role as landlords and she knows they need money, and so she gives them any work she can."

Jessica added, "Glynis hired my mom to scout samples for her. I think Steph's mom dropped a hint that my dad is a sweetheart, but not exactly the universe's most reliable provider. Glynis probably has a few other people collecting for her. Finding an analyst would be a lot harder."

"I could go talk to Herman," Scott offered, "but if he is doing anything illegal, he's not going to talk to me. He might let something slip to one of you, though."

Cordelia grinned at Karl and Stephanie, "But not to the SFS rangers. Looks like this is a job for your undercover partner. Jessica, just in case something is hinky, I'd feel a lot better if I didn't go alone. Do you have time?"

Jessica nodded. "We're staying here tonight, and I'm off tomorrow until late afternoon. Shall we go see Herman first thing?"

Cordelia sobered. "Definitely. There are too many accidents going on for this to be chance. Despite how bad it looks for him, I can't believe Herman is the one who beat up Nosey. To be honest, that doesn't seem to fit in with Trudy's worrying about Stan running with the bad crowd, either. Maybe all of them are in over their heads."

✧ ✧ ✧

When Jessica and Cordelia went to brace Herman Maye the next day, they weren't precisely alone. Stephanie had wanted to set them up with both panic buttons and audio-visual links so that she and Karl could listen in and record the conversation, but Karl had shot that notion down instantly.

"Can't do it," he'd said firmly. "For that matter, I can't even officially 'listen in' on a conversation, even one I *don't* record, without consent from all parties or a warrant. The Constitution is deadly serious about privacy rights, Steph, and you know it. And I can't get a warrant because we still don't have any sort of probable cause to take the magistrate."

"But what if they need *help*?" she'd demanded. "We can't just send them in there without keeping an eye on them, Karl!"

"Didn't say we would," he'd assured her. "Just that there are limits on how we can do it."

He'd turned to Jessica and Cordelia.

"We can't listen in, but there's no reason you can't send out a ping on your uni-links if things get dicey," he'd reassured them. "Normally, I'd consider letting you go in alone to question a possible member of a drug gang a really bad idea, but Steph and I will be parked discreetly out of sight, ready to come to the rescue, the minute you ping. And you won't be alone, anyway. You'll have Valiant and Athos with you. People who don't know 'cats tend to underestimate just how dangerous they can be when defending their friends."

"As I remember very well," Cordelia had said, reaching up to scratch Athos behind his ears.

On the drive over, she and Jessica talked about anything except drug gangs and treecats. This was the first time since they'd met that Cordelia had had an extended time to visit with the younger woman, and she found Jessica fascinating. Jessica had lived a hand-to-mouth existence much of her life, and she appreciated the stability her family was finding on Sphinx.

"I think even my dad is settling down. I was too young to realize it before, but I think a lot of his inability to hold down a job came from his feeling that—other than a paycheck—he didn't have a lot to gain from hard, steady work."

"There's something to be said for a paycheck, especially when you have a big family," Cordelia commented.

"True," Jessica agreed. "But I think that my dad was a big-hearted dreamer before Sphinx. Now that he sees that he can have *both* the paycheck and a chance to earn us a little place in the history of a new world, he's more content. There are so many 'firsts' still left: first one to discover a new plant or animal; to found a certain type of business; to build something. He's working harder than ever and he's happier than ever. Even if my bond to Valiant hadn't made it impossible for me to leave the Star Kingdom, I would never have taken Anders up on his offer. I want to be part of making a future here."

Cordelia had been really small when her dad had died, so she didn't precisely remember those days when her mom had done a bunch of data entry and other unglamorous work so she could bring in necessary extra cash and stay home with her own small children and the Kemper boys, but she'd heard the stories—especially when someone was careless with money.

Mom really was a hero. I don't think I ever realized just how much she did to keep our family going and together. Sure, she had a lot of support from the community, but at the end of the day, she got into a bed that should have held her husband, and fell asleep, wondering just when baby Natalie would start crying.

"How is it going with Anders?" she asked Jessica, hoping she wasn't treading on a delicate topic.

"Not too terrible." Jessica shrugged. "He's actually a really decent guy. His dad can make mine seem like a prize, so Anders has seen up close and personal how destructive only thinking about yourself and your own goals can be. I think Anders is about ready to start hanging out with the gang again, and I'm glad. Romance is all well and good, but friendship is better."

And romance and friendship would be best, Cordelia thought. *Let Dia Zivonik do the emo brooding. I want someone I can feel all tingly about, but also talk to and share interests with.*

She knew perfectly well that she'd been thinking about romance to keep her nerves in check, but now that the air car was approaching Mr. Ack's, she had to focus on Herman—odd, nerdy Herman, who just might be dealing drugs.

Jessica was checking the handgun she had tucked in a pocket of her jacket. "I know you like Herman, Cordelia. Don't forget, though, even if he's completely innocent, he might be scared and scared people do stupid things."

Cordelia surveyed the area. "Gotcha. Parking field is empty. Herman's air car is around back where he keeps it, so likely he's in." She checked that her own gun was where she could get it, wondering if she could actually shoot someone she thought of as a friend. Herman wasn't exactly a near-weasel.

But if he attacked me or Jessica, he wouldn't be behaving very friend-like, would he?

They found Herman washing up his breakfast dishes. He blinked in surprise, but didn't seem particularly wary at their early arrival.

"Cordelia, what's up? Do you and your friend need something?" He did a double take when Valiant emerged from examining one of the small herb gardens Herman had started for his own use. "That isn't Athos, but you aren't Stephanie Harrington, so you must be Jessica Pheriss, right? From the fire season. Herman Maye, I'm pleased to meet you."

Jessica smiled and gave him a firm handshake. "Can we come in, Mr. Maye? We have a couple of things we'd like to talk to you about."

Herman glanced at the wall chronometer and nodded. "Sure. I have a bit of time before I need to begin my rounds of the propagation sheds. Come on in. I still have some coffee and the better part of a breakfast cake."

Cordelia felt relieved. She'd been worried they'd find Herman in one of the propagation buildings. She and Jessica would likely be invited in, but not the 'cats. Last night, the group had spent a lot of time discussing the best way to approach Herman, and in the end, they had all—with varying degrees of hesitation—agreed that a direct approach would be best.

Cordelia accepted the coffee Herman offered, lifted her mug to her lips, then realized she was too nervous to swallow, and set it down. "Herman, what can you tell us about the new drug that's contributing to the rise in accidents?"

Jessica added, "Some people are calling it baka bakari, because it makes you think stupid choices are perfectly reasonable."

They'd made up the name the night before, because giving the drug a name made it seem as if they were talking about something they were sure about, rather than something they weren't even sure existed.

They'd also discussed the next move, depending on Herman's reaction. The one thing no one had believed would happen was that Herman would completely crumple.

"Baka bakari!" Herman said, nearly falling back in his chair, setting down his coffee mug so unsteadily that the dark brown liquid sloshed over the sides and started to drip onto the floor. "They can't be branding it! I never agreed. It's all wrong!"

He's not only involved, Cordelia thought, amazed. *He's also in seriously over his head. I think we know who Nosey Jones got beaten up to warn what would happen if he talked about baka bakari.*

Jessica put on what Cordelia recognized as her bedside manner. "Hey, Herman. Why don't you tell us how you got into this? Maybe we can help you."

"They'll..." Herman began, and Cordelia would have bet anything that he had been about to say, "They'll hurt me" or "They'll kill me." But he impressed her by visibly stiffening his spine. "I'll tell you. I've been wanting to tell someone, but I didn't know if anyone realized that there *was* a drug. I've been cross-eyed afraid, but I couldn't see how I could both convince someone that there was a problem and admit I was part of it. I just didn't have it in me."

"Go ahead," Cordelia said, trying to seem calm and matter-of-fact, although she wanted to cheer "We've got a lead!" "Tell us. Maybe we can help you figure a way out."

12

HERMAN SWALLOWED SO HARD HIS ADAM'S APPLE rippled the skin on his throat. Then he leaned forward and, folding his hands between his knees, began talking.

"It goes back some T-months ago. I'd had a really busy day. I'd put the order together for the Câmaras' restaurant, and I thought I had enough time to grab a late lunch before Frank dropped by. You've got to understand, I work hard, really hard, and even my meals are often part of my work, because I use them to taste-test samples that we've cleared as nontoxic. On the day I'm telling you about, I'd intended to do just that, but I was rushed so I decided the systematic testing could wait until dinner or maybe the next day. So I hauled out my wok, splashed in some oil, and put together a stir-fry using a mixed batch of the samples. Frank arrived just as I was finishing up my cooking and, since I was just about starving, I invited him to join me for lunch."

Cordelia chuckled. "For a new recipe? Wow, you're braver than I am."

"I really *am* quite a good cook," Herman said,

relaxing slightly, "and I'd done a little sampling as I cooked, so I felt certain there was nothing that would taste horribly bitter or musty or anything. Actually, later, I wondered if even then the concoction was influencing me. One of the first things it does is mellow you out."

Mellow enough to want to have lunch with Frank Câmara? Cordelia thought. *That's amazing.*

"Anyhow, by the time we were done with lunch the drug—what did you call it? Baka bakari?"

Jessica laughed. Cordelia knew her well enough by now to know that the laugh was forced, but Herman didn't twig to it.

"That's Japanese for 'nothing more than an idiot,'" Jessica explained, not adding that Karl had come up with the name. His girlfriend Sumiko had been of Old Terran Japanese descent, and her family had been into preserving some of the language and traditions. "Most people wouldn't know that, though, so I'm guessing it's an inside joke."

"Well, it's a pretty good name," Herman said, growing serious once more, "because when Frank told me my cooking was terrific and asked if he could he have some leftovers, I gave them to him quite cheerfully. Normally, I'd never have done that, and when I—sobered up, came down—whatever term you prefer, I was horrified. I commed Frank and asked him to bring the leftovers back, since I hadn't finished my tests. Not only wouldn't he bring them back, he told me he'd already shared them with a friend, and he wanted more. When I protested, Frank offered to pay me, really generously. Since I had no idea, then at least, what sort of person he was, I agreed.

I was actually a little pleased, and even found myself thinking that maybe I could copyright the recipe and make something from it."

He shook his head, as if astonished by his own naïveté. "This went on for a while, a couple of weeks, maybe? We always have more mushrooms than we can use, which is why we started selling the safe ones. I was pleased to be making some extra money—Glynis pays me a good salary, but this job won't last forever—and I felt clever for making money off of what would have otherwise been discards."

"Were you still regularly eating your special stir-fry?" Cordelia asked, carefully avoiding the drug-related name.

"I was," Herman admitted. "A fair amount, actually, because as long as I was supplying Frank, I might as well not cook twice."

"Did Frank always ask for you to cook it for him?" Jessica asked. "Or did he ask for the ingredients so he could make it himself?"

"It might seem odd," Herman said, "given the family business, but Frank doesn't like to cook."

"I get that," Jessica said. "Kids either seem to follow what their folks do or reject it entirely. Frank definitely strikes me as a rejecter."

Or reject, Cordelia thought.

"So," Herman said, obviously forcing himself back to the subject, "let's fast-forward. Frank started asking for more special stir-fry. Several times, I had to tell him he couldn't have any, because one or another of the mushroom crops needed to replenish. That's when Frank started asking just which mushroom created that nice mellow feeling, hinting that maybe he could just buy some of those. I had to admit, I didn't know. I'd been curious myself, see? By then, I'd cooked each type separately, and none of them on their own created the buzz. Frank didn't believe me, and insisted on coming over for a taste test. Well, by then, I was beginning to realize that he was the sort of spoiled rich kid who, if his folks weren't so well off, would be called a 'bully,' but because they are pillars of the community is instead said to be 'strong-willed' and 'someone who knows his own mind.' When we did the taste test, I changed the names of as many of the mushrooms as I could, because I didn't want him to try making the stir-fry himself. I didn't need to bother. He just ate each one and got increasingly peeved when none gave him a buzz."

Jessica grinned. "I believe I heard Frank described as 'strong-willed' myself, back in the days when I was hanging out with Trudy Franchitti and her gang. Frank's best friend, Stan, is Trudy's beau, and a couple of times I got set up with Frank. Not my best memories ever. He definitely knows his own mind and isn't happy when you don't want to do what he wants."

Encouraged by being believed, Herman hurried to conclude his tale of woe. "So, clearly, the mellow feeling was caused by an interaction between one of more of the ingredients in my stir-fry. The thing is, I didn't know—I still *don't* know—which ones. I can't even eliminate the cooking process. An all-fresh batch didn't do it."

"Did you use meat?" Cordelia asked. "I don't think you mentioned that?"

"I didn't," Herman said. "I'm pretty much a vegetarian, actually. Fungi can provide an amazing variety of nutrients, including proteins. And I love tofu."

Cordelia nodded gravely, although she'd never been very enthusiastic about vegetarianism. She wasn't Stephanie, whose genetically modified metabolism made low-calorie food unappealing, to say the least, but she *did* agree with Stephanie about tofu. The only tofu she liked was in a frozen dessert, and that only as long as it was served as part of a sundae, with at least chocolate sauce and whipped cream.

Herman went on. "When Frank started pressuring me to find out which combination created the happy, mellow euphoria, I realized that I was in trouble. As long as I could fool myself that he was just sharing with a few friends, I felt fine about taking his money and cooking party foods. When I realized that he was probably selling it, then I started getting scared. I got more scared after Frank mentioned in passing that one of the kids who'd had a weird accident—that skimmer dude—was someone he knew from another club. I started wondering if, all unintentionally, I might have been complicit."

He unfolded his hands and slurped deeply from his rapidly cooling mug of coffee.

"You didn't realize you'd created a new drug," Cordelia said sternly, "one that was perfectly legal, because no one realized that it existed, but nonetheless could be dangerous?"

"I didn't think about it that way," Herman protested, gripping the mug. "People brew beer or make wine out of all sorts of astonishing things. No one calls the end result 'drugs,' even when they're pretty high proof. I didn't think I was making a drug, just a meal with a nice extra spice."

His shifting gaze gave lie to his words, but Cordelia

didn't push him. While Herman might be the source, he wasn't the problem, she realized. What if she called Karl or Stephanie in, and they ordered him to stop dealing with Frank? Would that be enough to stop the problem?

Probably not, she reflected. *Frank was there for at least one sampling session. He might have a harder time finding some of the ingredients, but given that his dad's in the food business, it would be easier for him than for a lot of people. I hate it, but we've got to let this go on, at least a little longer.*

"So, how's your analysis going?" Jessica asked, very much the inquiring young scientist. "You told us that cooking was necessary. Does dehydration change the effect?"

Herman nodded. "Raw ingredients dehydrated remain inert or, at best, provide a slight glow. Something in the heating process either releases the chemicals or changes them or something. The problem is, I'm not enough of a pharmaceutical chemist to know what to look for."

"That's a pain," Jessica said sympathetically. "It's like analyzing traditional herbal remedies—something my mom really got into. A lot of those traditional remedies work, but unreliably, because maybe a certain herb is more potent when harvested at a certain time of the year. Maybe the original directions say to harvest in the 'dark of a summer moon' and this gets changed to 'dark of the moon.' There are also cautions about using certain tools or even who can do the harvesting. Like with when to harvest, those cautions may have made sense originally. Saying 'should only be harvested by a nimble-fingered maiden between the ages of ten and twelve' might simply have meant 'small fingers and a light touch,' but over time it gets changed to a 'delicate virgin' and the actual, perfectly practical, directions get lost."

Conversation went on in this vein for a time, with Jessica eliciting details as to how Herman was methodically testing the various mushrooms in different combinations, how he was beginning to suspect that one or more of his spices might be providing a contributing element. They were discussing the medical properties of capsicum when a tone sounded over the bone conductor mics Karl had insisted both young women wear.

"There's an incoming air van on my cruiser's sensors," Karl said over them. "Its transponder is registered to Câmara Comestibles. I'm willing to bet it's Frank." Cordelia and Jessica glanced quickly at one another. Karl and Stephanie might be legally barred from listening to their conversation, which meant they hadn't heard Herman's confirmation of Frank's involvement, but from his tone, he clearly didn't think Frank "just happened" to be flying in.

"Whoever it is," he continued, "it's coming in fast enough that I don't think you could clear out before it lands—even if that wouldn't make Herman wonder if you'd been warned. But I don't want you two hanging around *after* he lands, either. So why don't you start making your excuses now?"

"Do we move in?" Stephanie said from her own place beside him in the cruiser, feeling every muscle in her body tighten with the desire to be there to help her friends.

"Not until Frank's on the parking field," Karl replied. "Then I'll ease us closer, using the forest canopy for cover. Hopefully, we won't be needed."

"I *hate* waiting," Stephanie said from between clenched teeth.

"But you can do it," Karl reached over and patted her arm. "We both know that."

Meanwhile, Cordelia had glanced at the chronometer, and interrupted the increasingly technical discussion between Herman and Jessica—a conversation in which Jessica had held up her part, even as Karl's briefing had come through.

"Hey, Jess, I just got a look at the time. Didn't you say you had to meet your mom and then go by the hospital? If we don't hurry, we're going to need to six-leg it to get you there in time. Remember, we're not in Twin Forks."

Jessica jumped to her feet. "Ooh . . . Am I going to get it. Thanks for talking with us, Herman."

"You've given me a lot to consider," Herman said. "Maybe we can talk again."

He was walking them toward the parking area when, turning a bend in the path, they would have slammed directly into Frank Câmara if Valiant, pacing them along the rooftops, hadn't bleeked warning. Cordelia and Jessica pulled up short, so fast that Herman nearly ran into their backs. He was starting to say something when he saw Frank and the words vanished.

"Frank!" Jessica said, giving the burly young man a playful swat. "Still rushing from place to place. I never would have expected to see *you* here."

Frank managed to regain his cool with a swiftness that would have done credit to the maître d' of his father's most expensive restaurant.

"Hey, Jess. What brings you here at such an early hour?"

"Hanging with Cordelia," she said. "Cordelia's brothers asked her to drop off a few things they'd fixed. I came along because I'd heard how amazing this place was. I think these buildings are *so* cute! Don't you?"

"They're all right," Frank said. "Kinda weird, really."

Karl's SFS cruiser lingered in hover, just below the treeline, while Stephanie watched the conversation on its directional camera. Now she melted in relief as Jessica swatted Frank.

"Jess is going to get them out of there. She always was cool-headed. Even the short time she's been working at the hospital has added to that. I think we can relax."

"For now," Karl said, looking worried. "But Frank isn't stupid, for all he acts like a hulking gorilla. If he started remembering that Jessica and Cordelia both know us—if even only because of the treecats—Herman Maye could find himself getting a Nosey Jones style warning."

"Certainly nothing like that," Stephanie protested. "They need him."

"I wish I could put cameras up here like we did at Nosey's," Karl said, "but we'd need permission."

"Can't you just ask Mack and Zack Kemper?" Stephanie was asking, when Cordelia and Jessica pulled up alongside Karl's cruiser.

"Let's get out of here," Stephanie said over her uni-link. Then, leaving the connection open, she repeated her question. "Can't you just ask Mack and Zack Kemper if we could put observation cameras around the place? It's their land."

"That's a legal gray area, at absolute best," Karl said just a bit repressively, "as I'm certain you remember from our law classes on Manticore. Yes, the Kemper boys own the land, but Glynis is the tenant and Herman is her representative. Ask Jessica how she'd feel if the Franchittis gave the SFS permission to put a remote watch on her family's house, especially if they had done nothing at all illegal."

"Seriously creeped out," Jessica responded. "But Karl, Stephanie doesn't want to spy on Herman. You and she want to keep him safe."

"And with good reason." Karl nodded. "We can ask the Chief about it—we have to brief him on this fungus cocktail of Herman's, anyway. He may be able to give us a little more insight. Like I've said, we probably *could* get a warrant to set up surveillance if we had evidence a crime had been committed. But we don't—not really—so I'm pretty sure we'd have to have Herman's permission even if Chief Shelton thinks it would be a good idea."

"Should we just go ahead and ask him, then?" Jessica asked.

"I . . . don't think so," Karl said slowly. "While I agree with you that Herman seemed to be lying to himself about just how complicit he is, that doesn't mean he isn't actually perfectly aware of it. Maybe he's an excellent liar. Maybe at this very moment, rather than him being intimidated by Frank, they're actually collaborating on how to keep fooling the stupid kids. If I felt absolutely certain about Herman, I'd ask him if he'd mind if we put up surveillance equipment, but I don't."

"What if," Stephanie said, thinking out loud, "we put the cameras where they could observe the area, but not exactly Mr. Ack's? So we could see what vehicles were approaching, like that?"

"Still a gray area," Karl replied, "especially with so little justification for doing so. Remember, Herman isn't doing anything illegal. That baka bakari he's making might never be made illegal. It might end up classified a permissible recreational drug, like alcohol or tobacco, or be ignored entirely."

"We could put them up for an SFS study, tracking wood rats or something, and they could 'just happen' to be placed to cover the parking apron," Stephanie suggested.

"And if any imagery they captured ended up being part of a criminal prosecution, the defense counsel would subpoena the paperwork on the study." Karl shook his head. "Since there wouldn't be any, he'd argue—correctly, by the way—that the real purpose had been to set up an illegal surveillance, which would automatically make anything we learned from it—directly or indirectly—inadmissible in court. Not going to happen, Steph."

"But . . ."

"Stephanie," Karl said more sternly, "just accept that this is one of those times when you can't go by your 'It's better to ask forgiveness than permission' creed. Maybe you need to remember there are reasons for rules, even for clever people like you. Anyhow, you're not eleven anymore."

Stephanie nodded, knowing that he was perfectly right, adding silently to herself, *But things were a lot easier when I was.*

✧ ✧ ✧

Although the night air was crisp, Heart Stone chose not to wear the made-fur that Life Shaper had given him when he went out to explore. The made-thing was very useful for keeping him warm during those times that he was sitting still, working on a scraper or knife, but it did have an annoying habit of collecting bits of twigs and leaves in a manner his natural coat did not.

Earlier that afternoon, there had been a large gathering at Second Nest, one attended by many two-legs, some of whom Heart Stone recognized as visitors to Life Shaper's home, including several young males who seemed to have interest in bonding with some of Life Shaper's littermates, or so he speculated, based on behaviors he had witnessed when the pairs thought themselves unobserved.

Climbs Quickly and Fierce Fighter had come to the gathering, as had Sharp Sight and Determined Defender. Even Plant Fancier and Feels Strongly had come. Heart Stone had spent a very enjoyable time helping the quiet plant-loving Person tuck a variety of little tubers into sheltered areas near the bases of various trees. When the right season came, these would blossom forth, with the added benefit of providing tasty treats for the two-legs. Only Strikes Like Lightning and Flame Crest had not joined the festivities, but this was not uncommon. They lived very far away, and Heart Stone had gathered that Flame Crest's calling as a healer kept him very busy.

All in all, it had been a pleasant day. When night drew on, the guests departed, leaving Life Shaper and her littermates to finish restoring order to the friendly chaos. Well-fed and guessing, based upon the presence of the carry-thing that Life Shaper brought with her whenever they were going to be long from the central nesting place, that she was sleeping here tonight, Heart Stone set out to explore.

During their many other visits, he had familiarized himself with the immediate area around Second Nest, but had not ventured too far because—especially after the intrusion of Stench—he had not liked to leave Life Shaper unguarded. Tonight, he felt free to range farther. One of the great problems with always going places in the flying thing was that he had no clear idea how various important places were situated in relation to each other. Based on travel time, he knew that three places—Life Shaper's central nesting place; this secondary nesting place; and the Rich Dirt Grove—were, as the flying thing flew, closer to each other than many of the others.

From his explorations of the area after he had left Bright Water, he had a sense of the relationship between Second Nest and Central Nest. Tonight's goal was figuring out the relative position of Second Nest and Rich Dirt Grove. For all that Rich Dirt Grove had many structures, he knew it was a newly built place, having watched Life Shaper and her friends help create one of the structures in an amazingly short period of time.

An added benefit of his exploration would be testing how great a distance he was comfortable going away from Life Shaper—something that would be useful to know if he did decide to accept Sings Truly's invitation to visit Bright Water. In his youth, like many male People, Heart Stone had been a hunter. Even after he had discovered his passion for working in stone, he had often gone to hunt for food for his family. Although the clan would have been happy to support him in exchange for his stone work and his teaching the art to others, he liked feeling he had not completely lost his touch.

One of the advantages to being an older Person was that the distance one could travel from one's mate tended to increase with the length and complexity of the relationship. Having young also often strengthened the bond. Mind singers speculated this was because when the female was nursing a pair's kits, she had to remain behind while her mate did all of the hunting. For these reasons, before the gray death had taken his Golden Eye, the then Stone Shaper had been able to range quite widely without the least anxiety.

Is that why I left my voice behind when I nearly followed Golden Eye into death? Heart Stone wondered. *Perhaps I called after her until I had worn my voice thin into breaking, but the glow of her passionate desire that I live after her kept my mind-glow alive.*

Life Shaper had a powerful mind-glow, as, he had noticed, did each of the two-legs who had bonded with a Person. The mind-glows were different, even as the colors in a rainbow were different. If mind-glows were colors, Fierce Fighter's would be a brilliant yellow. Determined Defender's would be the deep violet that is least often seen but most beautiful when glimpsed. And Life Shaper's? Red, perhaps, or bright orange, like a warming fire. Whatever the "color," her mind-glow did not fade as Stone Shaper leapt from tree to tree in a gradually expanding exploratory spiral. He chose this pattern rather than a straight line because, although he was confident of the direction in which Rich Dirt Grove lay, based upon the times they had taken a flying thing there from this point, he enjoyed creating a mental map of what he felt was part of his new territory, if for no other reason than that no other People were currently using it.

The area proved very interesting. Here and there, he found definite indications that two-legs had once dwelt in the area in larger numbers—quite possibly the reason no clan had settled in such a pleasant area. He was not Plant Fancier to have carefully studied plants, but People did eat nuts and berries as well as fresh meat, so he had some sense of how long it took some of the faster growers to spread. Based upon that, he guessed that the time when many two-legs had lived here was long enough gone that Air Dancer, Life Shaper's youngest sister, might well have been a squalling kit.

Although the People had not chosen to show themselves to the two-legs, that did not mean that some of the bolder scouts had not watched them. Heart Stone recalled memory songs, shared when he had still been Stone Shaper, of a great sickness among the two-legs. Some People had speculated that at the rate they were dying, they might soon vanish from the People's lands.

A *plague, then,* Heart Stone thought, *one that may have killed some of Life Shaper's clan. Our hearts have sung similar songs of loss, our spirits have had to learn how to live when dying would have been easier than grief. No wonder we meshed so simply. We are alike in other ways than in that we both chose to fight a battle when the odds were so against us.*

Even as he grieved that Life Shaper, who he gathered was not among the oldest of her clan, should have suffered so much, Heart Stone felt happy to know that if they had both possessed mind-voices, they would have discovered shared experiences beyond those that had brought them together.

Life Shaper's mind-glow was still a strong fire, if perhaps one that flickered a bit with distance, when Heart Stone scented the unmistakable scent of Rich Dirt Grove. It was not an unpleasant scent: rich and loamy, damp, promising tasty bark chewers, interesting insects and grubs, and the sort of rot that meant new growth, rather than sickness and death.

He angled toward it, and was on the outskirts, near where Mends Things and Colorful Splotches had built a thing that put dirt into carry bags, when he heard the hootings of two-legs in contention. When he had been broken Stone, foraging among the leavings of the two-legs for tools and bits of food, this would have been a signal to flee, but he was Heart Stone now, and he thought that the thinner, shriller hooting and howling belonged to Rich Dirt Grove's resident, and Life Shaper's friend, Musty. The other...

He sniffed the air and the fur along his spine rose as he caught the unmistakable odor of Stench. Two males clashing. That was as natural as night following day. Even among the People the ability to share feelings and thoughts did not eliminate disagreement. Among those many creatures who did not use mind-speech, disagreement frequently culminated in violence. And, as Sharp Sight's scars showed, even among the People disagreements could degenerate into physical violence.

Heart Stone considered fleeing the budding conflict, but a shift in the wind brought him the scent of other two-legs. Stench hadn't come alone. This was worrisome. Two-legs seemed to be largely diurnal, so several two-legs coming together well after dark to a place where one two-leg lived alone did not bode well for the solitary two-leg.

Heart Stone felt a growl rising unbidden deep within his throat. He knew how it felt to be alone, facing off attackers without a clan to call upon. He'd survived, but sometimes just barely. Moreover, this was Musty's territory. Was Stench trying to drive him away from it and had brought herd members to aid him? Having Stench settle so close to where Life Shaper's clan nested seemed like a very bad idea.

Despite the ingrained caution that had kept him alive during the many season turnings of his self-imposed exile from Bright Water Clan, Heart Stone crept closer. He knew what he was doing was dangerous. The healing scars on his battered hide reminded him of the cost the last time he had decided to assist a two-leg, but he didn't hesitate.

And this time I am not alone. Life Shaper and I are bonded. If she is not asleep, she will feel my mind-glow. Knowing her, she will be concerned.

Springing lightly from tree limb to tree limb, Heart Stone came to where he could get a better view of what the two-legs were about. There were a hand plus one in all, not including Musty, who stood a bit apart. One of the intruders was smaller than the others—all of whom were much larger than Musty, and reeked of excitement and malice—and one particularly large one stood near the dirt-eating thing. That one had his—Heart Stone felt fairly certain that this one was a male—foot raised, resting on the edge of the thing, pushing just hard enough to rock it. Musty was making mouth noises at him, frantic and rapid, so that Heart Stone did not believe that what Kicker did was at Musty's request or to his liking.

Stench stood a short distance away, beside and

slightly behind the smallest of the two legs. Heart Stone was still learning two-leg body language, but he thought that this position meant that Stench was subtly deferring to this other. That was interesting, given that most of the time Stench swaggered like a horn blade in rut. From this, Heart Stone decided Little was probably the leader, perhaps a female as dominant as any old memory singer.

The two remaining two-legs seemed content at this point to stand back and let Little, Stench, and Kicker interact with Musty, but they were no less a threat. Musty was outnumbered, and one did not need to be as experienced in life as was Heart Stone to understand what was happening.

Little wanted Musty to do something—probably give over this nesting place into which he had put so much labor. Musty did not wish to do so. Little was escalating the conflict, threatening the thing that bundled the dirt, and using Kicker as her extra legs. Stench's role was less certain. Did he belong to Little's clan? If so, he was a very junior member. Perhaps he was present because he had been the scout who interacted with Musty to prepare for this hunt.

In the distance, Heart Stone felt a warmth that told him that Life Shaper was awake and aware of the shift in his mind-glow. That was good, although he hoped she would not come out into the night alone. Nonetheless, he did not dampen his apprehension or his determination. He did not wish to frighten her, but she should know that this was a problematic situation.

Below, Kicker rocked the dirt bundling thing harder, so that it swayed like a branch in the wind. The shiny legs creaked in protest as they strained against their anchored feet. Musty wailed in frustration or fear or both.

Life Shaper's brothers made that thing, Heart Stone thought. *They were very pleased that day. I don't think they would be happy if Kicker broke it. Perhaps I can at least stop that. Life Shaper is definitely coming, but if I wait she may arrive to find her friend driven from his home. That would not do.*

Mind made up, Heart Stone rippled the length of his spine down to the tip of his tail. Then, pushing off from the tree limb, he leapt down into the midst of the warring two-legs.

13

CORDELIA SPRAWLED HAPPILY ON THE RUG IN FRONT of the big fireplace in the high-ceiled living room of the Kemper residence. Today's housewarming party had been a tremendous success. Now she enjoyed the pleasant feeling of having worked hard, hit all the marks, and earned her rest.

Mack and Zack wouldn't be completely moving out of the Schardt-Cordova home for quite a while to come. The housewarming celebration had been more to mark the long vacant house as ready for occupation. It was likely they would move in stages. Doubtless Mack and his new beau, Brad Abrazo, a handsome, olive-skinned youth who, despite being a computer game wizard, was not in the least adverse to hard physical labor, would start spending more times alone together here.

At this moment, Brad and Mack were cuddling on one of the reupholstered sofas, softly talking. From the stray words Cordelia caught, they were discussing their very ambitious plans to set up a custom fabrication facility in what had originally been built as a livestock barn. The idea sounded like a good one to her. Ranching on Sphinx, with its long winters, was not feasible as a small business. The outlay for winter feed alone could be shockingly high.

Zack was half-drowsing on the other sofa, gloating over a colorful box of paint tubes. Danette had presented these to him to encourage him to follow through with setting up an art studio in one of the many vacant rooms, then more seriously pursuing his long-held dream of a sideline in landscape and portrait painting. Marjorie Harrington, who had attended the party with Stephanie and Richard, had promised Zack art lessons, an extra gift, in addition to the flat of hardy Sphinx-adapted herbs that had been the Harringtons' housewarming present.

Cordelia stretched luxuriously, pillowing her head on her arms as she considered whether the effort of migrating up to the guest room that was hers for as long as she wanted to use it was worth the effort. Maybe a nap here, first . . .

As her eyes drifted shut, she reached for that awareness of Athos that had been with her since that first miraculous awakening in the vet clinic. There he was, somewhat more distant than usual, but close enough that she felt no panic or anxiety. She let her mind unfocus, more testing her nearness to sleep than seeking the treecat. In that uncluttered mental space her sense of what he was feeling came more strongly.

Athos was curious, worried, something else . . . Cordelia felt uneasy. He wasn't angry. Not precisely. Defensive? Not quite. Ready to defend?? Keeping her eyes shut was an effort, but she did so rather than break the fragile awareness. She pretty much always knew in what direction Athos was in relation to her, but she couldn't see through his eyes or any of those pretty storybook conventions. Even Stephanie, who had a tremendous rapport with Lionheart, admitted she often had to guess what was feeding the emotions she felt through their bond.

Eyes shut, mind racing, Cordelia considered. Maybe it was just extreme distance panic, nothing more, but she no longer felt in the least drowsy. What she wanted to do was jump up, toss on outdoor clothes, and race in the direction where Athos was until she had reassured herself that he was okay. That would be pure stupidity, even worse than refusing to set the fall alert on her uni-link. Even in relatively settled areas, Sphinx had plenty of predators, and the Kemper hold was far from settled. And, if Athos was defending something, that argued there was something threatening to attack.

How to handle this? she thought, mind twisting through mazes of possibilities and rejecting most half-formed. *How to get at least Zack to come with me without giving away that I have this link to Athos? I might trust the boys in a pinch, but Brad—sweet as he is—is still more or less a stranger.*

The tempest of ideas seemed to take hours, but in reality they took only long enough for her to open her eyes, and get to her feet.

"I'm going to find Athos," she said, trying to sound casual. "I want to make sure I know where he is before I go to bed."

Zack looked at her quizzically. He'd always been sensitive to nuances of mood. Mack blamed it on his younger brother's artistic temperament, but Cordelia thought it had more to do with being a younger sibling, careful to judge the moods of his elders.

"I'll come with you," he said. "It's pretty dark out."

Mack frowned, obviously unwilling to uncuddle, but equally unwilling to let his recently injured sister and sixteen-year-old brother go out alone.

"If Athos doesn't come back when you call," he said, "don't go wandering off into the woods with just Zack."

"Agreed," Brad added, running a finger along Mack's jawbone. "Besides, a walk in the woods by starlight would be very romantic."

Cordelia was grateful. She tossed on her jacket, grabbed her rifle by reflex, made sure the fall alert was set on her uni-link, and tried to look casual as she headed outside. Zack snatched up his shotgun as he followed her. As the door shut, she heard Mack and Brad getting up off the sofa.

No questions, though. The Great Treecat Conspiracy might be semiofficial, but just about everyone on Sphinx realized that treecats were at the very least the most interesting wildlife located so far, and, maybe a whole lot more. Having one to foster was a serious responsibility, one that was embraced by not just the bonded human, but—at least so far—by the entire family.

Athos didn't answer when Cordelia called. She confirmed her sense of what direction he might have gone, then had an inspiration as sudden as she was certain it was correct.

"I wonder," she said, "if he's gone to Mr. Ack's? He really likes poking around there, and I saw him fussing at Herman at the party, as if wondering if Herman had brought him a treat."

The last was pure fabrication, but there had been so many people wandering all over the house and grounds during the housewarming, admiring what the Kempers and Schardt-Cordovas had achieved and making offers of further help, that there was no way Zack would know for sure.

"We could hike over that way," Mack said, coming out onto the porch, Brad on his heels. "It's not that far, now that we've opened up a good trail since we're back and forth so often. We can call for Athos as we go."

Cordelia wanted to jump in an air car and get there as fast as possible, but there was no way she could justify that without revealing too much. She considered using her formerly injured ankle as an excuse, but that would definitely make the boys suspicious.

"Sounds good," she said, heading for the trail and calling Athos's name. "He'll probably hear us and come romping over, showing off whatever he was eating or a new rock for his collection."

But Athos didn't show up as they tromped along the trail through the towering Sphinxian forest. Something of Cordelia's sense of urgency must have communicated itself to her brothers because neither Mack nor Zack made any of the sensible suggestions she feared: that they go back and check in another direction, or call the Schardt-Cordova house to make sure Athos hadn't gone "home," or split into two groups so they could cover more ground.

I wonder just how much the boys have guessed, Cordelia thought. *Certainly they would have noticed that Athos is never far from me, and that I always take him with me when I go somewhere. They're good guys, not asking awkward questions.*

The trail to Mr. Ack's ended near the parking area. They were still hidden within the shelter of the trees when Zack said, "Whose air van is that? I hope Herman doesn't have a sweetheart visiting. That could be embarrassing."

Cordelia looked, half-expecting the now-familiar Câmara Comestibles and Produce van, but this was a different vehicle, built for hauling passengers, not groceries. Its finish was a deep silvery gray that melded into the shadows. It lacked any of the personalization that most privately-owned vehicles on Sphinx acquired, as a result of their owners spending long hours in them, going between widely scattered destinations, so that vehicles became extensions of "home."

"*A rental maybe,*" Cordelia was about to say, when from a short distance away, a shout more of surprise than anger broke the stillness.

"What the blazes is that?"

At the same moment, Cordelia felt a surge of smug satisfaction along her link with Athos.

"That wasn't Herman's voice!" she said, wondering what trouble the treecat had gotten himself into. "C'mon!"

Not wanting to give herself away, Cordelia switched off her flashlight. The others did the same without question. Given how well Cordelia and the Kemper boys knew the layout of Mr. Ack's the pale glow from the lights along the paths were sufficient to guide them. Brad dropped to the back, letting them lead. Cordelia liked him even more for this unspoken evidence of support and trust.

If he and Mack stay together, I'll definitely dance at their wedding.

Happily for Cordelia and those with her, the outburst that had alerted the group as a whole that something unusual was going on had continued, providing them with both noise to cover their approach and a very neat distraction. They were still a distance away when a new voice spoke, a woman's, cool and authoritative.

"That's a treecat, Willinski. They were covered in your briefing."

A guffaw, then the first voice said, "No way! Treecats are fluffy, kinda cute. If that's a treecat, it's got a serious case of the mange."

Herman's voice, trembling but determined. "That's Athos. He doesn't have mange. He was injured saving my landlords' sister from an attack by wild beasts."

Willinski barked another crude laugh. "And now the little fuzzy has come to save you?" There was a creak of protesting metal. "Save yourself and keep the beast from getting shot. Quesk won't miss at this close range. Tell Dr. Orgeson what she wants to know and we'll be on our way. Don't tell, and you'll be explaining to your landlords how a valuable piece of equipment got busted and their sis's pet got hurt."

Cordelia wanted to race forward, but she didn't need Zack's hand on her arm to remind her that at least one of the people threatening Herman and Athos had a gun at the ready. Her mind raced, and she came up with a plan. There was no way to brief the others, but Mack and Zack were her brothers, and they'd played a lot of games together. She's just have to hope they'd take her cue.

"I heard something over this way," she said, pitching her voice so that it sounded as if she was farther away. "I bet Athos is over near the compost heap. There are all sorts of wood rats there that he likes to hunt."

The three young men all had their firearms out and

readied. Mack nodded crisply, a gesture that said, *Go for it! We'll cover you.*

Cordelia swallowed over a sudden lump in her throat and called, "Athos? Athos? I've got some celery for you, boy! Time to come in for the night."

"Bleek!" came the instant reply. "Bleek! Bleek!"

Lowered voices, then Herman called, his voice tight. "Cordelia? Over here, by the compost heap. Athos and I were doing varmint control when some late visitors arrived."

Very neat, Cordelia thought. *I bet someone fed him the lines. That doesn't sound in the least like Herman.*

"Oh! That's whose air van we saw."

"We?" Herman's voice squeaked on the single syllable.

"My brothers and Brad are with me. When I said I was going out to try and get Athos to come in for the night, they decided to come with me. Brad absolutely wouldn't believe us when we told him how Glynis decorated this place."

The exchange had brought them to the composting area. Cordelia bet anything that the pleasant, social scene before them bore no resemblance to the reality of a few moments before. Herman stood with his back to the compost bagger. Athos was perched nearby on the raised housing that protected whatever mysterious mechanical wonders Mack had cobbled together.

Facing them were four strangers—three men and a woman—and Frank Câmara. Despite their business attire, the three men's body language screamed "thug." Frank, acting as if they were all old buddies, set about making introductions—and it was telling that he only bothered to introduce one of his companions, a petite, neatly-coiffured woman in what Cordelia thought might be a fairly expensive suit.

"Hey, this is Dr. Lyric Orgeson. She's visiting Sphinx. Turns out she's really into mushrooms, and wanted to talk to Dr. Bonaventure, so I brought her out here, but there was just Herman, so we were getting ready to split."

As explanations went, it was thin, but Cordelia had no desire to push matters, not since it looked as if they just might be able to squirm out of this without anyone being shot. The boys hadn't put their firearms away, but then they *were* settlers on Sphinx, out for a stroll at night. Being unarmed would be far more unlikely. It helped that at this moment, Athos chose to come leaping over to nuzzle Cordelia's hand. Was it her imagination or did the curl of his whiskers and swish of his tail indicate more than just pleasure at seeing her? She could almost imagine him saying, "Yeah, right. You tell 'em, Frankie."

I am overtired, Cordelia thought as she pulled the stick of celery out of her pocket and gave it to him. *Just a cute little animal, boys and girls. No need to worry.*

"We'll take our leave now," Dr. Orgeson said. "Thank you, Herman, for showing us this fascinating facility. I will definitely be in touch."

With a nod to the new arrivals, she trotted toward the parking field, trailed by her thugs.

Because, no matter how neatly they were dressed, I have no doubt that's what they were. I'm going to need to update Steph and Karl before I sleep tonight.

"Oh, Cordelia, before you go," Herman said, sounding like the very bad actor he clearly was, "I have the excess butter-and-eggs I promised you at the housewarming. You might as well pick them up now, rather than me dropping them by in the morning."

"Thanks," Cordelia said. She didn't think they *quite* looked like they were seeing Dr. Orgeson and company off the grounds as they went along with Herman, but they certainly didn't step inside Herman's cottage until the rental air van had lifted off and sped in the direction of Twin Forks.

"Okay, Herman," Mack said once they had crowded into Herman's living room. "What was that about? We heard that Willinski threatening you, seems on Dr. Orgeson's behalf."

Herman glanced over at Cordelia, his pleading expression all but begging her to not tell the others about the baka bakari. She gave a slight nod, and, collapsing into a chair, he started talking.

"I know you think Glynis and I are completely nuts about fungi, but the fact is, they really are tremendously interesting and—unlike most living things—they can be grown in all sorts of different situations, as long as you know how."

"Yes," Mack said patiently. "We could probably qualify as graduate assistants in mycology by now. Go on. We didn't get the impression that Dr. Orgeson was here on a friendly scientific visit."

"Scientific, yes," Herman said. "Friendly, no. She wanted me to turn over our research—and some samples—related to some very interesting fungi native to Sphinx that, if we can work out the right supplementary medium, could augment or even pretty much replace the waste recycling hardware aboard spacecraft and orbital platforms. These have the capacity to transform and cleanse both organic and nonorganic waste, and they're very efficient. Even better, they can do so leaving very little excess beyond their own fruiting bodies behind. The cleansing beds would probably require a little more volume than the hardware they'd replace, but their fruiting bodies are compact and, if not exactly tasty, can serve untreated as edible matter. Fed into a synthesizer, they could provide a supplemental food supply."

Brad gave a low, musical whistle. "That would be remarkable. A great deal is already done with hydroponics tied into the life support systems, but fungi like that—something that killed two birds with one stone—could be worth a bundle! This Dr. Orgeson learned about it somehow?"

"We thought our database was secure," Herman said, more relaxed now that he knew Cordelia wasn't going to give him away. "But either it isn't or someone who had access spoke more freely than they should have. In any case, Dr. Orgeson saw the potential where—much as it pains me to speak ill of my employer—for Dr. Bonaventure this fungus is just one of many wonderful discoveries we've made."

And I bet Herman's telling the truth about this poop-to-produce fungus, Cordelia thought, amused now that she was no longer scared. *He wouldn't dare make up something like this. And I know that his frustration with Dr. Bonaventure's love for discovery rather than the tedious work of analysis and development is real. The best lies are mostly true.*

"So they were threatening you?" Zack asked. "That seems stupid."

Herman shrugged, got to his feet, and unasked,

started pouring tall glasses of a slightly fizzy beverage that tasted rather like a mixture of apple cider and lemonade, but was actually the by-product of a fungus grown in vinegar. "Zip" was already on the market as a wholesome health drink, low calorie, high in nutrients, but very few people knew just how it was made.

"It was stupid," Herman agreed, "and they didn't start that way. First were compliments to our work. Then a request for samples. Then, when I said I wasn't cleared to give samples out—and was even unwise enough to indicate that we didn't know enough to make sharing safe or prudent—Dr. Orgeson offered me a very lucrative position on her staff."

The look Herman gave Cordelia as he handed her a tumbler full of Zip said, *"This is true, except substitute baka bakari."*

Cordelia thanked him and said, "You must have been really tempted."

"I was," Herman admitted, "but not enough to screw over people, like Dr. Bonaventure, who've given me a break. I said I'd need to consult with her first. Then, well, the velvet glove proved to have an iron fist inside. When the job offer came up, I'd been giving them a tour of the grounds. I'd told them about how Mack and Zack had built our compost bagger, then that Willinski suggested that jury-rigged equipment was so vulnerable, and very difficult to replace. Things were getting a little rough when Athos came plummeting down from the trees like a *deus ex machina* in a melodrama. You folks showed up not long after."

"And we're glad we did," Cordelia said firmly. "I bet Athos thought those people were trying to horn in on one of his favorite hunting grounds, and decided to defend both it and you. We don't know a lot about treecats, but they surely understand the concept of the hand that grows the celery or makes the nice, smelly dirt that attracts the wood rats."

"Herman, you can't stay here alone," Zack said firmly.

Herman looked nervous. Cordelia bet he hadn't thought beyond how he'd explain the basics. "You're right. But I don't want to leave GBMRAC. I'm responsible for it."

"Then I'll stay with you," Zack said. "You're probably right that you won't be bothered again tonight but, after this, no more one person at the facility, at least at night."

Mack nodded crisply, like someone far older than his eighteen years. "We'll talk with Dr. Bonaventure. It was one thing to leave you alone here when this was a two-building operation, but now that you have valuable samples, she needs to think differently."

"And it wouldn't be a bad idea," Brad added, "to get a security system up, both visual and alarms. Happens I know someone who can do the work on the cheap because he likes a certain Mack Kemper."

His wickedly playful grin left no doubt that he was speaking about himself.

By the time they started the walk home, minus Zack to whom Herman was lending pajamas and a toothbrush, Cordelia was physically tired, but her mind was racing. Up in her room, under Athos's watchful green gaze, she put together a report to send to the members of the Great Treecat Conspiracy.

"There's been a development," she began, supplying details. She ended, "We should meet."

✧ ✧ ✧

"Well," Stephanie said, "at least now we have surveillance on Herman, and completely legal, too."

She, Karl, and Cordelia had met in Twin Forks at midafternoon of the day following Cordelia's report on recent events at Mr. Ack's. The lunchtime rush was over, so they had the "treecat friendly" side room of the Red Letter Café to themselves. All three had ordered milkshakes. Stephanie had a large slice of cheesecake, too. The three treecats were up in the boughs of the artificial picketwood Eric Flint had recently installed along the walls, a furnishing that not only made them more comfortable, but also limited where they dropped bits of whatever snack they were enjoying. There was even a hatch near the ceiling that the 'cats could use to let themselves in and out.

"We do," Karl agreed. "And I had another thought last night. I was thinking about the way Herman admitted to Cordy that he's the original source for baka bakari, but he's not having any luck figuring out why it has the effect it has. Well, now that we know where it's coming from, I think he needs to cook up a little batch for *us*."

"What?" Stephanie blinked. "Why?"

"Because I want to send it back to Landing." Karl's expression was grimmer than it had been a moment before. "I'd like to get some of it to Scott, right here on Sphinx, but I bet Dr. Flouret knows somebody—probably right there at the university—who could analyze it for us, maybe even give us some idea about the 'why' and the 'how.'"

"That's a great idea!" Stephanie said, then grinned as she saw Cordelia's perplexed expression.

"Sorry! Karl's talking about Dr. Flouret—Mordecai

Flouret—the head of the Forensics Department at Landing University. We met him when Chief Shelton sent us off for forestry training last T-year. If anybody would know who to have look at this stuff, it's him."

"I don't know how happy Herman would be about that," Cordelia said. "When I went over to talk with him this morning, he wanted to refuse to have anything more to do with Frank or any of Frank's associates. I finally convinced him that it was too late to hope that burying his head in the dirt would make the problem go away, but I don't think he wants to get any deeper—or admit anything else to anyone else—unless he has to. I talked him out of trying to back out by pointing out this isn't about one druggy teen anymore. He was already nervous, but that's a lot heavier than anything he'd thought he was mixed up in, even now. I don't think he'll want to go official about this—even with you two—or be handing over samples of his stuff and officially admitting what's been going on."

"He's going to have to," Karl said, so firmly even Stephanie looked at him in surprise.

"Look," he told them, "we can't keep dancing around forever. I'm a sworn law officer—for that matter, Steph is, too, even if it's 'probationary' in her case. That means there are things we can do and things we *can't* do, especially where Herman's rights are concerned. But he's the one real lead we have, and we need to follow it up. I can justify not filing official paperwork on this—treat it as a 'confidential informant' sort of thing—so he doesn't have to come in and make any official statements. But we need to tell him what's going on, and we need to get him onboard with helping us. And I think what happened last night gives us an opening, if we approach it right. Dr. Orgeson clearly represents a group of some sort—probably the same that attacked Nosey. They aren't going to just take no for an answer and go away, whatever he wants, so if he doesn't want to end up facing some kind of drug syndicate on his own, he's going to need our help."

"A drug syndicate?" Stephanie said dubiously. "You really think that's who Orgeson is working for? Would Sphinx provide enough of a market to make it worth anyone's while?"

Cordelia sighed. "Steph, I'm glad you love Sphinx, but it's not a frontier paradise. Two major and several lesser waves of the Plague mean that anyone who's not among the recent immigrants is living with a history of loss, and loss of someone close to them."

"Like your dad," Stephanie said, "and both of the Kemper boys' parents."

"You see us 'coping.' Well, here're two things. One. 'Coping' doesn't mean an absence of grief or loss. My mom cries every holiday and on Dad's birthday. She's not mopey, she's not ungrateful for what she has, but you don't just put love 'behind you' like a bad haircut. And we're the lucky ones, because we can cope pretty well. But there are a lot of survivors who cope because, at the end of the day, they have a glass of something or a smoke or whatever."

"And baka bakari," Karl said, "especially if it was made more convenient to use, would be a perfect addition to the pharmacopeia. It might even be prescribed as a form of antidepressant. We're not necessarily looking at the dark-shades-wearing thugs of a crime holo, Steph. We're looking for people who smell money, and don't really care who they run over while on the trail of it."

"Are you saying, then," Stephanie said, "that Herman needs to go work for this Dr. Orgeson?"

"No," Karl said. "Oh, if I trusted her at all, I'd suggest exactly that. In fact, she'd be the logical person to be analyzing his samples for him . . . and us! But I *don't* trust her—not as far as I could throw her right here on Sphinx—because of the way she operates. If she really was a legit pharma person who'd somehow gotten wind of this, then she'd have gone to Glynis. This stinks. After I got Cordelia's message, I did a background check through the SFS. Nothing we can use. At least according to her official credentials, she has a doctorate in biology and is a representative of a company that's interested in investing in Sphinx."

"What about the other two names I got?" Cordelia asked. "Willinski and Quesk?"

"Both are listed as personal assistants, both have carry permits. No listed criminal records. Willinski was slow to pay off a few traffic violations on Manticore, but that's it. Orgeson's group is relatively small: seven people. That would account for the four last night and a few more."

"Did you tell Chief Shelton about them?" Jessica asked.

"Of course we did, and he's seeing if he can dig up anything more on her background. Not much more the SFS can do at this point. He agrees with us that Willinski and Quesk have to be the ones who beat up Nosey, but there's no way we could prove it. For that matter, Nosey still hasn't 'officially' changed his original story about what happened. The fact that they were directly threatening Herman confirms they were the ones who attacked him—and who their 'message' was meant for, for that matter—as far as the Chief is concerned. But it doesn't *prove* it in the legal sense. Not without imagery or at least someone else to corroborate Herman's version of what was said and done yesterday. It's too bad Athos can't talk! He's the only 'friendly witness' Herman had. Herman could still swear out a complaint, but it would be one of those he-said-they-said things. The magistrate would laugh us out of court without at least *some* supportive evidence, and that would leave Herman in an even more dangerous position with them."

Silence fell as they slurped milkshakes. Stephanie's cheesecake vanished in little delicious bites. As she ate, Stephanie contemplated "her" Sphinx in comparison to Cordelia's and Karl's. On one level, she was actually a little ashamed because—since the Plague had led to the recruitment program that had let her family acquire a large chunk of land, and help setting up new businesses—she, well, she hadn't exactly felt "friendly" toward it, but she'd thought of it in terms of benefits, not losses.

Now that she'd made friends among the long-time settler families, she was coming closer to understanding the other side. Maybe people like Jordan Franchitti were such zorks because they felt they'd paid for their lands and titles not only in money and time, but in the family members in the cemetery plot that just about every older homestead had.

Stephanie knew how devastated she'd be if she lost her parents to some natural disaster, but—like the Schardt-Cordovas, like the Zivoniks—she'd stay here. Sphinx was home.

Which brought her back to how they could deal with the people causing other people to get hurt right here in her home.

"I think you're right about approaching Herman openly and officially, Karl," she said. "And your idea about sending Dr. Flouret some baka bakari is a really good one. It'll probably take time—months, at least—for them to figure out anything definitive about it, but that only underlines the need to get them started as soon as possible. That's all in the future somewhere, though—assuming we can talk Herman into all this—so what do we do right now? Immediately? We can't tell Glynis Bonaventure what's going on without getting Herman into trouble, and we need Herman to keep doing what he's doing as bait. But we have to do *something*."

"I don't disagree, Steph. But for right now—just this minute—I really don't see much of anything else we *can* do. Do you?"

"No," she said unhappily. "No, I don't."

"Well keep thinking about it. We all will. But if something does occur to you, don't go charging off on your own without talking it over with us, first. Clear?"

"Clear." She sighed, and slurped up the last of her milkshake. "I don't like it, but clear. I just wish we could come up with some fresh way to attack this before somebody gets *really* hurt!"

"Well," Cordelia said encouragingly, "maybe Nosey will have something fresh to add to the picture, Steph."

✧ ✧ ✧

Stephanie went by herself on the next visit to Nosey. They weren't sure yet if they would need to maintain the perception that she and Cordelia didn't get along, but they'd decided it was best to play it safe. And Karl, like Jessica, was spread thin between family responsibilities, school, and work.

Nosey came to the door, calling cheerfully for the benefit of any snoopers, "I'm so glad you came by. I really want to see the physical mock-ups of the SFS Explorers gear."

Stephanie, arms wrapped around a large box, Lionheart loping at her side, called back, "They're looking really good. I've got hats and sashes in here."

Once inside, they actually did take time to review the contents of the box. The current plan was to have several levels of membership, related to achievements, rather than age. These would be named for various Sphinxian animals, although they hadn't settled exactly on which. Stephanie had a lot of reasons for wanting to avoid treecats, but admitted that "treecat level" might be inevitable.

"And we don't want all predators, either," she said. "That's sending the wrong message, but I've been outvoted on hexapumas. They're just too cool—at least if you've never been mauled by one."

Nosey laughed and perched the prototype of a hexapuma hood on his head. He was mostly recovered by now, a tribute not only to the medical professionals, but also to the men who had beaten him up, while taking care not to do anything that might lead to a charge of manslaughter or murder if something went wrong.

"So, what's the latest wrinkle?" he asked, and still wearing the hood, went to get snacks and drinks.

Stephanie knew Nosey and his phenomenal memory well enough by now that she launched into an account of what Cordelia had discovered without worrying that he wasn't taking notes.

"That fits in all too well with my own research," Nosey said when she was finished, setting a tray laden with various snacks on the coffee table. "I've been going over the accident reports and mapped them. Let me pull up the holo. Okay. First I'll show you points without any coding other than that an accident occurred in the last six months. Now, let me overlay one for the same period a year ago."

"Wow!" Stephanie said, the hand holding a cheese puff dropping into her lap as she studied the image. "The comparison can't be perfect because environmental factors make certain times of year—fires during summer droughts like this year, heavy snow, flooding—more likely to contribute to accidents, but still..."

"I corrected for that," Nosey said smugly. "Okay. This image has accidents coded according to cause. Natural situations are in green. Still a gain, but not as much in other situations, like in sports, recreation, vehicle-related. It skews even further when we correct for age of victim. And then there's this—"

He punched up another chart, this one overlaid on a map of the entire planet, and Stephanie frowned. Then her frown disappeared.

"Wow," she said again, this time almost softly. "Accidents are actually *down* everywhere else on the planet!"

"Exactly." Nosey nodded vigorously. "Yawata Crossing's our biggest town right now, but Tanner's Port and Mountain Crest are almost as big, and there are a couple of dozen smaller towns scattered around. A million people can cover a lot of ground when they start spreading out. But this upturn in accidents has been happening *only* in the area around Yawata Crossing and Twin Forks."

Stephanie nodded, frowning thoughtfully, and they went through a bunch more charts. At the end, the snacks were hardly touched because Stephanie had been completely absorbed in the story unfolding in the charted data.

"That's pretty conclusive," she said finally. "Especially the geographic spread. Twin Forks and immediate surroundings show the first increase, with a later increase in Yawata Crossing. That makes sense if Frank was involved, because his family is based here, but does a lot of business in Yawata Crossing."

"I have one other holo to show you," Nosey said, "and I admit I may be biased on this one. I decided to look at various areas specifically focusing shortly before, then after the date of my being attacked. What I found was both interesting, and deeply unsettling. In both cases, incidents dropped off after they beat me up. They're still well above average, but they've definitely dropped. At first I couldn't make sense of it, but with what you've learned about Frank, Herman, and all the rest . . . Well, you tell me what you think?"

Stephanie glanced at the man, wondering if he was playing teacher, wanting her to find the solution for herself, but Nosey's expression was completely serious. He was consulting her, colleague to colleague, and didn't want to lead her to the "right" conclusion. She carefully reviewed the images, clicking between them, and creating overlays before speaking.

"You're right; there's a definite drop-off in both locations, more in Yawata Crossing than in Twin Forks, since they attacked you. Somehow, though, based on yesterday's events, I don't think this means everyone's stopped using baka bakari."

"Neither do I," Nosey said when she paused. "But did you notice the shift in the *age* demographic?"

Stephanie looked at him, then turned back to the data. After a moment, she frowned.

"It's skewing upward, isn't it?" she said slowly. "A lot fewer kids Jake Simpson's age, and a lot more older ones. It's still mostly kids, but it looks like someone's deliberately marketing to older customers, too."

"Which suggests what?" Nosey pressed.

"Well..." Stephanie rubbed her nose. "What I think is that it looks like someone—probably Dr. Orgeson or whoever she works for—came down hard and is now controlling where the drug is being used and how. Like maybe they're doing lab tests or something. I know that if *I* was thinking about investing a lot in a new drug, I'd probably want to field test it, even if only in a raw form."

She felt fiercely disappointed. If that was the case, they weren't going to be able to get anything incriminating on Orgeson, probably the opposite. The woman would come across as a serious scientist doing controlled testing, not as someone who was willing to advocate the use of an untested drug.

She said as much, then started thinking aloud, "But if that's the case, then why not just talk to Glynis? Dr. Orgeson wouldn't be worried about protecting Herman. In fact, she'd be happy to look like the good guy, showing Glynis that her assistant had been behaving badly. I think they're still doing something hinky."

Nosey nodded. "I agree. You're forgetting one thing. It's not easy to get permission to test a new anything on human subjects. Computer modeling comes first, then careful testing on analogs, then reviews, then, only after all of that, testing on humans. *And* the testing has to be consensual. Legitimate testing would be public, too, which would mean advertising for volunteers and possibly agreeing to pay them after they sign up. A group interested more in making lots of money, rather than in benefiting society, would cut to the chase."

Stephanie brightened. "That's terrific. I mean, it's horrible, but it's terrific because that means we have a chance to catch them. Even if the drug isn't illegal, providing it to people when you know it can lead to injury or death—especially if you're not warning them it could—still constitutes criminal negligence. I'm betting these people are doing their best to keep the situation contained to avoid just that charge. And the fact that they threatened you, both to create an example and to keep you from making someone else decide to take a look, suggests they *did* know it could get people hurt or killed. Then they started controlled testing. But how?"

"Well, they'd have to find some way to slip it to people without their knowing it. Or else find a distribution point they could control that would still have enough traffic to give them a big enough sample of test subjects. And somewhere they could find people actively looking for some sort of new 'experience.' The kind of people with both the money and the inclination to try something new if it was offered."

"And the ages are skewing upward..." Stephanie said slowly. She frowned at the chart for several seconds, and then her eyes narrowed.

"I think you're right about the kind of 'distribution point' they'd need," she said. "And maybe that explains why we're seeing what looks like older users. If *I* had some new drug I wanted to market, I think I'd be looking for something like a nightclub or a dance hall. That would be one place to find the kind of 'customer' you were talking about. And it might explain the uptick in ages, if they're using the club scene."

"That could work," Nosey said. "It would probably appeal to Orgeson's group, too, to have people paying for the privilege of risking their lives and health in the name of the cartel's future profit. And you're right—it would help explain the shift in age spread. If they're using something like nightclubs for their cover, there'd be fewer minors with access to the source." He nodded, slowly, at first, and then harder. "I like it."

Stephanie beamed. "Can you find it for us? The club or clubs, I mean? Once we know that, we can figure out what next. I really want to get these people, but we don't dare take too long because, as what happened to you—what nearly happened to Herman—shows, these aren't nice patient people. They're callous, hard-hearted, and about as cuddly as a hexapuma."

✧ ✧ ✧

"Nosey really is good at this sort of thing, isn't he?" Cordelia said a few days later, and Stephanie nodded.

"Yes, he is," she agreed, without a trace of her onetime resentment. "The question is what we do now that he's come through for us. Again."

"An excellent question." Karl nodded. "And answering it is still the problem, isn't it?"

The three of them sat in the Red Letter, with Stephanie—inevitably—chowing down on cheese fries and a burger while her friends kept her company with mere milkshakes. Nosey had indeed come through for them again, compiling a list of nightclubs that might be involved in testing baka bakari. All but one of them were in Yawata Crossing, not Twin Forks, unfortunately. Which did little to solve the question upon which Karl and Stephanie had just agreed.

"All of this is still just speculation," Cordelia pointed out. "Oh, I agree with you guys that Nosey's nailed it, but it's not anything like proof. It looks to me like the only way to get that would be for someone like the SFS or the local cops to actually send someone in to investigate."

"Yes!" Stephanie nodded vigorously.

"Um." Karl tapped his chin thoughtfully. "You're right about that. But even if they *are* selling this stuff to people, it's not illegal—yet, at least. And even if it was, SFS doesn't have jurisdiction off public lands."

"Does that mean we can't follow Cordy's idea up?" Stephanie sounded unhappy, and Karl gave her a quick grin.

"I didn't say that, Steph. I don't think he'll be in any better position to sanction an official investigation—especially in Yawata Crossing!—but I'll run it by the Chief. At the very least, he'll be a good double check on our enthusiastic speculations, and he may just have some additional insight of his own to offer. For that matter, he might run Nosey's list by Chief Chuchkova. She's smart, and you know what close friends they are. She'd probably listen a lot more seriously to him than to a bunch as young and excitable as *we* are."

Stephanie rolled her eyes, but she also nodded. Olivera Chuchkova was the chief of the Yawata Crossing Police Department. It was a small force—only a couple of dozen officers—but nothing happened in

Yawata Crossing without Chuchkova hearing about it eventually.

"Could Chief Chuchkova help us chase it down?" Cordelia asked.

"Not beyond helping us figure out where to look." Karl shrugged. "Still no provable crime connected to all this, so she'd have the same problems Chief Shelton would where warrants or anything like that was concerned. She doesn't even have probable cause to open an official file on it yet, especially since all the wrongdoing we *think* has happened is way outside her jurisdiction. I'm sure she'll be willing to ask her people to keep their eyes and ears open, but that's about as proactive as she could get at this point, and she's almost as shorthanded as *we* are. I don't know how much manpower she could devote to it without making it a formal investigation. Which brings us right back to that probable cause stuff."

"Well, that should still be *some* help," Stephanie said, but her tone was less than happy, and Karl shrugged.

"There's other places we could look, too," he pointed out. "Chet and Christine have continued working as tour guides, you know. They might already have heard rumors of hot spots for chemically enhanced nightlife."

"Would that mean filling them in on what we suspect about baka bakari?" Stephanie said. "We may want to, just to warn them, but I don't want them getting into trouble with someone like Orgeson and her thugs!"

"I think we do have to warn them," Karl said. "And I also think they'd be a good secondary source to check Nosey's list against. But eventually, we're going to have to figure out how to get some actual proof of what's going on, and Cordy's right; that's going to mean sending someone in on the ground, with or without official sanction."

"Really?" Stephanie smiled at him, and the gleam in her brown eyes filled him with instant trepidation. He'd seen the Harrington smile entirely too often, and he realized he knew what she was going to say next before she even opened her mouth.

"What are you thinking about now, Steph?" Cordelia, who'd had less experience with Harrington exuberance, asked incautiously, and Stephanie's smile expanded.

"Well, I was just thinking that if we're going to ask Chief Shelton to talk to Chief Chuchkova anyway, he might ask her how she'd feel about a little unofficial, independent, um . . . fact-gathering expedition in her backyard?"

Karl's trepidation turned into a sinking sensation. Part of him wanted to stop her right there, but the problem was that she was probably right. And even if she wasn't, stopping the Harrington in mid-scheme was far more easily said than done.

"What I was thinking," she continued, "is that—"

14

THE GOOD NEWS, KARL ZIVONIK REFLECTED AS HIS SFS cruiser bored through a beautiful, sunlit sky, was that Chief Shelton hadn't shot down Stephanie's plan entirely. Or Karl *thought* that was good news, anyway. He still didn't see any better approach to the problem, but he knew only too well who Stephanie envisioned as their "fact-gathering expedition," and he was definitely in two minds about that. Unfortunately—or perhaps he meant fortunately—Shelton had pointed out that they still had nothing like any actual crime to investigate, beyond Nosey's beating and the apparent attempt to intimidate Herman, and they had no admissible evidence or even criminal complaints in either of those cases. Without at least a little more to go on than a spate of accidents which might or might not be caused by the ingestion of a substance that wasn't illegal in the first place, neither he nor Chief Chuchkova had the basis to open an actual investigation. And absent that sort of basis, Chuchkova was less than enthralled by the notion of turning a bunch of underage amateurs loose on her turf.

Karl couldn't really blame her for that, and he

had no objection at all to keeping Stephanie out of as much trouble as he could, but—

The sudden, shrill scream of an alarm jerked him upright in his flight couch. He was sixty kilometers north of Twin Forks, headed for the Harrington homestead, and the lurid, crimson icon of the crash beacon glared in his head-up display. It was barely ten kilometers off his flight path, and he turned sharply to port even as he keyed his com on the dedicated SFS frequency.

"Dispatch, Zivonik!" he said crisply.

"Dispatch," Carla Jensen, the duty Forestry Service dispatcher replied almost instantly. "What do you need, Karl?"

"I'm showing an air car crash transponder," he told her tersely. "Fifty-seven clicks north-northeast of Twin Forks. Grid Alpha-Kilo-Two-Niner."

"Hold one." Jensen's voice was crisper, and he pictured her checking the planetary net.

"We don't show it on the net," she told him after a moment. "You're sure about those coordinates?"

"Yes," he said. "Positive."

"I believe you," she said, and he wondered just how emphatic his own tone had been. "But we don't show it."

Karl frowned. That didn't make any sense. If he was seeing the beacon, then why weren't the satellites picking it up? Beacons were short-ranged homing devices, intended mainly as backup for an air car's regular transponder, and those were specifically designed to be tracked from orbit. So why—

His mouth tightened as he came up on the beacon site and saw the line of tangled wreckage plowed through the trees.

"I don't know why you're not picking it up, Carla," he said flatly, "but I'm eyes-on now, and somebody's definitely down. It . . . doesn't look good. I'm setting down. Switching my transponder to ground mode. Does *it* show on the net?"

"Got it," Jensen said. "Strong signal. Twin Forks first responders are saddling up now."

"Tell them to hurry. If anybody made it through this, they're likely to be in pretty bad shape."

"Copy," Jensen said grimly.

Karl landed in the trough the other air car had torn through the tree canopy. It was a good thing his cruiser was designed for rough field landings most civilian craft couldn't have handled, he thought, as jagged, snapped off branches and trunks crunched under his fuselage. And it was also a good thing—probably—that this section of forest was mostly picketwood. Judging from the damage around him, the wrecked vehicle must have been traveling at well over a hundred and fifty kilometers per hour when it hit. Not even modern synthetics could handle that kind of impact energy, and the picketwood had ripped the incoming air car to bits as it slammed through the trunks. But if this had been crown oak and the hapless pilot had hit one of those enormous trunks squarely, his air car would simply have disintegrated.

Air cars were designed to be as crash-survivable as possible, and at least the safety features designed to prevent the hydrogen reservoir from exploding must have worked, since there was no sign of fire. Despite that, his stomach tightened as he realized how unlikely it was that anyone could have survived *this*.

He pulled on his SFS helmet and activated his air

car's search-and-rescue drone. As it deployed from the side hatch, he slid back the canopy, grabbed his emergency medical kit, and turned up his personal counter-grav. He vaulted to the ground, his landing softened by the counter-grav, and turned up the drone on his helmet's visor as Survivor landed beside him. The drone's field of view was much wider than anything he could manage from ground level, and if anyone *had* lived through this, he needed to find them fast. Because—

An icon blinked on his visor, alternating green and amber, and his eyes widened. That was an ejection seat's transponder! Had someone punched out before they hit?

He turned to charge through the debris field, cursing as he stumbled over uneven ground, ripped and torn foliage, and an unholy tangle of broken branches. Survivor had wheeled in the same direction and gone darting through the wreckage even before Karl detected the transponder. The 'cat was a blur of cream and gray, scurrying through and over the litter of shattered greenery, and Karl felt a moment of bitter envy. Even with the counter-grav, it was hard going for someone his size and with only two legs, and he wished he had one of the thruster packs that could have propelled him above the tangled terrain on his CG. But he didn't, and he reminded himself—not for the first time—that, unlike Stephanie, he didn't have the Meyerdahl mods, either. Muscles, yes; those he had. But his bones were just as fragile as Cordelia's or any other unmodified human's. If he fell and broke a leg, he wouldn't do any possible survivor any good.

There!

Survivor bleeked urgently at him as he slithered down a sharp slope into the ravine where the ejection seat had crashed to earth, and his stomach tightened when he reached the bottom and found his companion perched atop the seat.

Whoever was in it must have ejected at the last possible second, he thought. Its built-in counter-grav clearly hadn't lifted it above the picketwood canopy before momentum carried it into the trees right behind the air car. But its attitude computer must have had at least a sliver of time to react, because it had gone into the trees base first, and it had clearly been climbing when it did. Instead of the heavier, lower trunks which had demolished the air car, it had crashed through the upper, thinner branches, and its protective shell's armored base had survived the impact more or less intact. Whether that had been enough—

Karl clambered toward Survivor, up the tangled mass of broken limbs wrapped around the ejection seat. It was even more badly damaged than he'd thought. The panels that automatically deployed when someone ejected were intended to protect a passenger from the airstream at relatively high velocities, not from high-speed impacts with the ground. They were twisted and torn, and at least one branch stub had slammed right through them.

Karl punched the button that was supposed to retract the panels, but he wasn't surprised when nothing happened. Not given how badly wrecked they were.

He unhooked his SFS issue bush knife from his belt. The audible alert whined as he brought the vibroblade to life, and Survivor recognized the sound and leapt clear. Treecats might not understand how human technology worked, but he'd seen bush knives in action often enough to stay out of the way. Despite which, Karl waited a beat to be sure he was clear. And to consider angles. That blade could cut through almost anything, including whoever was in the ejection seat, if he wasn't careful. Every instinct screamed that he had to move faster, but he made himself stand back. Made himself plan *exactly* what he wanted to do and how. Then, and only then, he cut away the tangle of broken picket wood and sliced a rectangle out of one side of the protective shell with quick but careful strokes.

He grabbed the rectangle as it came away and tossed it to one side, and his eyes widened in recognition as he saw the blood-soaked young woman in the seat. Its base hadn't absorbed all of the crash energy, after all. The entire shell had telescoped when it hit, but one side had taken a lot more damage than the other, and her right leg was twisted, bleeding heavily around at least one compound fracture, She'd been hit by the branch which had penetrated the shell, as well. Fortunately, it hadn't hit her squarely, but the channel it had ripped through the left side of her torso looked bad.

But she was still breathing, and it was his job to keep her that way, he told himself fiercely, and heard—and felt—Survivor humming in agreement.

The last thing she needed, especially if—as seemed likely—there were internal injuries he couldn't yet see, was him dragging her around. But she couldn't survive that much blood loss for very long, either.

He was vaguely surprised to discover that his hands were perfectly steady as he pulled out the med kit's tourniquet. He got it under and around her right thigh, as high as he could and jostling her shattered leg as little as possible, and hit the inflation button. The tourniquet hissed as it pressurized, and he tapped the pressure pad, watching the numbers as he tightened it far enough to slow, and then stop, the heavy blood flow pulsing around the broken bone which had pierced her skin. Unless he overrode it, the tourniquet would periodically loosen briefly, long enough to let blood reach the leg's tissues, then tighten again, but hopefully the Twin Forks EMTs would be here before he had to worry about that. In the meantime—

He used the bush knife to cut the branch that had penetrated the seat's shell, pulled it free, and tossed it aside, then ripped away enough of her shirt to reach the wound in her side. It didn't look quite as bad as he'd thought it was, but it was bad enough. At least it hadn't penetrated her abdominal or chest cavities, but the ribs which had taken the brunt of the impact, and probably prevented it from ripping right through her, were badly broken. He could actually see two of them where the branch had driven into her, and the inside of her upper left arm was also badly torn. The arm didn't appear to be broken—or no bone fragments had broken the skin, at least—but the tissue damage was too high on the limb for another tourniquet.

His eyes were grim as he sprayed coagulant into both wounds to stop the bleeding, He didn't know if it would be enough to save her, but there wasn't anything else he could do without at least one more set of hands, and he felt suddenly useless. He knew he'd done everything anyone could, but he ought to be able to do *more*, damn it! What *good* was he, if he couldn't—?

Violet-blue eyes slitted open in a blood-streaked

face. They were unfocused, tracking without seeing, but he touched the side of her face.

"Trudy?" he asked gently. "Trudy, can you hear me?"

"He flew into the trees." Trudy Franchitti sounded almost calm but as if she were speaking from a long, long way away. "He just flew into the trees. I told him. But he flew into the trees."

"Who? Who flew into the trees, Trudy?"

Those blue eyes blinked slowly, as if trying to focus on him. He didn't know if she'd actually heard him at all, but then she rolled her head.

"Stan," she said, in that same, detached voice, but it was thinner, wisping away. "Stan . . . just flew . . . into . . . the . . ."

Her voice disappeared into silence, and Karl's eyes burned as he brushed bloody hair from her forehead while Survivor stood on the base of the ejection seat, leaning lovingly against him, and the Twin Forks EMTs' incoming sirens wailed behind them.

✧ ✧ ✧

Jessica sat in the bedside chair, stroking the treecat curled in her lap as she watched the monitors and waited.

She and Trudy were no longer as close as they'd once been, and there'd been a time, especially when Trudy had been so eager to acquire a treecat "pet" of her own, when Jessica had actively disliked her, almost as much as Stephanie had. But, also like Stephanie, she'd been forced to amend her opinion of the other young woman as Trudy became more and more deeply involved with Wild and Free. Jordan Franchitti despised "bleeding hearts" and "enviro maniacs," and he'd actually forbidden Wild and Free to "trespass" on his land. He'd certainly never concealed his contempt for it, and Jessica had seen how much tension that had created between Trudy and her father. And her brothers, for that matter. But Trudy had made it clear that she knew her own mind in that respect. Given her own large, boisterous, close-knit family, Jessica could sympathize only intellectually with the degree of tension that must create within the Franchitti clan, but she'd come—grudgingly, almost against her will—to respect Trudy for the stand she'd taken. That hadn't made them bosom buddies again, but Jessica was constitutionally unable to hold grudges against people who at least tried to make amends.

Which was why she'd volunteered to sit in ICU with Trudy as she drifted back toward consciousness. It wouldn't be much longer, she thought, watching the monitors, but until Trudy said she was ready for it, the hospital had no intention of admitting anyone but staff to her room. Besides—

Trudy's head moved on the pillow. The tip of her tongue licked her lips, and her eyes drifted open. For three or four seconds, they only gazed blankly at the ceiling, but then, slowly, they focused.

"Trudy?" Jessica said softly, and Valiant crooned from her lap.

Trudy rolled her head, blinking, then smiled a fragile smile.

"Jessica." Her voice was barely above a whisper, but her right hand rose, reaching out, and Jessica took it. Valiant sat up in her lap, patting their joined hands with a gentle true-hand, and Trudy's tiny smile wavered a bit wider. "And Valiant," she said. "Of course."

"Well, of course 'of course,'" Jessica replied, squeezing her hand. "He sort of comes with the territory."

"I know." Trudy smiled again. But then her face tightened and she closed her eyes again. "Stan?" she asked, and Jessica inhaled deeply. She'd dreaded this moment, and Valiant's comforting purr buzzed higher as he stroked Trudy's hand.

"He didn't make it," she said simply, as gently as she could. "I'm so sorry, Trudy, but he's gone."

A tear leaked from the corner of Trudy's eye and she bit her lip, her hand tightening almost painfully on Jessica's. She turned her face away, shoulders quivering, and Valiant leapt lightly from Jessica's lap to the hospital bed. She started to reach after him, but he moved with delicate precision, avoiding Trudy's injured left side, to curl beside her and lay his chin on her shoulder, his nose against the side of her neck, while his entire body quivered with the force of his purr.

Trudy lay still for a long, trembling moment, then turned her face back toward Jessica. She tugged her hand free of Jessica's, wrapped her arm around the treecat, buried her face against his coat . . . and sobbed.

✧ ✧ ✧

"Better?" Jessica asked five minutes later.

"Better." Trudy nodded, still stroking Valiant's coat. It was quite a bit damper than it had been, and she smiled gratefully. At Valiant, Jessica noticed, not at her. "Still a long way from *good*, but better." She transferred her smile to Jessica. "Thank you. Thank you both."

"Hey, somebody had to keep an eye on you. Just the luck of the draw that it was me."

"Sure it was." A spark of actual humor glinted in the depths of Trudy's voice. "And you just happened to be sitting here when I woke up."

"Well, maybe it was a little more than 'just happened,'" Jessica confessed.

"How bad is it?" Trudy took her hand from Valiant and waved it in an arc that encompassed the entire hospital room.

"Let's just say you're lucky it wasn't a whole bunch worse." Jessica shook her head. "You almost lost your right leg entirely, Trudy. It's going to be okay, eventually, but the soft tissues and muscles got ripped up really badly. The bone damage was worse, though. They decided it was best to just go ahead and replace the tibia and fibula with synthetics, I'm afraid, and they had to almost entirely rebuild your femur. You're going to be stuck here for a while, even with quick heal, over that one, and after that you'll be doing a lot of PT."

"Which Sphinx's gravity's going to make a real pain in the ass," Trudy observed with a grimace.

"Oh, I think you could probably put it that way," Jessica agreed. "The good news is that your leg's still there to *be* a pain in the ass."

"I know." Trudy nodded. "And this?"

Her right hand indicated her immobilized left arm.

"Hopefully the painkillers mean you're not noticing it, but every one of your ribs on that side were broken. Not only that, you've got heavy damage to the external oblique and intercostal muscles, and the crash peeled your left tricipitus muscle completely away from the humerus. They got everything reattached, but that's why they don't want you moving it yet. Like your leg, it's going to be okay, eventually."

"With more of that PT."

"With more of that PT," Jessica confirmed, and if

Trudy's response was more grimace than smile, at least there was a smile wrapped inside it. Then it faded.

"How?" she asked. Jessica raised an eyebrow, and Trudy shrugged, careful of her damaged side. "How did I make it?" Her voice was darker than it had been. "From the sound of things, I shouldn't have."

"It was Karl," Jessica told her. "He just happened to be passing by, literally, on his way to Twin Forks when you and Stan went in. He was close enough he picked up the crash beacon, and he got to you on the ground in time to at least stop the bleeding." She met Trudy's gaze steadily. "You wouldn't have made it without him."

"I figured." Trudy closed her eyes briefly, and her nostrils flared. "I owe him."

"Maybe. But, Trudy, he picked up the short-range crash beacon, not the one from the air car's transponder. If he'd been forty kilometers farther away, nobody would've known what happened until it was way too late."

Trudy opened her eyes again, looking at her, and Jessica leaned forward in her chair.

"They recovered the transponder," she said. "Why was it manually disabled?"

Trudy didn't answer. She only looked back in silence, her lower lip trembling ever so slightly, and Valiant stirred. He touched her face lightly with a long-fingered true-hand, his croon so soft Jessica could barely hear it, and Jessica felt . . . something. She didn't know what, but she knew it came from Valiant, and she watched Trudy's eyes widen, and then soften before they moved back to her.

"Stan disabled it," she said then. "I told him not

to. I reminded him how much trouble he'd get into if anyone found out. He just laughed and said no one would. Stupid." She shook her head, fresh tears gleaming. "So *stupid.*"

Jessica nodded. It had, indeed, been stupid, and in more than one way. Intentionally disabling an air car transponder carried a hefty fine and a one T-year license suspension. That was for the first time it happened. After that, the penalties got stiffer. Up to, and including, jail time for repeated offenders.

But those were only the legal consequences. Stan Chang had just discovered—briefly—what the other ones were. With the transponder down, only the short range, omnidirectional crash beacon intended to help on-site rescuers zero in on a downed air car whose location they already knew from the transponder had remained to guide Frank to Trudy in time to save her life.

"But why did he do it?" she pressed.

"I didn't know he had until we were already in the air." Trudy's voice was stronger, clearer, now that she'd admitted Stan had shut it down deliberately. "He was so . . . so *pleased* with himself when he told me about it. I told him it was the dumbest thing he'd done yet, and he only laughed harder. He said his dad had threatened to ground him the next time he tried any 'fun' aerobatics. But without the transponder to 'rat him out' his dad would never know.

"I guess he was wrong about that." Her voice was lower, hoarser, and another tear trickled down her cheek.

"Yes, he was," Jessica agreed softly. She leaned closer to blot the tear with a tissue, but even as she dried the tear, she frowned internally. She'd never really liked Stan, even when she and Trudy had originally been close. He was a braggart, with a streak of bully, and she'd wondered even then what Trudy saw in him. But, despite that, he truly had been an excellent pilot. He'd always enjoyed pushing the limits, and she didn't doubt that his father had threatened to ground him, but this . . .

"Trudy," she said after a moment, "you told Karl Stan 'just flew into the trees.' What did you mean?"

"I said that?" Trudy blinked.

"To Karl." Jessica nodded. "Just before the EMTs got there."

"Well, he did." Trudy closed her eyes again. "He was buzzing the treetops. So fast and so low it scared the hell out of me. I told him that. And he just laughed that *laugh* again. Like it was the funniest joke he'd ever heard! And the more it scared me, the closer and faster he went!"

"That . . . doesn't sound like Stan," Jessica said.

"Oh, yes it does." Trudy didn't open her eyes, but her tone was bitter. "He *liked* scaring people. He thought it was funny, and sometimes, I have to admit, after I got done being scared, *I* thought it was funny, too. Not always. But sometimes." She bit her lip. "Maybe if I'd yelled at him more about it, told him I'd walk if he kept doing it, then maybe . . ."

Her voice trailed off, and Jessica touched her hand again.

"Stan was always Stan," she told the other young woman. "You weren't going to change that part of him, Trudy. I don't think anyone could. What I meant was that he could be a complete zork sometimes, and he was awfully full of himself where his flying was concerned, but you guys went into those trees at almost two hundred kilometers per hour. That kind of speed, that close to the treetops?" She shook her head. "I don't remember him ever buzzing the ground at that speed. He was more into high-altitude craziness. Or that's what I always thought, anyway."

"Mostly, yeah." Trudy opened her eyes with a sigh. "But lately, the last few months, he's gotten—he *had* gotten," she corrected herself with a wince "—a lot... cockier, I guess. Started doing a lot of really dumb stuff. I think—"

She cut herself off, but Jessica's eyes widened as a connection clicked in her brain.

"Trudy," she said carefully, "do you think Stan was doing drugs? Is that what happened?"

Trudy said nothing for almost a full minute. Then she sighed again.

"Yeah," she confessed. "He always did some, and to be honest, I did them with him, for a while. I quit back when the fires first got so bad and I got involved with Wild and Free, and I told him he had to, too. Oh, we didn't do anything heavy. And Stan never drank. He said he didn't like what it did to his coordination, so he'd never do anything like that. But we'd sniff a little dust, sometimes. Maybe smoke a little more weed than was good for us. I didn't quit because I was scared of what it was 'doing to me.' I quit because I was... kind of crawling into it. Using a lot more of it, and not just to party. I was pretty unhappy about then, you know." She looked Jessica in the eye as she made the admission. "I figured out I was using so much more of the stuff we did to pretend I wasn't, and I've seen too many people do that. So I knew I had to quit, and I told him he had to quit, too, if we were going to be together. Because I didn't trust myself, Jess. I was afraid I'd slide back into it—no, I *knew* I'd slide back into it—if I was around him and he kept doing it."

Jessica nodded, with more respect than she'd ever thought she might feel for Trudy Franchitti, as the other young woman admitted that. She'd known Trudy's life had gotten a lot more stressful in light of her strained relationship with her family, but she'd never realized Trudy had that much self-awareness. Or the strength of will to do something about it.

Of course, if she'd thought Stan was still doing drugs anyway, she should have gone ahead and walked away from him. But it wasn't easy to just walk away from someone you cared for. Especially not if you were trying to help them with a problem they might not even be willing to admit they had. But . . .

"But you think he *was* still using," she said, and Trudy nodded unhappily.

"I couldn't prove it. But, yeah. That was why I've been spending so much less time with him. Until today." Another tear leaked down her cheek. "It was . . . tomorrow was his birthday, you know. We were supposed to grab something at the Red Letter to celebrate, but—"

She broke off, lower lip trembling, and drew another deep breath before she resumed.

"But whatever he was doing, I know it wasn't the kind of stuff he'd done before. Weed always just sort of . . . mellowed him out, you know? And dust made him high as a kite, convinced him he had the greatest sense of humor in the world, but it didn't make him *stupid*.

He did yellows, once in a while, but once you've done a couple of those, you can hardly even *move* till you come down. This . . . this was different. It was like . . . like dust on steroids, but it never affected his coordination. He just got wilder. It was like whatever it was, it just made him really, really *stupid*. It was like he was convinced he could do all the things he would've known he *couldn't* do if he'd been straight. I mean—"

She broke off, shaking her head in frustration at her inability to nail down what she was trying to describe.

"I understand what you're trying to say," Jessica told her, and Trudy's eyes narrowed at something in Jessica's tone. "In fact, I think I understand *exactly* what you're trying to say."

✧ ✧ ✧

"The drug screens were completely clear," Chief Shelton said, his expression grim. "Absolutely nothing any of the med scans could identify. No alcohol, no dust—nothing."

Stephanie and Karl nodded, their expressions as unhappy as his. They sat in his office, facing his desk, Survivor and Lionheart on the backs of their chairs, and the accident report glowed on Shelton's display.

"Karl," the chief ranger said now, "you did good. That girl would be dead if you hadn't been there, hadn't acted as quickly as you did. I've put you in for a commendation for it, and you damned well deserve it."

Karl nodded soberly, and Stephanie reached across to lay one hand on his forearm. He hadn't wanted to talk about it much, but she knew the wreck site haunted him. Trudy's injuries had been bad enough, but he and Survivor had also been the first to find what was left of Stan Chang's body.

And all of it had brought back what had happened to Sumiko. She knew that, too. He'd made a lot of progress dealing with those memories, but not enough to protect him from the echoes of something like this.

"And Jessica did well to get what she got out of Ms. Franchitti," Shelton continued. "For that matter, I have to admit that I was a bit surprised Ms. Franchitti was prepared to make a formal statement about Chang's condition. Or what she *thinks* was his condition, anyway."

It was Stephanie's turn to nod. She'd been at least as surprised as Chief Shelton could possibly have been, and she didn't like admitting that to herself. She'd always known her mom was smart, but in Trudy's case, at least, she hadn't paid enough attention to Marjorie Harrington's observation about hidden depths and the ability of human beings to surprise you if you only gave them the opportunity.

"Unfortunately, we still don't have any proof that this baka bakari was involved. And Ms. Franchitti can't tell us who was supplying it to Chang, assuming someone actually was. Which"—he added dryly as Stephanie straightened in her chair—"I *do* assume someone was, Stephanie. But assumptions on my part, despite my vast wisdom and innate brilliance, do not constitute legal evidence. And neither do yours, young woman."

"Point taken, Sir," she said after a moment.

"Ms. Franchitti *thinks* he was getting them from Frank Câmara or someone else in that circle, but she never actually saw it happen. And, given that we're talking about something that's not a prohibited substance, even if it should be, I can scarcely hand this over to the sheriff or go to the magistrate myself and ask for a search warrant. At the same time, though, we're beyond just personal injury, even *serious* personal injury. This is the first time—that we know of, anyway—where someone may have actually been killed because of this stuff, but it's entirely possible it won't be the last. So, I think you two are probably right. You have no idea how little I *want* you to be right, and not just because of how many ways this could go sideways. But you're right that this has gotten to a point where just collecting anecdotal evidence isn't enough. So, much as it pains me, I've screened Chief Chuchkova again, and this time she's agreed—assuming certain conditions are met—to let you young idiots try it."

"'Idiots,' Sir?" Stephanie repeated. "Isn't that just a *little* strong?"

"Oh, excuse me." Shelton rolled his eyes. "I meant to say 'you overly enthusiastic young overachievers.' Does that sound better?"

"Much better!" she agreed brightly.

"Of course it does . . . you young idiot," he told her with a smile.

✧ ✧ ✧

"Dead?" Herman Maye stared at Karl and Cordelia. "He's *dead*?"

"I'm afraid so," Karl replied as Herman sat down—collapsed, really—on the plastic bench. "It happened late yesterday."

"And . . . and it's confirmed that baka bakari was involved?"

"Not officially, no." Karl shook his head, and saw a flicker of what might have been relief in Herman's eyes. "But there's not much question," he continued unhurriedly. "Trudy Franchitti's testimony is pretty damning, Herman. And she's made an official statement to SFS."

Herman swallowed, hard.

He'd been clearly unhappy to see Karl's SFS cruiser land on the landing apron, for which Karl couldn't blame him, given his concern that Orgeson and her goons might hear about Karl's visit. But that visit was safely unofficial, if anyone asked, because he'd simply agreed to "drop Cordelia off" with Zack and Mack, since it was "on his way." If anyone was keeping a close enough eye on Herman to know Karl had visited him at all, they should also be able to discover that fact.

Not that Karl had any intention of mentioning that—yet, at least—since the real reason he was here was to hit Herman as hard as possible with news of Stan Chang's death. They'd figured that having Karl deliver the news in his official capacity as a law enforcement officer would be the best way to do that, and from Herman's ashen expression, they'd been right.

"Eventually, this is all going to come out, one way or another, Herman," Karl said. "Surely you've always known that."

"But if I—If people think *I* supplied him with it..."

"Well, indirectly, you *did*," Karl pointed out.

"But I never *wanted* to do!" Herman half-wailed. "And I never thought anyone would get killed!"

"Of course you didn't." Cordelia's tone was much more sympathetic than Karl's had been as she stepped into the "good cop" role. "But," she continued a bit more sternly, "whatever you may have thought, you always knew this could happen." He stared at her mutely and she shook her head. "Eldora Yazzie shattered her ribs and damaged both lungs, Herman. And Jake Simmons broke his back in that skimmer park accident! It's sheer luck that he wasn't killed, then."

"Sphinx is a high-risk environment," Karl said, pulling Herman's eyes back to him. "It always has been, and probably always will be. Couple that with something like baka bakari, and it was inevitable someone was going to get killed eventually. Why do you think we've been trying to find a way to get on top of this?"

Herman stared at him for a long, still moment, then drew a deep breath.

"You're right," he said. "And I guess I always knew that. But I never wanted anyone to get hurt at all. For that matter, I never wanted to be involved with this at all! It just . . . happened. And now . . ."

He leaned forward, his elbows on his thighs and stared down at his interlocked fingers.

"I'm responsible, aren't I?" he asked in a low voice.

"Legally?" Karl shrugged. "I honestly don't know how that would shake out, Herman, but I doubt it. It's not a legally prohibited substance—yet, at least—and you didn't personally provide it to Stan. Or did you?" He frowned. "I know Stan hung around with Frank a lot. Did you ever hand any of it directly to him?"

"Never." Herman didn't look up, but he shook his head firmly. "Oh, he made a couple of collection runs with Frank, so I probably handed him a carton of it once or twice. But I never gave it directly to him; only handed it to him when he was here with Frank."

"In that case, I'm not sure about the legal liability aspects of it." Karl shrugged. "There is a moral aspect to it, of course, but you didn't make Stan fly while he was using it. But, Herman, ultimately you *are* responsible. You're the one who cooked it up the first time, however accidentally, and the one who's gone on supplying it to Frank. And to Orgeson, now."

Herman nodded wretchedly.

"I'll stop," he said. "I'll stop right now." He looked up at last, and his eyes were hard. "I'll go to Dr. Bonaventure. I'll tell her about it. And I'll make a formal statement to Chief Ranger Shelton. Orgeson and her thugs can do whatever they want about it, but I'm not going to get anyone else killed."

"No." Karl shook his head, and Herman blinked in surprise.

"Frank knows which mushrooms and other ingredients go into your 'special stir-fry,' doesn't he?"

"Well, yes," Herman acknowledged. "He knows which mushrooms, at least, and he watched me cooking it a couple of times. But I don't think he knows *all* the ingredients, and he doesn't know the proportions, because I was careful not to tell him after I first realized what he might be up to."

"But he does know the mushrooms—which means Orgeson does by now, too," Karl pointed out. "And he *may* know the other ingredients. He definitely knows at least some of them, anyway, and I suspect a good chemical analysis of the final product could crack the basic recipe for the rest of them. For now, they obviously prefer to . . . encourage you to cook it up for them, but I'm pretty sure that if you just stop, they'll find someone else to experiment until they come up with the right recipe and cooking times. And the problem is that this stuff still isn't illegal, and nobody knows enough about it to decide whether or not it ought to be. So, we need you to go right on doing what you're doing. I'll take you up on that formal statement for the chief ranger, and I think we need one that details what Orgeson and her thugs were really threatening you with before Cordy and the guys turned up that night. It would only be your word against theirs, of course, and there's four of them, but it would go to establishing a pattern if all of this ends up in the courts. And I promise we'll keep it completely confidential until and unless there is a formal investigation of Orgeson. But in the meantime, you have to play along with them until we can get some kind of break. And I need a couple of kilos of baka bakari to send to somebody I know in Landing for a complete analysis."

"But somebody's been *killed*," Herman said stubbornly. "I don't care whether it's illegal or not—not anymore! Like you said, I'm ultimately responsible for anything that happens because of this stuff. I know that now, whatever the courts may finally say about it. I can't pretend I'm not, and I don't want to contribute to any more deaths. Or even 'just' any more accidents that don't happen to kill somebody!"

He meant it, Karl realized, and put a hand on his shoulder.

"I understand," he said. "I really do. But look at it this way, Herman. There's no way to prevent Orgeson from finding another cook. It may take her a while, but she will eventually, and you know it. So even if you stopped providing it to her tomorrow, more people are going to get hurt by it down the road, anyway, unless we can figure out if—and how—it ought to be regulated. If you really want to make up for any responsibility, you need to help us get a handle on it, figure out just how dangerous it really is, and stop Orgeson and Frank from going right on peddling it. And that means you have to go on working with them while we put together the facts we need to figure out how to stop *them*, too."

Herman stared at him for another long moment, and then, slowly, he nodded.

15

THE YOUNGER MEMBERS OF THE GREAT TREECAT Conspiracy, plus one, met at Stephanie's for one of the Harringtons' over-the-top cookouts. The plus one was Anders Whittaker, who had arrived unannounced with Jessica. This was clearly not going to be an issue as far as food went. The Harringtons always cooked as if prepared to entertain at least three times as many guests as they had invited.

Which wasn't to say it wouldn't be an issue at all.

After general greetings, Anders joined Karl and Richard over at the grill, where they were cooking a variety of interesting meat items under the watchful supervision of three—four now that Jessica and Valiant had arrived—treecats.

Stephanie hissed at Jessica, "Why did you bring Anders? You know we've got sensitive things to discuss."

When Stephanie was upset, she reminded Cordelia of a treecat in battle mode; she half-expected to see her short, curly hair bristle with fury. Jessica, however, was completely unfazed. She crooked a finger to draw Stephanie closer, winking to make sure Cordelia knew she was welcome to remain.

Just girl chat, Cordelia thought, amused, *and what more natural since The Boyfriend has arrived?*

"It's *because* we have sensitive matters to discuss that I invited Anders along," Jessica said. "We're looking at the club scene for possible baka bakari distribution points, right?"

"Right," Stephanie echoed, bristling somewhat less.

"And all of them are in nightclubs or similar places, right?"

"Right."

"Trust me," Jessica said. "Okay? Anders may have jilted you, and be in the process of being jilted by me, but that doesn't change that he's the same basically decent guy who kept his father's crew alive in the middle of a massive forest fire. The same guy who helped us out not long ago, when we began to suspect the treecats were killing each other. He's never let anything he learned or suspected then slip, not even when it would have put him in good with his crazy dad. So, trust me on this. I think he can help us now."

"Okay..." Stephanie agreed, a bit reluctantly. "Trust your judgment, and his. You got it. Let's go join the party before they eat all the bratwurst. It's a new type Mom got in trade from someone. It's going to go great with ice-potato salad."

The party was pleasant, the food plentiful, and when Stephanie offered to handle the cleanup, the elder Harringtons left the younger people to their own devices after dessert, both claiming the demands of work.

But really, Cordelia thought, *Marjorie and Richard*

are just over the moon to see their daughter happy to hang out with people her own age. I wonder what they'd think if they knew we're planning to discuss how best to get evidence to stop a group who just might have something to do with the recreational drug trade? Who knows? Being Stephanie's parents, they just might take it in stride.

Once Stephanie had gotten over her initial surprise at seeing Anders, she had gone out of her way to be friendly, asking about what he'd been doing (mostly helping his dad's crew) and bringing up a graphic novel series of which they were both obviously big fans.

Cordelia caught Karl watching the pair a couple of times, his gray eyes slightly hooded and basically unreadable, but she didn't think it was because Karl didn't like Anders. The two of them talked easily, bouncing jokes off of each other and getting into a friendly argument over their differing interpretations of a new study they'd both read.

So, Karl's fine with Anders. Is that watchfulness Big Brother watching to make sure Little Sis doesn't get in over her head, again, or something else?

Cordelia wished she knew. The rapport she had felt might be building between her and Karl had taken a serious hit after Dia's accident. Dia was still grounded for not telling the truth about where she had said she'd be, and for leaving the two younger girls unsupervised while she went chasing off with Loon. That had removed the easy excuse of picking up the kids as a reason for meeting up, and Karl's busy schedule left him very little free time. Even days like today he was on the clock. Officially, this gathering was in part to plan the launch of the SFS Explorers.

However, Chief Ranger Shelton knew they'd also be working on the baka bakari issue as well.

Stephanie called the meeting to order by saying, "So, everyone here knows that Nosey gave me a short list of places where baka bakari may be being given unofficial human testing, right?"

Everyone, including Anders, nodded. Stephanie absently cut herself another thick slab of a triple decker chocolate fudge cake, and, licking a bit of frosting off one finger, went on.

"First, Karl and Cordy had a long talk with Herman. He wasn't at all happy to see Karl turn up in uniform, but he was also just as worried as Cordy and Jess thought he was. And Karl and Cordy agree he's genuinely devastated about Stan. He doesn't want anyone else getting hurt, either, but we've convinced him he can't just pull the plug by refusing to cook up any more baka bakari for Frank and Orgeson. Not before we find out what's really going on and how many people are really involved. He's given us a kilo of it to ship off to Dr. Flouret, and we've promised not to tell a soul—yet, at least—where we got it. Well, he knows Chief Shelton's in the picture, even if he hasn't made any *official* statements, but he doesn't want us telling anyone else, and I don't see any reason we have to."

She looked around the table and saw a chorus of nods.

"Okay," she said. "Karl went ahead and contacted Dr. Flouret, and he's agreed to help us. *And* to keep everything under wraps until we tell him differently. He's not any happier about the idea of a drug that gets people hurt or killed than we are.

"In addition, Chief Ranger Shelton's agreed to let

us run with Herman as a 'confidential informant.' The rules about what Karl has to report about him are a lot looser that way, and what happened to Stan—and Trudy's statement about it—confirms our suspicions that drug use is contributing to the rise in accidents, as far as the Chief's concerned. Unfortunately, he still doesn't think he can assign an all-up SFS team. Part of that's because he's still short-staffed, part of it is that he still doesn't have probable cause to assume anyone's committed any criminal actions, and part of it is because of jurisdiction, since all the clubs Nosey flagged are in Yawata Crossing. It *does* constitute a possible public safety issue, though, and that opens the window just a crack. He's not investigating anyone for criminal activity; he's just trying to determine the cause of a fatal air car crash that *did* happen in his jurisdiction. It doesn't change his investigative options a lot, but it gives him a hook for anything *we* might turn up, if and when he's able to go to the magistrates."

She paused to let them digest that—and to shove a largish bite of cake into her mouth—and heads nodded around the picnic table.

"He's brought Chief Chuchkova into the picture, too," she continued then, "so the Yawata PD knows what we're thinking, and Chief Chuchkova's asked her people to keep an eye out for any evidence that might support our theories. But most of her officers are uniform. She doesn't have much in the way of plainclothes staffing—she's as shorthanded as the SFS, really—and most of the plainclothes officers she has are currently assigned to what are honestly more pressing cases. So she's agreed Karl"—she flashed Karl a smile—"can take his one-man investigation into

Yawata if we see a thread to pull. I think she and Chief Shelton both figure Orgeson—assuming that's who's behind it, of course"—she rolled her eyes—"is less likely to be worried about a bunch of 'kids' than she'd be if she saw uniform officers suddenly poking their noses her way."

"What exactly do you need next?" Anders asked. He was also working his way through a slab of cake with the enthusiasm only a teenage boy about due for a growth spurt could show. Cordelia envied him. "Just so I'm clear on that."

Karl replied, "Basically, we want something, anything, that would indicate that if baka bakari is being distributed, it's not just in 'good fun,' but in the way of a test. Especially in the way of an unauthorized test on people who don't know they're being used as test subjects and most of whom are still legally minors. That whole informed consent thing can bite Orgeson hard if we can prove she knew it had possible dangerous consequences and never told anyone. Hold that thought—we really should resolve first who's going in, because who is on point will definitely influence our tactics.

"I'm out, because I'm officially SFS. Even if I just said I was on a date"—his gaze drifted, apparently without noticing, to Cordelia, and she felt her heart leap—"the people we think are behind this know I'm a ranger. A lot of them—maybe *all* of them, for that matter—have seen me in uniform, even if they don't know me personally, like Frank. They'd be really careful about giving themselves away if I was there."

Stephanie leaned forward, but Jessica cut in before she could speak.

"Anders?"

Anders took the cue. "Look, the reason Jessica briefed me is because she thinks I'm just what you need. Dad is based out of Yawata Crossing now, so I'm local to the town. I'm not part of your treecat club. I haven't even been hanging out with you much, and I'm going home to Urako soon. That means I'd be a great test subject, because I'm not going to be around to talk about what happened to me when I tried an interesting euphoric. And, if I develop a sudden interest in nightclubs, what of it? I'm having girl problems"—he gave an appealingly crooked smile—"as everyone knows."

Jessica patted his hand. "Those problems won't last long, Anders. You really are a great guy." She turned her attention to the rest of the group. "Most of us have seen firsthand that Anders knows how to keep a cool head in a crisis."

"But Anders *is* going home soon," Stephanie broke in. "So, if we need him to testify firsthand about his experiences, that could be a problem."

"Recorded statement under oath before he leaves," Karl countered. "And it's not like he's leaving the day after tomorrow or something. If we can break this open, give Shelton and Chuchkova what they need to go all-in on an investigation, then Anders will be available for questions."

"Point," Stephanie reluctantly agreed.

Jessica grinned at her. "It's obvious you were about to make a case for you going in, Steph. That's why I was rude and cut you off—I wanted to suggest Anders before it would be a case of him being a better choice than you. Now it's just an alternate option. Go ahead.

How can the Girl Wonder of Sphinx, discoverer of treecats, the young woman for whom the SFS created a new position, co-founder of the new SFS Explorers, and someone known to have about as much of an interest in the joys of the nightlife as she does in catching neo-ticks justify going to a shady nightclub?"

Cordelia was impressed. Just about anyone else saying all of that would have sounded as if she was mocking Stephanie, but Jessica's honest admiration for what Stephanie had done and was still doing was clear—even as she noted that those very achievements were going to cause problems.

Stephanie grinned back at her friend and took the challenge.

"Undercover. I can even pose as someone from off-planet, if we want. After all, I lived the first eleven years of my life on Meyerdahl. As for me not being experienced with nightclubbing, well, so what if I look awkward? Wouldn't that make me an even better target for someone pushing baka bakari? Herman reports that it eases anxiety, right? So if I disguise myself as someone my age, but trying to look older, trying to act sophisticated, failing entirely, then wouldn't I be a great target? We'll get me an ID that shows my real age, so I can't even buy a drink to ease my nerves. Again, that makes me a target."

Anders chuckled. "How about we *both* go? Me as me. Steph undercover as Awkward Angela. That way we can look out for each other. Double the chances of being contacted or recruited or something."

"Just one minute," Karl said a bit sharply. Indeed, his tone was sharp enough Cordelia's eyes widened slightly, and she realized he was looking very sternly at Stephanie. He waited until Stephanie looked back, then pointed an index finger at her.

"No unauthorized hang-glider expeditions," he said flatly. "I already told you that, Steph. Either your parents know about this—and *approve*—or you don't go anywhere near any nightclubs."

Stephanie started to say something sharp of her own, then visibly stopped and drew a deep breath instead.

"Contrary to what you may think, Karl, I *have* learned a few things since Lionheart and I met," she said then, her own tone just a bit edged. "One of which is that sneaking around behind Mom and Dad isn't exactly the smartest thing I ever did. I don't intend to go to any nightclubs without their knowledge."

"So you've discussed this with them?" Karl pressed.

"Of course I have . . . sort of." Karl's eyes narrowed, and Stephanie shrugged. "I've told them everything Nosey has turned up, what we've found out from Herman, that Chief Shelton has you looking into it, that I've been helping, and that it looks like this stuff is being handed out in nightclubs in Yawata Crossing. *And* I've told them we need to put someone young—like me—in to see if the bad guys approach her. Or if she can just see something hinky herself. And they know this is really a strategy session. I haven't told them *I* want to be one of the 'kids' we send in, but come on, Karl! You think *my* mom and dad can't figure out who I'm talking about?"

"And they were okay with that?" Karl asked skeptically.

"Well, there was that Mom-to-Dad-and-Back look," Stephanie admitted. "I won't say they seemed thrilled by the idea. But they didn't say no. I think both of them know how dangerous something like baka bakari could really be, especially on Sphinx. Mom knows all about how dangerous plant products can be, even when they seem harmless, and Dad's a doctor. His patients mostly have four feet—or six—and not two, but he's still a doc. They'll make me make all kinds of promises about how careful I'll be—and I really will be careful, Karl, and you know it!—but they'll sign off on it."

Karl still looked less than happy, Cordelia thought. Not surprisingly, given how protective of Stephanie he was. But she could see his resistance crumbling.

No, not crumbling, she corrected herself. *It's just that he knows Steph. And he also knows that if she promises her parents to be careful, she will. And now, thanks to Jessica, he doesn't need to send her in alone. He's not giving up on protecting her—he's just choosing his fights.* Her lips twitched on the edge of a smile. *I'd pick 'em pretty carefully, too, where Steph is concerned! Hold out for the best support team we can get her, since she probably* would *head out on her own, whatever she may have "learned" since she and Lionheart met, if Karl tried to freeze her out. I wonder if he'd have asked me to go in as her backup if Anders hadn't come along? Well, now he doesn't need to.*

"All right," he said finally. "*If* your parents sign off on it, Steph!"

He gave her that stern glower again, and she looked back so innocently Cordelia had to suppress a giggle. Karl gazed at her a moment longer, then sighed and turned his attention back to the rest of the group.

"If the Harringtons *do* sign off on this, then I think we have the basis of a pretty good plan. But if we don't hit pay dirt the first couple of times we can't keep trolling Steph through the clubs on the list without somebody wondering why she's spending so much time there."

"In that case, we put me in next," Cordelia offered.

"That's definitely a thought!" Stephanie said. "And we could talk to Chet and Christine, if we needed to, too."

"Both excellent thoughts," Karl said approvingly. "But there's no need to refine future plans yet when we may score the first time out. Besides"—he flashed a smile at Cordelia—"it's not as if the rest of us won't be playing a part. We're going to need to have someone hanging around as backup, just in case something goes wrong."

Cordelia suddenly felt a whole lot better.

Discussion turned to which of the clubs on Nosey's list would be best for their first try. There were several, but they decided to begin by narrowing down to two that used Câmara Comestibles to provide food service.

Cordelia tried to think like someone unethical enough to test an unregulated drug on a minor, then said, "I vote for this one—Enigmatic Riddle. It has advantages that the other one—Lighter Than Here—doesn't have. It's attached to a hotel, which means the clientele will have a lot fewer regulars who might notice something hinky going on. Also, because it's attached to the hotel, the dance floor and social area are open to hotel patrons and their guests, which means no getting stopped at the door for being a minor. For our purposes, it's better, too. A lot more coming and going at all hours, which means we can set up surveillance without worrying about being noticed hanging around a nightclub before it opens."

"My thoughts, exactly," Karl agreed. "Again, as with teams, this doesn't mean we're ruling the others out, just that this will be our starting point. I have enough budget to get a room at the hotel for Stephanie's identity, which will have the added advantage of giving us a base."

They refined their plans a while longer, then Cordelia and Jessica started getting ready to go home.

"Anders," Stephanie asked, "are you going all the way back to Yawata Crossing tonight?"

"That or getting a room in Twin Forks," Anders replied. "Jessica's family is sort of packed in at their place."

And besides, Cordelia thought, *staying with your not-really girlfriend at her family's house would be super awkward. That would go for staying here, too.*

She cut in before Stephanie could make the polite offer she clearly intended.

"Come back to my place? We have a spare room and the house sort of rattles now that Mack and Zack are spending some nights at their place. We're south of Twin Forks, but I could take you wherever you left your car in the morning."

Anders looked surprised, then pleased. "Actually, I took public transport to Twin Forks, and Jessica picked me up. If I can get back to Twin Forks tomorrow, I'm good. But don't worry about it. We're not too late for me to catch a lift."

"Really, I'm serious," Cordelia said. "Besides, if we're going to be up to our necks in skullduggery together, I need to get to know you better. I'm the only one who hasn't had a chance."

"Okay," Anders said, then added with a solemnity that did not hide the twinkle in his eyes, "but I just want to warn you. I'm not planning to fall in love with you, too, no matter how much it seems that I have a thing for girls with treecats."

✧ ✧ ✧

Stephanie tried not to show that she was watching to see how Karl reacted when Cordelia offered to give Anders a place to spend the night. To be honest, she couldn't quite tell.

After the others left, she and Karl gathered up the dessert plates and drifted toward the kitchen. She could hear music playing from her mom's art studio, but otherwise the house was quiet. Lionheart had appeared briefly with Athos and Valiant when the others were leaving, then he and Survivor had vanished back to somewhere up in the trees. She knew he was well and content, and felt very happy that he, too, had had a party with friends today.

"That was good of you, checking to be sure Anders had a place to stay," Karl said. "I was going to ask him if he wanted to spend the night in my room, here, but I wasn't sure how you'd feel about it."

"It's good," Stephanie said. "Jessica was right to recruit him; righter to just drop the situation on me like that. I would have fussed. I deal better with problems than with anticipation. Jess is smart about people."

"She is. I'm glad she's on deck with us on this baka bakari thing. We talked a bit, and she's going to make sure she's available." Karl stretched and smothered a yawn. "I think we should get a suite at the hotel and all plan to crash there."

"Um. I sorta thought that myself, but then I remembered something else: the 'cats. You know Lionheart's not going to be any more willing to stay home than

Survivor would be if you tried to leave *him* behind. Not as far away as Yawata Crossing. But if I'm undercover, I can't very well have a 'cat in my room with me! So I think we may need to get two rooms. Or one suite to use as HQ and another for 'tourist me' to use. Of course, that still leaves the problem of how we smuggle them into the hotel in the first place. I know it's got a 'pets welcome' policy, but still—"

She shrugged.

"Hadn't thought about that," Karl admitted wryly. "I love the 'cats, but they *do* make undercover harder." He rubbed his chin for a moment, thinking hard. Then he raised his uni-link and punched up a map of Yawata Crossing. He scrolled around it for a few seconds, then nodded to himself.

"Thought I remembered that," he said, and looked at Stephanie. "There's a Yawata PD precinct office one block over from the Enigmatic Riddle. It's in a city-owned building that's supposed to house an EMT center, as well, but they haven't had the budget to set it up yet." He grimaced at the familiar refrain. "That means half the building's standing empty, but it's got power and running water. Bet if we ask Chief Chuchkova—or get Chief Shelton to ask her—we could use that as our HQ. Not as close as right in the hotel, but almost as good. We borrow one of the SFS vans, opaque the windows, fly all of us and the 'cats in to the precinct house, and set up camp there. Then we rent a suite at the hotel as planned for 'tourist you.' It'd be big enough we could sneak Cordy and Jess in without anybody noticing, and Anders could rent a room of his own on the same floor. Think our furry little shadows would go for that?"

"I think it's about the best idea we're likely to come up with, anyway," Stephanie said with an enthusiastic smile. "We were separated by a lot more than a block when you and I were attending class on Manticore, so Lionheart *should* be okay with it. Of course," her smile turned into a grin, "getting him to *stay* there might be a little iffy if he decides I'm up to something that could get me into trouble!"

"Yeah, I know." Karl rubbed the back of his neck, then shrugged. "Truth is, that might not be a bad thing, Steph." He looked at her very seriously. "We don't want him dashing to your rescue and blowing the whole operation if you're *not* in trouble, but I'll be honest and admit I'd rather have him around to help keep an eye on you. I'm not kidding. I don't want anything happening to you. Not on this operation. Not ever."

"Sounds good to me," Stephanie said as lightly as she could, a bit taken aback by the intensity in his voice. "As long as he doesn't get squashed in city traffic, anyway!" she added perkily.

"Not much chance of that," Karl assured her. "Lots of green belts in Yawata Crossing, remember? A 'cat could get all the way across town without ever touching the ground once!"

"Then I think—" Stephanie began, only to stop and look up as the kitchen door opened and Marjorie Harrington walked in.

"Did you have fun, Steph?" she asked.

"Yep."

"I had the impression Anders showing up was a surprise," Marjorie said, glancing back and forth between Karl and her daughter.

"It was, but it turned out not to be a bad one," Stephanie said.

"And that *other* little project we discussed?" her mother said.

"That's one reason it wasn't a bad surprise," Stephanie said with a grin. "He's willing to help us out."

"Oh, so you won't be doing any clubbing of your own?" To Karl's ear, there was a touch of relief in Marjorie's voice, but Stephanie shook her head.

"No. If you and Dad agree, we still want me to go, too." She met her mother's eyes levelly. "I know I'm young. That's a big part of why I'd be a good pick. But I promised Karl I'd only go if you and Dad *do* sign off on it, and we'll be really careful, I promise. I'll leave my uni-link open so Karl can hear every word. And a couple of Chief Chuchkova's uniformed officers will 'just happen' to be close enough Karl can call them in a hurry if we need them."

Marjorie's hazel eyes were dark, but she nodded slowly.

"Maybe it's silly of me, but I can't help worrying, Steph. You're my daughter, and part of me still thinks of you as my little girl. But if you've taught me and your dad one thing, it's that kids grow up fast on Sphinx. If I'm willing to let you traipse around the bush visiting treecats with that hand cannon of yours strapped to your hip, I don't suppose there's any reason I shouldn't let you traipse around Yawata Crossing. And I already let you go off to Manticore without me, didn't I?" She smiled with a tiny edge of sadness. "You really are growing up, whether I'm ready for that or not. And Karl did a pretty good job of looking after you when those thugs tried to kidnap Lionheart, too. I guess he can do that again. And you will, won't you?" she asked, looking directly at Karl.

"I won't let anything happen to her," Karl said, putting an arm around Stephanie as he faced her mother.

"No," Marjorie said with another, broader smile. "No, you won't." She reached out and touched Karl's cheek, then inhaled.

"All right, Stephanie. You have our permission. When are you planning on launching this operation of yours?"

"Pretty soon," Stephanie replied. "Anders is going to help keep an eye on me"—she flashed a smile at her mother's nod of approval—"so we have to fit it into his schedule, as well. Probably in the next couple of days?"

She made the last sentence a question and looked up at Karl, who nodded.

"All right," Marjorie said with a serenity Karl suspected was just a little forced.

"It should be pretty simple," he said. "For that matter, we may not turn up anything at all. In which case, we'll just have turned it into a sendoff night out for Anders!"

"I hope neither of you will be too disappointed in me if I say I'd almost prefer that," Marjorie said with a headshake. "I know that's not what *you* two want, but once you get to be my age, you get a little tired of adventures and the way they make you late for dinner."

"Yes, Master Baggins," Stephanie said demurely. Karl looked puzzled, but Marjorie laughed out loud and reached out to give her a hug.

"I knew reading you those stories would prove useful

one day!" she said. Then she stood back a bit, her hands still on her daughter's shoulders. "And speaking of Bilbo, he knew how to throw a party, too, didn't he? So if we're going to be thinking about sendoffs for Anders, we'd be happy to throw him a going-away party, too, here at the house."

Stephanie grinned, knowing she was about to startle her mother.

"Maybe we could follow through on the Baggins model and combine it with my birthday party?" she suggested. "He's leaving not long after."

Last birthday, Richard and Marjorie had needed to all but threaten Stephanie to get her to agree to invite anyone over to celebrate it. Stephanie knew her parents had been being *very* tactful about this year. Now she had the pleasure of watching her mother's face light up, but Marjorie replied carefully, as if afraid that showing too much enthusiasm would make Stephanie scamper like a frightened range bunny into the brush.

"That would be nice, dear, and very generous of you to share. I'll talk with your father."

"Okay, Mom. I'm off to do some studying."

"Don't stay up too late. You know you'll be up early to see Karl off."

"Promise."

16

SEVERAL DAYS LATER, THE NEW STEVIE BITTS, TOURIST from Manticore, although originally from Meyerdahl, was ready to make her debut. They'd chosen this backstory for a variety of reasons. It let Stephanie disguise her speech with Meyerdahl slang and accent, while not necessarily being up to date on the latest trends. She'd been called "Stevie" by some of her friends on Meyerdahl, so would automatically respond to it. And short-term tourist IDs were widely available and easy to alter.

"And, if anyone notices it's been altered, they're just going to think I'm younger than I'm claiming to be," Stephanie said, looking with satisfaction at the end result.

They'd researched, and learned that while Enigmatic Riddle was open to all hotel guests, children under fourteen were excluded unless in the company of their guardians. "Stevie," at the edge of seventeen, should have no difficulties.

The club's evening dress code encouraged "dressy" attire, which suited their purposes perfectly, since Stephanie Harrington expended her clothing budget on clothing that wore well outdoors. Indeed, footwear had been a problem, since she owned exactly one pair of very neutral flats for when hiking boots wouldn't do. Attempts to get her to walk in high heels were a disaster. However, it turned out that low dress boots were back in style, especially when worn with ankle-length skirts.

Jessica, who, because of her family's size and lack of disposable income was skilled in getting good deals second hand, put herself in charge of costuming for the project, while Cordelia—who was also the "outdoorsy" type, and nearly as hopeless as Stephanie when it came to dressing up—snitched some of her sister, Dana's, cosmetics and brought them along when the three girls met in "Stevie's" room at the hotel to do the final preparations.

The outfit Jessica had designed was built around a black ankle-length skirt worn with a sleeveless top in an abstract "leopard" print in a shimmery, silky fabric and a golden vest. Over this ensemble, Stephanie would wear a black, cropped-waist jacket that, for now, waited on a hanger. On her feet were black suede ankle boots, whose six-centimeter wedge heel made Stephanie feel amazingly tall, but which had proven much easier to walk in than the ten-centimeter spike heels Jessica had initially offered.

Waiting on the dresser were a pair of three-centimeter diamond-shaped hammered gold earrings, and five bangles, similar in size, but with distinctly different textures that caught the light in fascinating ways. There were also fingerless net gloves to disguise what even an hour-long manicure had been unable to repair regarding Stephanie's work-hardened and scratched hands. But, before she would don these, came hair and makeup.

Stephanie had always worn her curly brown hair

relatively short, because she didn't want to be bothered "messing with it." Jessica had come up with a surprisingly easy-to-use set of extensions, in a shade similar to Stephanie's natural hair, so that the two could be blended. The longer hair worked amazingly well to change Stephanie into someone else.

"The best is yet to come," Jessica cackled. "Cordelia, my paints, please."

Cordelia produced several flat boxes that, even unopened, promised beauty. With a flourish, she handed them to Jessica.

"Here they are. As you requested, an ample selection from Dana's chest of wonders."

"Dana won't mind?" Stephanie asked nervously.

"She probably won't even notice," Cordelia assured her. "She loves buying the new color palettes each fashion season, and then rarely looks at the others."

"These are pretty," Stephanie admitted, looking over a selection of glittery pastel and metallic hues. "Like butterfly wings."

She stretched her hand out to dab a vibrant blue eye shadow on a sponge applicator, but Jessica intercepted her.

"Not that! Especially not with the outfit we chose for you. That blue would really clash!"

Stephanie frowned. "But I'm not supposed to look supersophisticated, am I? And that blue's the prettiest color there."

"There's a difference between 'unsophisticated' and completely ignorant," Jessica countered. "Sit still. I'll show you how even apparently muted colors can make you look amazing."

The process of being made up tickled, so Stephanie

had to resist a constant urge to rub her nose. However, if Jessica's absorbed expression hadn't been warning enough that such actions would be unwelcome, Cordelia's increasingly fascinated gaze made Stephanie willing to hold still, just so she could see the end result.

"There you are," Jessica said, adding a final touch of something to one of Stephanie's cheekbones. "Stephanie Harrington, meet Stevie Bitts."

Stephanie turned the mirror to face herself and saw a stranger's eyes widen in astonishment. She'd always thought the combination of brown hair and brown eyes made her completely unexciting, but Jessica's skillful work with the cosmetics had brought out flecks of gold she hadn't realized were buried in the rich brown of her eyes.

For the rest, a medium beige foundation covered Stephanie's outdoor-weathered complexion. Cocoa-colored eye shadow, highlighted with soft cream near the brow bone and inner eye near the nose, made her eyes mysterious, even (dare she think it?), a little sexy. Her eyes had been further reshaped with black eyeliner that extended into a slight cat's eye, and her lashes accented with black mascara.

Rose-colored blush and a pearlescent highlighter along the cheekbones subtly changed the shape of her face. Her lips had been lightly outlined, then tinted a glossy shade of rose like, but not identical to, that on her cheeks. Overall, her new appearance was simultaneously natural and sophisticated.

"Wow!" Stephanie said, wondering what Karl and Anders would think.

She jumped up to put on the jacket, but Jessica waved her back.

"We've got to work on how you move," Jessica said. "Remember, you're wearing a skirt, a full one, sure, but you've got to pull your stride in. No, no . . . Don't mince, just don't walk as if you're trying to cover as much ground as fast as you can."

Stephanie did her best but, in the end, both Cordelia and Jessica agreed that it was a good thing she wasn't trying to look as if she went out dining and dancing every night.

"Steph, can you even dance?" Jessica asked. "I don't think that's ever come up."

"A little," Stephanie said. "Well, shuffle to music."

"Don't worry about it," Cordelia offered encouragingly. "You're naturally light on your feet. Trust that and the fact that 'Stevie' isn't local, so she won't be expected to know the music or the popular steps."

"Do you dance a lot?" Stephanie asked, heart thumping a little at this unexpected complication.

"Sure! It's fun. Mom always had us dance to work off our fidgets when the winter froze us in. Anyhow, if you look like you're having fun and you don't step on your partner's feet too often, you'll be fine."

"Either of you want to take my place?" Stephanie asked, only half-joking. "Cordelia? You have the right coloration to wear the same things that I am."

"Sorry," Cordelia replied with an impish grin. "You're stuck with it. You're short and petite. Neither Jess nor I could wear your clothes. Anyhow, you're going to do just fine. We believe in you."

And she really does, Stephanie thought, heartened as she submitted to Jessica's final primping. *Treecats really do know how to pick the best humans.*

17

WHEN STEPHANIE WALKED UP TO THE ENTRY FROM THE hotel into the Enigmatic Riddle, her mind was a jangling confusion of various instructions.

Don't stride. You're not in a hurry. You're actually a little nervous. Well, Stevie is, but differently than I am, you are. She's nervous because she wants to have a big adventure. Meet people. Maybe find a holiday romance. Don't think about why you're nervous, Steph, up to and including that your first boyfriend is going to be in there. And you're trying to get something on dangerous drug dealers, of course.

As she drew closer to the moment when she'd need to talk with the hostess, she nearly worked herself up to the point of turning on her fashionably booted heels and running toward where she could feel Lionheart's comforting presence. The only thing that kept her from bolting was thinking about how Karl would react to her sudden appearance. He had Lionheart with him and Survivor in his air van, somewhere out on the parking field, because it was closer than the precinct house.

Right. I can't act like a kid racing for safety. But why oh why is this so much harder than facing down a forest fire?

The hostess scanned Stephanie's room key, then glanced at her ID.

"I'll have to give you a bracelet indicating you're underage," she explained, following this with a conspiratorial wink, "but it doesn't have to stand out. Here. This one will mingle well with the bangles you're already wearing. Have a lovely evening."

The team had scouted the floorplan of the club earlier, and Stephanie had already earmarked her destination: one of the high tables that gave a good view of most of the club, including the dance floor. The club was comfortably full, but not crowded. She found a small table and claimed it, remembering at the last minute to step up gracefully into the long-legged chair, not hoist herself on her hands as would be more usual.

Sound buffers around the dance floor kept the music at a comfortable level for those who didn't care to immerse themselves in the current dance number. The piece playing now was perky, so Stephanie didn't think it was out of line to tap her booted toe against the footrest while she scanned the in-table menu and placed an order for a provocatively named "Ruby Houri (virgin)," which was basically a blended juice drink served in a glass with more curves than Stephanie could ever hope to be gifted with by nature. The photo showed it as quite pretty, with swirling layers of reds and oranges that managed to evoke the veils of the dancing girl drawn in the illustration.

She longed to order a slice of an amazingly rich-looking confection that alternated layers of whipped cream, cherries, and yellow cake, but suspected that would not look sophisticated—and would probably ruin the elaborate artistry that Jessica had made of her lips. Instead, she settled for some little squares of dark chocolate she could place directly onto her tongue, while promising herself a slice of that cake some other day.

So equipped, she scanned her surroundings, deciding that this would only be natural for a young woman out on her own, hoping to make a connection or two. While there were numerous couples, the majority of the clientele seemed to be unattached. Many had come in groups, but didn't necessarily restrict themselves to interacting with their friends. A few times she saw someone apparently being dared to go talk to someone in another group.

Human courtship rituals, Stephanie thought, trying to look cool and a little detached, not scared out of her mind. *Or maybe "mating rituals" would be a more accurate term, because courtship is meant to go somewhere farther than just an evening's fun right? But not all these people are looking for someone to have sex with, right? So mating isn't fair, either. I wish I understood better. Maybe I am, like Trudy always said, just too much of a dumb kid.*

In her pensive survey of the room, Stephanie completely missed Anders the first time, but she spotted him the second time, less for himself than because he was attracting a lot of attention from a mixed group of locals—she felt certain of this from the body language—who had just come in and were looking about, clearly seeking who was new and interesting this evening.

When Stephanie caught her initial glimpse of Anders, her heart flip-flopped, much as it had that very first time back in much less glamorous circumstances, when Dr. Hobbard had been introducing her—and more importantly, Lionheart—to the newly arrived Whittaker xeno-anthropological team. Then Anders had been dressed casually, but tonight... She fumbled with her Ruby Houri to keep herself from messing up her makeup by burying her face in her hands.

Oh! I'd forgotten how completely gorgeous Anders is.

And he honestly was. His button-down shirt was an indigo that drew attention to the dark blue of his eyes. As usual, he wore his wheat-colored hair pulled back, but tonight, instead of the usual utilitarian tie, he had it bound with a thick band of silver, printed with angular geometric holograms that sparkled in the shifting lights from the dance floor.

As Stephanie watched, a redheaded woman at least five years older than Anders came over and leaned on the table in front of him in a fashion that showed off an expanse of cleavage. She said something to him, and Anders laughed, tapping his wrist where a solid silver cuff showed.

Saying "Thank you, but I'm underage."

Whatever the red-haired woman said next made them both laugh. In a few moments, Anders was leading her out onto the dance floor where a thudding bass and drumbeat-heavy piece was starting up.

Stephanie squelched a fierce flood of jealousy. *Remember, you're here to work. Can't do that if both of you just sit around and watch. Now that Anders is working the crowd, what can you do?*

Even with her resolve, it was hard not to feel like

a wallflower, to wonder if, despite Jessica's best efforts, she wasn't very attractive. Stephanie knew she could get up and ask someone to dance, but here she hit a basic snag—she wasn't very good at reaching out to others. She knew perfectly well that if her parents hadn't insisted she socialize with people her own age, she would never have bothered, considering the majority of her age-mates "zorks" and "nulls."

And how wrong I was, Stephanie scolded herself. She caught herself reaching up to pat Lionheart, as she often did when in an uncomfortable situation, and let her hand drop, thinking how odd that would look. *Well, if anyone noticed, maybe they thought I was playing with my hair. I certainly have a lot more of it now.*

Postponing the moment of truth just a little longer, she sipped her Ruby Houri and studied the crowd, hoping to find someone who she wouldn't be scared to ask to dance. She also looked for signs that something other than alcohol and snacks were being dispensed. Certainly nothing strange seemed to be going on: no one was being whispered to by mysterious concierges in immaculately stylish evening attire, then being escorted to a slightly screened doorway, or anything else indicating secret transactions. Stephanie was just about to push herself into at least mingling, when she noticed someone drifting toward her table.

The person approaching was elegantly androgynous, with short-cropped dark hair that swept in wavelike bangs, overshadowing dark, slightly almond-shaped eyes framed with velvety dark lashes. It was a look that went amazingly well with close-cut white dress slacks, a dark purple shirt with pearl buttons, a white cutaway jacket with long tails, and high-heeled boots. Stephanie saw no jewelry, except for pearl button earrings that echoed the buttons of that shirt. When the fashion plate spoke to Stephanie, it was in a voice as subtle and soothing as Lionheart's purr.

"I am called Xadrian."

"I'm Stevie." Stephanie felt very proud when her voice didn't squeak.

"You are new here, perhaps? Would you like to dance?"

Stephanie wondered if Xadrian was on the club's staff, someone paid to make certain that even wallflowers had a chance to bloom. Nonetheless, she was happy to accept the courtesy.

Hey, maybe Xadrian will prove to be a lead.

"Thanks, Xadrian. I'd enjoy dancing, but I don't know this music and," Stephanie decided she might as well confess her shortcomings up front, "I'm not a terrific dancer."

"Then here, where the Enigmatic Riddle echoes, is where you can express yourself," Xadrian assured her, tucking a beautifully manicured hand under Stephanie's elbow. "Here, away from home, where there will be no one to bear tales."

Stephanie forced a smile. "I'm game. It's okay to be shy in a strange place, right?"

Xadrian nodded and smiled a silky smile. "Precisely right."

Although Stephanie felt as if everyone must be staring at her, she knew that was her own self-consciousness speaking. She remembered how Cordelia had spoken of dancing as fun, had praised Stephanie's natural grace.

All right. Let's think of this as a new sport rather

than me making an exhibition of myself in public. I wouldn't be shy about not flying a new type of glider right the first time, would I?

As she and Xadrian moved onto the dance floor, the music was easing from something throbbing, slow, and romantic to a lighter, perky, tune that defied the listener to not at least try to dance. Under Xadrian's subtle coaching, Stephanie felt she didn't make a complete fool of herself. When the song ended, she didn't feel the least desire to scurry back to her seat. The music was segueing into something whose introductory notes elicited squeals of delight and a general scurrying toward the dance floor.

"Ah!" Xadrian said, flashing white teeth. "This is a group dance. Not all that different, really, than some you might have done when much younger and in school. The steps are included in the lyrics." Xadrian gave Stephanie a melting smile. "But don't worry. I won't abandon you."

"Okay, coach," Stephanie said. "I'll give it my best."

"Let me stand to your left, then," Xadrian said. "That way I will be behind you and can whisper instructions if you miss a line of the lyrics. Besides"—a smile with a definite twinkle to it—"this way I get to put my hands on your waist. Ready?"

Stephanie found her hand drifting toward the non-present treecat at her shoulder and covered the gesture by playing with one of her earrings. "I'm set."

The dance, which was apparently called Sixy-Snakey, did remind Stephanie of line dances she'd done in school back on Meyerdahl. She wondered if it might have been aged-up from a similar origin, because she was absolutely certain that none of those dances had contained such provocative hip and hand gestures. Here, though, performed by a lighthearted crowd, the hip thrusts and butt wiggles seemed less provocative and more a mockery of studied seduction.

To her surprise, Stephanie realized she was actually having a good time. Then the dance line curled around, Xadrian's hands on her waist subtly steered Stephanie into a turn, and turning to face another coil of the line she found herself face-to-face with none other than Frank Câmara.

Frank was dressed up, at least for him, wearing a snug shirt that showed off his muscular upper body and arms. Heavy leather cuffs at his wrists all but hid his "underage" band. He'd not only combed his hair, but swept it back and plastered it down with some sort of styling product. To Stephanie's surprise, he was wearing jewelry: a tough guy stud in one ear that looked like a bit of iron ore. He had his hands on the waist of a woman at least as voluptuous as Trudy Franchitti. Unlike Xadrian, whose touch was feather light, Frank kept a firm grip on his partner and all but publicly groped her when the opportunity presented itself.

The woman doesn't seem to mind, though, Stephanie thought.

The steps of the dance required that Stephanie face Frank, while the Sixy-Snakey curving line moved two steps to one side, two steps to the next, before whirling around and continuing to weave around the dance floor. He didn't appear to recognize her, though, and there was something vague and disconnected about his expression that made her doubt that he would recognize his own mother. Nonetheless, Stephanie barely managed not to sigh in relief when the tide carried Frank away. Soon after, the song ended.

She thanked Xadrian, then let her guide choose another partner, a choice made easier because Anders was using the general shifting as groups reformed to ask Stephanie if he might have the next dance. Stephanie knew Anders had probably spotted Frank as well, and wondered if it was wise for the two of them to be dancing together, in case Frank had recognized her after all.

A single dance can't hurt, she thought, and accepted Anders's gesture toward the dance floor with a shy nod that wasn't entirely feigned.

When we were dating, we never went dancing. This is a first, and probably a last.

"I noticed you as soon as I came in," Anders said, a perfectly normal opening line that nonetheless made Stephanie feel very happy, "but someone got in before me."

She smiled. "This is fine. I haven't danced so much in a long time."

They'd steered themselves deeply enough into the crush that it was natural for them to move closer. Stephanie also felt fairly certain that even if someone was watching them, it would be unlikely that they could read their lips or anything.

"Frank," she said, and Anders nodded.

"Yes, I saw, and he brought a pal, too. Rod Gállego." He snorted at Stephanie's grimace. Rodrigo Gállego, Frank, and Stan Chang had always been very much birds of a feather. "They're hanging in a back corner, close to the bar."

"Just them?"

"A couple of others came and sat for a bit. Your old teammate doesn't seem to be a stranger, here."

"What next?" Stephanie asked.

"I'm here as me," Anders reminded her. "I'm going to pretend to notice them for the first time. Go over, establish my role as pissed off and looking for trouble."

"Me?"

"Keep on as you have. Mix, though. Xadrian asking you to dance was good, raised interest."

"What? Xadrian's just hired help, right?"

Anders snorted. "Not from what I heard. More like Pharaoh who interprets the Sphinx's Enigmatic Riddle. Xadrian showing interest in you means others will, too. See what you can learn."

The song—three minutes or so of focused activity—ended. Stephanie had meant to go to her table, finish her drink, catch her breath, but apparently what Anders had said was true. Her stock was on a rise. Three or four dances later, when something slow and cuddly came up, she was able to make the honest excuse that she needed to catch her breath.

Her current partner said all the polite things, but let her go. Stephanie took a moment to slip into the ladies' room, and check her costume. Jessica had done a good job, and despite Stephanie's fears that some cosmetic might be running or have smeared, she thought she still looked pretty good.

"Her" table was slightly altered from when she'd left it. Her partially drunk "Ruby Houri" was gone, but the chocolate remained. As she pulled up the table menu, a server arrived, bearing a fresh drink.

"The other was getting stale," she said, "and a patron asked that it be refreshed when you returned."

Xadrian, Stephanie thought happily. *I bet.*

"Thank you. Could I trouble you for some ice water?"

"No trouble at all."

She tried to sip daintily, though every ounce of her longed to down the sweet, sugary drink in a few gulps. She followed the Ruby Houri with the best part of the ice water, looking about with a new eagerness and enthusiasm.

I can do this! I can!

She didn't notice that she'd lost track of exactly what her goal was, nor that her heart was racing far too fast, nor the self-satisfied smirks on the faces of two hulking young men who watched from the shadows near the bar.

Boldly, defiantly, Stevie Bitts sashayed forth, ready to conquer.

✧ ✧ ✧

Climbs Quickly was not precisely certain why Death Fang's Bane had wanted him to stay with Shining Sunlight, but by now he had learned that there were certain places where the two-legs did not care for People to go. This tall, sky-touching nest which held the mind-glows of many, many two-legs must be one of those places. But Death Fang's Bane had entered it willingly and, although he tasted apprehension in her mind-glow, he caught the tang of excitement and anticipation, as well. A new experience, then. She had felt like this often when they had gone to the place of blue trees and many, many different scents.

At least the mostly empty nesting place where Death Fang's Bane and her friends had set up camp meant they were separated by less distance than had often been the case on the other world he had visited with her and Shining Sunlight. But he had been greatly relieved when Shining Sunlight had invited him into the flying thing and they had moved still closer to his two-leg. It was not that he thought she went *seeking* trouble; it was just that she seemed to find it so easily.

Still, he trusted Shining Sunlight. He knew how determined Shining Sunlight was that nothing evil would ever happen to Death Fang's Bane, and although Shining Sunlight was focused and intent, his mind-glow tasted of anticipation, hope, and a familiar trace of the exasperation he often felt when Death Fang's Bane was involved, but only the tiniest edge of concern. So, although he kept alert, Climbs Quickly knew the situation was under control. Besides, he had Keen Eyes as company, an assortment of tasty treats, and while he would have preferred not to be restricted to the interior of Shining Sunlight's flying thing, he was not at all unhappy.

Climbs Quickly was pleased when Death Fang's Bane's mind-glow shifted, losing a great deal of its apprehension and instead taking on tastes that he associated with her being immersed in learning. At one point he felt a spike of fear, but that dulled quickly. Not long after, he felt the confusing blend of emotions that he associated with her usual reaction to encountering Bleached Fur. These were a little more intense than she had been feeling lately, but no matter for concern.

Climbs Quickly was contemplating whether—now that darkness had spread and the movements of People would not be seen by the night-blind two-legs, especially if the People in question kept to the shadows—he and Keen Eyes might convince Shining Sunlight to let them go exploring, when he felt Death Fang's Bane's mind-glow begin to shift. She had been growing increasingly happy and confident, but this came after a lull, when he thought she might be taking a break from whatever exertions she had been about.

The change was so sudden that had the emotions he tasted been those of fear or anger, he would have believed she was being attacked. This though . . . This was something he had never felt from her before. Even when Death Fang's Bane launched herself into some danger—as when they had rescued the Damp Ground Clan from the spreading fires—her mind-glow was never without a core of calculation. The only time she did not think was when she was angry—and she was not in the least angry now. She was, instead, ebullient, the shape of her mind-glow reminding him of how a waterfall might feel as it launched itself over a precipice, to plummet in a perfect dive that created rainbows and mist.

Climbs Quickly bristled. Whatever this new mood was, it was wrong, very, very wrong. He hissed as he would at a death-wing that threatened the clan's kittens, causing Shining Sunlight to turn from where he had been studying something on the make images thing that came and went within the flying thing. Keen Eyes, who had been stirred from a drowse by the sudden agitation in Climbs Quickly's mind-glow, looked at him, his own hackles half-risen in reaction.

<What troubles you?>

<Death Fang's Bane. Her mind-glow. It is wrong.> He shared the sensations with Keen Eyes, and saw his friend's fur rise in response.

<Wrong. Yes. And so sudden. She does not seem unhappy or frightened, but . . .>

<She does not, yet I sense in her something of the intensity she brings into a fight, but this time without any of her usual prudence. There is no anger, so I do not think she is actually threatened, but... She feels as if she is running?>

Keen Eyes turned to Shining Sunlight, who was making mouth noises at the two agitated People. As with all mouth noises, these were meaningless, but clearly the young male two-legs was trying to comfort them. Then there was a sharp alert from the thing all the two-legs wore and into which they frequently made mouth noises. Bleached Fur's voice, tight and measured, backed by some sort of loud, rhythmic noise, came forth. Shining Sunlight made short, clipped mouth-noises, and began to get out of the flying thing, motioning for the People to remain within.

Climbs Quickly was having none of this. He snarled at Shining Sunlight. As he had anticipated, Shining Sunlight, who was no fool, hesitated in the face of those bared white fangs and Climbs Quickly slipped past him and ran, ducking over and under the host of flying things at rest in the large hard field. His route was the most direct line to Death Fang's Bane. She was still ebullient, but that ebullience was now colored with annoyance. Climbs Quickly hoped he could reach her in time because, better than most, he knew what damage Death Fang's Bane could cause if she became truly angry.

Climbs Quickly doubted he could successfully moderate such an extreme mood from a distance. Her mind-glow felt almost as if another Person was there before him, muddling the channels of her mind. As he raced to her rescue, he heard Keen Eyes behind him,

Shining Sunlight's pounding feet, his mouth noises coming between breaths, snatches of Bleached Fur's voice, more muffled since they were carried by the noise thing. Then, miraculously, stronger, ahead of him, an outline in a shape of multicolored light that proved, when Climbs Quickly angled toward it, to be a large opening such as two-legs made in their structures.

Normally, Climbs Quickly would avoid such a place. Too many two-legs, too noisy, but this was the way to Death Fang's Bane. He dodged stranger two-legs, followed the trail of Death Fang's Bane's increasingly chaotic mind-glow, a mind-glow so turned in on itself that it hardly seemed to hold the brilliance that was Death Fang's Bane at all.

Around Climbs Quickly, two-legs shrieked, screamed, shouted: a pack of crazed grass runners in full panicked cry. They parted about him, and he was glad because he did not wish to hurt a single one of them, but he would if they kept him from Death Fang's Bane. Close as they now were, Climbs Quickly could feel her heart was racing faster and faster, her ability to form coherent thought vanishing in a whirlpool of giddy confusion.

Then there she was, smelling not quite like herself, but herself, her beloved, beloved self. She was being restrained by Bleached Fur and a stranger two-legs, and they were having difficulty doing so. Tiny as she was, Death Fang's Bane was fierce and very strong.

Gathering his five legs beneath him, pulling in his claws, Climbs Quickly leapt, first hitting onto one of the raised things upon which humans put what they ate and drank, then kicking off to launch himself, soft-pawed onto Death Fang's Bane. Every fiber of him wanted to merge with Death Fang's Bane in her crazed, heart-racing, joyful insanity. He remembered what Keen Eyes had shared of the madness that had driven the Trees Enfolding and Swaying Fronds clans to war not long before. Privately, he had thought he would be able to resist an emotional intensification loop, but now that it was his bondmate, his heart, his dearest beloved, friend, partner, life-light, he felt himself nearly drawn into her madness.

Only one thing kept him from being swallowed. Death Fang's Bane needed him to anchor her. She needed him to be a rock to dam the raging, cascading waterfall she had become. She needed him, and he would not fail her. He would not, would not, although the power of her mind-glow, brilliant as the sun, was enough to blind them both.

Climbs Quickly leapt into her light, stumbled, felt Death Fang's Bane's warmth, beneath him. That physical contact centered him. He had dealt with her anger and moodiness since she had been but a youngling. Now with her smell around him, the touch of her, her arms automatically gripping him close, he was where he must be. He was in his truest home.

Now that he was here, Climbs Quickly could put all that he was into calming her. Distantly, he was aware of Bleached Fur making rapid mouth noises, of the noise ebbing around them, of new, familiar sounds and mind-glows: Windswept, Dirt Grubber, Awakening Joy, Stone Shaper. These felt as distant as the bright lights in the sky, for his journey was inward, riding the currents of Death Fang's Bane's unnaturally exhilarated mind-glow. He purred, he patted her with his tail and true-hand. He sent calm and rest and quiet memories to her.

Gradually, something of her manic mood receded, but he could still feel her heart racing, her breath coming fast. He sniffed: that scent he knew from Healer's place, from where Darkness Foe worked upon the injured. Healers had arrived, healers who knew how to help a sick two-leg. Reluctantly, refusing to completely leave his bondmate, Climbs Quickly released enough of Death Fang's Bane's body that the healers could inspect her with things from their healer's kit.

There were many mouth noises all around, but Shining Sunlight made the most. Windswept was helping the healers—no surprise that. Bleached Fur had stepped back and was gripping hard onto Dirt Grubber, while the wise old gardener did his best to soothe the frightened young male. Awakening Joy stood holding Stone Shaper, shoulder to shoulder with a stranger two-leg that Climbs Quickly thought might be the one who had assisted Bleached Fur in restraining Death Fang's Bane.

Climbs Quickly felt the change after the healers gave Death Fang's Bane something that calmed her racing heart as he had her drifting mind. She slept then, breathing only a little faster than she should. Eventually, under Shining Sunlight's guidance, all of them except for the healers—even the stranger and all the People—went out of the now nearly deserted gathering place, to a smaller nesting place.

The mouth noises rose and fell as the two-legs consulted. For once, Climbs Quickly felt none of his usual curiosity regarding what it was they did. He curled close to Death Fang's Bane, guarding her, even in her dreams.

18

UP IN STEVIE BITTS'S SUITE AT THE HOTEL, CORDELIA and Karl tucked Stephanie and Lionheart into bed. Anders and someone named Xadrian, who had been of great help down in the club, waited in the sitting room. Jessica had stayed behind to talk to the EMTs. As Cordelia and Karl stepped out of the bedroom, shutting off the lights, but leaving the door open in case Stephanie should need them, Jessica let herself into the suite.

"We're clear," she said. "Since Stephanie's blood work didn't show anything illegal—not even alcohol—and her vital signs stabilized, the EMTs didn't see any need to rush her off to a hospital. Based on what they didn't say, they think she was acting up, trying to get attention. Apparently, they see a lot of that sort of thing."

Karl sighed. "Richard and Marjorie didn't ream me out or anything when I commed them." He shook his head, his expression less than happy. "I almost wish they had."

"Hey, it wasn't your fault!" Jessica said, giving him

a quick hug. "We were all watching her like hawks. And Chief Chuchkova's people were there almost as quick as you and Lionheart!"

"I know. I know!" Karl shook his head again, then closed his eyes and drew a deep breath. "I know," he said again, "but it's *Steph*, and if anything happened to her—"

"Something did happen, but we were waiting, and we caught her when she fell, Karl," Anders said. He reached out and squeezed Karl's shoulder. "And the reason we were there to catch her was because you'd insisted we do this right. So stop kicking yourself, okay?"

"But—" Karl began, then stopped. "Okay. You're right," he admitted. "And at least the EMT doc was able to tell Richard and Marjorie she's going to be fine before they climbed into their air car and headed for town."

"Exactly," Jessica said firmly. She gave him one last squeeze and stood back, and he smiled at her, then looked at the others.

"In that case," he said in a deliberately brisker tone, "we need to start figuring out what happened. Anders, any thoughts?"

Anders gave them a quick summary of events earlier that evening, including how he'd seen both Frank and Rodrigo. At this point, the newcomer, Xadrian, leaned forward from one end of the sofa.

"I have seen those two before," Xadrian said, "usually accompanied by another."

"Oh?" Karl looked at her for a moment, then punched up an image on his uni-link and showed it to Xadrian. "Would that have been this guy?"

"It would, indeed," Xadrian agreed, looking at the image of Stan Chang. "And I wondered what they were doing in the Enigmatic Riddle. Clearly, even though they tried to look as if they enjoyed themselves, it was not the sort of place they would choose to socialize."

"Do you think they could have done something to Steph?" Anders asked, pacing restlessly around the room, picking up and putting down things, clearly unaware of what he was doing.

Xadrian nodded. "They might have put something in her drink. When Stevie left the dance floor and returned to her table, one of the waitstaff brought her a fresh Ruby Houri. Stevie looked just a little surprised, but then she caught my eye and smiled at me. She drank the entire thing fairly quickly."

Jessica drew in a sharp breath. "That's Stephanie all over, especially if she was thirsty from all the dancing and the drink was at all sweet. Was it?"

"Oh, definitely," Xadrian said, "a Ruby Houri is essentially a mixed fruit punch with spiced rum. The 'virgin' version would use a rum flavoring instead. What if someone gave her a drink with alcohol and she downed it that quickly? Does she hold her liquor well?"

"Steph doesn't really drink," Anders said, "but, y'know, we sampled a little when we were dating. She'll get just a little buzz, but she doesn't hold it. She says she guesses her metabolism burns through the alcohol too fast."

"But what if the drink was spiked with . . ." Jessica stopped in mid-sentence, turned to Xadrian. "Look, Xadrian. I gather you took a liking to Stephanie, and Anders said that you were the one who signaled the hotel EMTs that something was wrong, that Stephanie wasn't just making a spectacle of herself, but we don't know you. I'm inclined to trust you..."

Cordelia saw her gaze flicker to where Valiant—along with the other treecats—was keeping vigil over sleeping Stephanie, and understood. Athos also seemed completely comfortable with Xadrian.

"...but maybe you should tell us about yourself."

The elegant figure in the snowy suit brushed a hand down the line of pearl buttons that closed the deep purple shirt. "I am... By day, I am a humble worker behind the scenes, employed in a government office. By night, I am the guardian of the Enigmatic Riddle, keeper of the sacred dancing floor..."

Anders frowned, puzzled by this odd introduction. "So, you're a paid host at the club? Stephanie thought you might be."

"No, no, not at all." Xadrian seemed slightly offended. "I simply feel at home there, as a treecat does in the shadowed greenwood. If the wilderness has those whose souls resonate with it, so must the urban landscape. The Enigmatic Riddle is my favorite haunt, that is all. When I see a promising acolyte, I reach out to draw that one into the mysteries. So it was with Stevie—Stephanie, as I must now call her. She was waiting, intense but shy. I would not have her leave my temple feeling unwelcome."

Karl made a sound somewhere between a snort and a laugh. "All right. Believe it or not, I can buy that. So, how would you feel if someone did spike Stephanie's drink?"

"Annoyed. Extremely. That is bad behavior."

"And," Jessica said, returning to what she had been about to say, "what if they spiked it with something other than booze? A drug that causes euphoria, for example?"

"I would be deeply offended, but not . . ." One perfectly manicured nail tapped an upper lip while Xadrian searched for the right word. ". . . not surprised. However, the EMTs would check for euphorics immediately. That is part of what they are trained to do, given how such substances can be abused, since they are hired by the club. They found nothing."

"Possibly because there was nothing to find," Jessica said, "either because it cleared Stephanie's metabolism quickly or because the drug wasn't programmed into the analyzer."

Xadrian did not look surprised. "There have been rumors of something new, but I have not pursued it. My 'high' comes from the rituals of the nightlife. I drink very sparingly, take nothing illegal." She dropped her elevated manner for a moment and grinned. "If I'm going clubbing at night, and expect to go to work in the morning, I need to be careful."

Then she became serious again. "None of you seem at all surprised by the idea of a new party drug. May I assume you know something about it?"

"Not enough," Karl said, "and we need to know more. Look, Xadrian. I think someone slipped a drug to Stephanie. I've known her since she was a kid, and she's never acted like Anders reported, like we saw after we got in there, before she went down. I don't know if you believe me but—"

Xadrian interrupted. "I believe you. The Stevie I danced with was charmingly awkward in some ways, definitely not the sort to begin racing about like a mad woman, as some patrons have been known to do to draw attention to themselves. I will help you learn what was done to her. I may be able to learn whether one of those two—Frank and Rodrigo, you say—arranged for Stephanie to be sent a new drink. However, I doubt that even I can get a server to admit to knowingly delivering something that had been spiked. Still, if one of them did, it would be a confirmation of your suspicions, and that might be helpful."

Karl looked pleased. "I'll send my contact information to your uni-link. Thanks for the offer. Also, if you can get a line on whether Frank and Rod are doing more than being inept barflies, that would be great. Are they meeting with anyone specific? It's too much to hope that you can get anyone to admit those guys are actually selling or distributing drugs but, if you can, that would be fantastic."

"I will do my best," Xadrian bowed deeply. "They have profaned the temple of which I am self-appointed hierophant. Punishment should come swift and sure."

Xadrian rose from the bow and swept theatrically from the room.

"Quite a character," Cordelia said. "But I like her. And so do the 'cats. That counts, right?"

"It definitely does," Karl agreed. "Okay. Deep breath time. Four treecats are very rarely seen in a Sphinxian nightclub, so it's inevitable someone is going to post about tonight's adventure. I've already brought Chief Ranger Shelton up to speed, and Marjorie and Richard are comming *my* mom and dad and about it. Cordelia and Jessica, I'll leave what you tell your parents up to you, but we need a public version, especially if Frank and Rod were involved, because they'll darned well figure out *exactly* who 'Stevie' is as soon as the word 'treecat' comes up! So what I suggest is that we stick with the send-off party for Anders. I offered to 'cat-sit with Lionheart so Steph could party a bit with Anders and you two, since none of you could take your 'cats into the Enigmatic Riddle. But then Lionheart thought something was wrong and ended up getting inside after all to reassure himself that it wasn't really an issue. Turned out she'd just gotten a little overheated and overexcited dancing, since she doesn't do much of that."

"She is *so* going to kill you for that one, Karl Zivonik!" Jessica chortled. "'Over*excited*? Our Steph? Oh, this is one comeuppance I've *got* to see!"

"Hey, it beats drugged without even knowing it!" Karl shot back with a crooked smile.

"Actually, that sounds like a pretty good cover story," Anders said thoughtfully. "I'm sure some of this is going to turn up on social media, but the lighting wasn't too good and Lionheart got to her quickly enough we don't really need to cover anything else." He nodded. "I think it'll work, Karl."

Cordelia agreed, and saw Jessica nod and reach for her uni-link. Once messages were sent, Jessica went in to check on Stephanie.

"She's sleeping peacefully. Heart rate back to normal, breathing, too. I'd say that by checkout time, probably even by morning, she's going to be fine."

They sat up a while longer, discussing possible future courses of action, much of which depended on what Xadrian was able to find out for them. When they finally crashed, Cordelia and Jessica took the spare bed in the room where Stephanie still slept within her guardian circle of treecats. The last thing Cordelia heard as she drifted off was Karl and Anders arm-wrestling for who got the sofa, and who the rather lumpy extra cot.

Somehow, Cordelia had no doubt that Karl would win.

✧ ✧ ✧

Stephanie awoke to find Lionheart snuggled close to her, his tail wrapped around the top of her head. She felt no disconnect at being in a strange place, and extraordinarily clearheaded. The room was very dark. In the other bed, Jessica and Cordelia, with Valiant and Athos curled at the foot of the bed, slept.

Obviously, all of them had moved from their secret HQ in the YCPD's building to the hotel, she thought. That said interesting things about the hotel management.

She rose as quietly as possible and tiptoed to the bedroom door. She peeked through it into the suite's living room, then sighed silently as the two largish, snoring lumps confirmed what she'd already known. Everyone was here, which meant Operation Undercover was history, one way or the other, whatever happened next. Five teenagers and four treecats in a single hotel suite was about as un-undercover as things could get.

She shook her head, eased the door shut, and went into the bathroom adjoining the room the girls were sharing. Lionheart padded after, leaping lightly onto the countertop, his green eyes sparkling in the light from the nightlight. Once she had the door shut, Stephanie turned on the overhead light and surveyed the remnants of Stevie Bitts.

Someone—probably Jessica—had taken off her hair extensions and outer clothes, as well as somehow getting Stephanie into the sleepshirt that had been in her overnight bag. However, most of the makeup remained, so the face that looked back at her was in many ways still that of a stranger.

Well, I can deal with that, she thought.

The small bag in which Stephanie had packed her toiletries was set on the counter, alongside similar bags that doubtless belonged to Jessica and Cordelia. There was also a container of cold cream, which Stephanie remembered was used for removing makeup. So armed, Stephanie set about reverting to her more usual self.

Teeth brushed, freshly showered, her curly hair finger-combed, Stephanie realized she was ravenous. She was debating whether she could order something from room service without disturbing everyone else, when there was a light tap on the door.

"Need the toilet," Cordelia said, yawning around the words. "And everyone is awake. Karl's ordered bagels, cream cheese, bacon, and a bunch of other stuff."

Stephanie had the door open before Cordelia had finished speaking. Impulsively she hugged the older girl. "Thanks for everything!"

Karl had seen her in her nightshirt many times, but with Anders there, Stephanie decided she could wait to eat long enough to change into street clothes. Jessica, veteran of a large, very informal family, had no such qualms, as Stephanie saw when she joined the others in the main room of the suite. Karl and Anders wore shorts and not much else, so Stephanie ended up feeling overdressed.

She covered her momentary embarrassment by pouncing on a large pumpernickel bagel, smearing it with cream cheese, topping it with bacon, then plopping down on the floor. They'd brought 'cat kibble, and the space under the table was occupied by a line of treecats, munching away. Lionheart patted Stephanie before going to take his place at the one unemptied bowl.

Another proof they're "people," not "just animals," Stephanie thought. *His pals left him his breakfast, even the bacon garnish. Heck, not even all humans would do that.* Her stomach growled in agreement.

Stephanie knew she was thinking about other things to distract herself from having to ask exactly what had happened last night. Her memories after leaving the dance floor were distinctly blurry and part of her wanted to leave them that way, but she had to find out.

"So," she said, once several large bites of bagel had been washed down with black coffee, "what happened last night?"

"What do you last remember?" Karl countered.

"Dancing with Xadrian, then with Anders, then with a couple other people. Really needing something to drink. Going back to my table and . . . That's where it gets foggy. I do remember feeling as if I knew the solution to the problem of Frank and Orgeson, but what that was . . . I can't remember."

"We're not sure exactly what happened to you," Anders began. He'd never been much of a breakfast eater, she remembered, and now he was sipping a mug of coffee and toying with some melon cubes. "But I can tell you what I saw. I was doing what we'd agreed on during our dance. Keeping my distance, seeing what gossip I could pick up. I'd located the woman Frank had been dancing with, and was just about to ask her to dance when I realized there was sort of a ripple in the crowd. I turned to see what was going on, and I was amazed to see that you were, well, stalking around, looking for someone or something, and getting seriously pissed off when you couldn't find it."

"Ouch," Stephanie moaned, envisioning the scene all too easily. "Go on."

"I didn't watch for long, because you clearly weren't yourself. Xadrian and I converged on you in time to keep you from assaulting a bartender who you seemed to think was holding out on you. Although why the bartender and what you thought he could tell you, I'm not sure. I'm not sure *he* was certain either. You were articulate, but cryptic. Anyhow, we got you pulled back—which wasn't easy, let me tell you."

He held up an arm to show a line of bruises that looked remarkably like small finger marks.

"About then Lionheart came racing in from the direction of the garage. The door was open because people had started trickling out when it looked as if you were going to start a brawl. Then it was you and treecat and people screaming and more treecats and club security, and about the time we were going to get thrown out, you collapsed. Xadrian, bless her heart, had already figured out that you were drunk or stoned or something and alerted the club's very discreet, very helpful EMTs. By then, Jessica and Cordelia—with more treecats—had come in. Jess set herself up to liaise with the medics, speaking some sort of medico babble that reassured them that you weren't in any danger."

Jessica said, "I mentioned Meyerdahl mods, accelerated metabolism, and since their job is to make sure the club doesn't have scandals, and the sedatives they'd given you were dealing with the crazy heart rate, and we were willing to sign a waiver. Well, Karl was willing—"

"After I checked in with your dad and mom," Karl added, and shuddered dramatically. "I popped the EMTs' data to your dad on my uni-link, but I still had to face 'em. Believe me, that was a bad moment."

"—we all left peacefully, and came up here and that's it."

Stephanie finished the pumpernickel bagel and smeared more cheese on a cinnamon raisin one, mostly to give herself time to review this.

"My—"

"—folks," Karl finished for her. "I told you; they're up to speed. I do have instructions from your mom that you're supposed to screen home 'as soon as she's finished eating,' but I don't *think* they're likely to tear your head off. Besides," his eyes darkened, "if anyone's head needs tearing off, it's mine, not yours."

"Don't go taking *all* the credit," Stephanie said in a deliberately light tone. "Some of it's mine, you know. I was just as involved in setting this all up as you were."

"Maybe," Karl said after a moment, then shrugged. "Anyway, Chief Shelton and Chief Chuchkova are up to date, too. I had to promise them we'd bring you down to Chief Chuchkova's HQ for a formal statement before we head home. And she wants copies of the EMTs' notes, too. Your parents have to sign the release for that; you can't because you're a minor and I can't because I'm not your guardian. Xadrian messaged me and said she's been checking. There's been some chatter on social media about the young woman with the treecat who wigged out, and it didn't take much for people to connect that with you. But apparently no images of you actually collapsing have gotten out. We're putting it down to your overheating and getting too excited in a crowd like that, then passing out, since the fact that the EMTs were called is already out on the feeds."

"To *what*?" Stephanie stared at him. She heard something like a smothered chuckle from Jessica, but her friend's face was admirably serious when Stephanie darted a look her way, so she returned her glare to Karl.

"We needed a cover story," he said, meeting that glare levelly. "And if we don't want them guessing we're on to them, mentioning anything like drugs or spiked drinks would be a pretty bad idea. Chief Shelton and Chief Chuchkova both agree with that, by the way. That's why you don't see any cops parked outside the suite; they're keeping a low profile. I know it's, uh, a little embarrassing, maybe, but the Enigmatic Riddle's not exactly your usual stomping grounds, Steph. Not mine, either. So the possibility of you being . . . a little out of your depth, maybe, will work. Especially for the people we're interested in, since most of them think of you as a nosey, troublemaking kid with a twitchy temper. You know they do."

Stephanie gazed at him balefully, but he had a point, she admitted.

Maybe.

"Anyway," Karl continued, "someone with the club's management pinged the EMTs, even though you really didn't need them, and I was out in the parking lot, 'cat-sitting until one of you spelled me for my turn on the floor. But when the EMTs got into the act, I hopped out and Lionheart and the others got past me and went scooting ahead to find out what the stupid humans were up to. Which only added to the excitement when they arrived about the same time the EMTs did, of course. Naturally things got pretty confused, but there weren't any *drugs* involved. We can sell that with the right help, Steph."

"What sort of 'help'?" Stephanie demanded, still regarding him with a fulminating eye that promised eventual retribution.

"Xadrian's already doing damage control, and so is Nosey. The story going out is that the treecats wanted to be with their owners and got into the club, which caused some confusion.

"Nosey is amazing. The signal's already down to 'amusing animal story' and he predicts that, without further material, it's going to vanish by noon. He's been boosting the signal on a story about a city counselor caught with her hand in the till, too, as well as the touching story of two high school sweethearts who each thought the other had died in the Plague, and who are getting married next week. He said something about 'Move along! Nothing to see here!'"

"Nosey," Cordelia stated, coming to join them, her hair damp, "is amazing and terrifying. Karl, please pass me the bagels before Stephanie eats them all, and I have to steal Athos's crunchies."

She gave Stephanie a pat on that back that took away any sting from her words, and said, "You feeling better, kiddo? You look good. Clear-eyed and perky. Any chance you remember anything we can add to the data file?"

Stephanie grabbed another strip of bacon. "Just a little. I remember I was trying to find Frank and

Rod. I was going to ask them some very pointed questions. What questions, I don't remember, but I had this idea that I knew exactly what would break the whole case open. Then, when I couldn't find them, I started getting really pissed-off. No one was going to stop me when I was right on the edge of success. I don't remember talking to the bartender, but I guess I thought he was hiding them and got upset."

"Fits," Karl said, leaning forward, resting his elbows on his knees. "Your increased heart rate—doubtless caused by the baka bakari—was probably interpreted by your mind as anger, anxiety, annoyance. We already suspect the stuff makes for overconfidence, and you've never really been great about keeping your temper when you think you've been crossed."

"Truth," Stephanie admitted. "I'm getting better, but if this stuff removes common sense, then . . ." She shrugged, reached for a third bagel, then stopped in mid-reach.

Karl grinned. "I ordered extra. Go for it. You haven't had anything but some sweet drinks and a bit of chocolate since dinner last night."

"And that was early," Jessica commented, "because we had to doll you up. Hey, make this future doctor happy and have some fruit with your carbs and fats, okay?"

✧ ✧ ✧

Stephanie thought about dolling up when, as the gang was packing up, preparatory to checking out, a very different Xadrian showed up at the suite. She was still androgynous, but gone was the exotic figure of the night before, replaced by a soberly clad, completely forgettable civil servant.

The forgettable civil servant in question flashed a bright smile more in keeping with the nightclub Xadrian. "I was sent out on an errands that brought me this way. I couldn't resist seeing if you were still here. May I come in?"

Anders, who'd answered the door, stepped back. "Sure. It's a bit cluttered, but there's always room for you."

Xadrian gave Anders a wicked grin, which made him blush. "Good to know..." Once inside, she turned to Stephanie. "I see I am not the only shapeshifter in our company. You look charming this way, too, I assure you."

Their guest took the seat that Karl gestured toward, and didn't flinch when Lionheart leapt over to give her a solid head butt. Stephanie knew the gesture was a friendly greeting, and was pleased by Xadrian's understanding, and evident pleasure.

"I was able to gather a little information last night," Xadrian went on, patting Lionheart gently, "although not as much as any of us would like. The order for Stephanie's second Ruby Houri came electronically, paid off a pre-paid chip, so no information there... Except." Xadrian flashed another brilliant smile. "I managed to get a look at the night's receipts and that same pre-pay was used to purchase several drinks as well as some snacks for Frank Câmara and Rodrigo Gállego."

"So, it *was* them." Stephanie fought not to bare her teeth and growl. "But there's nothing illegal about buying a girl a drink."

"Nothing," Xadrian agreed, but she still seemed very pleased, so Stephanie guessed there was more. "I located the server who brought the drink to you.

I know her—I know everyone at Enigmatic—and I told her I had a bet on that you'd been drunk when you flipped out. She denied it, even showed me the order, and told me that she'd made the drink herself. I got her talking, challenging her, you know, because I had a bet on, and she challenged me back, saying she remembered every step, even how, when she had the drink ready and on the tray, she'd had to stop because two young men came up to her with a bunch of questions. She'd been glad that the Houri doesn't melt quickly, because she would have had to remake it. From whom she described, I would say that the young men were this Frank and that Rodrigo."

"And that while one distracted her, the other put something in Stephanie's drink," Karl said. "That's very useful. I didn't actually see the drink. Would it show if something was dropped in, especially if that something needed to dissolve?"

"Sadly not," Xadrian said. "It is multihued, more opaque than translucent, and very strongly flavored, the virgin actually more so than the straight because of the rum extract."

"Can't have everything," Karl said philosophically. "It's good to know who ordered the drink and that it could have been tampered with. It's too easy to start blaming things on people you don't much like. Any luck with what they were doing there?"

"I'm working on that," Xadrian said, "but nothing definite so far. I'll message you one way or the other, whether I learn anything or not. Now, you must check out, and I must scurry back to my duties. I did want to speak to you in person, and reassure myself Stephanie was recovered. Be well! Be careful!"

Then, with a flourish of the hand more suited to her nighttime self than the soberly clad individual currently before them, Xadrian rose, patted Lionheart a final time, and slipped out the door.

✧ ✧ ✧

Olivera Chuchkova was a tall woman, with straight dark hair and sharp, equally dark eyes. She wore the Yawata Crossing PD's dark blue uniform without any rank insignia, which Stephanie supposed was actually its own insignia, given that she was its chief.

At the moment, Chuchkova sat behind the desk in her Yawata Crossing office, tipped back in her chair, elbows on the armrests and fingers steepled under her chin as Karl and Stephanie finished bringing her fully up to date. Chief Ranger Shelton was in his own office but attending the conference by com, and Chuchkova had turned her com display so that all of them could see one another.

"So we got Steph up to the suite and put her to bed." Karl had chosen to stand as he made his report, and he faced Chuchkova and Shelton square-shouldered, hands clasped behind him. "The EMTs were right; she turned out to be just fine. But we still blew it, at least in terms of catching anyone red-handed. And we don't have a sample of whatever they put in her drink, either, so we can't match it against the baka bakari Herman gave us."

"You mean what they *allegedly* put in her drink," Chuchkova said dryly, and Karl flushed ever so slightly. "Even if these two bought the drink for her, we don't have any proof they put anything in it. And, for that matter, we don't have any proof Ms. Harrington was given anything at all, according to the blood panels."

"As far as a court of law is concerned, maybe, Ma'am," he said. "But I know Steph. She can be a handful, but not like that. Her behavior was completely outside her normal parameters. So even if we can't prove it, someone did put *something* into that glass. Under the circumstances, it almost had to be baka bakari. And I may not be able to prove Frank and Rod were the 'someone' who put it there, but I know them, too, and that's why I know darned well they were."

There was more than a little grimness in his level voice, and his eyes were hard.

"A good cop—or ranger—knows when to listen to her instincts," Chuchkova said. "Just between you and me, I think you're absolutely right about who did what, but there is that bothersome little thing called 'proof.' You know—the thing we don't have any of?"

"No, Ma'am. We don't," Karl acknowledged.

Stephanie wanted to pipe up, but she'd decided it would be best to let Karl carry the ball. She didn't know Chief Chuchkova anywhere near as well as she knew Chief Shelton, and Chuchkova had said very little to her, aside from greeting her courteously and asking how she felt. She wondered if the police chief was one of those people prepared to write her off as a troublemaking kid, but she wasn't about to horn in on the report of the single sworn ranger on their investigating team and risk confirming that view of her. So she'd sat in her chair, Lionheart in her lap and on his best behavior, listening, with her mouth—uncharacteristically for her—firmly shut.

Which was why she was a bit surprised when Chuchkova raised an eyebrow at her.

"You were the one they got to with this stuff, Ms. Harrington. I've viewed Karl's initial report, and I've obviously talked to my own department medical staff about the EMTs' notes. But you're the one who experienced it from the inside, as it were. So is there anything you'd like to add?"

"Well," Stephanie said slowly, "I can't say completely honestly that my behavior was as totally outside my normal behavior as Karl seems to think." She quirked a brief smile. "He tends to go easier on me than he probably should—when he's not yelling at me for something *really* stupid, that is."

Chuchkova snorted.

"My memory's nowhere near as clear as I'd like," Stephanie continued, "but I do remember being completely confident that I had the answer to everything that's been bugging us about this. I don't remember what I thought that answer *was*, but I knew I'd figured it out, and all I needed was confirmation. I didn't *think* that, Chief Chuchkova—I *knew* that, without any doubt at all."

"And you think that's especially significant . . . why?" Chuchkova asked, regarding her intently.

"Because that's what I wanted most in the world last night," Stephanie said very seriously. "I've been talking to my friends a lot lately about what could make someone—someone young, someone my age—abuse drugs. Until last night, I didn't really understand what they were saying. But there are a lot of young people, a lot of kids, here on Sphinx who're carrying around a lot of pain. People they've lost." Her eyes flitted ever so briefly to Karl and her arms tightened around Lionheart. "Boredom. People who don't want to be here, can't do the things they really want to do. I think what makes this baka bakari so attractive is that while you're using it, you think you're solving whatever your problem is, fixing whatever's wrong."

"I'm not sure I follow you," Chuchkova said.

"I'm not sure I'm explaining it right," Stephanie said. "But—I don't drink, and I don't do drugs, unless somebody else puts them into my drink." She quirked another smile. "But from what I understand, aren't drugs usually... I don't know, an *escape*? A way to distract yourself from whatever's making you unhappy? To help you forget about it, at least for a while?"

"That's probably fair enough." Chuchkova nodded. "The 'distraction' works in different ways, of course. False euphoria—happiness, I suppose—is probably the most common, but just sending yourself into a stupor will do it for some people. Why?"

"Because the one thing that *didn't* happen to me was to distract me from what was bugging me or send me into a stupor. I wasn't 'escaping' from anything." Stephanie looked back and forth between the two chief officers and Karl. "I was completely, a hundred percent *engaged* in what I was doing. I was *that* close"—she held up her right hand, thumb and forefinger a centimeter apart—"to actually solving the case. And there's a little part of me that remembers being that close. That thinks I really was. I know I wasn't, but it *feels* like I was, even knowing what actually happened."

"Really?" Chief Shelton asked thoughtfully from the com display.

"Yes, Sir." Stephanie nodded. "And if I was a kid in a lot of pain, someone who didn't think she could cope with all the stuff coming down on her, someone who didn't think she had any way to accomplish what was really, *really* important to her, that would make this stuff *awfully* attractive to me. I'm not running away from my problems when I take it; I'm *solving* my problems. I'll bet you that even someone who's done something really stupid while she was using it feels the same way. And if her memory's as . . . hazy as mine, she may not remember the stupid, but she darned well remembers solving the problem!"

"That's a very good point," Chuchkova said after a moment. "And it may well indicate that this stuff is more addictive than I'd first thought."

"The kind of addictive that attracts competent, capable people, not just people stuck in ugly situations," Shelton said slowly.

"We already suspected some of that from the people we think have been using it, Sir," Karl pointed out. "Jake Simpson, for example. He's really good with a skimmer, so it's not like he needed to get drugged up to feel confident about using one. But if Steph's typical, then maybe the baka bakari makes him feel even more competent, *more* confident. Maybe what it's really doing is making all the outstanding stuff he can do with a skimmer an even bigger triumph for him?"

"That's all very interesting—I mean that sincerely." Chief Chuchkova brought her chair upright and folded her hands on her desktop. "And it probably does help explain a lot about the usage patterns we think we've been seeing. Unfortunately, it doesn't get us any closer to Orgeson, assuming she's the one really behind this. Or, for that matter, any closer to what 'baka bakari' really is!"

"I think it does indicate that it is—or has the

potential to become—a really serious problem, though, Olivera," Chief Shelton said from her com.

"I have to agree with that." Chuchkova nodded. "Especially if it really was involved in the Chang air car crash. We still aren't able to prove that linkage, though, and we're still up against that limitation of budget and manpower. And jurisdiction, for that matter. But despite that, I think I have to get officially involved at this point. It's not illegal to buy someone a drink, but it *is* illegal to put any sort of emotion-altering substance into it, and especially in the case of a minor." She smiled briefly, and with very little humor, at Stephanie. "It doesn't matter whether or not the 'emotion-altering substance' is legal for consensual use, either. And given what you people have had to tell me about this Câmara and Gallego, I will be astonished if they, at least, haven't seen the date-rape potential for a new, untraceable drug." There was no humor at all in her expression now. "So I think I have grounds to start looking very closely at our suspects—and Enigmatic Riddle. We do have the minor problem that we can't find any traces of something like that in Ms. Harrington—Stephanie's—bloodwork, but the EMTs' description of her symptoms clearly suggests that something was affecting her physically, and that's enough reasonable cause for me to at least start looking. *Probable* cause to justify a warrant, no. Not yet. But if we turn anything up just looking, that could change. So I'll put some extra surveillance in there—not just more cameras; I've got one undercover officer who'd be a perfect fit—and my uniforms will keep an eye on the other clubs. But, frankly, I think your friend Xadrian is more likely to turn up any real evidence."

"I hope the people who beat up Nosey don't go after Xadrian!" Stephanie said quickly.

"I don't think Xadrian's clumsy enough to get caught poking a nose where it shouldn't be," Chuchkova reassured her. "I know her, and we'll keep an eye peeled where she's concerned.

"But for now, all we can really do is pursue the 'endangering a minor' side of things, and that's judicially iffy," she continued, looking at Shelton. "Before we can go any further, we've got to be able to demonstrate what this stuff is and how it's getting from your mushroom research facility to Yawata Crossing. That's your jurisdiction, not mine, Gary."

"I know." Shelton rubbed the tip of his nose, then shrugged. "I know," he repeated, "and I don't like how close Steph came to getting hurt last night. But despite that—and I know I'm going to regret saying this—she and Karl and their passel of friends are probably still our best chance of figuring that out. Karl, I think you two need to move your focus back to Twin Forks and chasing down the link between Herman and Câmara and Orgeson, especially if Chief Chuchkova's going to be able to put some of her people—officially—on the distribution end in Yawata Crossing. I'm going to bring Frank and Ainsley up to speed on what you've been doing, and I want you to feel free to use them as a sounding board. We've all got our hands way too full for me to pull them off of their regular patrol duties, but they know you—and Stephanie—so we know they'll take the 'kids' seriously, and they'll be available for backup.

"Aside from telling you to keep doing what you've been doing, I don't have a lot of new advice or direction for you. Make sure you keep me fully in the loop, and I'll keep Chief Chuchkova up to speed. I know it doesn't seem that way to you right now, but you've actually made a lot more progress than you probably think you have. We know where it's coming from, how it was discovered, and who first started distributing it. That's a lot, when you consider where we started. I'm confident you'll get to the bottom of it all eventually."

Karl nodded soberly, and so did Stephanie, although she wasn't all that fond of Chief Shelton's final adverb. If they didn't get to the bottom of it sooner than "eventually," somebody—somebody *else*, she corrected herself—was going to get a lot worse than just hurt.

✧ ✧ ✧

Stephanie spent the trip back to Twin Forks considering what to do next. She was glad Chief Shelton was making Frank Lethbridge and Ainsley Jedrusinski available. They were both very good at their jobs, and they were also old friends. They knew her and Karl well enough to trust their judgment as they proceeded, but they'd come running in a hurry if they were needed.

That still left the problem of what rock to turn over next. They could try a different club. They should see if Nosey had come up with any more rumors. But although she didn't want to admit it to the others, she was getting worried that last night's fiasco might drive their quarry into hiding, and they'd need to start all over again.

✧ ✧ ✧

A few days later, Nosey Jones cross-examined Stephanie about the incident at the Enigmatic Riddle. "And this Xadrian says that neither Frank nor Rod have been back to the club since, and the best she can get are rumors that something might have been being experimented with, but that's it?"

Stephanie rotated her cup of spikethorn tea between her palms and nodded. "Xadrian hasn't given up, though. She's also checking other clubs."

She was about to say more when her uni-link chimed. She glanced down. "Cordelia, and she's flagged it 'urgent.' Do you mind?"

"Not at all."

Stephanie moved to where she could take the call in private.

"Hey, Cordelia, what's up?"

"I just left Mr. Ack's, and I'm worried about Herman," Cordelia said tersely. "I dropped by with some stuff and stayed to chat. He's still really upset over what happened to Stan, and I think he was lonely. Glynis still hasn't gotten him a full-time assistant, and he's alone during the day a lot. I think that gives him too much time to worry and beat himself up over this whole thing.

"Anyhow, Herman welcomes visitors, at least if he isn't working in one of the contained growing buildings, and we talked for—I don't know, maybe thirty or forty minutes. I think I cheered him up some and he gave me a big basket of new edible mushrooms to take home to Mom. But then, as he was walking me out with the basket, we heard an air car incoming. Guess who it was?"

"No guess."

"Dr. Lyric Orgeson and two of her goons. She was all sweetness and light. So were the thugs, best as they could manage, and, well, I moved to where I knew a camera would pick us up. I've copied over the feed, and I'm sending."

Stephanie saw the zipline indicating a download,

and said, "Cordy, I'm over at Nosey Jones's. Can I show him this?"

"Absolutely!"

Stephanie moved back to where Nosey had been waiting without even the least attempt to eavesdrop—incredibly admirable restraint for anyone, but especially for him—and gave him a quick summary.

"Can I link this to your holo projector so we can both watch?"

"Do it!"

A moment later, Cordelia's shoulder appeared, showing that she'd chosen an angle where the new arrivals would be clearly visible.

Lyric Orgeson extended one hand and smiled as Cordelia stepped forward to shake it. "Cordelia Schardt-Cordova, isn't it? We met some time ago."

"Dr. Orgeson, right?" Cordelia said with a very good facsimile of shy and overwhelmed. Stephanie approved.

Polite duty done, Lyric Orgeson turned her attention on Herman. "Hello, Herman. I'm afraid this isn't a purely social call. Something's come up back on Manticore, and I'm going to have to catch a shuttle home a lot sooner than I expected. I just thought I'd pop out and see if you've decided to take that job I offered you. I don't like to sound pushy, but we really are running out of time for you to decide. I'm afraid I need to know if you're still interested."

Nosey hissed softly under his breath, and Stephanie didn't need to ask why. While the words were matter-of-fact, something in the tone and emphasis turned what should have been persuasion into a threat.

"Oh, yes." Herman swallowed, and his eyes flicked ever so briefly in Cordelia's direction. "I didn't realize

I might need to make a final decision so soon, I'm afraid."

"Yes, I understand. But, as I say, something's come up." Orgeson's tone never changed, but her eyes hardened slightly.

"I see." Herman swallowed again. "I didn't know that, though, and I haven't spoken with Glynis about it, yet. I don't think I could justify just walking away and leaving her without an assistant."

"I can see where that would be inconvenient for her," Orgeson said. "But I'm sure she can find someone else. And let's be honest here, Herman. I'm not only offering to pay you more, I'm offering you a job so much less wasteful of all you know."

Her voice, like her gaze, hardened on the last three words, and alarm flickered in Herman's eyes.

"Herman, are you really thinking about taking another job?" Cordelia broke in. "The boys and I would really miss you!"

Her interruption diverted Orgeson's attention from Herman, and annoyance flickered in the older woman's expression. She banished it quickly, however.

"Well, I'm rather *hoping* that he is," she said with another surface-only smile.

"Uh, well, yes. I have been considering that. Really, as it stands, this job here is a dead end, you see. You *do* see, don't you? Glynis is an admirable woman in so many ways, but really more an explorer at heart. I have a lot of skills that aren't being fully, uh, exploited in this job."

"And I plan to fully exploit him," Dr. Orgeson purred. "I'm sure he'll find using his many talents on my behalf so much more rewarding than being stuck here in a jungle on a world that physically drags you down."

Stephanie knew Cordelia well enough by now to recognize her friend's irritation at hearing her part of Sphinx called "a jungle," but she only looked back at Herman.

"Gee, Herman. That does sound like it might be a great deal! But, like I say, we'll really miss you. Will there be time to throw a proper going away party for you? I'm sure the boys would love to host it."

"Probably not," Dr. Orgeson cut in. "As I already said," she continued, "I'm rather shorter on time than I expected to be. That's one reason I flew out here, instead of just screening Herman. I wanted to tell him in person, because if he's taking my offer, he'll need to start packing... Packing *everything* he'll need for his new job. But *so* sweet of you to think of a party. Really, Sphinx may be an absolutely uncomfortable planet, but the people are so nice, so interested in everything. But you were on your way out, I think. I shouldn't keep you. Have a lovely day, Cordelia."

So bluntly dismissed, Cordelia had little choice but to give Herman a finger wave, tell him she hoped he'd like his new job, if he decided to take it, and leave.

The feed continued for only a short while. Lyric Orgeson said, "Lovely child. So very nice to see her again, her and her little cat. Now, Herman, perhaps we can go into your charming cottage and discuss details. There's a weight allowance, but..."

The rest of the words were lost as the humans moved out of range of the cameras, which had been set to watch the perimeter of the GBMRAC—not specific buildings.

Cordelia's image took the place of the recorded feed. "Hey, Nosey. Good to see you. What did you guys think of that?"

Stephanie inclined her head to indicate that Nosey should speak first.

"Well," drawled the Nose for News, "we already knew she'd 'offered him a job' cooking up baka bakari for her, but it looks like something's made her change her timetable. Maybe she's figured out the Yawata Crossing PD's keeping a closer eye out for new euphorics and she's decided she'd feel more comfortable experimenting back on Manticore, where nobody's likely to be looking over her shoulder." He shrugged. "I don't know about that. But it looked like this came as a surprise to Herman?"

He glanced at Stephanie, and she nodded.

"As far as we know, she hasn't approached him directly since that night Cordy and the Kempers interrupted them."

"I thought it looked that way," Nosey said. "And you notice what happened when he suggested he needed to give his current boss a reasonable time to find a replacement? Charming Lyric threatened him with something then, at least by implication. If I had to guess, she was suggesting that she'd make sure everyone found out he was the one who originally developed baka bakari. If she did that, especially if she's realized it was involved in Stan Chang's death, and if she added the way he sold early samples to Frank Câmara, she could make Herman look very bad indeed."

"But Herman is working with us and the SFS, now," Stephanie pointed out.

"But she doesn't know that, now does she? She probably figures that while Herman might not be liable for anything criminal, he'd probably find it nearly impossible to get a job in his field here in the Star Kingdom, if the right rumors spread. Even Glynis might find it unwise to keep him on, lest her operation be tainted by association. With all of that, Charming Lyric might not even have seen any need to drop reminders about stupid reporters who got beaten up for sticking their noses in where they shouldn't have. But then again, she might have, once she got rid of Cordelia. That's the stick."

He motioned to Stephanie, which she took as an invitation to fill in the other end of his analysis.

"The carrot is a well-paying job," she said. "One that pays a *lot* more than Glynis is paying him. We already know she wants to move him off Sphinx into his own lab, and from what he's said, she's dropping hints about publication in his own right, not just as someone else's lab assistant. And given how much she's offered to pay him already, I won't be surprised if she doesn't offer to cover any penalties he might incur for leaving Glynis without notice."

"I'm a bit surprised he didn't take her up on it when she first made the offer," Nosey said.

"Not me." Cordelia shook her head. "I think he'd started really regretting getting in so deep with Frank even before Jess and I got him to come clean with us. I don't think this new move of hers is a reaction to what happened to Stan, either. It might be, but I think if she'd figured that out—that anyone might even suspect baka bakari might be involved, I mean—she'd have made it even sooner."

"You're probably right about that," Stephanie agreed. "And it's probably a darned good thing—for him, too—that she hasn't figured that out. And that she doesn't know about the statements he gave Karl. We still don't have any proof she actually threatened him, only his unsupported word, but if she had any idea we were looking so closely at her, she'd cut her losses and just disappear right now. Especially if she even guessed he's voluntarily working with us now."

"I know." Cordelia nodded. "And let's face it, Steph. Herman's not the bravest guy in the world. I can tell he's worried she can still get to him somehow, and I hate that."

"Probably something to that," Stephanie granted. "But I think he's really determined to help stop her," she added, mentally replaying her and Karl's conversation with Herman. "He really took what happened to Stan hard. And from a more selfish perspective, helping us get on top of this is the one thing that might get her off his back for good, too."

"I agree!" Cordelia said. "But that doesn't mean he's not scared to death of them. And whatever's going on in his head, I think we have a new problem of our own. Timing."

"Yeah." Stephanie nodded. "I wonder if my shenanigans at the Enigmatic Riddle have anything to do with this, because Nosey's right that it looks like Orgeson's planning on pulling up stakes here on Sphinx. And if she moves her entire operation back to Manticore, there's no telling how long it would take for law enforcement there to get back to the point we're already at. We might still be able to get Frank and any of his local cronies, but if she gets loose with it someplace like Landing..."

"Exactly!" It was Cordelia's turn to nod vigorously. "And I think that's exactly what she has in mind, Steph. I've kept an eye on the feed from Mr. Ack's since Lyric and cronies left, but her parting words were another reminder for him to pack *everything* he'd need." She imitated the mycologist's flirty way of speaking to perfection, then sobered. "I'm betting 'everything' includes samples for growing all the ingredients in baka bakari. From what I've learned, many fungi propagate well in controlled environments. And they're small. They're not like, oh, crown oaks or hexapumas or something. It would probably be ultra easy to smuggle out samples and set him up with his own greenhouses on Manticore."

"They might not even need to smuggle," Nosey put in. "Control of what goes planet-to-planet isn't as carefully managed as you'd think it might be. As long as what was being taken wasn't officially restricted, it might not even be an issue, especially for someone like Dr. Orgeson, who's here on an R&D visa."

"Well, we already know we're not going to let Herman be bullied into taking this 'offer.'" Cordelia's tone made it perfectly clear where she stood on that idea.

"No, we're not," Stephanie agreed, reviewing all the things she'd learned in her jurisprudence courses. "But we're going to need to tread carefully. We don't want Herman to land in the exact sort of trouble Orgeson could still land him in if she manages to deflect blame for what happened to Stan on to him. And we don't want her getting away, either. But whatever we're going do instead, we've got to come up with it pretty darned fast! And—"

Her uni-link chimed with an incoming call. She looked down at it and grimaced.

"Guess who?" she asked as she tapped the icon to open the new call in a separate window without losing the connection to Cordelia.

"Hello, Herman," she said.

19

"ALL RIGHT, HERMAN," STEPHANIE SAID, SEVERAL HOURS later.

Sphinx's long day had segued into darkness, and the Kemper brothers had invited her and Cordelia—and Herman—to a "potluck dinner." Mack and Zack had been brought fully onboard, at least as far as baka bakari was involved, and their dinner invitation had offered the best cover for her visit. She could have screened Herman rather than flying out to the Kemper claim, but she and Karl had agreed that this was a conversation best held in person.

They fully intended to eat that dinner, too, and interesting aromas wafted from the hot pots with which she and Cordelia had arrived, but no one seemed really interested in eating. Not yet, at any rate. Not even the treecats. Athos and Lionheart had discovered the mantel above the living room's old-fashioned fireplace, and they perched there like guardian gargoyles, green eyes bright.

"Like I said when you screened me, right after Orgeson left," she continued, "you can't just tell them no."

Herman opened his mouth, but her raised hand stopped him before he spoke.

"I know you want to, but all the reasons you can't still hold true. At the same time, though, we're taking Orgeson's threats seriously, I promise."

Herman looked unhappy, but he also nodded, and Stephanie looked at the Kempers as the botanist sat back in his chair.

"I don't think you guys are completely up to date," she said. "After Cordelia left, Orgeson got down to brass tacks with Herman. She told him that he's got three days to make up his mind before she goes home, and that if he *doesn't* take her 'generous job offer by then,' she'll not only go to the authorities and reveal that she's just discovered that Herman's been selling untested drugs to minors, but her thugs will beat him up, too. Badly."

"Really?" Mack looked at Herman sharply. "They actually said that, Herman?"

"What they said is that they'd beat me up so badly I wouldn't be able to give my version of events for months. If ever."

"Wow," Mack said. "Steph and Cordy told us they'd threatened physical violence, but I didn't expect them to have been that explicit. And I sure didn't think they'd threaten to murder you!"

"I'm not sure they'd really go that far," Herman said. "On the other hand, I'm not sure they wouldn't, either!"

"I guess not." Both Kempers shook their heads.

"One thing we're pretty sure of, though, is that they don't know we think baka bakari was involved in Stan's death," Stephanie continued. "If they did, then Orgeson certainly would have threatened Herman with that!"

"I thought about that," Herman said. "But *I* know about it. I can't *forget* about it, however hard I try!"

His expression was so unhappy that Cordelia reached out to pat his knee.

"That's why we're trying to do something about it," she told him.

"Yeah." Stephanie nodded vigorously. "And, before we get into that, there's been another development in Twin Forks that may play into all of this. Not so much where Orgeson is concerned—not directly, at least—but where Frank and Rod are."

"Really?" Cordelia raised an eyebrow at her. "And you didn't think to share this with me earlier?"

"Only found out on the way here," Stephanie told her with a grin. "Chief Chuchkova screened Chief Shelton. It looks like Xadrian really is the chief hierophant at the Enigmatic Riddle. It turns out that one of the regulars she hangs out with was recording a birthday party the night we were there."

She paused, and Cordelia smacked her hands together.

"They actually caught Rod spiking your drink on *video*? Oh, that's just too perfect!"

"Oh, no." Stephanie's grin was even wider—and much more predatory—than before. "They caught *Frank* spiking my drink. And they already tied him to the drink order. And it doesn't matter whether or not baka bakari is legal. It's still a euphoric, and he still provided it to a minor without her consent or knowledge. It's only a misdemeanor, not a felony, since nobody got hurt, but if we can tie him to Orgeson, then we have somebody else we can squeeze to testify against her and corroborate anything Herman can tell us."

"That sounds good to me," Zack said.

"But it's still not bulletproof," Stephanie cautioned. "So far, Orgeson hasn't done anything—so far as we know, anyway—that a clever lawyer couldn't talk her way around. Frank, yes. But, like I say, even in his case, we can only get him on misdemeanor charges right now. We want something . . . more permanent than that. And if Orgeson is willing to have Nosey beaten up, and to actually threaten to *kill* Herman if he doesn't do what she wants, then we want to hammer her as hard as we can. I mean, preferably, we're talking some serious prison time here."

"That would be great," Mack said. "But you just finished saying we don't have evidence of anything that heavy."

"We don't have evidence of anything that heavy *yet*," Stephanie corrected, and her expression was much more serious as she looked back at Herman.

"Karl and I talked it over with Cordy, and then we ran our idea by Chief Shelton. Chief Chuchkova's ready to ask for a bench warrant against Frank whenever we tell her to, based on the video Xadrian's turned up. That still leaves Orgeson, but she made a mistake being present and personally threatening you instead of just letting her thugs handle the intimidation. That way she could have denied she'd ever told them to go that far to convince you to cooperate. And the fact that she's made one mistake makes us think that we might be able to get her to make *another* one."

"What kind of mistake?" Herman asked, his eyes narrow.

"Based on something Karl's turned up, we think she might be prepared to go as far as to kidnap you and haul you back to Manticore. Hopefully, that's because she figures that she could convince you to actually take the job once you were there, but it's also possible she figures she could just get the full recipe out of you, one way or the other, and then get rid of you."

"Get *rid* of me?!" Herman's narrowed eyes flared wide.

"She wouldn't have to be thinking in terms of killing," Stephanie pointed out. "As far as she knows, she still has all of that stuff about selling drugs to minors to hold over your head to make you keep your mouth shut. Plus the fact that at the very least, you'd lose your job with Dr. Bonaventure! If that happened, you'd need a job from *somebody*, so why not take hers? And worst-case scenario, they could always say you'd come voluntarily, with nobody able to prove you hadn't."

"Wait a minute," Cordelia said. "There's no way they could just kidnap Herman and drag him off to Manticore and then claim he'd come voluntarily! They'd have to drug him or something to get them onto one of the shuttles against his will, and there's too big a chance something would go wrong along the way."

"Ah, but that's not how she's planning to get home," Stephanie said. "When Karl heard about her three-day time limit, he put in an official SFS request for information on her reservation date, and there isn't one. Turns out she arrived aboard a privately owned ship, the *Priscilla*, that's still in parking orbit around

Sphinx. Chief Shelton's trying to run down its real owners, but the company it's officially registered to is obviously a shell, a front for someone else. Which means our Dr. Orgeson's past may be even sketchier than we thought. But it also means it would be a lot easier for her to smuggle Herman off-world, which probably makes the idea of kidnapping him even more attractive to someone like her."

"Wonderful," Herman muttered, and Cordelia patted his knee again.

"We're going to get you out of this," she told him.

"Absolutely." Stephanie nodded vigorously. "One way or the other."

"I'd really rather just come clean." Herman looked around the living room unhappily. "I mean, I don't want to. It's going to be bad enough when I have to tell Dr. Bonaventure about this. She's going to be really, really pissed with me, and she should be. I've abused my position here, and for all I know, I've exposed her and GBMRAC to potential liability in all those accidents. And even if she doesn't fire me on the spot, if I go public, my career's pretty much over. But if that stops Orgeson from getting away with this, stops anybody else from getting hurt or killed when they don't even know they're using drugs, then that's what I'll do."

"I know it is." Stephanie smiled at him, much more warmly than she once ever thought she might have. "But we'd really rather not wreck your life."

"Actually, I did that all on my own." Herman managed a crooked smile of his own. "On the other hand, it sounds like you think there's a way to avoid it."

"Sure there is." Stephanie's smile segued into a treecat's grin. "We *let* them kidnap you."

"What?" Herman blinked at her.

"Look, unlike providing a mind- or mood-altering substance to a minor, kidnapping is a Class A Felony. The *minimum* sentence is ten T-years; the maximum is thirty. Unless violence or threats of violence are used, in which case the judge can tack on up to another fifteen T-years. And in the eyes of the law, it doesn't matter whether or not the kidnapping was *successful*, Herman. All they have to do is make the attempt, and we've got them."

"But—" he began, then broke off.

"Just how do you see this whole thing working?" he asked slowly.

"Well, the bad news is that if we bust her for attempted kidnapping, everything about the baka bakari's almost certain to come out. Especially if we bust Frank for spiking my drink. And, to be honest, we need that to happen, because it's unlikely baka bakari's going to be ruled illegal right away, if at all. So we need to be able to warn people that it's out there and what its effects are. That's pretty much a minimum, Herman."

He nodded glumly.

"I know. And that means I'm going to have to fess up to Dr. Bonaventure before we go any further. I can't blindside her with the way this is going to splash on GBMRAC."

"No, you can't," Stephanie agreed. "And telling her will also at least mitigate some of the damage to *you* when this goes public, too. You'll have told your boss everything, including that you tried to fix matters, only to discover that they'd gotten out of control when Frank made contact with Orgeson. After that, you only collaborated because of her threats of violence. Which brings it all right back to her as the prime mover."

"That's true." Herman's shoulders sagged, but there was an edge of relief in his tone. "I'll come across as a complete naïve idiot, but at least not as a drug pusher to innocent young people. What next?"

"Next, you contact Dr. Orgeson. You let her know you've confessed to Dr. Bonaventure, and what the end result was. Then you let her know that—even if you've lost your job—you're not interested in taking hers. That's when we figure they'll try to kidnap you. Maybe not that instant, but within no more than a day or so."

"And then?"

"And then we let them go far enough that there'll be no wiggling out of the charge of kidnapping. At which point Karl and I pounce."

"Just the two of you?" Herman looked like someone trying hard to avoid sounding skeptical, and Stephanie chuckled.

"Actually, I think we could handle it. But, like I said, we've discussed it with Chief Shelton. He's authorized Karl—well, me, since Karl didn't want to fly back out here in case Orgeson's keeping an eye on you—to arrange a sting operation. We can't manufacture evidence against Orgeson, but we can sure as heck let her incriminate *herself*. And the Chief has agreed to make Ranger Lethbridge and Ranger Jedrusinski available as backup. They'll be close enough to intervene if we need them to. But we'd just as soon be sure we keep them out of sight unless we do need them."

"I see."

Herman's relief was evident, although it was equally evident that he remained far short of enthralled by the entire notion. Stephanie couldn't blame him for that, but she only smiled sympathetically, leaned back, and waited.

He sat in silence for several minutes, then nodded and straightened in his chair.

"All right," he said. "Let's do it."

✧ ✧ ✧

Stephanie was pleased when Herman asked if Cordelia would sit in when he had his interview with Glynis Bonaventure "Because you can confirm that I told you and Jessica that I regretted what I'd done before anyone threatened me."

The interview with Glynis was just as painful as he'd feared, though, even just to watch. As expected, she felt angry, betrayed, and even guilty that her own obsession with discovery over development had led to Herman making some unwise decisions.

"I'd like to believe that concoction of yours—what are they calling it? Baka bakari—had something to do with you acting so unwisely. From what you said, it does seem to lead to overconfidence."

"It may well have," Herman admitted. "Ever since I stopped making it, I've found myself questioning how I could ever decide it was a great idea to make it for anyone else without checking if it had any long-term cumulative effects. I believed what I wanted to believe."

"Which seems like a common side effect," Glynis said thoughtfully. "Very well. I won't fire you. That's enough for now. Give me time to think about the next steps for GBMRAC."

The meeting had ended with repeated apologies and promises of good behavior, before a thoughtful Dr. Bonaventure took her leave.

When her air car was a dot on the horizon, Cordelia turned to Herman. "Now for the next part. You need to screen Dr. Orgeson."

"Right! There's no good reason for me delaying and a lot of bad ones." He coded in the call, which was answered promptly. "Dr. Orgeson, this is Herman Maye, but you know that. I'm sorry. I'm a bit nervous about this, given what you said at our last meeting."

It had been agreed that Herman should give Lyric Orgeson any opportunity to incriminate herself, but the woman was far too smooth an operator.

"Yes, I remember our meeting. Do you want to suggest any changes? A raise in salary, perhaps?"

"No, nothing like that. In fact, I... I'm... I'm turning down your offer. Dr. Bonaventure was here earlier, and I found myself feeling terrible about not at least giving her notice, so I told her I'd had another job offer. She, well, she's very persuasive, and even after I told her what an idiot I'd been, she told me she didn't think the situation was nearly as bad as I was making it out to be. She wants me to keep working for her, although, of course, I won't be mixing any more mushrooms except in controlled settings."

There was a long pause, then Lyric Orgeson said in a low voice that was more terrifying than any shout, "I see. Well, that is a pity. I really feel that being stuck in a painted hut in a jungle is a waste of your talents, but it's your life."

Something in how she said those last words made Cordelia shiver. Herman, however, carried on as if he hadn't heard the implied threat.

"Thank you for being so understanding. I hope you have a good trip back to your home."

"Thank you."

The call was terminated on that abrupt note. Cordelia rose.

"As much as I hate to do this, I've got to get out of here. We're pretty sure they didn't leave any cameras of their own to keep an eye on you, but we can't be positive of that. So we need everything to look as normal as possible. But don't worry! We'll be watching through *our* cameras, and someone will always be close. And Mack and Zack were pretty adamant. They plan to take turns spending the night here."

"I hate to think that anything could happen to one of them," Herman said with a distressed expression.

"The fewer changes to our routine, the less likely Orgeson and her goons will get suspicious. Don't worry." Cordelia sounded confident. "We've got this under control."

But when Cordelia screened Stephanie later, her first words were, "I *hope* we've got this under control, Steph. If we don't, this could get seriously ugly."

✧ ✧ ✧

Not only had the Kemper boys insisted on continuing their night vigils with Herman, they'd also insisted on using their house as a base for the kidnap attempt watch.

"We have enough outbuildings that vehicles can be parked undercover," Mack said, "and the tunnels will make sure a casual observer won't realize extra people are hanging out here."

Underground tunnels were common on Sphinx, where heavy snowfall during the almost sixteen T-month-long winters made them the logical solution to going between buildings. Everyone was grateful for Mack's suggestion, since a glimpse of a camouflaged air car in the forest might raise suspicion. The next job was setting up shifts for keeping an eye on Mr. Ack's during the wait for what Anders had dubbed Operation Save Herman From the Vermin.

They felt fairly certain Orgeson's gang wouldn't go for Herman today, or even in the next few days. Now that he'd turned them down, they no longer needed to maintain the pretence of a three-day time limit, and he was likely to be wary, for at least the next little bit. And they'd want some time between the job offer they knew Cordelia knew about and Herman's disappearance, because they wouldn't want anyone wondering if they'd made him an offer he couldn't refuse. Karl's investigations had determined that *Priscilla* carried an atmosphere-capable shuttle of its own, which meant they wouldn't even have to smuggle him through security at the port, assuming *Priscilla*'s crew was willing to make an unauthorized landing to pick them up. And they probably would be, given how little of Sphinx's skies were covered by radar.

Even so, as Karl said, "We need to keep watch starting right now. We'd feel like complete zorks if they snatched him sooner."

Anders didn't have anything to keep him in Yawata Crossing, so he joined Cordelia and the Kemper boys monitoring the feed. They'd rehearsed until they could get someone over to Mr. Ack's within minutes, and Chief Shelton had shifted patrol assignments to move Frank Lethbridge and Ainsley Jedrusinski closer to the Kemper homestead. Neither of them could just drop their regular duties, but they'd be available as a heavier, quick-response reinforcement, if they were needed, although everyone hoped the two senior rangers wouldn't be.

Aside from Karl, who was more or less camped with the Kempers, all the rest of them continued with their usual routines. It was unlikely Orgeson would be worried enough about a bunch of "kids" to keep an eye on them, but no one was taking any chances.

Despite their carefully laid plans, Stephanie grew extremely edgy as the days crept past without Orgeson making a move. It was one thing to believe you'd calculated the odds properly. It was another to have someone else's safety—maybe even his life—resting on the choices you made.

This is why I want to be a ranger, not go into the military. My life will be fluffy range bunnies. Our friend the hexapuma. The circle of life. All that nice gentle nature, red in tooth and claw stuff.

✧ ✧ ✧

Stephanie's uni-link buzzed. She looked at it and tapped the "ACCEPT" icon as soon as she saw it was Karl.

"Yes?" she said a bit sharply. Eight of Sphinx's long days had slipped past without anything at all happening.

"Hey, Steph! Chief Chuchkova says Dr. Orgeson and her thug friends just checked out of their hotel in Yawata Crossing. So if they're going to try anything, it'll be today."

"I'd better get over there!" she exclaimed.

"Don't panic. Zack's on his way to pick you up now. You'll have plenty of time to get back here with him before they can fly all the way from Yawata Crossing to grab him."

"Great! And Frank and Ainsley?"

"They're going to be waiting on the ground right next door. Official story is that they're inspecting that abandoned near-beaver dam where Cordy almost got eaten. They can be from there to Mr. Ack in under seven minutes if we need to call them in."

"Sounds good!" Stephanie said with a sudden burst of elation and relief. Worrying about one of her plans was one thing; once she actually got the chance to put it into motion—

✧ ✧ ✧

Stephanie waited, hunkered down in cover where she had a clear view of Mr. Ack's public parking field. Zack Kemper was covering the lot from the other side. Mack Kemper was around back, where the composter was, since there was enough open area to set down a vehicle there. Cordelia, Jessica, and Anders were positioned around the perimeter. The four treecats were up in the forest canopy, lying low.

Nosey wasn't on site, but he *was* watching all the spy camera feeds, so he could give them advance warning of any approaching vehicle. At the same time, he was recording the visual feeds, and thanks to Chief Shelton's warrants, those recordings would be admissible in court, if it came to that.

Stephanie could sense Lionheart's watchfulness, and was glad. Of the assembled treecats, he had the most experience dealing with dangerous humans, having helped her with the poacher Tennessee Bolgeo, and, more recently, with muggers on Manticore.

But what if there's shooting? How many of the other 'cats have actually been where there was more than target shooting? Athos was there when the Kemper boys showed up to help Cordelia, when the near-weasels were attacking her, but by all reports, he was in seriously bad shape by then. He might not have made the connection between the weapons and the result. But maybe they haven't figured it out that guns are dangerous to more than targets? Maybe they just think firearms are worth avoiding because of they make so much noise. We suspect that treecats can communicate with each other, but can they share something as abstract as "loud noise here is connected to splattered target there"?

All I can do is hope everything will go down just fine. I can hope that there won't be any shooting, that I just worry too much. Concentrate on the moment, Steph. Don't get distracted by "might be's."

She scanned the area in her line of sight, avoiding the urge to get distracted by her uni-link feed. She had to trust her allies, and Nosey had proven himself very reliable. As arranged, Herman was working outside today, taking care not to stray out of where one or more of the security cameras would record his actions.

At the moment, he was turning over the soil in a new garden bed. A barrow filled with mushroom compost stood to one side, waiting to be dug in, and a flat of herbs had been set in a shady spot to one side. If, to Stephanie, Herman's actions looked studied, like an amateur actor doing busywork on stage at the opening of a scene, she wasn't all that worried. Herman wasn't the most poised person. Well, except when he was talking about fungi and their cultivation, of course. Then he was like a different person.

And thinking he looks awkward is probably just my imagination. I can't believe only five minutes have gone by since I last checked. I could have sworn it had been at least half an hour.

Her stomach rumbled, and she eased a granola bar out of her pocket and slowly pulled back a section of the wrapping. She was still chewing her first mouthful when Nosey's voice sounded in her earbud.

"Large, nondescript air van coming in from the north."

Stephanie took another bite, then shoved the wrapping over the rest of her granola bar and slid it back into her pocket. In a moment, she heard, then saw the air van. It was a commercial model, like hundreds used every day on Sphinx for routine deliveries. However, they knew from Herman that he didn't expect any deliveries that day.

The air van slowly circled overhead. Maybe it was just looking for where to set down, but Stephanie would have bet her right eye that it was making sure there were no other vehicles in the vicinity. Karl's cruiser was stashed in the Kempers' barn, so she wasn't worried about that. Yet even though she knew she—and the rest of her team—were invisible from above, Stephanie felt like a hexapuma dropped in the middle of a snowfield.

She breathed deeply, slowly, remembering years of lessons in woodcraft and tracking. A moving target is much more visible than one that holds still, so as much as she yearned to peek out and see where the air van was, she contented herself with glancing at the map image on her uni-link. After circling several times, the bright dot that indicated the vehicle began to descend, eventually setting down with apparent innocence in the public parking field, not far from where Stephanie was hiding.

It was crucial to their plan that Herman actually be kidnapped so, as much as she longed to break cover,

Stephanie froze in place. She hoped the 'cats wouldn't race to Herman's rescue, as Athos had that memorable night. That was definitely a risk, but the humans had decided to trust the 'cats ability to read their bond-mates' moods, and hope that they would understand the game was "Hide" not "Seek and Destroy."

The air van's doors popped open, and Dr. Orgeson and three henchmen emerged.

No Frank this time, Stephanie thought. *That's good. If they didn't bring a local witness, they probably mean business.*

According to plan, Herman had walked over to the parking lot, as he would if he happened to hear any new arrival. However, also according to plan, he stayed out of easy reach.

"Dr. Orgeson! I didn't expect you."

"I know." Lyric Orgeson's lips shaped a bright, utterly sharklike smile. "But we'll be returning to Manticore this evening, so I thought I'd give you a last chance to come with us."

Herman shook his head. "Sorry. Really, no. Maybe some other time, but I really couldn't leave Dr. Bonaventure with no warning. Really, now that I've thought it over, I really couldn't leave my work. There's really just too much potential here."

Too many "reallys," Stephanie thought, *but Herman's doing well. It's perfectly reasonable that he'd be nervous. Now to see what they'll do in the face of a flat-out refusal.*

"Can't we even talk about it?" Dr. Orgeson asked, her tone reasonable. "I brought a snack basket at that charming Red Letter Café in Twin Forks. We can chat over tea and muffins."

Herman hesitated. Stephanie thought he was going to refuse. Then he forced a smile.

"That's very sociable of you," Herman said, leaning the neat little spade he'd been using against a nearby tree. "I can pause long enough for a cup of tea, but only to be polite, because you and I are in the same field. Who knows? We might want to work together in the future. I'm simply not interested in a new job at this time."

Very nicely stated and right where the bug will record it. Okay... How far will they go?

A short distance from the parking field, there was a long, narrow table with benches alongside. Herman trotted over to it, moving a few buckets and an assortment of tools to create an area large enough for the five of them to sit. Lyric Orgeson walked over to join him, picking up a short-handled broom and brushing dirt from the benches.

"That should do just fine. Willinski? Will you get the snack basket from the back of the van?"

When Stephanie saw the assortment of oversized muffins set out for everyone to select from, her traitor stomach reminded her that two bites of a granola bar wasn't much for a growing girl with Meyerdahl mods. She wondered if she could sneak a nibble from her granola bar without being seen but, remembering that motion is what betrays someone in hiding, she restrained herself.

"Tea? Sugar? Milk?" Lyric acted the role of hostess, handing around disposable cups and plates.

Herman chose to neither sweeten nor to add milk to his tea, and selected a muffin at random. Dr. Orgeson both sweetened *and* added milk to her tea, then took a muffin of the same sort as the one Herman had chosen. The subsequent conversation was about what one would expect. Lyric being persuasive. Herman holding steadfastly to his resolve not to take the offered job. Before long, though, he began to stumble over his words. Lyric's smile broadened, but it wasn't until Herman slumped forward, his head nearly bopping into the table, that she said anything.

"Excellent! If Herman was at all suspicious, I don't think he anticipated the knockout drops could be administered by contact from his cup. Quesk and Underwood pick him up—gently, mind—and get him into the van. I'm going to see if any of the doors are unlocked, and I can get onto one of the computers. People can be so sloppy about protecting data when they work alone. I won't be more than a minute."

She found the doors all locked, though, and with an "oh, well" shrug trotted toward the parking area. Willinski waited on the driver's side, while Quesk and Underwood loaded Herman into the back of the van.

Once Herman was in the van, and there could be no doubt that he was being removed from the scene, Zack stepped forth, just as if he'd just been coming down the trail from the Kemper house. Stephanie joined him, a few steps behind, as if they'd been together.

"Where are you taking Herman?" Zack asked, his tone sharp and accusatory. He had his shotgun held with casual comfort. Even day-hikers on Sphinx were usually armed.

For a brief, crucial moment, Lyric goggled. At that moment, Willinski overreacted.

"What the hell?" he said, and a large firearm appeared in one beefy hand.

Dr. Orgeson was a quick thinker. Stephanie had to give her credit for that.

"We were having farewell snacks," she said, "when all of a sudden, Herman keeled over. We were taking him in to Twin Forks to see a doctor."

But she might as well have saved her breath. Wilinski's pulling his firearm had caused Quesk and Underwood to do the same. They hardly looked like a farewell party. Instead, they looked like exactly what they were—paid muscle.

Stephanie, behind Zack and partially screened by his body, drew her own pistol and eased off the safety, though she was careful to keep it out of sight. They'd hoped the fact that all of them were armed would keep the thugs from threatening actual violence until Karl got into position, but it didn't look like working out that way, after all.

Mack, coming down the path from the other end of the complex with Cordelia, Jessica, and Anders, did his best to defuse the situation.

"No problem. Jessica here is a trained EMT," he said, slightly exaggerating Jessica's credentials. "Let her have a look at Herman, then she can teleconference directly with the hospital in Twin Forks."

Dr. Orgeson might have cut her losses, but her henchmen, seeing their chance of getting off-planet doubtless vanishing when knockout drugs were found in Herman's system, reacted.

"Drop your weapons!" Willinski shouted, his gun covering Cordelia. Quesk leveled her weapon at Stephanie, Underwood at Zack. "Get flat!"

Stephanie's group was also armed, and she doubted that Orgeson's thugs had the faintest idea of the determination—or marksmanship—of the "kids" they were threatening. She was coldly confident she and her friends could take them, but none of the others were law officers. Even she was only a "probationary" ranger, and the chance that one of them would be hurt if shooting started was too great.

Besides, we have backup.

"All right," she said. "We're putting them down."

She stooped and laid her pistol carefully on the ground. (As Frank Lethbridge had explained to her when he taught her handgun safety, "Only idiots in really bad holodramas actually *drop* a loaded weapon. Too much chance of an accidental discharge!") An instant later, the others followed suit, and she straightened again.

She knew Karl was working his way around behind Orgeson's group, and Frank and Ainsley had gone airborne—although they were still discreetly out of sight—the instant Herman keeled over. The situation was under control, whatever the thugs might think. All they had to do was stall for another minute or two, and—

But a snarl of raw fury rent the sudden stillness, and an apparition in gray and cream dropped from the tree branches, hit the roof of the van, and swifter than sight could follow, leapt to where Underwood held his gun on Cordelia.

20

OLD AS HE WAS, EXPERIENCED AS HE WAS, HEART STONE felt like a kitten whose eyes had just opened as he tried to understand the actions of Life Shaper and her friends. First they had gone with great caution to Rich Dirt Grove, but they had not spoken with Musty. Instead, they had stalked him, taking up positions from which they were well-hidden, even from above. From this he had concluded that they were hiding from more than Musty.

Very well, he understood hiding, even if he did not understand why they were hiding, nor why they maintained their vigil for so long. He wished he could ask Climbs Quickly or one of the other People, in case this was some sort of game that the two-legs routinely played. However, as long as Life Shaper's mind-glow remained as it was: focused, a little nervous, but not frightened, Heart Stone was content to wait, watch, and learn.

When the big flying thing arrived and disgorged the unpleasant two-legs whom he had encountered that night near the dirt heap, Heart Stone understood;

Life Shaper's two-legs were stalking these other, very unpleasant two-legs. He tensed, ready to join in the hunt when the moment came.

But even after the prey had arrived, there was no springing forth, no pouncing. Even though Climbs Quickly's mind-glow remained calm, Heart Stone could tell that Sharp Sight and Plant Fancier were relying more on whatever Climbs Quickly was telling them than what they understood about the developing situation. This did not exactly reassure Heart Stone. He liked Climbs Quickly. Over these many hands of days during which they had become friends, he had learned to appreciate the scout's sound judgment and insight. Even so, Heart Stone could not dismiss memories of the talented young scout who, despite his much admired skill, had been frequently scolded for taking undue risks.

Heart Stone knew where his responsibility rested, and concentrated on Life Shaper, waiting for any sign, no matter how small, that she needed him. He tasted as the odd blend of exhilaration and dread in her mind-glow soured into tense awareness, then anxiety. When Musty fell forward, his mind-glow cloudy with something other than natural sleep, Heart Stone felt Life Shaper's mind-glow shift again, bright with a readiness to do something, even as she held her place.

Only when a pair of the prey two-legs lifted Musty and carried him toward the big flying thing did Life Shaper move stealthily from cover. She froze in place when Little, the leader of the enemy band, walked over to Musty's nest structures, rattling the openings, and snorting in annoyance when none of them yielded to her. When Little moved to join her band near the flying thing, Life Shaper began to creep forth again, joining several others of her clan as they moved rapidly—although belatedly, to Heart Stone's way of seeing things—toward where Musty was being bundled into the flying thing.

But since Life Shaper did not call for him, and the other three People kept their positions in the branches, Heart Stone kept his place as well. Then it happened. After an exchange of mouth noises between Little and Mends Things, the mind-glow of the biggest and meanest of Little's followers—Kicker—reeked with a dangerous mixture of rage and panic. Kicker bellowed and suddenly there was a thunder barker in his hand. It was not the largest thunder barker Heart Stone had seen, but he had seen far smaller things of this sort make practice targets explode into flinders.

At their herd bull's cry, the other two males reappeared, thunder barkers in their hands. That was bad, but worse came when Kicker pointed his thunder barker at Life Shaper.

Although she kept outwardly calm, Life Shaper's absolute terror washed through their link and she dropped to the ground in supplication. Heart Stone had endured enough. He had lost Golden Eye, and this rampaging he-bull of a two-leg was threatening the one who had given him back his soul.

With a shrill cry of rage, Heart Stone leapt down from his arboreal perch onto the flat top of the flying thing. From there he launched himself so that he could smash into the thunder barker in Kicker's hand, knocking it from its target. Then, with his true-hands, Heart Stone grabbed hold of Kicker's shoulders, counterbalancing himself with his true-feet and tail. Even in this moment of extreme fear for his beloved, Heart Stone managed to keep all but the tips of his claws pulled in, although he longed to rake with his hand-feet and true-feet, disemboweling his prey. Instead, he extended his claws only enough to assure his hold. Then he grabbed hold with his hand-feet onto of the naked skin of the hand in which Kicker held the thunder barker, all too aware that although he'd pushed its angry mouth from Life Shaper, it might now be pressed into his own gut.

Heart Stone screamed a furious warning directly into the two-leg's unprotected, furless face, causing Kicker to momentarily loosen his grip on the thunder barker. In that moment, Heart Stone ripped the thunder barker from Kicker's grip. When it clattered to the ground, the aggression in Kicker's mind-glow transformed into purest fear. With Heart Stone still clinging to his shoulder, he began to stumble away from Life Shaper, perhaps to seek refuge in the cavelike interior of the flying thing.

Heart Stone decided this would be fine. Kicker's hand was streaming blood. If he was anything like most two-legs, he would want to stop the bleeding before doing anything else. Satisfied, Heart Stone released his hold, then sprang back to crouch in front of Life Shaper, hissing and spitting warning. He knew well he was at risk, for he had seen how the thunder barkers spat destruction from a distance, but he maintained his defensive stance and surveyed the roiling interactions of two-legs and People.

Thus far, none of the many thunder barkers had roared. The only blood he smelled was Kicker's. The two-legs were making many and varied mouth noises, some of the sort Heart Stone suspected held meaning for the two-legs, many more the inarticulate sounds of rage, fear, and threat that seemed to be the same no matter what sort of creature made them.

Then a new sound entered the mix. Mouth noises—coming from Determined Defender, he realized, recognizing the other two-leg's mind-glow. The Little and her remaining two-legs drooped and sagged like newly sprouted plants beneath the worst of the sun's summer heat, and Heart Stone heard more mouth noises from Determined Defender. Nothing happened for a moment, but then it was the members of Little's band—including the still oozing Kicker, who crept from the flying thing to join his clan—who laid down their thunder barkers and fell to the ground, facedown, limbs splayed, bodies offering surrender in a language that even one without mind-speech could understand.

The fear in Life Shaper's mind-glow had spiked when Heart Stone attacked Kicker—fear for Heart Stone, far more acute than what she had felt for herself. Now this ebbed, and her mind-glow tasted of satisfaction, even happiness. She crouched down and patted Heart Stone, making many mouth noises, including "Athos," the sound that she most frequently directed at him. Heart Stone had long wondered if this sound might mean "Come here" or "I have food," but he was beginning to suspect that, for her, it was his name.

<*I am Heart Stone,*> he thought at her, although even if he had possessed a mind-voice, she would have been unable to understand. <*And you have given shape to my life.*>

✧ ✧ ✧

If Cordelia had been frightened when Willinski leveled his gun at her, she was absolutely terrified when Athos dropped out of the trees and assaulted the thug. If the treecats started attacking as a group, Cordelia had no doubt that Dr. Orgeson would turn it to her advantage. But although Athos could be horribly dangerous—as dozens of near-weasels would never live to remember—he showed amazing restraint. When Willinski dropped his gun and backed into the air van, he was only dripping blood, not disemboweled, with his face ripped off, as Athos could have managed far more easily than simply disarming him.

As if Athos's move had been a signal, the other three treecats plummeted from above, each hitting the roof of the air van with a solid thud, then crouching to attack. However, at that critical moment, Karl Zivonik had stepped out of the trees on the edge of the landing ground, shotgun at the ready, behind Orgeson and her men.

"Freeze!" Karl's voice was always deep; this time it crackled with a hard, authoritative edge Cordelia had never imagined coming from him, and the two still-armed thugs' heads whipped around in his direction. They took one glance at that rock-steady shotgun's muzzle and froze.

"SFS." Karl identified himself formally, as the law required, although he knew they'd recognized his uniform "Put down your weapons! Then facedown on the ground." They hesitated, and the shotgun's muzzle rose a centimeter or two.

"Now," he said flatly, and suddenly they couldn't move fast enough.

"Oh, thank goodness you're here, Ranger!" Orgeson began. "My associates—"

"That 'on the ground' applies to you, too, Ma'am,"

Karl said in that same flat tone. She looked at him for a moment longer, but something in his eye told her not to argue. She went to her knees, then lowered herself facedown.

"Good," Karl said, and looked at Stephanie. "First things first. Probationary Ranger Harrington?"

"Yes, Sir!"

"There seems to be an awful lot of weapons lying around. Let's get them collected. Over here behind me looks like a good place to stack them."

"Yes, Sir!" Stephanie said, as formally as she possibly could.

She collected up all of the firearms, beginning by retrieving and holstering her own pistol and careful not to cross between Orgeson or any of her men and the muzzle of Karl's shotgun. They made quite an armload, by the time she was done, and she piled them behind Karl.

"Now, you, with the injured hand," Karl said. "How bad is it?"

Willinski held out the freely bleeding hand.

"I've seen worse." Karl sounded remarkably unsympathetic, Cordelia noticed, but he looked at Jessica. "Ms. Pheriss, would you please take a look at this man's hand. And"—he moved very cold brown eyes back to Willinski—"I advise you to be very, very cooperative when she does."

"But—"

"I can put you in cuffs first, if you like," Karl said coldly, and Willinski seemed to wilt inside his own skin. He nodded, and Karl twitched his head at Stephanie. "Harrington, keep an eye on him."

"Yes, Sir." Stephanie drew her pistol again, careful

to keep its muzzle aimed at the ground but ready in the unlikely event that Willinski tried something—or something *else*, at least—stupid.

"Now," Karl turned his attention back to Orgeson while Jessica bent over Wilkinson and began slapping a pressure bandage onto his damaged hand. "You were saying?"

"Can I at least stand up, first?" she asked.

"You can. You other three, stay where you are."

Orgeson stood up, brushing leaves and gravel from her skirt.

"Ranger, there's been a tremendous misunderstanding here! I know what it must have looked like, but my associates and I were just attacked by that . . . that *vicious creature*!" she pointed an artfully trembling hand at Athos. "Then all of its friends just came swarming toward us!" She moved her pointing finger to Willinski's bleeding hand. "You can see what the first one did. We were only trying to protect ourselves."

Whatever else she might be, Stephanie thought, Lyric Orgeson was clearly a fast thinker. As cover stories went, that wasn't half bad. Unfortunately, it wasn't going to work.

"I see," Karl said. "And why would they do that? For that matter, how did you happen to be here *for* them to do that?"

"We came to see a colleague before going off-planet. He collapsed. We were taking him to the hospital when these young people—well-meaning, I'm sure—challenged us. Then that vicious beast, the one that looks like a treecat but must have the mange or be rabid or something, attacked my assistant." She waved a hand at Willinski. "And then the other ones came jumping down from the trees. Thank goodness you got here when you did!"

"So that's your story?"

"Well, of course it is!" Orgeson sounded indignant. "It's the truth!"

"No," Karl said as they all heard the sound of an incoming air car, "it isn't. Unfortunately for you, we can prove it isn't, too."

Orgeson closed her mouth with an almost audible click, and her expression went blank as a Forestry Service cruiser came slicing in to land beside her van. The canopy slid back and Frank Lethbridge climbed down, slung an SFS equipment bag over one shoulder, and strolled unhurriedly across to stand beside Karl.

"Looks like you've got everything under control here, Karl," he said.

"I don't know why you'd say anything of the sort!" Orgeson said. "This young man *clearly* doesn't understand what's actually happening here, Ranger—?"

"Lethbridge," Frank said in an amiable tone. "And I have to tell you, I misremember the last time Karl here misread a situation. Unless, of course, you're stupid enough to think I just happened to be in the neighborhood watching the feeds from that camera right there"—he pointed at the concealed camera—"when this all went down?"

Orgeson's jaw clenched, and Lethbridge snorted in amusement, then reached into the shoulder bag, pulled out a fistful of handcuffs, and offered them to Stephanie.

"Since you two seem to have the situation well in hand, Probationary Ranger Harrington, why don't you do the honors? And if you're through with Mr.—Willinski, is it?—Ms. Pheriss," Frank smiled thinly at Willinski as the other man realized that Frank knew exactly who he was, "why don't you check on Mr. Maye. Be sure to check his vitals, and you might want to draw a couple of blood samples. I'm sure the lab in Yawata Crossing will want to see if there's anything in his bloodstream that might account for his sudden, inexplicable collapse."

Stephanie's lips twitched in amusement as she pulled Willinski's hands behind him and slapped on the first set of handcuffs. She moved on to his fellow thugs before she approached Orgeson, and the older woman's expression would have curdled fresh milk as the handcuffs clicked on her wrists.

"Lyric Orgeson," Karl said then, lowering his shotgun at last and setting the safety, "you and your 'associates' are under arrest."

"On what charge?" Orgeson demanded. "For defending ourselves against your murderous little creatures?! Any judge will laugh that out of court!"

"No, for right now we'll settle for attempted kidnapping, criminal assault, and criminal coercion. There may be more later, of course."

"Assault?" Orgeson glared at him. "The only person assaulted here was Mr. Willinski, by that vicious treecat!"

"Oh, no." Karl shook his head with a knife-thin smile. "I'm talking about the formal complaint Mr. José Jones filed with the Forestry Service and Twin Forks constabulary three days ago. Oh, and the one Mr. Maye filed last week."

"What . . . what are you talking about?" Orgeson sounded significantly less confident.

"I think you know perfectly well what I'm talking

about, Dr. Orgeson. And before you point out that there weren't any witnesses to your actual threats to Mr. Maye the night the Kempers and their friends surprised you, you might want to rethink that. Frank Câmara was here, and I don't think he's really the loyal sort. We have him on video slipping a euphoric into a minor's drink—which may or may not have been on your orders, as part of your drug-testing program. Either way, I'm confident he'll be happy to cut a deal to testify against you if the Yawata Crossing city attorney makes it worth his while."

This time Orgeson only stared at him, and he smiled again, then waved at Lethbridge's cruiser.

"Think you've got room for all of them in the back, Frank? Or should I go get my cruiser from the barn?"

21

"I SEE A SPACE OVER THERE," CORDELIA SAID TO ZACK, who steered the Kempers' junker in the direction indicated. "Wow! Half the population of Sphinx must be here. I knew the Harringtons like to throw big parties, but this is amazing."

Zack, who was driving because Mack was coming with Brad, after they picked up Dana and her beau, laughed. Cordelia could tell he was feeling very grown up, with his mother riding shotgun and his two sisters in the back.

"Well, it's not just a birthday party. Or a going-away party, either. We've got quite a few other things to celebrate, as well," Danette Schardt-Cordova said, and Cordelia nodded. The Crown prosecutor had filed formal charges against Orgeson and her hoods two days ago, and word about baka bakari was spreading rapidly around Sphinx. No one knew whether or not it would be regulated—or how—but at least everyone knew it was out there, now.

"I wonder if Dia will be here," Natalie said. "She

messaged that her whole family had been invited to the party, but she wasn't sure if she'd get parole."

"Karl said he was driving over a bunch of his family," Cordelia said, "and I think Dia was on the list. How do you feel about seeing her?"

"Better," Natalie said, "now that she doesn't expect me to pretend not to notice she's sneaking off. There's a lot to like about her."

"The Zivoniks are a good family," Cordelia admitted.

She kept the rest of her thoughts to herself. She'd sort of hoped that Karl would suggest they go to the party together. She'd wondered if he planned to ask her, but then Stephanie's sixteenth birthday party had morphed into "Birthday Party Plus Farewell Party for Anders," and all bets had been off. Even though the Harringtons had set aside a large meadow as a parking field, they'd asked that people carpool whenever possible because space would be limited.

"Bleek!" Athos said, reaching up to pat her face.

Cordelia realized that Zack had set down the air car so lightly she hadn't even realized they'd landed. Athos seemed excited somehow, maybe even a bit edgy.

Maybe he's just excited because there will be celery. The 'cats always seem to like what Marjorie grows best.

Whatever the reason, as soon as they were near to where the party sprawled in and around the Harrington house, Athos gave her a firm hug with his tail, as if to reassure her that he'd be looking out for her, even if he wasn't in sight, and then scampered up the nearest crown oak trunk to where several other gray and white shapes could be spotted.

Although the invitation had said, "No presents," just about everyone coming in from the parking field seemed to have missed reading that line. Cordelia herself held a small bag containing a freshly-baked batch of treecat biscuits.

She presented these to Stephanie with a grin. "Since not even you are likely to be eating these, they qualify as a present for Lionheart, not you, so I didn't break the rules."

Stephanie laughed and gave her a hug. "We're going to be hang-gliding later. I hope you'll give it a try. The whole club's here, so you won't want for teachers. In fact, here comes someone who's really good, and we're hoping to get back on the team. Hi, Trudy!"

Cordelia looked up as the blond-haired young woman arrived. Like Cordelia after the near weasels, Trudy Franchitti was on crutches *and* a personal CG unit, but she looked a lot better than she had. Stephanie seemed genuinely happy to see her, too, Cordelia noticed.

Trudy also had a present for Stephanie, as well as an excuse.

"It's a hoodie promoting Wild and Free," she explained. "We're really excited about the new SFS Explorers, and hope we can do some presentations for you."

Stephanie shook out the dark green hoodie and admired the art that graced the back: a montage showing an assortment of Sphinx's wildlife. "You bet. Lots of presentations, and tours, and maybe some help cleaning habitats. We want the Explorers to understand all about wildlife, the dirty parts, as well as the cute and fuzzy."

Trudy dropped her voice slightly. "I've got something to tell you, and Karl, if he's around."

Cordelia made as if to excuse herself, but Trudy stopped her. "Hang if you want. This sort of involves your family, too. You're one of the Schardt-Cordovas, right? I saw the news articles about you helping that injured 'cat, and I know you were there when they arrested that Orgeson and her hoods."

Stephanie messaged Karl, and soon he emerged from the house with a towering sandwich balanced on a recyclable plate.

"I was just coming to make sure the birthday girl is kept fed," he said, putting the plate down near Stephanie. "Hey, Trudy. What's up?"

"I'd prefer that this wasn't spread around too much, but," Trudy shrugged, "if you think you need to use it, I'll go on record. I know you guys busted Frank for spiking Stephanie's drink in Yawata Crossing. Well, I found out why Loon and Dia acted the way they did, too. Loon ordered his fancy picnic basket from Câmara Comestibles. When Frank learned who it was for, he spiked the puff pastries with something. I can't prove it, but I know he did. I found a text from Stan where they were laughing about it."

"Well, that explains a lot," Karl said. "Thank you. Dia's admitted that she and Loon were sneaking off for a little romance, but she's sworn all the time that they weren't doing any drugs or drinking really heavily. It's good to know."

"Why would Frank do that?" Cordelia asked.

"Because he's a nasty bastard," Trudy said, her violet eyes flooding with tears. "And so was Stan. I knew it, too, but I looked the other way for a long time. Until . . . until—"

She broke off, and Stephanie looked at her for a

moment. And then, to Cordelia's astonishment, she put her arms around Trudy and hugged her tightly. Touchy-feely was the one thing Cordelia did *not* associate with Stephanie Harrington, and from Trudy's expression, neither did she.

"I'm sorry about Stan," Stephanie said softly. "I may never have liked him very much, but I know how close you were. I hate it that you had to lose him that way. But at least *you're* going to be all right, Trudy."

"Yeah." Trudy returned her hug, just a little awkwardly, then stepped back on her crutches. "Yeah, I am," she said. She scrubbed her eyes with one hand, then flashed a wicked, only slightly watery grin that showed Cordelia a glimpse of the former, less kind Trudy about whom she'd heard. "It'll be a while before I get off these," she indicated her crutches, "but when I do I'll knock your socks off on the hang-gliding field, Stephanie!"

"In your dreams!" Stephanie laughed.

"Just you tell yourself that," Trudy said. "And in the meantime, I guess I should get out of the birthday girl's way." She glanced at Karl flashed that grin again, one that *almost* hid the lingering pain in her blue eyes.

"Later, Karl . . ." she said, and sashayed off into the crowd. Even on crutches, that was the only verb Cordelia could think of to describe it, and she smothered a smile of her own as she and Karl, aware that there was a cluster of people waiting to give Stephanie birthday greetings, took their own leave.

"That sounded like an invitation," Cordelia said.

"Not my type," Karl laughed. "Definitely not my type, even if she's improved a lot."

Cordelia was tempted to ask just what Karl's type

was, but decided not to. Maybe she'd like the answer, but then again, she might not.

She was feeling happy and oddly excited. Somewhere, not very far away, she could feel that Athos was excited, too.

I already have a life partner, she thought. *I won't be greedy, just grateful.*

✧ ✧ ✧

<There is Stone Shaper.> Climbs Quickly looked down from where he was perched with Dirt Grubber, Keen Eyes, and Swift Striker, near where the two-legs were gathering their many flying things. *<He is coming to join us. Now to hope he will not flee when he senses the surprise we have for him.>*

When he had seen Death Fang's Bane, Healer, and Plant Minder begin preparations for one of their gatherings, Climbs Quickly had sent a message to Sings Truly that it was possible Stone Shaper would be in the vicinity within a small hand of days. She then had spoken with Fleet Wind, one of the heads of Bright Water's scouts, and requested that a relay be set up so that the news could reach her quickly and that she, in turn, could arrange for some of Stone Shaper's young to be ready to make the journey to meet with their long-absent father.

In the days that had gone by since her initial meeting with Stone Shaper, Sings Truly had worked hard to convince at least some of his family to meet with him and—more importantly—on how to not make Stone Shaper feel maimed in the presence of those who had not lost their ability to mind-speak. Climbs Quickly had helped by meeting with as many of Bright Water clan as cared to join in, so he could share first hand his own experiences with the Person that Stone Shaper had become since his departure turnings before.

Although he could not share precisely what had happened when Stone Shaper had met and bonded with Awakening Joy, since Stone Shaper had been the only Person who had witnessed the events, Climbs Quickly could share what he'd seen after, going back to his first meeting with the terribly injured Stone Shaper in Healer's clinic, moving from there to what he had seen of the battlefield where Stone Shaper had played a key role in saving Awakening Joy and the barker, Needle Biter.

Better were their experiences since then, and best of all was the tale of how Stone Shaper had bravely gone to defend his two-leg and, yet, when doing so he had kept within the bounds of the agreement the People had made long before to reveal as little as possible about how clever and dangerous People could be. Such behavior, Sings Truly had persuasively argued, showed that while Stone Shaper had taken himself away from where he could not be a full part of the clan, he had continued to live up to what he would have last been told about the policy of the People regarding the two-legs.

Happily, by now, most People were coming to accept that since Climbs Quickly had bonded with Death Fang's Bane, followed so soon after by several other bonds, the code of secrecy could no longer be maintained, although restraint was still in order.

Not all of Stone Shaper's children who still lived with Bright Water Clan would be coming to this reunion. Several had been unable to hide their emotions—especially pity, but also some resentment that Stone Shaper had abandoned them when they were still grieving for their mother—in check. Sings Truly had reassured them that if all went well, there would be other opportunities, that, for now, the goal should be helping Stone Shaper realize that while he had made himself a new life, a good life, he need not reject everything about the old.

In the end, three of Stone Shaper's children had come. The youngest was Frolics Merrily, from the last litter Stone Shaper and Golden Eye had produced. This young female was not yet bonded, and was concentrating on learning the many skills an adult female needed, for since the females rarely travelled far, they were the ones who maintained the clan. Clay Spinner was somewhat older, from a middle litter. He had not followed his father's path as a stone worker, but had taken an interest in pottery. He was also a strong hunter who provided not only for his own mate and kits, but for others.

The last, and most problematic, was sour Stone Biter. He was from Stone Shaper's first litter, and upon his father's departure had taken over as senior stone worker. Although talented, Stone Biter lacked his father's artistic flare. His tools were perfectly good and he made far more of them, but Climbs Quickly doubted that any young hunter or scout had lusted after one of his knives as Climbs Quickly had the one he now kept as a dearly held treasure. Worse, the advent of the two-legs and their not-stone tools, many of which could be scrounged from the places where the two-legs left their waste, had Stone Biter facing the before this point unthinkable possibility that his skills would become obsolete in his lifetime.

But although Climbs Quickly had thought that leaving Stone Biter out of this initial reunion might be best, Sings Truly had disagreed.

<Stone Shaper knows perfectly well that he abandoned not only his clan, but left his son to take his

place. If this is to be a healing meeting, those two must meet, so that for Stone Biter his father will cease to be a thunderhead he cannot get out from under, and so that Stone Shaper will have an opportunity to see how his son has carried on.>

Climbs Quickly respected his sister. Nonetheless, he had to shove his apprehension to where it would not taint his mind-glow, then let his honest excitement cover it as he loped down the limb of the net-wood to meet Stone Shaper and then led the way to the destined meeting.

✧ ✧ ✧

Heart Stone suspected what awaited him even before they arrived at the meeting place high in the net-wood. When she chose, Sings Truly could cause her mind-glow to be blindingly bright. In its blazing, Heart Stone decided there was a message.

<*I am here. I know you remember what I tried to share with you the last time we met, that Bright Water is open to you if you have the courage to face what once drove you away. We are not perfect. Not all of us have the imagination to face without pity and fear what you were condemned to when you chose life over the easy escape of death. You fled, only to discover that one cannot flee suffering and grief. You dove into battle, perhaps seeking death and instead discovered love and a new reason for life. Are you ready to face Bright Water? If not, turn back. I will not let you be tricked.*>

Closer, Heart Stone sought and found the taste of apprehension in Climbs Quickly's mind-glow. From Sharp Sight, a Person whose tragedy he would never know, there was the taste of determination. From Plant Fancier there was, as always, a slow, intense quiet that tasted of growing things. From all of these, Heart Stone took courage.

<Climbs Quickly, you are fearful that this meeting you have set up—for surely it was you who first contacted your sister—will drive me away from you, reducing this new clan you are making. Sharp Sight, I wish I knew what you suffered, but if after whatever it was you can live with a mind-glow that bubbles with laughter, then who am I to believe my sufferings are excuse enough to separate myself from other People? Plant Fancier, you are a strange one, but in you I taste how a dead and rotting tree is also a rich source of life. If I face those I abandoned, those who frightened me, perhaps my days of rot can be turned to use, because the song the memory singers will keep of me is one of regrowth, and that will be an inspiration into a future beyond my imagining. My friends, I can do this, because of you, and because my life has taken a new shape.>

And he ran forward, six strong legs leaping and jumping, doing his very best to fill his mind-glow not with his real apprehension but with anticipation, with hope.

In the joining of branches where once before they had met with Sings Truly, she waited and with her was Frolics Merrily, Clay Spinner, and, the taste of his mind-glow dour, bleak, and full of doubt, Stone Biter. Although he had been a grown Person when Stone Shaper had left to become Stone, Stone Biter's mind-glow was older, stiffer than it should be for one who had added only one more ring to his tail.

Young Frolics Merrily was tentative, but willing to meet the sire she really knew only through memory songs. Clay Spinner had memories of his own, and Heart Stone could taste the wistful hope that these would not be all he would ever have. To these he opened his body in a physical embrace, something People rarely offered except to mates after kittenhood, but which he had learned from Life Shaper could help wordless mind-glows to blend. They hesitated, but perhaps one of his friends explained, because they accepted his hugs and healing flowed forth.

Only then did Heart Stone face Stone Biter. He had wanted to give this most difficult of his younglings—no longer a youngling—a chance to consider. Rather than offering a hug, Heart Stone took something from the carry bag where he kept his stone shaping tools. As he had run toward the brilliance of Sings Truly's mind-glow, he had remembered something from a long time before. He could only hope that Stone Biter would remember as well.

On the broad surface of the tree limb, Heart Stone set the broken pieces of a stone knife he had been working on. It had been going well, then a hidden flaw in the stone caused it to split. Although he knew Stone Biter could not hear his mind-voice, Heart Stone shaped his intention as if he could.

<Do you remember when I was teaching you to work stone? You were very talented, and very proud of how you could shape tools better than many with far more rings on their tails. You were working on a knife, much like this one, when a buried flaw broke it. You would have flung the pieces away in anger, but I showed you how they could be worked into smaller pieces, useful for scraping the bark from branches.>

<I have proven myself a flawed knife, but I have remade myself. Can you accept me as I am? Even more, can you accept that you need not be so bitter? I feel that you see yourself as a bit of stone shaped too fast

and not as beautiful as you could be. Let this go. See yourself as the strong one you are.>

And as he shaped what his son could not hear, Heart Stone strove with all his might to pour his regret, his repentance, and, most of all, his love and admiration into his mind-glow.

Stone Biter stood as still as the bits of stone, but his mind-glow was a swirling clash of tastes, too complex for Heart Stone to understand fully. Doubtless Stone Biter's mind-voice shared things the others could hear, and doubtless Sings Truly replied with something, perhaps something very wise.

Then Stone Biter reached forward. He picked up one of the broken bits of the knife and carefully put it into his own carry bag. When that was done, he opened his own arms, inviting an embrace, wordlessly letting Heart Stone know that he was forgiven, he had been missed, and, even, <*Whenever you come to us, you are welcomed home.*>

✧ ✧ ✧

"I never knew," Stephanie said to Anders, "that there could be so many ways of saying, 'This isn't a birthday present.' The number one excuse is that the gift isn't for me, it's to help with the new SFS Explorers program. Number two is that it's not a present, it's just something to eat or drink that they brought for the party. Number three is that it's for Lionheart."

"Tell me about it," Anders replied. "At least in my case, though, the farewell gifts are pretty much all digital files. People did remember that I'm getting on a spaceship in less than a week and weight allowances are pretty strict—worse, Dad's taken over half of mine for his artifacts. Still, some are really amazing. Mack

Kemper did me a painting of Main Street, Twin Forks, which I plan to have printed when I get home. Nosey Jones gave me a subscription to his newsletter. It'll be out of date when I get it, but at least I can keep up with local events."

"Nosey's over learning to hang-glide," Stephanie said. "He's decided to do a series of columns featuring him trying out different sports. Since hang-gliding is becoming increasingly popular, he's going to start with that, but Jake Simpson has made him promise that skimmers will be next."

"Jake gave me a present, too," Anders said, laughing at the memory, "the schematics for making my own skimmer. I think I'll pass on that one. Urako's a little more conservative than Sphinx."

"You okay with going back?" Stephanie asked.

"I am, actually. This has been an amazing year or so, but y'know, I do miss my mom. I'm going to miss all of you, but it's not like I'm never going to come back. As long as Dad's working on treecats, there're going to be opportunities."

"I have a present for you, too," Stephanie said. "I've sent it to your uni-link. It's a bunch of images from your time here, sort of a scrapbook. A bunch of people helped me out. Chet and Christine even had images of you getting attacked by the rock ravens."

"Oh, joy," Anders moaned, but he was laughing, too. "It has been fun. Even when it wasn't, still, somehow it was."

They fell silent, standing shoulder to shoulder, comfortable now in a way that maybe they'd never been before, not even at the best of the short time they'd been dating.

There's something to be said for friendship, Stephanie thought. *To think that a year ago my parents had to all but threaten me to get me to invite anyone to my birthday party. This year it was my idea, and rather than having too few people I could ask, I just about ended up with too many.*

She looked to where Herman was having a conversation with Jessica's mom and Marjorie, doubtless discussing fungi, since Herman looked very animated. Jessica was over talking with Richard Harrington and Scott MacDallan, probably about med school. Zack and Irina were, judging from the way they kept sketching shapes in the air, chatting about something artsy. Overhead, the sky was bright with hang-gliders. Karl's emerald and gold striped wings were next to a pair of trainers. She guessed he was teaching Cordelia.

Without even realizing she was doing it, Stephanie reached out along her link to Lionheart. He was having a good time, too, and the glow of his happiness met and mingled with hers.

Once I thought that Lionheart was the only friend I'd ever need, she thought. *I'm so glad I've learned how great it is for us both to have friends.*

She looked out to where Buddy Pheriss had set up some speakers and was acting as D.J. to an impromptu dance party. Mack and Brad swayed in each other's arms, not far from Chet and Christine. Xadrian, in full club regalia, even for a midafternoon picnic, was marshalling a Sixy-Snakey line, which included Loon and Dia, Chief Ranger Shelton, and, Lev, Karl's youngest sibling.

Stephanie poked Anders in the ribs. "That looks like fun. Time's short. Let's dance!"